Contemporary Short Stories
from Central America

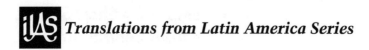 *Translations from Latin America Series*

Institute of Latin American Studies
University of Texas at Austin

Contemporary Short Stories from Central America

Edited by
Enrique Jaramillo Levi
and
Leland H. Chambers

Translations coordinated by
Leland H. Chambers

Translated by
Lynne Beyer, Pamela Carmell, Leland H. Chambers,
Elizabeth Gamble Miller, Sabina Lask-Spinac, Sylvia Schulter,
Charles Philip Thomas, Don D. Wilson, and Clark M. Zlotchew

UNIVERSITY OF TEXAS PRESS, AUSTIN

First Edition, 1994

Requests for permission to reproduce material from this work should be sent to Permissions, University of Texas Press, P.O. Box 7819, Austin, Texas 78713-7819

♾ The paper used in this publication meets the minimum requirements of American National Standard for Information Sciences—Permanence of Paper for Printed Library Materials, ANSI Z39.48–1984.

Library of Congress Cataloging-in-Publication Data

Contemporary short stories from Central America / edited by Enrique Jaramillo Levi and Leland H. Chambers ; translated by Lynne Beyer . . . [et al.].
     p.   cm. — (Translations from Latin America Series)
  ISBN 0-292-74030-1. — ISBN 0-292-74034-4 (pbk.)
   1. Short stories, Central American—Translations into English. 2. Central American fiction—20th century—Translations into English. I. Jaramillo Levi, Enrique, 1944– . II. Chambers, Leland H., 1928– . III. Series.
  PQ7087.E5C66 1994
  863' .01089728—dc20   93-38918
                                                        CIP

For permissions acknowledgments, see page 271.

*This anthology is dedicated to the young
writers of Central America.*

to write
to write even though it's froth
to speak
to speak extravagantly
pulling syllables
words from the mud
even the hilt of the necessary
scream

—Rigoberto Paredes, *Las cosas por su nombre*

Make no mistake: any literary work, on one of its
levels, is the life of the author himself as well
as of the society to which he belongs.

—Helen Umaña, *Literatura hondureña contemporánea*

Contents

Panama

Acknowledgments

Special gratitude is due Prof. Naomi Lindstrom of the Department of Spanish and Portuguese at the University of Texas at Austin. Without her critical comments and suggestions, the arduous labor of preparing this volume would likely not have been attempted. A Fulbright Research Fellowship generously gave Enrique Jaramillo Levi full support during two years' residence at UT-Austin. During this period (1987–1989), the Nettie Lee Benson Latin American Collection was indispensable in providing copies of materials.

The support of three others at UT-Austin should be mentioned here: Prof. Richard Adams, former director of the Institute of Latin American Studies, who made an office available, complete with typewriter, paper supply, and telephone; Prof. Robert Brody, interim chair of the Department of Spanish and Portuguese; and Prof. Carlos A. Solé, Fulbright adviser.

The following Central American writers offered mutually binding support in various ways: Jorge Kattán Zablah, José Roberto Cea, Ricardo Lindo, Carmen Naranjo, Carlos Cortés, Rima de Vallbona, Jorge Luis Oviedo, Arturo Arias, Pablo Antonio Cuadra, Horacio Peña, and Rosa María Britton.

Prof. Elizabeth Gamble Miller of Southern Methodist University provided much material by Salvadoran writers—her specialty—and was continually willing to be of assistance. And how could this book have come into existence without her fine translations of those writers? Or without the dedicated work of the other seven fine translators—Lynne Beyer, Pamela Carmell, Sabina Lask-Spinac (tragically killed in an automobile accident in June 1990), Sylvia K. Schulter, Charles Philip Thomas, Don D. Wilson, and Clark M. Zlotchew?

We are particularly fortunate in having the opportunity of working with our editors, Virginia Hagerty and Carolyn Palaima, of the Institute of Latin American Studies at the University of Texas at Austin. From the start they have been capable, thorough, and patient; moreover, the whole way through, they have maintained a high edge of enthusiasm for this book. What more could one ask?

And thanks are also due to Marck Beggs, formerly of the University of Denver, for technical assistance at the computer. We feel especially gratified that the University of Denver, through its Research and Creative Work Fund, has been able to make this possible.

And, finally, it is appropriate to call attention to those in Panama who, in the midst of the worst crisis in its history, always offered encouragement in this and other professional undertakings: Rodrigo Miró, Angel Revilla, Alberto Osorio, Humberto Calamari, Ricardo Ríos T., Ricardo Segura, and Manuel O. Sisnett, as well as the poets Elsie Alvarado de Ricord, Generoso Emiliani Villamil, César Young Núñez, Jorge Vélez Valdés, Viviane Nathan, Luis Wong Vega, Raúl Leis, and Ricardo J. Bermúdez.

Life takes strange turns; its apparently unseasonable, unforeseen movements often fail to realize what seem like our most reasonable expectations, or they then bring us into unlooked-for circumstances that can be appreciated only when one reaches a certain perspective—thought of as time and space that are different from other lived experiences—between the past and the present. So perhaps Luck ought to be acknowledged alongside the above-mentioned individuals.

A word about the respective contributions of the two editors of this anthology: Enrique Jaramillo Levi conceived this anthology, selected the stories, and provided the original draft of the introduction as well as the notes on the authors; he also secured permissions from many of the copyright holders before being obliged to return to Panama. Leland H. Chambers coordinated the team of translators, translated all the stories from Panama as well as some of the others as needed, revised the introduction, and took over the other editorial responsibilities after Jaramillo Levi's unfortunate departure. One of the most painful of these was reducing the scope of the anthology from its original sixty-five stories to fifty-one, *after* the translations had been completed.

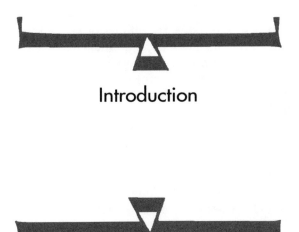

Introduction

Broad Historical Overview

The decade of the 1960s in the United States saw the assassinations of two Kennedys and one King (Martin Luther), the growth of the civil rights movement, the gradual buildup of the war in Vietnam. It was a time of large demonstrations and protests, rock music, bossa nova, an incipient drug culture, the beginnings of the sexual revolution.

It was also the decade when Latin American literature, particularly its fiction, suddenly became a visible current in the European/U.S. mainstream of modernist and postmodern literature. Important prizes went to Latin American writers: the Fomentor Prize of 1961 to the Argentinian Jorge Luis Borges (who nonetheless shared it with Samuel Beckett), and the Nobel Prize for Literature (1967) to the Guatemalan Miguel Angel Asturias, who had also received the Lenin Peace Prize in 1966. Novelists of astonishing range and technical virtuosity were quickly recognized in Europe and the United States. Julio Cortázar, Carlos Fuentes, Mario Vargas Llosa, and Gabriel García Márquez in particular seemed to be at the real center of the dominant literary tradition that included Proust, Joyce, Kafka, Mann, Gide, and Faulkner: the era of the "Boom."

It was a relatively short-lived period, actually, although with long-term effects. Writers like Borges came to influence the development of literary theory. Writers everywhere began to cultivate the techniques of magical realism. They also started exploring the self-referentiality of fiction. And a huge market for Latin American writers awaited further developments from the Latin American regions of the New World.

The post-Boom writers of Latin America generally narrowed their focus and many resorted to the techniques of realism, in part to make their works more accessible to a wider public. But, taken all in all, those who came after the Boom moved in directions laid out by the Boom novelists (who themselves continued to produce influential works, sometimes apparently to satisfy a market for the mode of writing they had established). Pop culture informed the novels of such as Manuel Puig (Argentina) and Guillermo Cabrera Infante (Cuba). Other novelists made language itself the focus of their fiction, arguing as did Severo Sarduy (Cuba) that language by its nature could never be dependably referential. And women writers suddenly became accepted and taken seriously in this most macho of worlds: Elena Poniatowska (Mexico), Isabel Allende (Chile), Marta Traba (Argentina), Julieta Campos (Mexico), Clarice Lispector (Brazil), Luisa Valenzuela (Argentina), and the like.

The writers of Central America did not benefit very much from the newfound respect accorded other Latin American writers of narrative fiction. Asturias is an exception, of course. But the colonial legacy of dependency cast a long shadow over the struggling republics—democracies in name only—of the region. The region remained economically behind, without significant industry, in part due to the continued domination by oligarchical families and a parallel exploitation by foreign—mostly U.S.—business interests, and it has suffered bitterly from political repression as well as from U.S. military interference in national affairs. Moreover, Central America lacks any of those luminous centers of intellectual excitement such as Havana, Buenos Aires, and Mexico City.

But writers of narrative fiction in Central America persisted. And that is why this anthology is important—as a record of high achievement against serious odds, during a period of turmoil, upheaval, revolution, and war. The twenty-five years covered by this anthology have seen the Somoza dictatorship overthrown in Nicaragua and the subsequent ten-year rule by the left-leaning Sandinistas, a regime the United States saw fit to oppose in every way but all-out invasion; a continual state of guerrilla warfare in El Salvador and eventual rule by death squad, with the United States giving its support once more to a government unable to govern except with the aid of bloodshed; in Guatemala, a succession of military governments followed by a civilian government that has ruled only through the courtesy of the military, and all of them fanatically opposed to any show of movement toward populist aims; in Honduras, a series of military governments succeeded by civilian governments that ended by providing a haven for thousands of Contra troops engaged in the war against the Sandinista regime in Nicaragua. In

Panama, strongman Gen. Omar Torrijos successfully renegotiated the treaties concerning the Panama Canal (1977) and managed to win back a good measure of control and eventual political hegemony over the Canal Zone, while the years following his death were marked by Panama's development as a commercial center in many enterprises, some of them reprehensible. United States opposition to the Noriega regime culminated in the celebrated invasion of Panama in December 1989, just after the period covered by this anthology (1963–1988) comes to an end.

Only Costa Rica has been reasonably free of severe political and economic disruptions during this period, and, in fact, it has been governed through a real, functioning democratic process that has been a model for the region, though possibly destined to remain unique.

The Short Story in Latin America

The short story, in its various forms down to the present time, is adaptable to any set of circumstances where narrative fiction is wanted. Throughout Latin America, realism and naturalism have provided a theoretical framework dominating short fiction in the first half of the twentieth century and still find capable adherents. One thinks of the legacy of Maupassant, Chekhov, O. Henry, Stephen Crane. Models for a more imaginative kind of story are to be had in Poe, Hawthorne, and especially the great Nicaraguan poet, Rubén Darío. With the stories he published in an iconoclastic little volume, *Azul* (1888), Darío initiated important and lasting new directions within both Latin American and peninsular Spanish literature. He eschewed the urge to write about the material world of everyday life—in contrast to all the writers mentioned above—and cultivated instead a nostalgic, aristocratic world of dream, in which the language of metaphor took on an importance it did not have with any of those writers. And, most important, he elevated the artist above the world of practical concerns, social inequities, and middle-class values—an attractive concept for many, even down to the present day.

Throughout Latin America, the period between the two wars saw an increase in the number of short fiction writers turning out quality material. Seymour Menton distinguishes two basic tendencies: *criollismo* (from *criollo*, meaning native-born as apposed to peninsular Spanish) and cosmopolitanism. The first (some critics, Gerald Martin in particular, would call this social realism) focuses on the portrayal of common people and their immediate environment; the writer sets the action in a particularized, often remote, and sometimes picturesque spot and asks readers to visualize events that are very likely far removed from their own experience. The second often involves urban settings, the usually middle-class characters are engaged in the same things their counterparts in Paris, London, or New York would be engaged in, and there is often some reflection of intellectual currents in the stream of contemporary Western European civilization (Menton, *El cuento hispanoamericano*, pp. 217–218).

Yet, though *criollismo* claimed most writers' allegiance in Latin America between 1920 and 1945, the cosmopolitan current initiated by Darío was not completely extinguished during those years, while in some writers earlier tendencies such as romanticism, realism, naturalism, and *modernismo* simply refused to die or else overlapped. But after 1945, according to Menton, in a trend that closely followed those in Europe and the United States, the movement toward the cosmopolitan replaced *criollismo* or at least became predominant in nearly every country. The goals of the two camps were clearly quite different. "For the *criollista*, literature served to interpret political, economic, and social conditions in his own country. On the other hand, cosmopolitan writers are much more concerned with the esthetic, the psychological, and the philosophical, even when dealing with *criollista* themes . . . They are more interested in the individual, urban life, and fantasy" (ibid., p. 23). And under the general heading of the cosmopolitan, the influence of several more precisely defined European "schools" can be discerned: surrealism, cubism, and existentialism (ibid.).

The decade 1944–1954 saw the publication of four collections of short stories that are fundamental for understanding the subsequent developments in all of Latin American short fiction: Jorge Luis Borges's *Ficciones* (1944) and Julio Cortázar's *Bestiario* (1951)—both from Argentina—Juan José Arreola's *Varia invención* (1949) and Juan Rulfo's *El llano en llamas* (1953)—both from Mexico. All except Rulfo are strongly touched by the notions associated with magic realism, a concept (frequently misunderstood) that posits the simultaneous existence of verisimilitudinous and nonverisimilitudinous events on the same literary plane. One finds the logic of realistic representation and the illogic of the fantastic intermingled in a sequence that may jar against the expectations of those whose basic assumptions about fiction are founded on the validity of representing cause and effect in the real, the physical, world.

Borges's and Cortázar's achievements are well known in the United States; the majority of their works have been translated and American readers and writers have proclaimed themselves disciples. It's not for nothing that Seymour Menton describes Borges as the "high priest" of the cosmopolitan spirit in Spanish America. His blend of scholarship and fantasy, of the exotic with the philosophical, written in uncluttered, ironic language, has brought major writers to agree with Carlos Fuentes's assessment that without Borges's prose there simply would not be any modern Latin American novel—even though Borges himself never wrote one! Cortázar's *Bestiary* presents a world filled with phobias and fantasy that impresses with its imaginative leaps. The two Mexican writers have caused far less of a sensation for U.S. readers than the two Argentinians. Arreola's *Varia invención* (Various Inventions) is a delightfully varied collection of sketches and short stories imbued with the satiric in an atmosphere of the absurd; the author uses his astonishing, offbeat erudition as a springboard for the illogic of the imagination. Rulfo's short stories—actually overshadowed by the resounding acceptance of his 1955 novel *Pedro Páramo*—preserve the closest links to his immediate historical background, in this case, the Mexican Revolution (1910–1920). That is, he is the most *criollista* of these four writers. But his stories clearly demonstrate the truth of Menton's claim that the cosmopolitan writer's handling of *criollista* themes shows off a prior and greater cosmopolitan commitment.

One of the basic assumptions behind the stories of these writers and that widespread group who followed and were promoted as the writers of "The Boom," primarily with their novels, is that asserted by Alfredo Pavón: "the literary tale does not represent reality but realizes it esthetically" (*El universo del relato literario*, p. 91). It is possible to extend this claim even to the fiction of those devoted to the techniques of realism, but its validity seems more obvious when applied to works where some of the "magical" elements occur. Thus, "the literary tale is not to be defined completely as communication—or at least it is not simply communication articulated through language—but as the production of a universe of signification which, drawing its nourishment from human substances, is presented as an intepretation of what human beings and the world mean" (ibid., pp. 42–43).

To achieve this end, the writers employed a marvelous, fresh array of themes and techniques: for example, Borges's depiction of the universe (in "The Library of Babel") as an interconnected series of hexagonal rooms filled with books, each room with an identical number of bookshelves, each shelf with an identical number of books, each book with an identical number of pages, but each page with an absolutely unique and chaotic combination of letters of the alphabet. Or take Arreola's playful description (in "The Switchman") of the Mexican railway system with its tracks leading nowhere, sometimes merely sketched in the sand, and its switchman-informer whose body eventually fades into the clear morning air while the red light of his lantern does not. Both writers touch on the universal as they invest their images with a convincing sense of their significance as metaphors for an absurd, pointless world. And this too is one of the qualities displayed so abundantly by contemporary Latin American fiction, for "it expresses anxieties and experiences shared by millions of human beings in countries very different" (Pupo-Walker, *El cuento hispanoamericano ante la crítica*, p. 19).

The Situation in Central America

Few writers of fiction from Central America have come near achieving the reputation internationally that the best novelists of the Boom have. Only Miguel Angel Asturias (Guatemala) has shared company with the likes of Carlos Fuentes, Mario Vargas Llosa, Julio Cortázar, Gabriel García Márquez, Alejo Carpentier, Augusto Roa Bastos. Nonetheless, one can agree wholeheartedly with the Puerto Rican critic Ramón Luis Acevedo:

> The scarce critical attention that Central American literature in general has received cannot be justified on the basis of a supposed lack of literary value. It is due completely to lack of familiarity. One only has to scratch the surface a little to become aware of the extraordinary richness and variety of the literature produced in Central America. Besides, both works and authors abound that, without being in the topmost category, nevertheless merit our attention because they are representative, or they offer some element of interest, or they simply provide the context within which the most outstanding works and authors are situated. (*La novela centroamericana*, p. 10)

It is nonliterary factors that in general have prevented Central American letters from being known and valued. One could cite the lack of economic development throughout the region, the low per capita income of the people, the high degree of illiteracy (consequently circumscribing a relatively small reading public), the preference among this constitutency for foreign works, the high costs of book production, a discouraging, inhibitive political situation—these are some of the negative factors that hinder the production of literary texts, their adequate distribution and promotion, and the critical process that ideally should stimulate interest in locally produced literary works. Consequently, few publishing houses exist in Central America, and editions that do come out tend to have small press runs.

In reality, writers in Central America often do not know whom they write for, but they may not be seriously affected by this if their vocations are firmly based. It is certainly the case that writers go on writing, often publishing, distributing, promoting, and selling their works themselves. The physical and mental waste entailed by these efforts siphons off energy for new creative work and often ends by forcing the writers to desert their profession and devote themselves to more practical things (Acevedo, pp. 10–11). But even if this does not happen, in the long run the writers' discouragement may well deepen anyway, for texts need to be read, decodified, pondered, discussed, analyzed, and responded to.

Critics and translators of late have gradually been directing more attention to short fiction from the region, but still only in very small doses. It is difficult to get a handle on it. Two important anthologies— one edited by Seymour Menton (cited above) and another by Sergio Ramírez (*Antología del cuento centroamericano*, 1973)—have helped greatly to make new and established writers known. They remain untranslated, of course, as do other anthologies, which, conceived on a lesser scale, have also contributed their share. And two works that deal primarily with the novel also provide a great deal of general information concerning Central American literature: *La novela centroamericana: desde el Popol-Vuh hasta los umbrales de la novela actual* by the aforementioned Puerto Rican critic Ramón Luis Acevedo (1982)—possibly the most complete study to date—and *La novela del imperialismo en Centroamérica* by the Panamanian poet Esther María Osses (1986).

The Stories in This Volume

As does any self-respecting anthology, this book sets out to be rigorous in its selection of representative texts; exhaustive in its search for writers, themes, and styles; and vehemently zealous regarding the motivations and goals that have brought it forth. We have made a serious attempt to make *Contemporary Short Stories from Central America* a showcase of literary and ideological tendencies, generational groups, and national contributions to the world of fiction today.

However, no matter how objective and critically scrupulous a work of this nature tries to be, in the long run it is the subjectivity, the personal taste, the interior "I" of the anthologist that decides which stories to include and which to reject from among so many possibilities available. That judgment, though in the long run subjective, has been based here on literary criteria—as it should be in a world governed by professional ethics instead of political and social conformity. Not only have the outstanding writers of the last quarter-century been included—many of whom are still producing—but also some from the active youngest generation, writers still in the process of development.

The most obvious characteristic of the stories included in this anthology is their perfectly representative variety. Variety of themes, variety of technical resources, variety of aesthetic goals. They run the gamut on both sides of the *criollismo*/cosmopolitan dichotomy. If we conceive of this dichotomy as a scale with "pure" *criollista* stories at one extreme and "pure" cosmopolitan stories at the other, we can easily place Bárcena's "The Sweetheart of the Spirits" and Kattán Zablah's "The Raccoons" close to the *criollista* extreme and Monterroso's "The Circumstantial or the Ephemeral" alongside Rovinski's "Metaphors" at the cosmopolitan end. But many stories lean in both directions and toward neither side absolutely, such as Chuez's "The Woman," with its *campesino* family so desperate that the father sells the rights to his prepubescent daughter to the local landowner (which points in the direction of the *criollista* camp) and its elliptical, "expressionistic" narration reminiscent of stories like the Russian Zamyatin's "The Dragon" (pointing toward the cosmopolitan end).

Predominant among the themes that these stories flesh out in their characters and events is concern over the condition of the poor (see stories by Barnoya García, Peña, Pinto, Britton) and the oppressed, whether by local landowners (Chuez, Leis), the military (Arias, Dobles), or the ubiquitous dictator (Escoto). As one might expect, these stories display some kind of fascination with dictator figures (Escoto, Ramírez, Del Valle) and with the usually futile struggles against them (Santos, Silva). Closely linked to these are stories that deal in some way with armed conflict (Quijada Urías, José Ricardo Chaves), military oppression (Arias, Bähr, Escoto), or rule by death squad (Liano). It may surprise some readers of this anthology that the preponderance of these stories do *not* place "war" front and center, for U.S. readers have heard very little about Central America in the last ten years *except* war in one form or another. But the truth is, of course, that many of these stories were written before these conflicts began to hit the front page, for the period this book embraces goes back to 1963.

However, national pride is something these writers know about. Cuadra's use of the jaguar attack ("August") to frame a view of an "essential," historical Nicaragua illustrates this, as does Arias's parallel depiction ("Toward Patzún") of the suffering Indian woman as symbolic of modern-day Guatemala.

Another set of themes has to do with middle-class preoccupations: love relationships, social expectations, conformity, bourgeois fatuousness, art, self-images, psychological obsession, fantasy, and the like (Monterroso, Cajina-Vega, Cea, Naranjo, Rovinski, Urbano, García Saucedo).

Finally, there is the absurd as a theme together with the approach (and techniques) of magic realism. Bermúdez's "The Horse in the Glassware Shop" is a classic instance of a story whose relentlessly logical outcome follows upon a blatant but significant impossibility divulged at the beginning; one presumes that Kafka's "The Metamorphosis" is a logical precursor in this mode. Endara's "Family Photograph" and Castillo's "The Attack of the Man-Eating Paper" are not far off. On the other hand, the very fabric of the experience created in Cortés's "Funeral Rites in Summer" becomes equivocal in the treatment of it, as also in Retana's "The Back Rooms," while the journey recounted in Chase's "The Path of the Wind" leans toward pure fantasy.

But fantasy is more a technique than it is a theme, and it has many uses. Other stories land squarely in this camp because the experiences related are so demonstrably at odds with the expectations we readers have (Ricardo Lindo, Méndez, Uriel Quesada, Bolaños Ugalde, Urbano, De Castro, Jaramillo Levi). Closely related to fantasy is allegory, a technique designed to convey a message on a level other than the literal. Here the messages inherent in Ramírez's brief "On the Stench of Corpses" and Escobar Galindo's "Restless" are perfectly clear (while pointing in quite different directions), and Arias's "Toward Patzún" seems to turn into allegory only at the end.

The basic notions of realism appear in many of these stories, along with the underlying assumption that whatever else literature may do, it certainly acts as though it intends to describe elements of our real material world while it interprets them. This is especially so among the stories that deal with the lower classes, whether urban or rural. Pinto's attention to particulars ("Disobedience"), Peña's accumulation of detail ("The House"), Turner's presentation of the world through the eyes of a totally inebriated peasant ("Carnival")—these three fairly represent the concerns and aesthetic goals of many others in this collection. However, one of the great concerns of realism (and one that much postmodern writing ignores) is the prominence given a verisimilitudinous, fully rounded central figure—and this concern is frequently absent from the stories here, even those in which the basic assumptions underlying "realistic" fiction otherwise prevail. But a few stories stand out in part simply because their central figures are sharply delineated as individuals: Monterroso's "The Circumstantial or the Ephemeral," Escoto's "Reality before Noon," Galich's "The Rat Catcher," and Britton's "Love Is Spelled with a 'G'" for example.

And what about satire, perhaps the most ubiquitous technique in this entire collection? This anthology is heavy with accusations. The targets are everywhere, and the charges are expressed in plots and situations, character depiction and dialogue, with a full panoply of tonal values, even when the satire may not be central to the story's thematic content.

Nearly all the writers represented here have published poetry, and three have earned worldwide reputations with their lyrics (Cuadra, Hugo Lindo, and Del Valle). Many are novelists; a few have written drama, television scripts, and literature for children. But very few of the writers of these stories make any pretense of being "professional": that is, they do not earn their living—or even a significant percentage of this—by means of their writing. Most have spent a significant amount of time abroad, as students, political exiles, or economic exiles. Some have connections with the world of publishing or journalism (Naranjo, Escoto, Oviedo, Jaramillo Levi, Cortés, Rivera, Cuadra). The largest number are academics, often teaching in disciplines other than the humanities, and many have published articles, monographs, and books in their specialties—philosophy, sociology, statistics, journalism—in addition to their short fiction. Physicians, lawyers, journalists, government officials, and diplomats are also represented here. Many have won literary prizes in their own as well as in other countries (though mostly in Central America). Some have seen their literary works translated into German, French, Italian, or English. And a few have gained international reputations because of this, such as Cuadra, Ramírez, Monterroso, Hugo Lindo, Dobles, and Naranjo.

References

Acevedo, Ramón Luis. *La novela centroamericana: desde el Popol-Vuh hasta los umbrales de la novela actual.* Rio Piedras: Editorial Universitaria, Universidad de Puerto Rico, 1982.

Martin, Gerald. *Journeys through the Labyrinth: Latin American Fiction in the Twentieth Century.* London and New York: Verso, 1989.

Menton, Seymour. *El cuento hispanoamericano: antología crítico-histórica.* Mexico City: Fondo de Cultura Económico, 1987.

Pavón, Alfredo. *El universo del relato literario.* Chiapas, Mexico: Universidad Autónoma de Chiapas, 1984.

Pupo-Walker, Enrique. *El cuento hispanoamericano ante la crítica.* Madrid: Castalia, 1973.

Contemporary Short Stories
from Central America

Toward Patzún

Arturo Arias
Translated by Leland H. Chambers

The road twisted so many times that I thought I would soon reach the top of the mountain. The cool, dense wind had now ceased picking up the road dust and was being enriched by the soft aroma from the rows of pines.

I had walked the whole morning and expected to reach Patzún before nightfall.

The long rows of pines at the borders of the deep ravines caused my heart to swell. I smiled with that involuntary smile that surges up like a jet of water whose drops burn into us unexpectedly when we contemplate the beauty of a landscape that at first seems alien to our nature but is then suddenly felt to be shot through with our own being. I stopped to listen for a moment and heard only the breeze among the leaves. I sighed. The humidity of the atmosphere was overloaded and I anticipated that within a short time thick drops of water would begin to shake me. I pushed ahead, trying to find the zig-zags of the shortcut without wavering.

It was then that I perceived a woman in the distance walking along the same path, going in the same direction as mine. With a graceful, playful step she was advancing rapidly through the trees, though not in a straight line, but in a roundabout way. It seemed as though she would run into the trees on one side and disappear, and then I would see her among those of the opposite side. With her head erect and proud she radiated a perfect harmony with all that was around her.

In the distance that separated us and given the angle from which the intense light of the sun bathed her, her skin seemed of pure gold. I imagined her as quite refined in her shape and manner of being. Slender, she was doubtless modest and restrained in her speech. Her black hair was well pulled back over her head and fell in two braids down her back. She was dressed in a typical *huipil*, a blouse from Patzún. It was bright red, loose and flowing over her waist. The fabric was a heavy stuff with green and yellow fringes.

I followed her with my eyes, turning my neck in order to keep from losing her. She walked at such a rapid pace that she rather appeared to be gliding between the branches.

The sky, which so recently had been perfectly limpid, unfolding luminously with a blue so blue that its very clarity dazzled, began to be covered with black clouds. Nonetheless, the leaves on the *chichicaste* nettle bushes still flashed intensely white.

I hastened my step still more. Allowing a sigh to escape, I matched my step with hers and continued on my way, maintaining the same distance behind her. All of a sudden the path was smooth before heading down into a gorge and from there beginning the last ascent that would take us almost to the town.

Swiftly, lightly, vaguely or densely, sometimes shining and bright, brisk and clear, thirty years of recollections went through my mind. That woman ahead of me, with her *huipil* filtering reddish bursts of light over the growing clouds, lighting up the air with a soft blaze of golden color spread palely toward the black clouds, embodied the perfume of the fragrant carnations, the resinous aroma of the conifers of my childhood. I had spent it happily far away in Antigua, that colonial city with cobbled streets. In those days everything was simpler. There were mountains, valleys, streams. I used to climb the mountains, wander through the valleys, sit down on the riverbanks. I would liken the hilltops to the breasts of wild turkeys, the rocks to calves. With curious eyes I sought to discover the wisdom that seemed to me hidden everywhere. And when from the peak of the Agua volcano I spied the white dots that comprised the former capital, my eyes opened even wider, my breast quivered, and I begged for that luminosity never to end: that intense greenness, the tranquillity of a breeze as soft and transparent as a crystalline drop of water. The kindliness, the beauty of my country at that moment seemed vast, infinite, and incapable of being matched. I saluted each peak, each star, as if they existed for me alone and would dissolve into smiles when they saw me, and on the cold, damp afternoons when it rained I would lie down on a blanket made thin by use in order to contemplate the flames of the chimney for uncountable hours, watching the white smoke given off by the firewood twisting around as if it wanted to avoid going out into the cold outside. The fire would burn with the sound of a satisfied cat spreading its warm breath throughout the whole room. It projected its tremulous light in the shape of a fan over the floor, frightening the shadows and forcing them to take refuge in the coldest and most distant corners. In that period, darkness was not safe anywhere, and I would hum the saddest songs with cheerful, harmonious sounds that lasted for a long while.

Now we were in tormented times. The sky was unrelenting, gray and clouded over. Cold bursts of wind beginning to descend in swirls from the sierra peaks seemed driven mad and were advancing blindly, crashing as often into the cornfields as into the slender cypresses, giving voice to howls like those of a wounded coyote. The mountainous countryside, whitened suddenly by the cold rain, lost all its depth. The stream that I had been hearing for some time now at the bottom of the gorge was bellowing, crazed and furious. The wind laden with drops of water flung them at my face as if they were whips.

Forced to nearly shut my eyes, I would try to guess where the path was. My only fear, in the midst of this sudden cold, was losing the woman from my sight. It seemed to me I could hear her shouts, and I was able to make out two or three children's voices. Strident shouts that bothered me, that made my hopes vacillate.

Anxiety gripped me. I felt dragged down into the darkest depths by the beating of the wind. I tried to open my eyes slightly, to understand the significance of this sudden violence over so gentle a nature; I trembled in distress because of its effect on the woman and the children who were obviously accompanying her. Grief was suffocating me and I became violently upset.

I started to run. Through the curtain of water it seemed to me I could make out three or four silhouettes almost floating amid all the mud. A little higher up the woman was running, shouting some words and lifting her arms toward what was even higher yet. When I saw her I felt as if cool water were running through me and, letting a profound sigh escape, I allowed my mouth to be transformed into a fleeting smile. Up there, higher up on the path, the red color of her *huipil* stood out over the brown ribbon of the path and above the green leaves.

She had scarcely disappeared over the hilltop when the three or four mud-covered silhouettes were rushing up behind her. One could see they were attempting to move much more rapidly than they were able to.

After the gorge where, struggling with the wind and rain, I was unable to prevent the mud from covering my lower legs, the ascent began again. It was a steep path that passed under the menacing shadow of the howling cypresses all covered with slippery dead leaves. I made all possible haste, furiously pushing my hands down on my knees in order to help my legs straighten out. My breath began to fail.

In a few moments I sensed I was drawing closer to the woman and the children. I could hear their voices through the trees.

Soon I reached a section still narrower and more torturous. I tried to move still faster and felt myself being invaded by an unknown calm, an artificial, treacherous peace, in keeping with the way the rain was getting gentler and the wind was abating its force. I thought I heard the steps of the woman and the children just in front of me, crushing the dry leaves, but the sounds seemed unusually strong, as if they belonged to some large animal.

It was a lengthy deliberation that had finally convinced me to walk to Patzún. I was no longer able to bear the melancholy that had gotten into me; I felt embittered by the surrounding situation.

In a slight clearing of the vegetation, I was able to see the woman's face for a single instant, up above mine. There was a point where the path went up in the form of a hook and I felt the reflection of her overwhelming proximity. Her large black eyes were severe, as if some disturbing fluids might any moment burst out of their long-suffering, dark depths. But what impressed me most was the coldness of her expression, so markedly indifferent that I instantly knew I would never dare to address a word to her. She seemed to have lost even the strength to turn her face down to look at me.

She vanished as quickly as she had appeared. For a moment I contemplated the shaded place where the apparition had been. It seemed to me I could hear a light sound of footsteps, almost abusively excessive, in the distance. I recalled again my childhood vista from the peak of Agua volcano, and, rejecting with an angry gesture the vision of the face that had so wounded me, I was unable to prevent bitter tears of rage and impotence from escaping my eyes.

I felt my body was empty. I lost the notion of time. I was unable to think anymore. Exhausted, I slowed my pace until I was almost dragging my feet over the dry leaves. Pressing my lips tightly together, I repressed the nostalgic need for coolness, serenity. Violently I yanked a branch from a bush and covered my eyes with it, as if this way I would be able to generate a state of mind in which everything might blend together harmoniously, like washing out the inside of my head with pure water which as it rinsed would leave nothing behind but a mollifying sweetness.

It was at that moment that I heard the shouts. They were the same as before but now they sounded desperate, heartrending, as if a tremendous squall had suddenly removed all the vegetation. The screams penetrated the thickest tree trunks and filtered through the earth by means of the same invisible cracks into which the water used to disappear. The screaming ceased and a silence as cold as it was brief began, like the grating calm of a big frost. And then I heard, with a knot in my stomach and an immediate weakening of my legs, a burst of machine-gun fire. And following that came another scream, still stronger, more cutting, a thousand times more heartrending.

I didn't know whether to run toward the point where the screaming came from or whether to hide in the underbrush. There was a sudden looseness in my intestines and a strange shuddering in my stomach. I was standing, very pale, leaning against a fragrant-smelling pine tree, shivering so that it seemed to me the very tree trunk itself was trembling and that some of its branches were knocking against the others.

The previous cycle was repeated once more. The screams, the icy silence, a new burst from the machine gun. The only thing different was the intense whimpering of the children, whose number seemed fewer with each burst.

It was so insanely inconceivable that I was unable to think of the woman in the red *huipil*, of the three or four silhouettes as muddy as my own legs, except with a superstitious horror. Suddenly losing my balance, or my strength, or my mind, I fell to my knees with the knowledge that now there was not a single probable certainty in life, not a single rational confidence, not a single human surety. Why kill them? Why? Why? Did it have to be this way inevitably?

And once again the screams, the silence, the new burst of gunfire.

A prisoner of panic, I burst into the underbrush, away from the path, and ran uphill headlong, paying no attention to the branches thrusting at me, the tears in my clothing, the stumbling, the thorns. I ran uphill with my mouth open, panting, like a desperate person who has run out of oxygen, as if appealing to the most brutal of means hoping to quell those screams, the inevitable gunfire, the muffled despair.

Not knowing how, with my feet unsteady, temples pounding, hands dripping blood, I reached the base of a large rock that seemed to mark the highest point of the hill. I wanted to go around it in order to pursue my violent and reckless flight, when I was stopped suddenly, absolutely jolted, and threw myself backward with such violence that my wrist struck hard against the rock. I let myself fall to the ground, weeping and cursing at once.

From that point I was able to observe what was happening. A military patrol had stopped the woman and the children. They were pointing their machine guns at them. Trembling like a leaf, the officer was swinging his arms back and forth like someone insane. His voice was hoarse.

"Where is he, you bitch? Tell us where he is!"

The woman screamed and shouted in her own tongue. For me, at least, it was impossible to decipher her words.

"You don't want to speak, is that it? Kill another one!"

Then I saw one of the mud-covered silhouettes, screaming with terror, being pulled around by a soldier. The woman tried to rush toward him but the officer grabbed her by the wrist. The woman attempted a slap toward his face with her free hand but the officer ducked it agilely and twisted her arm behind her back and forced her to fall to her knees. The other soldier threw the muddy silhouette to the ground and, almost in the same instant, fired.

"Let's see if you'll talk now, you turd-colored Indian!"

I let myself fall against the ground, sinking my face into the dry leaves. Again I clutched at my humble desire to love and be loved, howling pitiably like a dog recently beaten. At once my whole body relaxed and remained there on the ground, overcome. The dark dampness, the longing, the sorrow were interrupted only by the indecipherable screams, the quite clear "kill another one," the yells, the burst of machine-gun fire, while my body got accustomed to a strange laxity, a calm desperation, an insensibility that little by little was becoming adjusted to the shadow of affliction.

I felt like a captive wandering fruitlessly in darkness and monotony, never arriving any place, eternally alone, with the daily deaths of my compatriots as my only consolation and company.

Finally I heard the final sentence:

"Now there's only you. Are you finally going to talk or not? Where is he?"

Again the unintelligible shouting, this time without the chorus of whimpering anymore. And in the midst of the tormented crumbling away of lives, it seemed to me that once I heard her say in bad Spanish, "But I really don't know, I already told you he went away more than two years ago." As if in a half-dozing state, in the middle of a dream more terrifying even than reality itself, with its nebulous images of a life that has ceased being so, I heard perfectly when the officer said, almost disdainful and bored, "Let's finish her off once and for all." I made out the screams, the noise of a body being thrown violently into the weeds, the final deafening burst of gunfire of the day. Then the footsteps indicating a gradual withdrawal, and finally, of course, the reign of silence.

I remained in the same position for a long time, until the cold began to shoot through me and I started to feel achy and feverish. Only then did I get to my feet.

I saw the bodies clearly some distance away. And for a brief instant I shivered with fright on seeing there, stretched out in their midst, my own bleeding body. I could not take my eyes away from the place, as if the only way to drive away the image was to engrave it in my mind like a tattoo, down to the last detail of that macabre scene. In that way, before my own family eliminated with such impunity, I found a hopeless astonishment over my own destiny. I ran my hand over my hair and then lowered it to my mouth, kissing it with the serene generosity of feeling myself still temporarily unsure whether I was alive or dead. Then I hesitated an instant and lowered my eyes. Immediately I went down on my knees and, filled with anguished distress shot through with fierce hatred, I lowered my bare head utterly, respectfully, and wished for once not to have been born engulfed in this immense sea of misfortunes that used to be the most beautiful country in the world, while I felt for the bullet holes perforating my body.

Tránsito

José Barnoya García
Translated by Leland H. Chambers

For my country's starving children.

It was raining heavily. As it always did, and never like this before!
The drops became puddles, the puddles became lakes, the lakes
turned into rivers, the rivers into oceans . . . oceans of rain.

From the depths of a little hut illuminated only by the bolts of
lightning a howl broke out, prolonged, resounding, yearning. The crib
was simply a mat splashing about on the muddy floor, the roof thatch
was a filter for the rain, the stiff reed walls shook.

Vicente, the father, heard the crying. "Scream, you little scamp,
scream while you can," he said to him, whispering. "Later on you won't
even have the right to open your mouth. So scream away, you rascal,
scream. Scream."

The mother, Cayetana, resting from her exhausting work, shielded
her latest son with her firm, dark arms while a print of the Virgin of the
Forsaken Ones tried to protect the other three kids.

The little rascal's first days were happy ones. There was so much milk
for him to drink that it dribbled from the corners of his mouth and he
even had the luxury of spitting it out when his mother was burping him
over her shoulder, trying to draw all the air out of his stomach. Weary
from so much nursing of her offspring, Cayetana's generous breasts—the
breasts of a wet nurse—little by little became spent and no longer gave
very much. And that little rascal, no matter how hard he suckled, finally
was unable to extract more than a few drops of colostrum, and they did
not placate his longing for nourishment.

The tiny howl was soon transformed into a whimper, a sad, persistent, beseeching whimper. To quiet him down his mother began giving him swallows of *atol*, a drink made from cornmeal.

"*Atol. Atol de masa. Atole* on the tip of a finger, that's what they've always given us," his mother thought, remorsefully.

And to put him to sleep at night, she would dip the end of her shawl in a pint of aguardiente and let him suck it a few times, and finally the child would go to sleep, passed out.

Daydreaming, Cayetana could see her husband: he was drunk, weaving back and forth, saliva drooling from his mouth, voice heavy with aguardiente. . . . For Vicente got drunk quite often. He was drunk every Saturday, there was nothing else to do. He got drunk when she became pregnant again. He got drunk when the little rascal was born, all the more so because he saw the little one was just like him, even in the way he had of nibbling at her nipples. And he was drunk once again when they finally had him baptized.

It had been raining hard that Sunday. As it always did, as never before.

The church seemed like an anthill it was so swarming with people. She saw dark, beseeching faces on all sides, asking for favors with hands pressed together and bare feet twisted around.

On the altars coated with smoke and gold, the imitation saints in their luxurious robes remained silent before the prayers.

Dripping wax on the floor, the candles with their spiraling exhalations caused the hope-laden smoke of the prayers to ascend.

In a group they approached the baptismal font where a priest with his acolyte awaited them indifferently. Their turn came, and the priest began to read in nasal voice and bad Latin: "*Exorciso te creatura salis, in nomine Dei Patris omnipotentis, et in charitate Domine Nostri Jesu Christi, et in virtute Spiritus Sancti.*"

"Li mero Cagúa incá nanau aan, solo nanau li hi—" whispered Cayetana. Our Holy Father doesn't understand that, he only understands our looks, she repeated in her native Kekchi, "*Incá nanau. Incá. Incá. . . .*"

And the priest, continuing with another outbreak of Latin, "*Accipa sal sapientiae: Propitiation set tibi in vitam aeternam—,*" dipped his grimy, pudgy index finger in the salt and after pronouncing the name "Tránsito" he rubbed it lightly over the child's tiny mouth.

"More salt. The priest is putting salt in the wound already, he's fucking us over. Why more salt if he was already born fucked over? We've always been screwed and always will be screwed," Vicente thought at that moment.

"—*per saecula, saeculorum. Amen,*" the padre finished speaking while the altar boy held out his hand for the offering.

The joy of the Holy Cross festivals burst out like a giant skyrocket. Tránsito's belly began to show. His hands were plump, his skin was taut. Little fatso, fatso. . . . "Fatso my foot!" Vicente said to himself. "Swollen is what he is. Real swollen."

Like the firecrackers and bottle rockets announcing the bullfights, the joy of the festivities honoring Saint Anthony was scattered everywhere. His hair began to fall out and his color began to change. From the color he was born with, black as an ant, he was fading toward a shade of brown like a corn shuck. "Maybe this way, with his light-colored skin they'll respect me more and won't look down their noses at him," his mother thought.

Like the chords on a gourd marimba ran the joy of Saint Christopher's day. But Tránsito was deteriorating. From being swollen he gradually became more emaciated. He didn't play with his hands, nor with his feet. He no longer laughed, nor cried. He was no longer a child. He was a listless doll.

It was now the day of the feast of the Virgin of the Ascension. The crowing of the rooster announced that morning was near. Cayetana rubbed her eyes and stretched, pushed the bedclothes to one side, and paused for a moment pensively. She heard the muffled snoring of her husband. She didn't hear the breathing of her little rascal. On tiptoe she approached the mat where the baby was, as quiet as ever. Very pale, eyes wide open as if taking everything in. Mouth displaying tiny teeth like a gopher's, abandoned hands trying to grasp something. She woke Vicente by beating on him. They bundled him up the best they could and carried him toward the village. The doctor was half dressed when he received them. He placed the child on a table and with his stethoscope listened to him all over, trying to find some throbbing, at least a breath, a half-cut-off respiration. On a piece of paper, a form, he wrote: "Infantile malnutrition."

"Save him, Tatita," his mother was sputtering, while the father with tears in his eyes wailed in his native tongue, "*Dios Cagúa, kamenaq Li chinaal*—." He is dead. He is dead.

They dug a grave in the middle of their field. The defenseless body of the little scamp went down to the bottom and there it was covered over with their earth and their flowers.

"He's all right there," Vicente ended by saying. "He'll improve the soil and we'll have good corn. It'll be our best harvest."

It was raining hard. As it always did, and never like this before!

The drops turned into puddles, the puddles into lakes, the lakes turned into rivers, and the rivers turned into oceans . . . oceans of tears.

(*Translator's note*: "Tránsito," meaning "passing through, in transit," is a rather common name in the province of Alta Verapaz.)

The Rat Catcher

Franz Galich
Translated by Pamela Carmell

I started eating rats as long ago as I can remember. I think, I'm not really sure. I'm not going to say I did it because my parents taught me to. No. I would be ungrateful if I did, since I never met those people who were my parents. I don't know where I was born either, so I can't give them credit for anything—good or bad. Rats taste good. I like them better than other food, like for example: I'd rather eat a rat than an orange, the rat is juicier. I also prefer a rat to a snapper or a perch.

One of the reasons I didn't last long in the houses where I worked—I had to earn a living—was because cats ran away from me as if they saw the cat devil himself and because rats seemed to disappear by magic. People hate rats but when they disappear they begin to love them and miss them.

I never eat a single rat I don't need. I don't have a set number of rats I eat, no set time, but I like to eat at night and alone. I believe this is partly due to the fact that at that hour they know I need them and so they come out.

Another of my preferences, I think more a matter of habit—who knows where I got it from—is eating female rats. Better yet if they are pregnant, since the baby rats are very tender. I make sure no one is watching me when I'm eating. It isn't nice to watch someone eat; I don't like it. And it's worse if they want to ask for some. Anyway, there aren't many people like that.

I'd act like I ate the food that my bosses gave me but when they weren't looking I'd stick it in my pants pockets and take it to my room, the farthest down the hall, where I slept, and I'd give it to my friends the rats.

Usually, they didn't notice when I put the food in my pockets, since I ate by myself, far away from my bosses.

The dogs would come to where I was eating—where I was pretending to eat—but there was no way I was going to give them the food since the beings that were my fare really needed it. Besides, they put a little scare into me. No way am I going to eat dogs, though I know there are people who do. To each his own.

When each house starts to run out of rats, I have to go to another house and so on, from house to house, town to town. Since I don't have any sisters or brothers, or parents, or anyone watching out for me, not even a birthplace, much less a place to die, all this wandering doesn't matter to me. Why don't I have anyone—I already told you that, right? Well, just in case—none of that means anything to me, I don't have anyone or anything. The only things I own are a change of clothes and my painting of St. Martin de Porres, since he helps me keep from running out of rats, and the change of clothes because I like to go around looking clean and well-dressed. I like to be neat and clean.

I have wandered through many towns in Guatemala, mainly along the southern coast, and I have to say the taste of rats varies from one town to another. Of course, it's no big thing, but there is certainly a difference between the meat on the coast and the meat in colder places. Or a difference in animals with hot blood and animals with cold blood.

My stay in a church is where I get my devotion to that saint from somewhere down in Peru, according to the priest from Llano de Animas, the last place where I worked before getting arrested. Father Arango would tell me that the mice understood St. Martin and they paid attention to him, that he would talk to them and feed them. Sometimes I ask myself if he didn't like rats too.

I never tried to ask the father about that because I didn't dare, and I wasn't afraid that God would punish me either. It was nice in the church at Llano because there were enough rats. There were house rats and country rats. The house rats are little and gray, and the ones in the mountains are little and brown, with a few more scales on their tails. Father Arango was good to me but I killed him because he said I was going to hell for eating rats.

Let me repeat, I don't eat more rats than I need. The other guy who was a prisoner with me was afraid of me, not because I'd killed someone, but because I eat rats instead of all those hard beans, greasy, stiff tortillas, and that fucking water they call coffee that they give you here in jail.

To learn how to catch rats I had to practice a lot. It was hard. At the start, I spent many hungry hours and I had to catch them with trickery. First I spent all my time watching how the cats did it; too bad I didn't have their speed and size. Rats are very fast little animals. Speedy. I always feel bad when they get poisoned and even worse about the stuff they've come up with so the poor little things don't even realize they've been poisoned. Once I got very sick and nearly died. I didn't know it, but I was eating some rats that'd been eating poison. Then I got deathly ill and the worst thing was I couldn't go to the doctor. No way was I going to tell him I'd been eating rats. I had to cure myself with herb teas. The worst thing was I had to cover up my condition. In the afternoons I'd go to the edge of town to pick lemon tea leaves so I could wash my stomach and blood. Barley and Jamaican rose worked on the inflammation, but my liver was all torn up. In those days I went around in buggy, dirty old rags; it wouldn't have taken much to make me pull up stakes. And the worst part was I had to keep myself fed. That's why I went to another house.

Now I can't remember really well where that happened: in Palín or in Antigua.

They say rats eat anything. Even people. In the cemeteries they get into the graves and after they eat all the wood on the box they start to eat the corpse. The first thing they eat are the eyes and then they go farther inside, into the brain and the stomach until they get to the intestines and after that they go on eating the flesh until they strip the skeleton and clothes clean. It's a race against hunger: theirs and the worms'. I really think people say all those things because rats don't sit well with them. Since the time I was poisoned, I've hated people. None of them sit well with me.

The first days of my apprenticeship were hard. My tactic consisted of going into a dark room full of old worthless junk. Every house has those rooms, especially houses in the country. I'd stretch out on the floor and stay quiet, not making a sound, hardly breathing. I would open my mouth and put something to eat in it. I'd stay like that a long time. During those moments I had to concentrate as much as I could and think that the rats had to come. There I'd be. Thinking, thinking-praying, thinking, praying: "Blessed, holy, merciful rats, come to me, to my belly, blessed fruit, by your very precious blood I will live and will live for all eternity, to the end of time. Amen." Nothing more, nothing less. It was a prayer I thought up; I got great results with it. After I said the prayer over and over again, the first rat arrived and climbed up on my body and began to sniff around with its cold, little nose. I felt every little whisker and its soft skin. It walked along my shins, across my stomach and over my chest.

It nibbled at my hair. Things didn't always happen that way. Sometimes they ran up my face. Finally they would smell what I had in my mouth and they came toward it slowly. Carefully, little by little, they'd put their little head in the pit of my mouth, and when they'd gotten up their confidence, pow! I snapped my jaws shut and trapped one. I felt its warm blood run down my lips, my teeth and tongue. And I felt how the poor little things tried, with reflex movements, to get loose with their little paws and their little nails. Some would squeal, nearly all of them did that; others just struggled, trying to get away from my mighty jaws. Some scratched my face, but I tried to avoid that by letting my beard grow. It took me a lot of time and patience to perfect this technique, but who isn't going to be patient when he's trying to feed himself. The work was a little difficult, even dangerous, since sometimes I had to go up into the attics, but most of all I had to be careful of people, nosy, pushy people who like to go around checking out what someone is doing or not doing. That's why I hate everyone. I think I could only get along with someone like me.

I'm really sorry about the death of the late Father Arango, since in a way he was the one who paid for all my hate against people, built up all those years, especially against my bosses, who were the closest at hand and so the ones who checked up on me the most. The poor old guy was already so old. I really believe I did him a favor by helping him leave this world.

Another person who got some of my hate was that Micaila girl. That's what I called her, but her name was Micaela, Micaela Donis, I think, but I don't remember exactly. The poor woman was scared away by my habits. I met her at a dance in Escuintla or La Democracia, I'm not sure which. The only thing I really remember is it was very hot and our bodies were sweating from so much dancing and drinking. That very night I took her to a room and you won't believe this, but after being with her, that is to say, of having my way with her, using her for my manly needs— I have them too, you know—who would've thought it, but I had to get up in the middle of the night to eat my little rat. Micaila didn't know because she was tired from dancing and drinking, and, as if it were no big thing, she still attended to me in her womanly duty. I was tired too and I was just going to sleep when I hear in the distance, across the rafter, the almost imperceptible but unmistakable scamper of a little rat and, boy! I forgot about that Micaila girl's curves and how good it felt to be with that bubble head, and so without even getting dressed and still half in my cups, I got up to look for the little rat until I found it, nice and quiet, eating a newspaper. I swear it made my mouth water.

I started living with that Micaila girl. We rented a room in Siquinalá; she worked and I did too.

She didn't know about my favorite dishes. That day, around All Saints' Day, was some eight years ago, or is it ten? I can't remember anymore. She was pregnant by me and didn't have long to go when, one night, she catches me red-handed: I was eating a rat. On the spot she screamed at me, insulted me, and began to throw up. She twisted up her mouth, she scratched her face and beat on her belly, shouting the whole time that she didn't want a child that had been made with kisses from a mouth that ate live rats.

I feel sure that if the rats'd been dead it'd have been a different story.

That very night she left. I don't know where she went to but she told me she'd rather be dead.

I still don't know what became of her. Afterward the rumor went around that she had drowned herself; someone said she hadn't wanted to have the baby. That was one of my first pieces of bad luck. I've had a lot. Having to work isn't what you'd really call a hardship. Being a prisoner is. Being responsible for so many lives is, too. Not having a wife or children or homeland or anyone is too. The wife part can be taken care of a little bit by going to hookers and paying to spend the night with them, but that's not the same, my friend.

For a man like me there's no other choice left, since you've seen what happened to me with the wife I had. On the other hand, whores don't go around asking a guy what he eats.

When I was going to be with a woman, I would carry a couple of rats that were already dead in my coat pocket. (You ought to see the energy they give you for making love.)

There's no other way. Since the mess with that Micaila girl, I've gotten more careful because what I really can't do is quit eating my daily meal of rats.

Not having a wife means not having kids, because to have kids with a whore, well, there's enough of them around already.

Sometimes you think it's better not to have any, but it's a bitch knowing you'll leave this world and won't leave anything behind. It's not a pleasant thought.

In my case, just a bad reputation and on top of that, Rat Catcher! The business of not having a homeland to go back to is even more fucked up, since I don't even have any place to be buried in. The only thing that'll happen to me is what has happened to so many others. They just turn up along the roads, no one knows why, or maybe in a gully or in a river or in the ocean or in the Pacaya volcano or at best they'll bury me in La Verbena cemetery in an unmarked grave. All that bad luck has hounded me.

Think about it: first what happened to me with the Micaila girl, second with Father Arango, although actually I killed the priest first, since I hooked up with Micaila two years later. It was after that that I was in jail because of a ruckus in a bar where they killed some girl, but the truth is I didn't kill her, I swear. If they killed her on my account, that's something else again. But it wasn't because I wanted it. I was with her one Friday night. A policeman on patrol sat at another table. Because she wouldn't have anything to do with him, he, drunk on jealousy and brandy, shot her a couple of times when she got up to play "Cabaretera." While it was being investigated, I was a pris . . . ident.

Between times I think about the Micaila girl. . . .

There was a song I sang to her. It was a song I heard from some students who were drinking in Palín or Amatitlán, I don't remember exactly; the song goes like this (I'm going to sing it for you):

> For this baldy woo woo woo
> Miss Micaila cried woo woo woo
> for this baldy woo woo woo
> Miss Micaila cried woo woo woo
>
> When I put my hand
> on his bald spot,
> Micaila said
> this guy sure is hot.

Right here you repeat the first verse. You should sing it with feeling, because if you don't, it doesn't work with the ladies. Then the guy goes back to singing, a great big, fat-faced guy with a good voice, and he was good at drinking, too:

> When I put my hand
> On his broad chest
> Micaila said
> this guy points straight ahead.

It's a country song, a *ranchero*, and you surely know how those songs are sung in bars; those guys put a lot of feeling into it. The other students would sing the chorus. There were some who could really follow along with the tune, but some were too drunk—they were rocking in their boots—while the fat-faced guy went on, singing along with the guitar:

> When I put my hand
> on his belly button
> Micaila said
> this guy sure does come.

And to finish off the song, with all the guys who were knocking them back, listening close, the big guy would sing:

When I put my hand
on his turtle
Micaila said
goochy goochy goo

For this baldy woo woo woo
Miss Micaila cried woo woo woo
for this baldy woo woo woo
Miss Micaila cried woo woo woo.

But when they sang this part, some would double over, laughing. The women would get all worked up and would clap, some would shout and others didn't like it at all. I liked the song and I learned it, since in one way or another it reminded me of my Micaila.

When I think of the song I can't help remembering her and the kid she was going to have. It must have been mine, or else that night she wouldn't have scratched her face and screwed up her mouth, although she could've gotten it with some other son-of-a-bitch, I don't know.

After that I hooked up with María Antonia. Toña, I used to call her. She was like a cat, that hussy, but not because she had white eyes or because she had nine lives or because she was furry or because of all those things cats do, since she didn't even eat rats.

She was like a cat because she liked a guy to be on top of her all the time, she couldn't get enough. I left her because I thought that she was burning the barn down and because she liked a guy to do dirty things in bed. And I sure couldn't be one of those kind of guys, I'm such a sensitive guy, you know. A shame too, considering how she ended up. They say she was a whore in the "Cony" or in a bar in Mazate, I don't know which. At least that way she found an easy way to satisfy her desires. I don't hold anything against her, except a little disgust. When I was in the capital, one of the few times I went there, some woman asked me why did I let my nails grow so long and I told her "the better to catch you," because I sure wasn't going to tell her they helped me carve up rats better. Now, you may not believe this, but you need nails to get at this kind of food. Just looking at me here, I seem a little indifferent, but quick. But I can see in the dark and when I walk I don't make any noise. If I want, of course. This nose of mine is good at picking up smells.

What you're thinking is exactly right: a cat pure and simple. I let the mustache grow because it makes me look sharp, not because it does me any good, like my beard did in those first days way back when. Now, if I want to eat a rat the only thing I have to do is hunt for one and when I've found one, boom! one swipe with my hand and zap! into my mouth, alive, tail waving.

Father Arango I killed because he wanted to make me quit eating my little rats. He would say to me in a slow but authoritative voice: "It was no mistake that God made those animals disgusting, but to help souls go to heaven instead of hell, since those are some of the animals that live down there." Or if not that, he might say to me: "The rats are the opposite of doves since doves are white, pure, while the rats are gray, impure, the color of ash from the fires of hell. There aren't any white rats, they're agents of the devil that Satan has let loose so we'll fall into the trap of sin. Just like there aren't any gray doves either, they are rats disguised as doves that only serve to make the disbelievers go to dwell in hell. Doves dwell in heaven. And if that's not so, my son, why do you think that God chose to bring this dumb little animal into the world?" And so on, a lot of dumb talk that made me mad. What harm did I do the rats by eating them? What's more, I think I did them some good, if what the priest says is true about rats, hell, and Satan. So I began to plan how to kill him so no one would find out.

As I've said over and over, I began by wishing Father Arango would die. First it was a wish, then a need, and finally an urge that would come over me from way down inside, with all my soul. That's how I started to pray for help, with all my soul, from the only saint I was devoted to, St. Martin. I knew beforehand that I wouldn't kill him right out, the people loved him so much. I decided to get him to leave Llano de Animas, to kill him on the road, since hardly anyone traveled on it when there was no market, days when people go down to Amatitlán to buy and sell. Every night I went up into the attic over the sacristy where he slept, and made him listen to the squeals of rats and their babies.

Squeals from the rats when they saw me eating up their little baby rats and from the babies as I ate them up bite by bite. The poor priest suffered terribly, since he thought it was the devil's work. He would say the Devil was tempting him. The poor man would get up at all hours of the night to pray and to mortify himself to get a little relief. Afterward he beat himself for having drunk holy water. As I continued with the torture, he began to sleep in his cassock, with his rosary, scapular, and the magnificat. Then he would go to sleep with all the thingamajigs he used for saying Mass. Poor man. Poor old man. You should've seen him. The poor guy was looking even older than he was, but he never said a word to anyone about what was happening to him, not even me. He began to lose his confidence to an extreme, he didn't have any faith even in his own shadow, but he disguised it well. This went so far that people were saying that he was getting more saintly since every day he was kinder and more patient.

Finally, one day, without saying a word to anyone, after being tormented all night, he grabbed a gourd, filled it with holy water, and left for Amatitlán. I grabbed my machete and took off after him. When we got to the bend in the Matagusanos around Don Narciso's place, I spied him. He was walking along alone, muttering prayers.

When he saw me standing in the middle of the road with some sacks and my machete in my hand, he had to be thinking that he was dealing with the Devil himself. I looked him right in the face, the poor man raised his crucifix and ordered me to get back to my hell fires. He uncorked the gourd and raised it up to throw holy water on me. I raised my machete and brought it down hard. I had sharpened it the night before. There was a dull ring and the machete locked up on me a bit, I don't know if it was on the gourd or on his head. I only heard him praying. He didn't complain, he didn't cry out. He only prayed in silence. My arm hurt a little and it was splashed with blood. I put the dead man in my sack and carried him to the bank of the lake. The doomed man was so heavy. You wouldn't expect that from a thin guy like him, but it isn't the body that weighs so much, but death. Now at the bank of the lake, I looked at him for the last time; the last words of his useless prayers were still on his lips. His eyes shone with kindness, perhaps people were right, and I would have said that those eyes were beautiful except that the nasty cut between his eyebrows made him look ugly. I cut a cross in his stomach and threw lime in it. The living flesh, it still moved. I put some rocks in the sack and tied it up and let the bundle fall. Much later I came back to throw in my machete since I didn't want to keep it. Besides, it was nicked. I say that it was nicked up because the priest's bones were hard. The priest was already old, while I was young. He must have gone to heaven, while I'll go to hell. When all is said and done, I did him a favor.

I went back to the church and slept since I felt tired. After a month and the priest didn't turn up, the rumor began to get around that he had died; some said that he had gone to heaven body and soul. A few days later another father arrived to say a Mass for him and some very pious ladies prayed for him for nine days. It made me so sad tears ran out of my eyes.

But this isn't much for someone to go through. What is really a misfortune is when you think you've found happiness and pow! they snatch it away from you. That's what happened to me—plain and simple. So, I believe that's why I am the way I am, since there's never been any evil floating around in my blood.

Like I told you, my parents didn't teach me anything. Just like that. Nothing: not good or evil. To me, life was what made me bad. Bad luck. I got dealt a bad hand.

When I met Victoria something told me I was going to be happy, but not for long. You know, just a hunch. Like the ones you've had. She was employed by some old people with money. She told me they treated her well. That hussy was pretty, but that wasn't the best thing about her: she had a nice ass, wide and firm, good tits, and everything a woman could want. I bugged her with my habit of asking about her boss: your boss this, your boss that. She told me that she was an honorable woman, why was I thinking about that, and besides she wasn't in his league. At first I was jealous of her, I spied on the two of them, her and the old man, and I thought: "If she crosses me, piss on them both." But it turns out that she was good and honest. But the best thing about her, and the reason I got together with her, is that she ate rats too.

When I was living with her I didn't drink, I didn't go to bars with women either. This went on for three or four years. I thought finally I would be peaceful and happy. What worried me a little was the idea of having children, since the idea of a kid wasn't clear to her. Many nights I heard her crying quietly. One day I asked her why she was unhappy and she told me that she hadn't been able to give me a child. I told her not to worry, that we'd do whatever we could, but deep down I also felt something ugly I've never felt before. Her happiness returned; I knew it when I heard her singing:

Kitty, kitty,
Gentle cat,
In every corner
Finds a rat.

And I would sing back:

I would love
To be a cat
To climb in through
The open window
Hunting for
A girl like you.

But it turns out, see, that every day, day and night, we went at it, and nothing. The poor girl was wasting away little by little and she started to get old. She told me that she wanted to give me a son, that she wanted to go to bed with me, but how was I going to go to bed with a woman who was young but had gotten old already. Finally the poor thing died. She died crying. I was faithful to her always. The day she died I buried her. On the way back, I thought my bad luck was beginning to end. I went into the first bar I came to. I went all over town drinking, I don't know how many days. Drink, drink, drink. I said over and over to myself: drink, drink, drink. Life is short. All this happened to me a few days before I landed here, looking at the checkered light. After being in here a week with you, I began to feel a strange need to tell you everything that had happened to me. Now that I have, I feel better.

I always tried not to get mixed up in a fight. I don't have friends or enemies, I don't talk much and I don't like to be in any one place for long. I try to dodge, dodge all kinds of problems, but since bad luck follows me, it's better to keep your machete in your belt.

One night after my wife had died and a few days before I came here, I was having a drink when I heard some guys I didn't even know talking about her. They were talking about her female charms, they were talking about how beautiful she was, they were pretty crocked, there were two of them, I was crocked, too, the jukebox was playing "Deserted Lover" or "Marked Cards," I don't really remember, I touched the machete in my belt, one guy was telling the other guy that he'd had her before him, that she was real good but he'd gotten hold of her when she was a kid running the streets, the wench, that she liked him, that she didn't charge him. The brandy made my head spin, I felt her legs around my waist, her mouth made me drunk, her breath burned me, they were telling their macho stories, that's for sure: she had a good ass, she liked it, she didn't charge, they'd had her before me. I was certain that she had been faithful to me, she hadn't done me wrong, my machete cut into my waist, I felt like taking it out, I knew I shouldn't do it, I drained my drink in one gulp, and got ready to flee from my destiny, I didn't want bad luck to catch up with me. I stood up and made for the door, I closed my eyes so I couldn't see them, but oh! my friend! I didn't shut my ears, I didn't shut out the pounding of my blood. When I was almost to the door, one of them said, "That's him, the stud never learned what his wife used to be" (*Kitty, kitty, gentle cat*), the machete hurt me more than ever, my feet felt weighted down like bricks, my hand cramped up, but I took another step to flee and again the voice—it sounded like it was coming from a tunnel—"If she couldn't tell him, someone'll have to do him the favor" (*Sleep with me, I want to give you a son, a son from my belly and yours*). My head spun me around, the light in the bar blinded me, all the brandy I'd been drinking since the death of the only woman who had made me happy went to my head. My machete got in my hand all by itself, I saw two shadows that stood up and passed in front of me, someone called out to turn out the light, that was their mistake. I saw clearly how one went around to my right and the other to my left, one was left-handed and the other right-handed, one threw down his hat while the other took a pruning knife out of his belt. The guy with the machete tried to light up my face with a flashlight. That's when I heard the swish of my arm and the pirouette of the hand trying to grab the ceiling, another swish, more, fast, the light from the street hardly came in, shadows looked like the Moorish dances in Las Trojes, my hand didn't tremble anymore, my blood ran thick and fast, my head felt good, the drink made me feel hot, the guy with the knife took a couple of swipes at me, hard ones, but I got away from him just fine. In a second I got in front of him and threw him a backhand. When he stuck out his hand looking for my belly, the backhand that I had begun to make just moments before caught up with him. The rest was easy, he was weak in the knees and he couldn't turn around fast enough, but I could, and my whip-arm, and my sure hand, and my machete, too, finding the nape of his neck lowered a little in an attempt to get out of the way of the sweep of my arm, like the night Father Arango spent running through the streets, it was the same for both of them, split like big snakes with a drunken stare, I ran away by the river, I don't really remember but I think it was raining, I don't know, one thing is sure, drops of water were running off my face like pearls. I went on running about three days. I didn't try to stop the police, since I'd've had to kill them and I could have but, believe me, I give you my word, I'm not a bad guy.

Now, what I'm really not sure about is how I am going to handle it when I tell them you hanged yourself on account of me. They're not going to believe me.

That's the truth. I needed someone to know about my run of bad luck. Telling you now has really lifted a weight off my shoulders.

When I told my life story to the man who used to be in this damp, dark cell with me, he listened closely to me, but he couldn't stand it that the story took several days to tell.

Our first night in here together, when he woke up in the middle of the night and heard me eating, he said to me: "Give me some, pal," and I gladly handed over a piece of rat. So several nights went by, until finally he asked me where I was getting fresh meat, something he hadn't managed before. He even kidded me that I had connections with the chief of police, but when I told him the truth he began to throw up. The next day, he couldn't stop puking.

Yesterday, when I woke up he was hanging from the bars on the door. He'd made a noose out of his pants and hanged himself.

Poor guy, I thought it was a real shame. I can't tell you how it pained me to hear him puking—after he'd eaten too!—while he listened to the squeak of rats, too upset to eat them. Poor guy. Because he had the patience to listen to my story.

Now, it'll be just my luck you'll hang yourself, too, just because it disgusts you to talk to the Rat Catcher.

An Indolence of Feelings

Dante Liano
Translated by Sylvia Schulter

Some people have been upset by the death of my friend Ricardo Marel. I think I'm in a position to offer an explanation, the kind of explanation an assassin would give: Ricardo didn't deserve to live. Since I am aware that my declaration doesn't clarify anything, I think it also necessary to tell why and how I killed him.

I met Ricardo in high school. I was a very studious pupil and he was a professor of literature.

The stiff relationship between teacher and pupil dissolved when Ricardo suggested I manage the school paper. For years, whenever there was a class meeting, I would suggest to my friends that we put together a newspaper. But, while they would battle to be part of the school soccer team, the idea of starting a newspaper didn't excite anyone. That now far-off year, the idea came from the professor. In a few days, we put together the copy of the first issue, but with so few articles that we filled up the empty pages by cribbing from magazines or writing under pseudonyms.

With an anxiety I had not known before, after the third issue I showed Ricardo one of the stories I had written. Ricardo took it skeptically, but he promised to read it that same night. For the first time I experienced the torture of having to wait for someone else's opinion about one's own work. I thought it to be an excellent story; actually, I had been inspired by Salarrué's *Cuentos de barro* (Stories of Clay). This writer from El Salvador taught me that the great virtue of a good story consists in an unexpected ending, which leaves the reader feeling annoyed and at the same time joyful at having discovered an unexpected twist of life. But even though I felt the story to be a good one, I was sure my friend would chuck it right into the wastebasket if he didn't like it. The next day, class had barely ended when I went as usual to talk to Ricardo. I thought the first thing he would bring up would be my story. But instead he started to bore me with anecdotes concerning an erudite professor who used to dazzle everyone at the university with his knowledge. When the bell rang to return to class, I felt embarrassed as I asked him: "My story . . . did you read it"? He looked at me as if he had just been beamed down to earth. "Oh . . . your story!" he remembered. "I forgot to read it!" Throughout the next class I was unable to pay attention, I felt so let down.

The next day, Ricardo told me he had read the story. The enthusiasm he showed toward my literary virtues bothered me in the same way it would have had he told me I wasn't any good at literature. According to Ricardo, I was destined to fill the great gaps left void by other authors in our country; for him, from that moment on, I was to dedicate myself "solely and exclusively" to cultivating my talent as a writer. Sometimes, rereading the stories I wrote when I was seventeen years old, I ask myself why Ricardo made such a big thing of them. I think maybe he saw in me an image of himself, and he hoped, as always seems to happen, that I would do what he had failed to accomplish due to an indolence of feelings.

"An indolence of feelings": I think I've found a definition of my friend's soul. There are people who are capable of feeling impulsive passions, people who might enrich their lives by taking a small step forward. But instead, they put things off, let the grass grow under their feet. Ricardo was an indefatigable worker, a scholar full of promise who devoured books and wrote articles without ceasing. And yet he belonged to that category of people.

I first realized Ricardo's defect on an occasion that was quite harmless. The mother of a friend of ours was a mature woman, divorced and attractive. Whenever the woman came by for whatever reason, whether to pick up her son or talk to his teachers, a wave of sexual tension would sweep through the classroom, and only because we were afraid of getting an angry reaction did we refrain from making the lewd remarks we usually did on similar occasions. It was soon obvious the woman had her eye on Ricardo. He was young, with a fine, pale face, and a mustache that made him seem older than his thirty years. His delicate hands gave an annoying impression of uselessness. During her frequent visits to the literature professor concerning her son's poor performance, Ricardo didn't respond, so the woman decided to invite him to her house. Sometime after that incident, when it was all over, Ricardo told me that the last time the lady had him over, she greeted him—how pathetic and ludicrous her desperation, trying to imitate a scene right out of the movies—in a negligee exposing her firm, desirable body. But Ricardo was not inspired. He went on talking about notes and notebooks, and the woman never called him again. Naive as I was, I admired my friend's chastity.

I now realize this incident was related to what would later take place. Ricardo and I continued publishing the magazine until I moved on to the university. Other literary apprentices succeeded me but, according to Ricardo, no one but I really had what it took when it came to the art of writing. I disengaged myself from Ricardo so that I could live the university life more intensely, a life that opened up the world of politics to me.

One day, I was busy savoring an electoral defeat when a friend called. "Ricardo's brother has been killed," I was told.

I found out the details at the funeral parlor. The night before, Ricardo's brother was returning home late from a party. Some patrol officers signaled for him to pull over. He stopped his car and waited for the officers. The police asked him for his papers. When he reached into his coat pocket for his wallet, the officers fired, believing—that's what they stated, before disappearing into anonymity—that he was taking out a gun. Harsh times had set in, and the government had decreed a state of siege in an attempt to cover up the fact that it had caused nineteen union members to be assassinated.

With righteous indignation, I was infuriated with the police and the government. Ricardo, on the other hand, tried to calm me down by talking about "human errors" and "Christian forgiveness." At the funeral ceremonies in the church, when called upon to respond to the sermon, he said, after forgiving the assassins, that he hoped the death of his brother would contribute to the cause of peace. I was dumbfounded, because in those days I was absolutely certain that only the revolution could bring peace. In the following years the hoped-for revolution didn't take place, nor has there been peace.

My relationship with Ricardo became sporadic. But old friendships maintain a bond that the more or less calculated relations of later life rarely attain. The few times we did see each other, it was as if we had just seen each other the day before, and we carried on with long, banal conversations about the purpose of writing literature, the composition of a novel, the rhythm of a poem. Whenever the subject of politics came up, we would end up butting heads, because Ricardo was religiously afraid of communism. Whenever he mentioned "the communists," he gave the impression that he was talking about some unkempt, dark-skinned good-for-nothings with soiled shirts and purplish lips, foaming at the mouth with drunkenness and death. And it was useless to try to dissuade him, because he would tell me, laughing, that I was suffering from the cancer of the university.

Upon my graduation as a lawyer, the university granted me a six-month scholarship to Mexico. I prefer to forget those six months. I spent them trying to conquer loneliness and the sadness of being away from my country. That's the way I am.

When I returned, I didn't bother looking up Ricardo. He and I both knew the opportunity would present itself. What we didn't know was that it would be in the particular way it turned out. Often, as I relate certain incidents, I'm amazed at how contrived they seem, how strange. The government, in an attempt to fight the revolution, had decreed the death penalty for the insurgents. One day, a piece of gossip, a suspicion, or perhaps an inference caused the police to break into Ricardo's house. The family had been denounced. Ricardo wasn't living with them, and when he found out about it, he asked me to help him hide. A friend of ours, a very brave man, kept him in his house during the secret and hasty trial of Ricardo's parents and two sisters. The sentence was unbelievable, but not because we doubted the government's brutality—it was capable of worse; we couldn't accept it because it hit too close to home. But one day we saw Ricardo's family on the television screen being led in front of a wire netting where many sandbags had been piled up, oddly sensuous for the occasion. The execution of his parents didn't affect me. To some extent, one figures that older people are going to die first anyway. What overwhelmed me more than I can say was seeing the bodies of the two sisters, mere children, registering the impact of the bullets, their eyes all blindfolded, and falling slowly over the sandbags. It seemed to me I had been humiliated, that we had all been humiliated, and that this humiliation was linked to the difference between being a man or not.

Ricardo looked as if he were dead. We were all furious and it came into our minds then to join the resistance. I must sincerely confess that we decided to join the armed struggle not for ideological motives but out of pride, because it wasn't possible to continue being human beings in that manner.

Joining a revolutionary organization made me privy to many secrets, my own and others'. The worst of them concerned Ricardo. I found out, because I was destined to find out, that my friend was one of the closest collaborators with the police. He didn't do it for money or self-interest but for religious reasons: he had been converted by an unbelievable sect founded by an Asian whose fanatic beliefs called for fighting to the death against communism. For religious reasons, then, because of that obdurate blind faith that there is another life and that eternal happiness is won through combat, Ricardo had shown the final proof of his weakness: he had denounced his family. It was true that his parents and sisters had been fighting against the government, ever since his brother had been murdered. But only an extremely confused man could have rejected our ancient rituals to embrace vileness as a means to salvation.

I said I was destined to find out. In effect, I was informed about everything because I was the man chosen to eliminate the dangerous informer. Naturally, I could not refuse. I took him in my car to San Cristóbal. The highway was deserted, as always. We went down a desolate dirt road out in the middle of the countryside. I did not think it necessary to say or explain anything. He did not defend himself. All he did was open the door and take to the hills, running among the brambles. I saw him fall a few yards ahead. I then started up the car and left. A couple of days later the newspapers reported the discovery of his body, one of the bodies customarily found daily in the desolate areas of the country.

Don't anyone think I feel any remorse. I am disturbed by what I have related. When I was young, I never imagined we would come to this: I would like to know where so much evil comes from. What motiveless curse sinks us in blood and malice?

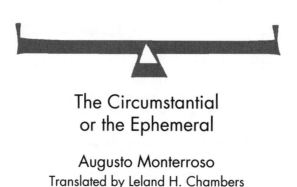

The Circumstantial
or the Ephemeral

Augusto Monterroso
Translated by Leland H. Chambers

From the first moment she saw him come in, she knew what it was about; but in any event she had to allow him to be the one who would say it. Then, waving a piece of paper in his hand, he informed her: "I won it."

"What was that?" she responded, persevering in letting him believe that she suspected nothing. Exceptionally good at her vocation, she knew that with her expectant attitude she was providing him with an extra joy. Of course, he knew that his wife knew; but he was just as certain that in a marriage, if you don't play this game, things end up by losing interest, since in that state, by a certain point both know so essentially that if one of them is thinking of something, the other one generally is thinking that same thing, and sometimes they both even say it simultaneously, to their mutual surprise, for they always declare, How curious, I was thinking that same thing, without either one knowing exactly how, but in such a way that both end up believing and on occasion being absolutely convinced that this means they love each other, and both discuss and chat enthusiastically about the topic, and even a few minutes later each one on his or her own goes on thinking that, of course, this really does mean they love each other.

"The prize in the contest. The car."

"No!" she said, thinking, we have to celebrate, I'm going to get the ice out for the rum. And, more convinced of it than ever, she added, "I can't believe it!"

In the face of his timidity and, more than anything else, in the face of the danger that his wife might suspect that he really felt himself to be a writer, he dared to remark, "For me the important thing is having written the story and sent it in to the contest. Even though I might lose. I don't care about the car."

"Oh? even though we need one?" she thought. And she imagined herself with her neck enveloped in a woolen muffler driving down Reforma and saying goodbye to her acquaintances with a careless movement of her left hand while out of the corner of her right eye she took care that the traffic was moving along without problems. But merely to continue with the machinery of the conversation, she proposed, without emphasizing it, "Well, if you don't want it we can sell it."

"You know it's not a question of that," he said. "Of course I want it. But, aren't you tickled? See, I write the story almost without wanting to very much, just to see how it would come out, like playing, and I win the prize. What do I care about the car? Now, I would like to be able to write more, yes, to read, write."

"Then let *me* have it," she said. And she seriously considered that possibility, though at exactly the same moment she began to recall that whenever she was at the window of a tall building looking down at the street she was afraid to think how she would feel down there the day she herself might have to be driving along among so many cars which from above seemed to be moving all by themselves, like toys or something.

"I repeat," he said, carefully taking another glass of rum and water with ice from her hands, "that for me the car is the least of it. The good thing is that from now on I really am going to write."

"Of course you are," she said.

"I don't want to go on my whole life long just correcting proofs. But neither of us knows how to drive," he added, as if he had just now discovered this fact, staring at his new shoes.

"All right, all right, you can't drive, I can't drive, what are we going to do, hire a chauffeur?" she made a pair of declarations and asked a question, secure in the knowledge that the first was as obvious as the second was absurd and that perhaps her husband's reply would be, "Hasn't it ever occurred to you that we might learn?" while he, in the meantime adding a little rum to his glass, waxed enthusiastic about how good it was that it had all been decided and now he was going to go write even though they hadn't eaten yet and she might not like it.

But she, adding just a little bit to her own glass, maintained, "When have I ever objected? Do your own thing, that's all that matters to you. I'm going to learn, and that's all there is to it. Anyway, who knows if you could even do it, with your nerves?"

"What's wrong with my nerves?"

"Well, you should just see yourself right now."

"Right now is another thing. Okay, okay, so I'm nervous. But as far as

I'm concerned I'm happy about the prize for the reason I gave you, not for the things they are going to give me. I don't think you understand that," he persisted, asking her if she wanted more rum and serving himself.

To direct the discussion she said that he knew very well that she was also happy for the same reason, but that what she was saying was only that either he would learn, or she would learn, or they both would.

"All right, then, you learn. From now on you do your thing and I'll do mine. If you want to, afterward we'll change around."

"Why do you have to be so sarcastic with me?" she said, suddenly really offended and adding that he just had an inferiority complex like the rest of his family that made him afraid to try to get ahead.

"I am not sarcastic with you," he responded. "Seriously: we'll change places if you want, from now on you write and I'll cook."

"See what I mean? What you really want is to keep me from using the car. You know very well you're never going to write because you're dying of fear, or vanity, or fear of failure, or being a success, or who knows what the hell else!" She let it ooze out, slowly and firmly, moved to cruelty by an unknown resentment and by the alcohol and filled with intent to cut really deeply.

"Are we starting again?" he questioned, certain that that was what they were doing, that they were in truth starting again.

"Yes; and hundreds of other times too, because you're so selfish."

Ever since he had come in, he hadn't done anything else but talk and talk about writing without giving a damn whether she was going to drive the car or not. And, coming back to reality, hadn't something just occurred to her? Where would they put the car? She was happy to have discovered this new difficulty and also the fact that of course it would have occurred to him as well, but she kept this in reserve.

"When do they give it to you?" she added instead.

She was beginning to feel tired, as if all at once she suspected that neither she nor he were anything more than characters in something written by someone else a long time before, not motivated by any incitement, not interested in satisfying any internal needs, not attracted by any prizes.

"Between the fifteenth and the twentieth."

While he was saying it he also began to feel the likely weariness the readers of his story would be going through, as if he lacked any real existence and as if what he was thinking were actually being thought by someone else. He shook his head before adding, "You should start taking lessons now. Let's not discuss it any more. It's a good thing there's no catch."

"And what if there is?" she said. After five years of marriage to a writer, or whatever, she was well versed in the kind of conversation where what one of them thinks seriously the other says as if making a joke—and vice versa. "You guys all know each other."

Despite the fact that he was certain this was just a case of a simple wisecrack, his wife's words did not cease to make him anxious. He remembered then the joking of his friends at the office when they were discussing the possibility of entering the contest. "Isn't there a catch?" one of them said craftily. "If there's not, I'm not entering," another said with a knowing smile, and they all laughed, putting out their respective strokes of wit while they mutually recalled how those things were done. It all depended: sometimes one would win because of a friendship, others lost because of enmities, and vice versa; and on and on ad infinitum, everything being illustrated with the names of former prizewinners that left no room for the slightest doubt and that put the finishing touches to their arguments. And then came all the slighting remarks about the obstacles found in the very rules of the contest, they were so vague and, apart from their vagueness, so funny. "The theme should have to do with any situation or development of events among persons or institutions, and these can take place when the satisfaction of needs is more than fulfilled, to the point of excess, waste, extravagance; when available resources, especially if they are limited or modest, are appropriated to superfluousness; when, in sum, a person or many persons or even an entire country deflect their resources toward excessive purchases under the influence of lack of foresight, imitation, vanity, appearances, the circumstantial or the ephemeral, instead of putting them at the service of the production of goods." This was the "theme" of the contest. A really nice theme, don't you think?

But leaving aside things and cars, the important thing now was that he had won, and above all, that he had written something and he had sent it in without fear of failure and he had won. Wasn't that at bottom what the contest was all about? Looked at properly, what was it they were trying to develop with their contest? The country's industry in general, and especially the automotive, or just literature? He knew that, in hopes of winning, many would try to follow those outlines in their coarsest form and try to please the automobile factories or the country's industry as a whole, and would forget the objectives of their art. But with this last argument, wasn't he himself, as one might think the protagonist was doing in the story he had submitted and never thought would win, trying to have an influence on the minds of the jurors—his friends, perhaps— by presenting them with the dilemma of deciding which side each was on, that of industry or that of literature? Again and again he repeated to himself that for him the important thing was not the prize but the fact that he had participated and won, with a worn-out joke, with the old foolishness of writing a story about the one who is writing the story, as a result of which he definitely succeeded in affirming once more that life is a foolish tale told by an idiot.

"Well, yes, probably. But not because I was after it," he said, as if coming awake again. "Why not? It could be that they realized it was mine and they liked it."

"And so?"

"And so what?

"And so what, what?

"Oh. The car. You take it. I tell you seriously, it doesn't matter to me."

"You see what I mean? Although you still don't want to accept the idea that the only thing that matters to you is the car, because you're a selfish person. All right then, take it and give it away to some whore," she said, thinking she would make him understand once again that what he liked were women who got money out of him, who deceived him, who were not as good as she was, and raising her voice a little, not with the idea that he should hear better but in order to draw his attention away from the fact that she was beginning to pour herself another glass.

"Do whatever you want with it," he responded in the same way, pouring one for himself too, and looking absent-mindedly at the shoes he had just bought and that he had been taking off because it had been a long time since he had broken in a new pair of shoes and his feet were burning. "Throw it away, give it away, sell it!"

While she was drinking her rum, she was thinking, he's all worked up, he always gets this way, he has to demonstrate that he is the stronger, that material things don't matter to him; that what he wants is to write, and that I should admire him for this, and I should love him not for what he has but for what he can do altruistically; that I should understand, and I do understand it, that he would be ready to let himself to be killed over this literature nonsense, or over a painting, or all those kinds of things that people rightly admire—but who would go so far as to think of doing the same over a war or particularly over the stupidities that others spend their time with, business or whatever. But of course what she answered was, "Oh, of course, that's what I'm going to do: buy what I can't have if my sister doesn't give me her throwaways, just to humiliate me, or if your friends don't do you the favor of granting you a prize."

She wasn't going to do anything like this, nor did she feel humiliated in the least, but in discussions of this sort that was the way one answered, even though what was inspiring the other was desire, or love, or tenderness perhaps, though one never knew why it was that all this was almost always blended with hatred.

"All right, let's not discuss it any more," he said. "Either you are married to a good writer or to a fool."

Just the opposite of what he thought, which was the latter, she was sure that in reality he was the former. But partly because they were beginning to get hungry and partly so as not to give any more importance to what each one was thinking at that moment, they made their way to the kitchen to look for something to eat. Once there, a silence occurred in the middle of which, while they were slowly chewing and with difficulty swallowing a little bread with some ham, since it wasn't a question of preparing a real supper, they thought about cars that were red or blue or any color really, and about new shoes, and long avenues filled with cars, and awful galley proofs, and garages for cars where one could leave them safely overnight, and literary reviews in which one's name appeared immortalized by a prize, and discussions enlivened by alcohol, and how you had to carry through with them and never give in, and love, and sex, and sentences of reconciliation, and who would be the first to say them, until the ham was finished, along with a couple more glasses, he said thank you, and she answered, you're welcome, both in the indifferent tone of voice of people who had never seen each other before this, after which he declared, with an air of determination or decisiveness, I am going to go write, and he got up and made his way to their room and sat down in front of his tiny writing desk and while she was getting undressed in front of him and into bed he took out a piece of paper and, pen in hand, stared at it for a long time, as if hypnotized by the color white, until she in her turn, after a long while of serious thought or, as can be imagined, serious examination of conscience, asked him from the bed, half imperiously and half in supplication, feeling herself abandoned and depressed as on most nights when he applied himself to that, "Aren't you coming?"

In general, at eleven-thirty at night one finds oneself more than weary of work, galley proofs, breaking in new shoes, the office, friends, oneself, arguing, eating ham on bread, winning prizes, one's own enthusiasm; apart from which, at that hour the alcohol makes one feel the next day will not only be less difficult but the glorious future a great deal easier, so that, thinking about the fresh white bedsheets and what awaited him within them, he responded in a conciliatory and hopeful tone while quickly tossing down a final shot, "Oh, yes."

Tarzan of the Apes

Eduardo Bähr
Translated by Clark M. Zlotchew

Well, you see, that was on the third day of the war. I was getting kind of nervous by about five o'clock.

I went up real close to him and pulled back and forth on the bolt a few times, smiling at him to "give him confidence"; but he didn't bat an eyelash. He sort of looked out of the corner of his eye, real serious, and didn't say a word. Actually, he hadn't moaned or groaned or made any sound at all from the time we grabbed him right up to this moment. And there I was, looking at him out of the corner of my eye too, trying not to make any eye contact, walking in circles around him, playing dumb.

To tell the truth, I can't explain what was the matter with me. I couldn't understand why a whole bunch of dumb things came into my head, as sudden as you please, one after the other, like pieces of words that friends or relatives had said; or parts of familiar faces but whose they were I couldn't say, and memories of things I had lived through a long time before. I started to think about the Angel of Death lurking in those parts and my hair kind of stood on end. The thing was, I was all alone on that mountain with that man who refused to make a sound and that dense fog and that fucking cold—pardon my language—that was freezing my face off.

But you've got my word on it, it wasn't that I was afraid, and I'll swear to that. Just to give you an idea, I could tell you, right here and now, about things I've gone through and come out of in one piece in this fucked-up war, because this little man you see standing before you has served on all three fronts, blowing up convoys of pack animals at Llano Largo and El Aceituno, switching sides at San Marcos and Agua Fría, in those mountains where the hail comes down in chunks, not drops, until they sent me out here, to the undefeated Colomoncagua front, to dig these trenches that guarded General López's territory. Anyone at all can tell you who I am, that my ribs look like a road map and I've got grenade fragments in me; anyone can tell you, except those who were left behind as dog meat.

What happened is what I'm telling you, that I'd been with that fucker for over five hours; although to tell the truth I didn't feel like talking to him at all, I just wanted to keep an eye on him. Letting him go was out of the question, because I was the one who had caught him in the first place. And you, tell me, what could you have done if you were I, out there with a prisoner who doesn't even make one little movement, or even a sound, eh? What do you say about having to guard him because that's what you've been ordered to do and not even being able to shoot him and put an end to it, because you can't make a racket and get everyone's nerves in an uproar and so on, and you can't even stick a bayonet in him because they didn't tell you to finish him off but to guard him until who the fuck knows when, excuse my language.

The thing is that there he was, just the way my buddies had left him, except that his neck was a little swollen, but hanging by his wrists and with the tips of his toes just about touching the ground.

Well, that day I held back from talking to him, like I said. A little after noon I opened a couple of cans of food and ate it all, right in front of him, without looking at him, and I drank from my canteen. Then I decided to take a little nap behind a rock, took the safety off my side arm and stuck it in my shirt. From there I noticed that the acacia tree was a big one and the branch he was hanging from had bent and some reddish brown blossoms were falling from the top. Then I kind of dozed off. It was a good sleep at first, but then I had nightmares and that night seemed pretty long to me and at dawn the mist was condensing on my helmet and running down to my ears. I was shivering under my blanket until the sun came out.

The Lieutenant said we had to look for Tarzan and I said, but sir, if Tarzan's been lost since last night, who knows where he took off for and he most likely deserted and the Lieutenant got red in the face and said we had to look for Tarzan and I was gonna say something else but he said take those three men and if you don't bring Tarzan back one way or another you'd be better off going over to the enemy and I kept my mouth shut just looking at him but then I took the three men and went off right toward the border but with plenty of weapons and after two hours of marching along the highway I noticed that nobody was talking so before heading into the mountains I told them to stop and then, nice and slow,

I told them that this guy Tarzan must be that son-of-a-bitch's mother and that from now on I'm gonna be *your* mother and I gave the order to strike out on the El Portillo side and the man with the compass took our bearings and we kept going in silence again until the afternoon when someone said let's eat and I said no and someone else said I don't know what we're doing, going to get ourselves killed and I said, boy, what's your name and he said Gúnera and I told him don't you know you shouldn't put up a fuss when you're on a mission to defend your country and he said to me excuse me sir but these mountains can defend our country all by themselves and who knows if we're coming out of this alive and I answered that he already was scared shitless, excuse my language, and he kept his mouth shut and I kept quiet too and right then I began to think about a dog I have back home and when I'm having dinner he comes up and puts his snout on my leg and I give him a piece of meat and I pat his head and I say Remington lie down and he lies down and looks up at me from the floor as if he were saying a prayer.

When it was just about dawn I asked the guy with the compass how we were coming along and he said fine, but I said then how come you could hear detonations like from a mortar and we stopped to listen to the thumping and I started to wonder if maybe we might have gone in on the Sabanetas side and I asked the guy with the compass if there was some metallic object near his instrument and he kept quiet and then took off his belt which had a cowboy buckle on it and I got this terrific urge to put a bullet through him but instead I told them we could eat while we kept moving and the blasts sounded closer and closer until by mid-morning the firing stopped and you could hear another kind of sound all around us and it started to rain like hell and we took shelter in a ravine and in spite of the cold I fell asleep in a sweat and so did they.

When we woke up it was already well into the day and I asked who had been on guard duty but I remembered that I hadn't given any orders, and taking all the necessary precautions I gave the order to move out and we made it up another hill and on the other side we saw some houses in ruins and a church and a cemetery and we also saw that smoke was coming out of the rubble and it was then that the asshole with the compass named Macuelizo said he'd lost the map, so I got up my courage and said we had to go down to see where we were because Macuelizo couldn't get a fix on our position and someone said there weren't any people in sight and someone else began to say that for all we knew we were in San Marcos and someone else said no that maybe it was Guarita or Junigual and Macuelizo said shut up, I see something moving and I said if you're bullshitting us I'm going to shove the M-1 barrel up your ass.

We proceeded down the side of the mountain to reach two objectives, an old house and the cemetery that was next to the church, and when the two men got into the house the rest of us went into the cemetery and seeing what we were looking at, which were some big holes and a pile of bones scattered among some wooden crosses, this guy Gúnera said it's a damn one-oh-five-millimeter howitzer and I told him to put a lid on it because near the side doors of the church and in the doorways blocked by some gigantic doors I had just seen the bodies of people who had died recently and they were Indian civilians because you could make out their sandals even though they were ripped apart and stuck to the bodies and all, and their guts were sticking to the whitewashed walls, then we turned around and pushed the main door open and saw there wasn't anything inside even though it smelled like manure and rotting flesh. Then we heard a noise and they were bringing this real skinny old lady with yellow teeth and eyes and who kept saying the ground was hard and someone informed me that there was a wounded man in the house and that he had tied him up because it looked like he was wearing the other side's uniform, so after sending Macuelizo up the hill again I went with the others and the old lady who kept saying the ground was hard, to see the wounded man but really to see if there was anything to eat but there wasn't anything on the stove but an earthenware pot of ice-cold black coffee and since the old lady wouldn't stop repeating that crap about the ground being hard I told them to make a stretcher so we could take the wounded man with us, and when the sentry came I ordered them to dump out everything they were carrying in their backpacks and to fill them with bones and with the parts of dead bodies that were in the cemetery and when we were back in the mountains, the man who had never opened his mouth to say a single word stopped and said excuse me sir but I want to know what we're taking these stinking pieces of dead bodies for and why we didn't kill this man instead of carrying him along and I was glad he asked me that because I was hoping someone would do that and I said what's your name and he said Patillo and I said Patillo my friend we didn't kill that man because he's my prisoner and what you're carrying in your packs are Tarzan's remains and I'm going to repeat that nice and clear one more time that what you're carrying there is what's left of Tarzan after a mortar shell landed on him but this guy Patillo had the balls to laugh in my face and say who was going to believe that that pile of bones came from just one person and that besides those bones had no flesh left on them, most of them, and right there I got pissed off and told them all nice and slow that those were Tarzan's last remains because Tarzan had been eaten by dogs and we kept on walking without saying another word.

Well, Tarzan sure must have known that it's every man for himself, because it's true that he had deserted, even if Lieutenant Vega didn't want to believe it. Look, here's how it was. Tarzan and I were together in the same battle zone, but I had never taken any real notice of him because he was one of those poor fuckers who never talk and who do everything they're told without even looking up at the officer giving the orders. When the invaders crossed over around Nueva Ocotepeque and took the towns of La Virtud and Candelaria, I was one of those at the command post in Jocotán and he was there too and we were together on some raids in which this fucker was one of the bravest. I remember that when the enemy piled it on with a humongous howitzer firing from Montecristo and Cayaguanca, he crawled right into the shell holes to get our wounded out and that's why we began to think of him as the hero of El Pedregal before we called him Tarzan. But I never found out what his real name was, and I didn't even hear his voice once. One thing sure, I remember he was one hell of a fighter and more than once we thought he was crazy. Lieutenant Vega always sent him to the most dangerous places and that's where he'd go. That's how it was that he distinguished himself at Llano Largo too and it was like this, the enemy's plan was to take all those little villages like Tambla, Candelaria, Cololaca, Tamalá, and Plandel Rancho and hook up at La Labor and Llano Largo and since they had said that they would reach the sea in seventy-two hours, then they were going to go from there to Santa Rosa and then on to San Pedro. The first of them to arrive at Llano Largo ambushed us as we were going along the gorge, and held us down with machine-gun fire; so we beat it out of there because we couldn't do anything with our M-1 rifles and the peasants who had come along with us had these Enfields and Mausers from the year one, and that's when Tarzan got lost the first time. After some hours of retreating I remember that the fucker showed up with two twenty-one-round G-3 rifles and Lieutenant Vega told us that they were the enemy's and that those rifles proved that Tarzan had killed two of the invading soldiers and when he was telling us this we saw he was turning red like when he would get excited or when he was happy about something, but Tarzan didn't notice when he cursed us out and called us slackers, and that was when we started to hate Tarzan, and I remember that from that time on no one would speak to him.

So we started to mess him over. When one time El Chivo got nervous and killed a horse thinking it was an enemy soldier, we all agreed to say it was Tarzan who did it. The same way when we found that lady high school teacher coming from San Marcos who told us she had slept with Medrano and that's why she was so happy and all thirty of us gang-banged her, we said that Tarzan was the first and we took our cue from him, even though he was the only one who didn't even touch her. Later we'd purposely mix him up with El Conejo, some dumb fuck who went around looking for jewelry and trinkets on corpses and shot their fingers off to get their rings.

With all this, things were looking bad. The invasion had been carried out on two fronts and the enemy had taken La Alianza, to see if they could reach the South Highway after advancing along the Pan American Highway. On the other side, Ocotepeque had been sacked and the Colonel had told us that since they were cutting the breasts off the women they raped, we could gouge their eyes out if they fell into our hands. But that stuff about the women, I can tell you it was just the same on our side, because any woman who crossed our path. . . .

At first we thought we'd had it, but when we retreated, the mountains stayed where God had put them and that was where the enemy became disorganized. They had this real screwed-up system that consisted of attacking in large groups; in other words, first they would bunch up like a swarm of ants, and then you heard a whistle and they would run like crazy shouting Up with the San Carlos Regiment, or the Such-and-Such Regiment or the National Guard, but they fought standing up and fell like flies and they always advanced shouting; that's why we thought they were drugged out, and it seems that one of our leaders protested about that and that afterward they didn't drug themselves up anymore. But we always had to give up a bunch of towns to them and we were only able to get back at them at El Ticante and Las Mataras. And the thing there was that our communications were handled by blacks and black-Indian halfbreeds who sent their messages in the Garífuna and Miskito languages; that's why they didn't realize they were putting their heads right into the lion's mouth and because they thought their vanguard and the bombardment of the fourteenth had cleared the way for them. At El Ticante there was hand-to-hand fighting in which the enemy suffered more than seven hundred casualties and since we were already surrounding them, they fell back and launched their last offensive on the eighteenth toward San Rafael and near the crossroads of Goascorán and Langue, this after some diversionary attacks out toward Santa Lucía and Aramecina. But in those simultaneous battles which lasted about five hours each we used another strategy and they had to ask for a cease-fire because they saw that we had the capability to take back the territory we had lost. In the afternoon we began to see how they were crowded together along the sides of some big camouflaged buses and dead bodies too behind the barricades they had formed with the bodies of their own men. You would have shit a brick to see that mess, keeping in mind that our artillery only consisted of eighty- and sixty-millimeter mortars, and the recoil-less cannons were fifty-seven millimeters. But it's how you use what you've got and since God helps those who need it most, that cease-fire stuff came up, because the army's seasoned troops remained dug in at the undefeated Colomoncagua front, defending the pass that leads to Cabañas, Sabanetas, Yarula, Santa Elena, and the Marcala highway, which later forks, with one road leading to Tutule and La Paz and the other to La Esperanza. But what am I giving you all these details for when, as they say, a pig knows nothing about saddles, all it knows is shit, excuse the expression. And, since what's born to eat swill always gets dumped on, what happened with Tarzan was that Lieutenant Vega, because he was messing him over too hard, always put him on guard duty in the forward positions as a lookout in the most dangerous places, until one night he started to yell the way Tarzan does in the movies, 'cause that's why we called him Tarzan, and he shot the whole camp up and thank God he didn't hit anyone because we were sleeping on the ground and he kept firing till he ran out of ammunition and then he threw his weapon away and began to run in the direction of the enemy as if he wanted them to kill him and we took off after him but we couldn't find him and Lieutenant Vega was about to bust a gut and that was when he sent me, the next day, to bring him back.

I see you there, I watch you, prisoner, I sense you, you're here, pal of mine, pal so fine, tied to a bent branch acacia tree with blood, without moving, sad early riser, dead man with glass eyes, a swollen neck, leggings hanging down to the center of the earth, I'm advancing, swimming, through the red leaves. They are heavy and scrape in a straight line, yours and mine, enemy line, sacks of mud, trench, where do you small talk at night you and your family, my house cup of coffee, tortillas, pocket? You, I see you, it fits you, the uniform made in USA, what weapons have you got on you let's see your G-3, kill twenty fuckers the ground is rotting no, I crawl along, by inches if you see me you'll kill me, I'll kill you I'll bury the bayonet in your throat, blood in torrents I swim guzzling it, I swallow blood coffee, I'll kill you, I jump you look and I'm nothing but air in a glass of water, blood wherever you look let's walk hand in hand, straw hat sleeping-mat sandal patched pants, edge of the bush scratches again I sink the blade in, spurt guzzler I drink swim it, and I finally come to your mud boot, your tongue hanging out I wasn't the one hanging you, or tongue burning branded, brandy, firewater, we go together drink at the marketplace mules tied up and we go down the road to the mountain and the pine needles get in my way again knife I slit your throat your teeth jump, you, they bite me in the eyes, I torture you, enemy, green cloth, man formed just like my legs and arms which fall off like peas from a pod. We march like peas in a pod. We march straight line to the right hulking sergeant, call me son of a bitch your first hitch, how many girlfriends and soldier's ointment, sweating in bath at three in the morning? Let's walk on the walkway of dirty white mud and hay grab on to the little pine trees, the abyss National Anthem in tune at attention motherland you fall and drag me right down to death real slow, down, down, sound of water panting like

dogs you wetting your pants with fear and you go and drag me to death
I won't let you go wise guy, by the scruff of the neck I stick the long
fingernail in you blood comes out I grab you by the nostrils, hard helmet
the fucking sun afternoon don't talk listen to me this is for my daughter,
for my mother, for my grandma climb up on my body little by little, you,
drool on my chest my face I swallow your saliva rum climb up, son-of-
a-bitch, damn you, get on the road, there I am crying whining like a dog
my chest feels heavy I don't hate you anymore I don't feel like killing
you, the transfer of command, general on the reviewing stand, hot hot
sun, seven hours, nine hours, days, standing at attention, pull in your
ass, stick out your chest a thousand knee bends, stinking prison cell
wallowing in the shit, I'm moving, advancing, a nice day for mopping
floors, they're the volleys in honor of Veteran's Day, cannon shots of
saliva, tall, tall acacia tree pieces of bone and rotten flesh fall and listen
here the country of gold and the cradle of talent, thank you, you are
dismissed, once more in formation this is an eponymic horse attention
the trench with guts falling out, you are hanging by your guts, the mist,
what a foul-up dead villager, eyes like slits, dried snot, blood, neck,
swollen, stiff hands, bones, you don't even look at how this force of
shrapnel fire stirs me up and in the air, blood-guzzling water, friend, foe,
dark skin, high cheekbones, olive drab fatigues is what you are, my God,
my God, on the black earth, hard as a greased pole, let's get on horses
and play yank the duck's head off at the festival, I feel like my head is
exploding the bullets are going into me, save me because you're
drinking water from the helmet that's the color of dead pine needles,
road snake aaaaah it's stuck to foggy sky, hard earth, hard old woman
get away with your yellow teeth go somewhere else look, you, enemy
seen from above, three-quarters view, you have haircream on you're
flapping your arms, seen from twenty meters away, black swallow
swooping down, rolling you didn't break your arm, I have blood poison
my belly split open save me I'm wounded only you, you, wait on us lady
'cause I'm a millionaire, the mule hitched to the post at the marketplace, again traveling toward the abyss skirting a cemetery at dawn
jack o'lanterns on the graves, you slide and I go with you inch by inch,
we fall in the air water you take a snapshot you hit the nail on the head,
blood in your eye, keep an eye on the blood, and I climb up your body
I take out a sledgehammer, knife long pack train I call you friend what
a laugh let's dig up a skeleton, we're crazy-drunk like never before, at
the marketplace we eat and pepper oregano tell me calaguala antican-
cer root, a jumping in my chest as if I had a big brick and finally you got
there, looking at you slowly to see what you're like and that you have
the same face as mine brutish olive-green Indian under our skin, I lock
and load the rifle bolt at you, death is hanging around in this fog my

*helmet is slipping off, you're only my prisoner Tarzan swims faster than
I do dammit I hit you with the decayed bones and I'm shivering on this
hard ground and the shell explodes with a flash and I fly through the air
water resounds and I wake up.*

I woke up with a bad taste in my mouth and shivering with cold, but
I went to the brook and put my hands into that icy water and kept them
there without saying a word, and what could I say, but I stayed that way
until I realized they were starting to freeze.

I was still there thinking I don't know what, it's a bitch this having to
guard a prisoner, don't think it isn't, only because they've told you he's
a prisoner of war who mustn't be touched, until I realized the pistol had
the safety off and a pistol shot at that hour of the day. . . . So I opened a
couple of cans and ate what was in them, and I drank from the canteen
and later I went down into the ravine to see if my buddies were coming
and I was there looking at the spring and the little brook bubbling along
and the mist that was lifting and the beautiful sun on my head.

I was touching my face like a fool feeling the stubble that was sticking
my fingers like cactus needles and I was looking at the milky water and
the white mud, until they got there. Guanizales came first all smiles and
I told him I could have shot him because he didn't say anything and he
told me lighten up will you, the war is over, why don't you feel happy,
and then the Lieutenant arrived thanking me all over the place because
he had handed over Tarzan's remains to his parents and I told him I know
the fucking war is over and he asked me how did you find out, the stupid
idiot, and later he told them to give me something to eat and he said that
an observer was coming to observe the prisoner and I was laughing a little
while they were asking me why I hadn't killed him nice and quiet before
this American got there and I started to beat my face, that time, I swear
it, against the ground feeling how cold it was and biting on the dried up
grass and shouting at them to go to hell and someone pointed at me just
as they were cutting down that stiff silent man.

The Last Act

Edilberto Borjas
Translated by Clark M. Zlotchew

Poor, self-important big wig brass,
such a bully and so hollow
such a he-man, a Fascist ass,
he can't make his own people follow.
—*"Pobre señor,"* by Mario Benedetti

Everyone attended the performances, not because of any interest in listening to the computer-codified words that the theater managers had provided for the actors, but to see how day by day the protagonist kept losing his own original behavior, his clear words, his authentic facial features, his smell of the fields or of buildings that used to be factories but that are now inhabited by laid-off workers. He, who had no familiarity with the extremes of luxury or the transparency of treachery, who was a labor leader, a comrade, as he used to be called by those who once saw in him the symbol of hope, appeared one day in one of the scenes, imitating salutes, trying out military heel-clicking, and kissing the rings of supposedly refined ladies. On that day, with hesitancy and remorse, he had allowed strings to be inserted in one leg; then people began to notice that his movements, as he walked, were off balance: the right leg grotesquely moved more than the left one. He began to march at the side of dishonest men. On that day he became aware that the applause began to diminish. Next another string was inserted in his right hand and he started to sign documents that were harmful to the human rights of his people; he wrote manifestos that praised to the heavens the unseen virtues of personages made of gold. Then he realized that not only did the applause diminish, but that the stage was filling with noises and with strange, ironic whispers. He totally distanced himself from the collective choruses and began to dream of kings and enchanted princesses and to believe in heavenly miracles. Another string was attached to his eyes, and he would open them only when the high muckamuck of the nation took part in ribbon-cutting ceremonies or unveiled the keystone inscriptions of buildings constructed through onerous contracts. Finally, a string was attached to his mouth; he now opened his lips—which used to demand justice and change—only to make known the latest arbitrary decrees of the Chief of State.

The theater lights dimmed, the curtain slowly opened to present the audience with the view of an exceedingly luxurious living room; in one of the easy chairs on the set was seated a sort of puppet. One of the strings moved and the marionette initiated its speech with a voice not its own: "Fellow union members, my brothers the field workers, I offer you my warmest greetings. I want to explain to you that I'm being accused of betraying the interests and the rights of the people, but all I've done is to fulfill the mandate that you yourselves granted me. . . . If I live in this little house in this little upper-class neighborhood; if I take trips from one city to another in one of my automobiles; if I deposit my savings—which is the same as saying your savings—in foreign banks; if my children—and, in a way, they are your children too—attend private institutions, it is to demonstrate this regime's fairness to our exploited working class, and if I collaborate with the regime, it is to stand by our historical principle of order and progress. Therefore, fellow workers . . . -low workers . . . -orkers . . . -orkers. . . ." While the puppet's voice—the voice of a ventriloquist—resounded throughout the theater like a poorly made tape recording, its body started to execute strange, almost deadly, steps. Through an intentional slipup made by the worker who was handling the marionettes of the little theater that day, one of the strings became entangled around the puppet-actor's throat so that he, never understanding what happened, collapsed and died.

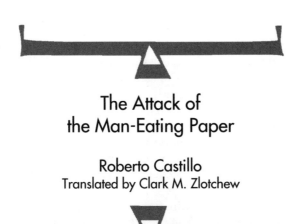

The Attack of
the Man-Eating Paper

Roberto Castillo
Translated by Clark M. Zlotchew

He gently tossed the white ball of crumpled paper, almost the size of his fist, into the wastepaper basket. Earlier he had sent for a cup of coffee and continued working as he sipped it. He had raised his cocker-spaniel eyes when the secretary who had brought the coffee was on her way out, and did not notice that two sheets of paper had been deftly placed on the left side of his desk toward the back. Meanwhile, the secretary's magnificent hips swayed with great skill as she passed through the doorway on her way back. The breeze caused the sheets of paper to move slightly, and he placed a paperweight on top of them. The telephone rang:

"They want to make an appointment. It's the real estate agency."

"Put it off for today. Make it for tomorrow morning. Have them confirm it for this same time tomorrow."

He continued working, at times energetically, at times half asleep. A gentle, unexpected, fleeting hand dropped three ponderous ledgers in front of him. A different hand—cruel, hurried, implacable—put at his left hand a mountain of invitations for him to sign. He picked up another paperweight and gracefully placed it on top of them.

The heat increased as the morning went by. He reached out and adjusted the setting on the air conditioner. Gazing through the window-pane, he thought how pleasant it would be to be in the position of that old man sitting on the little park bench: always ready to make small talk about anything at all with the first passerby.

He made up his mind to get the invitations over with. He had signed no more than five when he remembered that this very morning he had to dictate two URGENT letters. He was so exasperated that he accidentally knocked over the decorative books he had purchased to lend a touch of elegance to the office. Hardly out of their packing cases, they already formed a skyscraper rising from the surface of his desk. The luxuriously bound encyclopedia, its pages dipped in gold, sprawled out over the desk so slowly that by the time it was all over, he had already become furious. His hands were nervous now and reached beyond their capacity: instead of wasting their time with the beautiful gold-tipped volumes, with their illustrated Bible-quality pages, lying battered and bruised, they went straight to the briefcase situated at the opposite edge of the desk. At last, there were the references he needed for the urgent letters.

Once more, the telephone.

His right hand was even clumsier as he brought it back—it had shot out in a blind attempt to land on the receiver—destroying the little desk calendar. All those little pages were strewn indifferently across the floor.

"Yes, yes, dear. You'll have to excuse me for now, I can't talk right now. I'll get back to you later. I think I can make it for lunch. Wait for me to call."

It was the wrong time for another interruption, but the inevitable, inescapable visitor resolutely approached his desk, and did not stop until those great bundles of statistics he had requested the day before were put down, right in front of his nose. From his comfortable, warm, desperate, nervous location, all he saw was a pair of highly polished shoes advancing toward him with great determination. Then he heard a voice saying something about *the statistics you asked me for yesterday, sir,* and saw the pair of black mirrors violently turn as they began their return trip.

He would have liked another cup of coffee but did not dare ask for one until he solved the problem of the glue pot. He had overturned it trying to attend to the statistical data. The spilled glue adhered to everything on the desk. He set his pipe down in a safe place on top of the pile of statistics and, with great dignity, he retreated within himself to think of the correct solution.

The secretary with the fantastic hips came in once more, this time to leave him the confidential reports from the Ministry; she also brought him the Ministry's latest publications, which he loved to be the first to read. He saw her approach and thought that from the front those magnificent hips didn't look that great, but he knew the view would be different when she swung them around to leave. He saw them sway with pure sensuality toward his desk, and he noticed the girl's painted fingernails, which added a vision of pale pink to the strong scent of perfume this female gave off. He felt very small as he breathed in the aroma, and wished she would look at him again, even for an instant. But the secretary turned without seeing him, once more displaying those beautiful hips while walking through the doorway in that springy, sensual manner. He thought that her having been so close to him without seeing him must be like the solitude of death.

The spilled glue was becoming a deadly nuisance. He suddenly remembered that in one of the drawers of the file cabinet he had hidden away a substance that would effectively remove it. He violently pulled open the first drawer, where he was sure he would find it. He extracted folders and loose-leaf papers, which he threw onto the desk, as he became irritated and frustrated after groping in the drawer and finding nothing. Little sheets of paper were stuck to the sleeves of his suit jacket, to his lapels, and his tie. Then he hurriedly opened the second drawer.

His fury was uncontrollable when he had opened three drawers without finding what he was searching for. The desk was a mountain representing the Last Judgment of all papers, set out in all their sizes, colors, and places of origin. He finally emptied the two remaining drawers, putting their contents beside the rest of the filing cabinet material that formed the base of the mountain. His rage at not having found anything led him to sit down once more in his armchair, which, as he softly sank into it, emitted a discreet sound of air being expelled, reminding him of comforts he had struggled for all his life.

He raised his eyes, those cocker-spaniel eyes, to gaze at the mountain of papers that rose menacingly before him. With nostalgia he thought of his days as a law student, when his only love consisted of files and records, while his companions were interested in legal codes, pretty girls, drunken sprees, or elegant parties. Even then he had already discovered in those files and records the key to success in life, and now he was driven to desperation by nostalgia for the good old days, now that they had destroyed him, even though he had been faithful to them his entire life.

He began to feel an intense heat, and found himself sailing through a sea of torrential perspiration. He tried to breathe but found that his lungs were not up to the effort. At the same time, he calculated, correctly, that his nervous hand would not manage to undo his necktie. With his last ounce of strength, he pushed his chair backward, and the little wheels faithfully obeyed. He succeeded in reaching the air conditioner and attempted to put it on the highest setting. As he turned the dial, a strong current of hot air rushed in, sweeping everything before it, flinging the papers in his face, on his chest, forming a whirlwind of papers that stuck to the glue and the sweat. All that emerged from that mountain of papers completely enveloping him were a pair of clumsy hands waving about in the air, and a voice that never quite managed to call for help.

"Cardiac arrest due to excessive obesity, the heat wave and the malfunctioning of the air conditioner," the coroner declared.

Reality before Noon

Julio Escoto
Translated by Clark M. Zlotchew

Morning. General Fernández sprang like a tiger into a sitting position on the canvas army cot, the sweat-soaked blanket from a night of fever slipping to the dirt floor. He got to his feet and immediately felt the pain in his jawbone, the pain that sank its edge of broken glass into the area around his wisdom tooth. He started to bring his hand up to his cheek, but instinctively stopped it in midair and determinedly lowered it to his waist to ascertain that he was still wearing the revolver he had slept with during a night of stifled moans under the watchful eyes of his adjutants, crowded together beyond sleep and the suspicion of death. Inside the tent there floated an odor of bodily fluids blended with the fertile aroma of mint ointment, and a yellowish haze of dust glowed through the still walls, motionless since sunset. General Fernández stumbled lightly over his field boots, balancing himself with difficulty between the fog of pain and the first taste of an early awakening laden with suffocating heat and thirst.

"Damn!" he said, thinking of the bugler as he walked to the entrance, "they forgot to blow reveille, the sons of bitches."

At the tent entrance he shoved the mosquito netting sharply to one side and lifted the flap. A flood of salt-smelling light invaded the small space, spreading over the empty ammunition cases, the washbasin covered with mosquitoes, the field maps rolled up in tin cylinders and the saddle with silver riveting and guayaco-wood stirrups piled on top of a halter. A dun-colored locust reached him in three leaps and briefly fluttered against his face. The General's boots parted the coarse savanna grass that was covered with a film of volcanic silica. He spat thickly.

The first thing he saw in the distance, in the waxy glare of the April sun that ravaged the plum trees and stifled the beehives, was the reddish rust of his three field guns, set up with their backs to the mountains and with their sights trained on the tent in which he had spent the night in agony from a wisdom tooth wrapped in a poultice formed of chewing tobacco and lime. His vision was distorted by the shimmering waves of heat hovering over the plain, but when he was finally able to focus, he realized something he had never before imagined even along the twisting paths of his most intimate nightmares: he was alone. He had been left alone at the dawn of his day of glory, on the eve of the final battle, facing the firing squad of his own misfortune, under the already faded trappings of the mirage of power.

"What the hell is this?" He cursed as he chased the iguanas hiding under the cot, and picked up a bolt-action rifle over which his big, clumsy hands fumbled. "You don't pull something like this on the President of the Republic." And he fired three shots point blank at the pineboard tent frame. "Filthy pigs," he muttered, choking on the sulfurous soda ash of indignation.

Three aides came running in response to the gunfire, still wrapped in the rosy cocoon of morning, holding up their pants, adjusting their suspenders, hurriedly fastening their kidskin leggings in an aqueous cloud of dust that slapped them on the shoulders, whitened their moustaches, made them sneeze. "Commander," they said, "what is it? Just tell us what you want." But the General saw them from the distance of mistrust. "You bastards, weren't you aware of the general desertion? Look at this military disaster we have. Where were your hopes and dreams when you were asleep, you soldiers of the fatherland," he stammered. "You think the enemy is so easy to defeat, you bunch of tin soldiers?" "Not on your life, General, no, General, not on a stack of Bibles. What happened is that they weren't being careful while the eggs were being stolen from the nest, they had fallen asleep and we were singing on the hill without any regular soldiers or militiamen, the artillery men were off taking a walk, the men on guard duty dozing off. . . . Lazy was what they were, don't even think it was anything else, General." Right then they were re-forming the troops, impressing "volunteers," enlisting villagers, they were already out there persuading the deserters to come back.

"What's the trouble, *compadre*?" Colonel Sanabria entered, his spurs jingling, strapping his swagger stick to his belt. General Fernández turned to look at him with irritation; there was in the cordial distance between the two men a flow of electric energy originating in the pole of suspicion, and even though they had acted as godfathers for each other's children, and even though, in earlier campaigns against the guerrillas, they had shared the same trenches, the same women, the same state funds, their individual personal ambitions could not fit in the same room together. They both had the virtue of disturbing the other's sleep and troubling each other's waking hours by inventing ticklish situations, by putting affectionate stumbling blocks in each other's path and by diplomatic rivalry. In their embraces on official occasions, there always was the warm glow of a murderous love, something for which they were both eminently prepared by nature.

Seeing Sanabria and feeling the molar's stab of pain were simultaneous for General Fernández. Turning his back on him, although sensing the icy glare on his back emanating from that colonel with the superbly sturdy frame of a bull, his body pierced by three bayonet wounds received in the cavalry charge of the rebels at Acajutla, the General hurriedly opened the tobacco tin and extracted from it two plugs of the weed which he mixed with a pinch of lime and introduced into the hollow of his mouth. He softly clenched his jaw without betraying a sign of pain, certainly not in front of his *compadre,* and gradually began to feel the moistening of the poultice, the leathery flavor of the tobacco juice bathing his gum, its placid warmth making him spontaneously salivate. He rinsed his mouth with this substance and spat thickly.

Colonel Sanabria was observing the bullet holes, which had ruined the pine tent frame, when General Fernández cursed.

"Cowards," he said, his teeth clenched, his eyes glistening like a pair of hate-filled diamonds, "just like the time we fought at the Zelaya ravine. They all took off on us because they were scared."

"We've had some bad times together," Sanabria added, without seeming to insinuate a double meaning, "but we survived. We won that time, too, so don't let it worry you, Mr. President, *compadre.*" He slapped him on the shoulder. "I'll get them back for you right away; that is, if you give me a little time and permission to line a few of them up against a wall as an example, like last time."

General Fernández answered only with a thoughtful grunt. The last time it had been done with a decree from the Ministry, and by his own hand. But now . . . Was Sanabria trying to score points with public opinion? If he gave his permission, it would be he, Sanabria, who would appear as the just executor of the regulations, and after all, that was what counted, the regulations, in the eyes of those lawyers in Congress; if he refused permission, the guerrillas might arrive and find them without weapons, without men, powerless. The Colonel seemed to unravel the complicated reasoning of that secret thought, uncannily reading it in the air.

"*Compadre,*" Sanabria smoothly explained, with the conviction of one who has all the cards in his hand, "we believe what we want to believe, but reality takes over sooner or later."

"There you go again with your historical bullshit," the General interrupted. The exclamation knocked the piece of tobacco off position. He pushed the rough plug back into place with his tongue. "This is no time to be going on about the ancient Greeks again," he chewed lightly. "Get a move on," he ordered. "I'm giving you three hours to put me in command of another army."

Colonel Sanabria stamped noisily on the ground, knocking off the coat of dust that had been dulling the shine on his spurs. He walked out, touching his revolver with his fingertips, seeing the sides of the tent out of the corner of his eye. Once outside he was engulfed by a nitrous sunlight.

"And swing the cannons around, *compadre!*" he still heard his *compadre* shouting. The Colonel smiled with rancorous pleasure. "The poor fuckers," he thought, "they even have a sense of humor, these damned deserters."

General Fernández flung himself, exhausted, onto the old cot, an item inherited from the marines during the last military intervention. Was it the heat coming in from outside or was it the fever coming out again? He opened his uniform, unbuttoned his shirt; the puff of warm air, reeking of tobacco, made the hair on his chest dance, but he turned his face away with repugnance at his own breath. "A man who chews tobacco," he reflected, "hasn't got far to go to eat shit." In front of him no one smoked, no one drank; a theosophist could not afford to give in to corporeal needs, because they made the mind decay. His regime had reached a reconciliation of spirit and flesh, but how difficult it was to reform the customs of the Indians, to teach them the benefits of obedience, of making peace. If it weren't for the guerrillas, he thought, who have been making raids and setting off bombs for four years, who kept resisting the civilization being offered them, what an ocean of tranquility he would have. In his eighteen years at the helm, they were the most dangerous of those who had dared to raise their hand against him, to defy his reasons of state with their liberal ideas about elections and human rights: did they even realize they were human?

He stood up and loosened his boots with a couple of tugs at the laces, then went to a corner of the tent and began to delve into files and stacks of papers, notebooks, facsimiles of decrees and copies of agreements, stuffed into leather briefcases and cotton pouches. He put aside the small mahogany box containing his decorations and gold braid. Beneath an exquisite blue scrapbook, decorated with the most delicate drawings of doves in flight, he found the cups for mixing medicines. He took the album and blew off the film of dust that had begun to collect, forming a layer of volcanic soil. They were his love poems, secret voices written to be read only by two people, his chosen one and himself. Tenderly caressing that concealed vocation, he felt an ache in his heart and in his molar at the same time. He picked up the porcelain cups and poured into them the colored water from a lightproof opaque jug, and walked around stumbling against ammunition cases, emptying the water from one cup into the other and desperately breathing in the oxygen that sprang from the pink bubbles and the violet effervescence.

It was true, he recognized more calmly, that there had been bad times but also good ones. He suffered no aftereffects from the two attempts on his life, although he harbored a dull resentment, a minuscule ember of passion, because the poison had been put into the drink with which he gave a toast at the beginning of the banquet: a lack of elemental conspiratorial tact not to allow him to finish the supper of sumptuous partridges and steaming pork tamales. The other incident wasn't worth the scar tissue of memory: hiding a stick of dynamite among the candles on his birthday cake was an act of wretchedly vulgar imagination. If the chorus had delayed one second more, and if he had not blown out the candles with such robust lungpower, he would have been blown to smithereens, his atoms blending with those of the ice cream and the rice pudding. That was an offense to his dignity and he would rather forget it. Even so, the conspirators had left the country in such numbers after the failed assassination attempt that it had been necessary to classify them as "tourists leaving the country" in order to quiet the speculations of the foreign press, always inclined to see in his every act the odious mania of a dictator.

What did they know about his mission of civilization? Only his *compadre* was able to comprehend the greatness of the mission in which they had persisted, despite his idiotic fondness for the history of the Greeks, all that pedantic nonsense, famous quotations, adopting gestures, posturings, and imitations of a tropical tragedian. "Beware the Ides of March," he would repeat; the fool didn't even realize that it was a Roman saying. But still and all, even if it were only a fluke, his premonitions always came true. After the revolt at San Miguel, his advice was, "We must negotiate."

"Negotiate?! Are you out of your mind? Negotiate with the rebels?! Whose side are you on?" he had said accusingly.

"We must negotiate," he repeated. "That's a lot of people out there; there are thousands of them, *compadre*." And he was on the verge of having him arrested, thrown into a cell in the Central Castle dungeons, when he discreetly added, "It'll give us time, *compadre*, time to send troops and place the cannons on the high ground and make mashed potatoes out of them." He rubbed his hands together with malicious glee.

And after seven days of bombarding the city, when he promptly sent him a rose for each rebel he hanged, with little notes in which he proclaimed the loyalty of a brother with which he was defending the Constitution, "*Compadre,* you're an animal," he had joked with him when he received him in the atrium of the cathedral for the victory parade, "you've wiped an entire city off the map, you exterminator, you."

"I'm the instrument of God," he had answered, chewing each word behind the parched wrinkles of military exhaustion. "I'm your hand, *compadre,* nothing more than a plaything of the forces of destiny that you control." The two of them embraced with tears in their eyes under the sympathetic gaze of the bishop, surrounded by the masses of roses inundating the altar.

General Fernández heard footsteps outside the tent, the bustle of recruits, the whinnying of horses, and the placement of baggage. "They're returning," he realized, "little by little, but they are coming back."

After the uprising in San Miguel, nevertheless, he had to be open-handed about compensation. Congress requested permission of him to bestow upon Colonel Sanabria the highest honor, the National Condor Medal, making an exception, in his case, of the clause requiring the recipient to have died in combat, of course. Those slick lawyers were trembling with emotion at the audacity of his initiative and at the joy of being in his presence, which enveloped them in an atmosphere charged with intense animal charisma. That was the first time he seriously considered that now-recurrent idea that fertilized his dreams: to award his *compadre* the Grand Cedar Cross, but posthumously. Now along came that pack of fools suggesting he try to rise above his modest ambitions.

"Tradition, colleagues, tradition . . ." he began. The lawyers fluffed the colorful plumage of their flattered dignity, seeing themselves treated as equals. "Tradition imposes on us its sacred principles of organization: the highest honor will be awarded to the highest-ranking citizen." The Congress caved in entirely because of the fear inspired by the concealed message. On award day each man received his respective decorations.

"I defended you with iron and you pay me back with wood," Colonel Sanabria protested when he pinned the Cedar Cross to his uniform.

"The best gift I can offer you is to keep your ambition alive, to give you something to shoot for, *compadre,*" the General answered under his breath as he smiled for the cameras.

"Permission to enter, sir," an adjutant said, his voice issuing from the edge of the sunlit nebula extending beyond the mosquito netting of the entrance. "Volunteers are arriving, sir," he explained, coming to attention. He did not look directly at the cot on which the General sat. "We're pulling them in right and left, sir." The adjutant marched out, holding his breath.

In recent years they were mellowing. They were aging, and each one's fear of the other was diminishing. The private parties at which they would draw lots for women—and then have them on the couch in the hall reserved for consular receptions—were lasting longer. They were substituting sex with their appetites for power. They were getting old, and he suspected that what Sanabria missed about the ancient Greeks was the pleasures of wine rather than their philosophical baloney. He traveled a great deal and each time returned with peculiar ideas, unbelievable fabrications, fantasies from other worlds that could not exist as he described them.

"If everything you tell me is true, the whole world is becoming liberal," he once said to him.

"I'll bet money on it, *compadre*," he answered. Years before, it would not even have occurred to him to believe what he now saw with his own eyes.

The latest item that Colonel Sanabria had dropped into his little bag of distrust had occurred during the foolhardy attempt at revolt carried out by the proponents of a community land system. In the district of Morazán, news came concerning the mobilization the agitators were carrying out, brainwashing the people, forcing them to conform. "End the problem," he laconically ordered his regional commanders, but the inflammation continued and spread like wildfire, corroding everything, gnawing away at everything, undermining the long period of hard work during which he had built his government. Handfuls of secret agents became lost in the web of rumors and in the bursts of excitement that already threatened to explode, which were growing large enough to inspire fear. The mayors came and the governors went back. They awoke to find graffiti on the walls, the soldiers' women refused to make love inside the barracks lest the final hour come upon them at an inopportune moment, orders were sent out and then countermanded shortly after; ominous black vultures circled over Morazán.

On the weekend, Colonel Sanabria had hurriedly returned from abroad and reported to the President's office as soon as he left the airport. General Fernández stood at the huge window of his office, watching the light fall across the garden of voluminous gardenias and blossoming plantain, and gazing at the walls surrounding the city—that castaway of the sea—in the distance. December threaded its tiny needles of cold, and the north wind, spewed out of the cavernous mouths of the extinct volcano, beat against the windowpanes. The General sensed an air of circumspection in the room.

"What do the newspapers say out there?" he asked without turning.

"Bad, it's all bad," the Colonel answered, observing the curved spine, the sunken shoulders, the bulges at the waist of the President, as though he were being embraced by a snake, a female acrobat, a rubber tire. "They're calling it 'the barefoot rebellion'," he continued, explaining, "and they're sure that time has run out for your government."

"*Our* government, you mean," the General corrected, turning to face the Colonel. The glow of the evening sun, reflected against the window-panes, outlined for him a crystalline form of gigantic proportions, a monstrous aura of consummate will, and for the first time Colonel Sanabria felt that from the distance conferred by the power to make decisions affecting destiny, a man more powerful than he was speaking to him, a man who had come willingly to search out all the paths leading to death, and that his cruelty knew no bounds.

"They're ideas," the Colonel explained, "not men that are rebelling, *compadre*"—he dared to be familiar—"things of the times, changes being born. We have to adapt and come out on top by changing. We have to win by transforming ourselves if we're going to survive."

"So they're ideas, are they, *compadre*," the General assented with a trace of sarcasm clinging to his lower lip. "And the newspapers call it 'the barefoot rebellion,' do they," he sputtered with a tone of determination. Colonel Sanabria had never before seen him surrounded by that phosphorescent aura of tranquility and ire. "This man is destiny itself," he thought.

There was a prolonged silence in which the President scrawled on a sheet of paper with his desk-top pen, not breathing, never raising his eyes for a moment or being aware of the passage of time.

"We're going to immunize the barefoot boys against rebellion," he finally said, calling his secretary and handing the handwritten telegram to him. "You can go now and rest easy, *compadre*, we're going to have a peaceful Christmas," he added, dismissing him.

"What are you going to do, *compadre*?" he dared to ask, his hand on the doorknob. He did not fear for himself; he was afraid the General's heart would be flooded in a hatred that would suffocate him. The silence madly bounced around the four walls and broke into three little pieces of shadow.

The General murmured, "The people love me," as though he were talking to himself. He stood by the window once more. "The barefoot boys love me because I've given them everything," he repeated to himself in a monologue of conviction. "It's the educated and the cultured who oppose me, the ones who have done well, who read and learn to repeat liberal slogans. The real people love me."

Colonel Sanabria left the room unobtrusively, his hat in his hand. The secretary awaited him outside, his eyes bulging out of their sockets; he took the sheet of paper that was trembling in his hands: "Shoot the ones with shoes, every one of them," he read. The General's scrawled signature looked like a hairy spider.

It was true that it had all happened that way, the General reflected as he arose from the cot, but the stabbing pain from the molar made him sit down once more, sick with pain. His eyes half closed, he prepared a fresh tobacco poultice and doubled the dose of lime, then he leaned back and tried to get a little sleep. Yes, he thought, in the state between sleep and waking, it had been that way, but perhaps he was interpreting the events too drastically. Sanabria, he meditated, staring at the twin porcelain cups, was like a brother, although he was more diffident and more prudent than he. It was better that way. He wouldn't fail him, he knew he wouldn't fail him even though he might contradict him and brag about his own impulsive improvisations. Besides, in how many battles had he, the General, come out in one piece only because of Sanabria's sense of sacrifice. Those three bayonet wounds at Acajutla were meant for him, but Sanabria had allowed the bayonets to pierce the tender tree of his own enormous lungs. Furthermore, Sanabria had gotten everyone to sing a song that time with the birthday cake bomb. Sanabria took care of the squealers and gave confession to the informers. Sanabria deposited the money bags in Miami for him in his personal account. Without him, power would be more lonely, although he would not have to share it. His *compadre* had become a part of him, and the only problem was that they both strove for the same material goods; if only he could free himself from the ambition for worldly pleasures, make himself immune, purified forever from human temptation as in the splendor of the Greek gods, he now imagined, losing himself in a spongy spiral of drowsiness that silenced his pains and memories.

An hour later he was awakened by the distant sound of machine-gun fire. "The game is on," he said and got to his feet, all his worries and aches now soothed. He emerged calmly, his heart like ice, immune either to triumph or to disenchantment, every fiber of his being joined into one skein of willpower. Outside, shouting, orders barked by officers giving hasty battle instructions were heard. He smiled as he heard the neighing of horses. Sanabria must be returning with the powerful army that would crush the guerrillas forever. He strode to the tent entrance and brushed aside the mosquito netting; a flood of sunny-smelling morning clung to his inflamed cheek, to the white fire of his temples, his hands, the circle of his face, and enveloped him in luminous flashes that blinded and prematurely aged him. Above the esplanade of the encampment, on this side of the three reddish field guns that were now aimed at the mountains, the recruits were practicing their early apprenticeship for battle, but the General had the feeling he must be dreaming, that he was the victim of time's sleight of hand, a plaything of the mirrors of the mind. He saw old men dragging themselves along the ground, choking, in greasy rags, fainting in the suffocating heat, women lifting the heavy rifles of iron and lead, exerting their abdominal muscles more than advisable, children, adolescents, invalids, the sick, bearing on their contorted bodies the cases filled with mortars, bullet cartridges. He saw the calloused hands accustomed to the hoe practicing with the bayonet, polishing cavalry sabers, and he saw for the first time the tenuous imprint left in the dust by an unshod foot. The adjutants, with their mean and lonely faces, shouted threats, cocking their weapons behind the mob of forced laborers. Colonel Sanabria rode among them astride his horse like the angel of God.

Then he discreetly summoned to his tent three of the veteran officers and gave them the definitive order, in a manner as irreversible as a bolt of lightning: "Shoot my *compadre,*" he told them. The officers were thunderstruck with confusion and a sense of mystery, powerlessly watching the President sail beyond the ocean of compassion. Overwhelmed, they went to carry out the order.

When he heard the thunder of the rifles, General Fernández felt a great weight descend on him as he stared at the translucent walls of his quarters. "*Compadre,*" he wearily lamented, as though he were conversing with a dead man, "we believe what we want to believe, but reality takes over sooner or later," and he began to rummage around among the stacks of agreements and looseleaf notebooks containing decrees, hunting for the regulation concerning posthumous decorations for heroes who fall in battle under the burning sun.

The Final Flight
of the Mischievous Bird

Jorge Luis Oviedo
Translated by Sabina Lask-Spinac

After many years of incessant work, he succeeded in finishing his masterpiece.

The idea had begun to gnaw at him one morning when the teacher read us something about a character from Greek mythology who used to fly with wings that he had made for himself.

That same night Cesarín dreamt he flew over the town before the astonished gaze of relatives and friends who applauded him with noisy enthusiasm. The next day he abruptly decided to quit school so as to devote himself full time to the creation of a pair of wings, and, being as he was the scholar in the family, his stepparents had no choice but to give in to his flurry of madness.

"It's God's will," Doña Clementina would answer, with the satisfaction of being recompensed for the annoyance of her closest neighbors.

Almost two months later, with the help of a saddler and a carpenter, he had managed to construct wings out of cardboard. Cesarín contemplated them with a satisfaction that suffused his face and incidentally confirmed that they were as enormous as his madness.

On Sunday, the whole family got up at sunrise and, when the day began to get light, went on an outing to one of the properties belonging to Don Juan José de Jesús Antonio de la Sierra. When the peal of the bells announced the six-o'clock Mass, they had already arrived at the top of a hill. They watched the sun rise over the mountain ridge and, with the might of an oriental king, insatiably drink up the mist and frost of dawn, while they proceeded to bind the wings to Cesarín, who spread them wide with the clumsiness of a weary turkey buzzard and, trying to reassure himself, exclaimed, "We'll make it, Mother. You'll see, we'll make it."

"Yes, tomorrow you'll be famous," she replied in a tone of repressed doubt that she desperately tried to disguise with some early-morning smiles that were drawn across her face with the fragility of a bad portrait painter. However, she imagined Cesarín flying over the town and nearby villages supported by a magic thread and appearing photographed in full flight in newspapers all over the country, and the news about her adopted son's heroic feat spreading all over the world.

His stepfather, still skeptical, observed every movement from the hillside. He was calculating the size of the jolt as he watched the ravine that opened up at his feet like the belly of a vanquished woman; but, when Cesarín was ready, it only occurred to his father to say simply, "God's will be done." Almost immediately he saw his son make the final thrust and, on arriving at the edge of the abyss, attempt one useless flap. As for Cesarín, he did not have time to think about anything as he dropped swiftly like a useless object down the canyon's throat.

When, two hours later, he was aroused by the uproar made by the people his stepfather had engaged to rescue him from the branches of those trees that, almost by a pure miracle, had gotten in his way to save him from certain death, the only thing that struck him as an inexorable idea was that that was only his first try.

Don Juan José de Jesús Antonio de la Sierra tried to dissuade him, promising him that, when he finished his baccalaureate, he would send him to study aviation in the United States and for a graduation present he would buy him a small airplane to fly as he pleased.

Everyone believed that Cesarín would desist after such an offer; but he hadn't finished recuperating from his multiple contusions when he set about a new project (not necessarily just to be bold, as a journalist would say). It didn't take him long to build a new pair of wings, this time with the help of an ingenious tailor and a shrewd carpenter, who constructed wings out of bamboo frames and some printed cotton fabric. Although very similar to the previous ones, they looked lighter and more resistant.

Because of the experience he gained from his first failure, Cesarín preferred to wait a few weeks in order to do daily exercises designed to acquire the necessary strength for the day of his second performance. After almost a month, he invited his closest friends and relatives, who, attracted by his folly, showed up at the appointed time. The results could not have been worse than they had been the first time. Only this time he fell into a pool of incredulous swimmers who took charge of rescuing him. Almost all of them believed—according to what they confessed hours later—that he was a dead angel, but they soon discovered the unmistakable face of Cesarín, which only reflected some terrible and repressed desire to fly.

One dawn he woke up with a start, leaping about so joyfully that the spirit soon spread to his younger brothers, then to his whole family, and finally to his closest neighbors, who awakened thinking there was a fire. The tumult, however, was due to a brilliant idea (according to the qualifier that he himself had assigned to it). His mother, as always, opted to please him in everything and interceded with his father so that he would yield to Cesarín's plans. This occurred during the season when the herons had arrived to eat the ticks off of the livestock of Don Juan José de Jesús Antonio de la Sierra; his workers dedicated themselves to killing and plucking them, managing, in a short time, to collect a total of 2 million, 266 thousand, 729 feathers, a quantity more than sufficient to make Cesarín's wings.

"They are more beautiful than those of angels," Doña Clementina repeated in delight when she saw them finished. By then, no one doubted any longer that Cesarín was mad and that, within a couple of months, Doña Clementina, who completely abandoned her religious duties to follow her son's training in detail, had become infected with his folly. Her neighbor from across the street, Doña Azucena Martínez, much given to venturing opinions, said that Cesarín had more of the devil than the angel in him. Doña Clementina, however, maintained that it was all a matter of God's will. The rest of the people, more grounded in logic and reality, thought it was all due to the collective madness that had infected the entire family. Thus they were often heard saying, "It wouldn't occur to a sane person to support such wild madcap ideas."

Finally, at the end of interminable trials that threatened to become eternal, his parents arranged the date, time, and place for carrying out the final flight—"final" since Don Juan José de Jesús Antonio de la Sierra decided that if Cesarín didn't kill himself (which was most likely), he would no longer support him anyway; so it made sense to call it the final rather than the third flight. The people in general, moreover, agreed in a casual and spontaneous way to call it "the final flight of the mischievous bird."

By then, the news had spread to the surrounding area so that on the third Sunday of May 1968, at four in the afternoon, one hour before the flight, the town became impassable. Everyone went about searching for the best place to view the whole of the mad spectacle without missing a single detail (also as the journalist would say). Almost all of us were sure that this act of craziness would end in tragedy; many of our friends were saying, "Tonight there will be a wake in the rich man's house."

I remember that around five in the afternoon, the majority of the people had gathered on the lower reaches of the hill. There was one group that put out a large blanket just in case Cesarín fell, as was most probable. Only we, his two close friends, his stepbrothers, his stepparents, and the priest, went up to the top with him. Doña Clementina, in spite of the optimism she tried to express through her cheering words, was nervous. A wave of distress emanated rather violently from her plump, ashen face, while a stream of doubt and mystery bubbled from her languid eyes. Don Juan José de Jesús Antonio de la Sierra did no more than scratch his chin and, from time to time, pull hairs from his thin gray head as he scurried about in circles like a mole. His stepbrothers immensely enjoyed watching the trial flaps Cesarín made; the priest prayed without pause, asking repeatedly that God's will be done; Andrés, my other friend, had submerged himself entirely in a sea of amazement, observing every detail with a surgeon's precision. Since I was sure that Cesarín would again fall apart like a turkey buzzard struck by a rifle shot, I was thinking about how long it would take him to recuperate and the day we would all once again witness another "final" flight. Apart from that, I was sure he would not die.

At five in the afternoon, as had been anticipated, Cesarín began his run about fifty-five yards from the chasm. There was a favorable wind that swept away a cloud of yellow pollen. The afternoon continued clear and fresh. The sun had almost plunged beyond the highest mountains, and the crowd of people about fifty yards below kept its silence (which in this case had no reason to be funereal). After the first few steps, he slipped and almost fell, but he managed to keep his balance. He sweated so that it appeared as if a sudden rain were washing his face, which remained set, looking not at the ground but forward. Perhaps looking at the birds (a flock of parakeets, I recall) which at that moment passed above him, ignoring him. He had scarcely some fifteen steps to reach the edge when I saw him trip again (less sharply than before). His mother covered her face; the priest let out a scream, and his stepbrothers, who had begun running in the opposite direction, started to cut him off but were stopped by the unexpected shouts of their father a few steps from Cesarín, who at that moment extended his wings and threw himself into the abyss. Everyone was silent at seeing him give a few awkward flaps, like a young bird, that gradually became more intense and rhythmic.

When Doña Clementina, who had neared the edge to see the fall, confirmed that everyone had his face to the sky, she jumped up screaming like a madwoman, "He did it; he did it."

That night, if there wasn't a wake in the rich man's house, there definitely was a festival in the entire village, and everyone commented in his own fashion on Cesarín's incredible success. Doña Clementina, who never emerged from her state of shock, kept repeating to everyone: "He did it; he did it, and you all were saying I was crazy to support him. . . ."

A week later Cesarín still had not returned. Some people, among them the priest, maintained that he had been transformed into an angel and was already knocking on St. Peter's door; the more skeptical ones, that he was surely in some nearby town entertaining the folk or lying dead in some ravine. Doña Azucena Martínez, for her part, limited herself to saying, "I had it right—Cesarín had more of the devil than the angel in him."

What was certain was that after almost a month of searching for him through the whole region, he couldn't be found. This served to confirm the priest's suspicions. By then, Doña Clementina had begun making wings for herself (of turkey-buzzard feathers, due to the scarcity of herons) to go in search of Cesarín.

The Author

Roberto Quesada
Translated by Sabina Lask-Spinac

The young man who aspired to be a writer decided finally—after profound meditation—to take a firm step in the search that would bring him fame and convert all his ideas into reality; he already saw his name written in capital letters in newspapers, magazines, and books: BARTOLO TERCERO DIAZ. Other thoughts followed that, in his opinion, were of secondary importance, and it was only after he had made his decision that he put an end to his insomnia.

Upon waking, Bartolo thanked heaven, for now he could carry out the enterprise that would lead him to success. This enterprise consisted of going for walks along the busier streets and observing strange faces, those with distinct characteristics, following them and guessing their lives, and, as a result, writing the novel.

The idea for this enterprise was born after having failed in his attempts to write a story, then poetry, and later plays. And, as he saw himself manacled by total frustration, he needed only to recall a certain class in which the Spanish professor told some anecdotes about writers and painters who got famous through this method of observing strange faces.

When he arrived at one of the more crowded streets, he began to look at faces: men dressed in ties and shiny shoes, women draped with jewelry from ear to foot, girls imitating a dance step from the latest musical film, boys groomed like fashionable movie idols, children and old people walking in all kinds of ways.

He thought it would be easy to find the character for his novel, but it became more and more difficult, for it was no easy task choosing from among so many different faces.

After a great deal of walking and looking, he found one that appeared unequaled, and he stayed with it.

The guy was more than strange; indeed, he carried a suitcase and wore a formal suit, his eyes completely covered by dark glasses; he walked very swiftly and looked from side to side continually, as if feeling pursued.

Bartolo followed him, but avoided arousing the man's suspicion; the man turned through a desolate alley and entered a wooden house that was in very poor condition. Bartolo managed to get to the house, and through one of the cracks he could see that his character was meeting three others of similar appearance.

It was impossible to hear from where Bartolo was, and so he chose to move closer with the greatest caution.

"I only have part of it!" said the main character.

"How come only part?" said one of the three men, furious but not shouting.

"Next week," said the main character, his face full of anguish, "I'll bring the rest."

"It better be true," said the other three almost in unison.

The main character made a parting gesture and went out. Bartolo in his hiding place did not know whether to follow him or stay, but, thinking fast, he felt it was necessary to watch the other characters since they were also important to his story.

"Sebastian is not lying; he is sure to bring the rest next week," said one of the men.

"That's for sure," agreed the second, and the third only nodded "yes" without saying a word.

To Bartolo, finding out that the main character of his novel was called Sebastian was of vital importance, and it did not seem like a bad name to him; on the contrary, he found it worthy of an excellent novel. The three men decided to leave. Bartolo did not want to follow them since it sufficed him to know that the following week, on the same day and at the same time, this would be their meeting place.

As he captured the freshness of personal experience through his characters, it wasn't difficult for Bartolo to fill twenty pages, adding a few details that he invented, remembering that the writer must have imagination. The night well upon him, he put the final period on his first chapter; he would wait to write the second until after next week's meeting. Feeling the pride and optimism of a man who has fully accomplished his duty, he proceeded to dress and go out for a walk: "I've earned it," he thought.

The author did not like coffee at all, yet he sat in a small coffee shop having the obligatory cup, for to do otherwise would mean that everything about him was a lie; he remembered reading about the lives of great writers such as MacLeish, Hemingway, Dos Passos, and others who were frequently seen in the famous cafés of Paris. He adopted a pose of great concentration on something though even he did not know what that something was. He did not see the pedestrians who passed before the shop's window nor the rest of the café customers since he believed that if there was anyone who had to be seen by all without seeing all it was none other than BARTOLO TERCERO DIAZ. Still, no one paid him the least bit of attention. Bartolo moved mechanically, like one who knows he is being watched and wants to put on an impeccable performance. He ordered another cup of coffee, cursing his forgetfulness to bring along a book or a magazine or anything that would identify him as a man of letters. He left the café and walked slowly through the street, his face tilted as if searching for inspiration in the stars; he whistled a classical tune, one of the most common ones, those that almost everybody knows. He felt disgusted with himself for not having listened to other classical music that no one knew, for, though he had heard of Berlioz, Bach, Chopin, and others whose names escaped him—he had cited them on more than one occasion in some conversation or other—he knew nothing about them, had never heard them, and not until today, just when he was one step away from fame, did he realize this. He passed by a beggar who asked him for a coin. Bartolo gave it to him, and the beggar, in gratitude, told him he was a great man. Bartolo felt like giving him all that he had in his pockets, but, unfortunately for the beggar, it was only a feeling. Bartolo found it more and more difficult to keep walking; his face slumped, his neck ached, his spine could not bear the stiffness to which he was not accustomed, his legs trembled with the effort of maintaining his balance at each step. He arrived exhausted at his house and, in the middle of undressing, threw himself on his bed and fell asleep.

The following days were equally bad or perhaps worse until the day of his characters' meeting arrived. Everything was repeated as on the first occasion; only the dialogue had a few variations.

"I've got the rest," said Sebastian.

"Very good," answered one of the three men.

Sebastian handed over the contents of the suitcase. Bartolo needed extra eyes so as not to miss any movements since, in truth, he was incapable of imagination no matter how hard he tried. The main character took his leave. The three men were left alone, and Bartolo remained in his hiding place, wanting to know what those secondary three characters were saying because he already had names for them.

"We don't need that idiot anymore; next time we'll finish him off," said one of the men.

"Should we kill him right here?" asked another.

"Yes," answered the third, "and it will be easy if we use daggers instead of pistols."

"It's agreed," said the other and left.

For Bartolo this was a big problem. How is it possible to kill the main character in the third chapter? No, Bartolo could not go along with it; he wanted a novel with at least twelve chapters. He knew he had to do something, but he didn't know what. He found it impossible to sleep, yet at the same time this made him happy because he believed insomnia was a prerequisite to being a great author. "I could let them kill him," he thought, "but no, it's the third chapter, no, it can't be. Perhaps the best thing would be to look for Sebastian and warn him about his impending death. I know they are going to kill him anyway; but yes, it would be good to tell him so as to postpone the day of his death. But what about the professor who says that the writer must not become one with the character, that the character and the writer must keep their distance? No, I don't believe that becoming one with my character will ruin my novel; no, to the contrary, it will be an unusual thing, perhaps one to which my great triumph will be owed. What the hell do professors know? They don't know anything. Tomorrow I'll look for Sebastian, and now I better get some sleep."

Bartolo walked from place to place until he found his character reading the newspaper on one of the park benches. He came up to Sebastian, said hello to him, and sat down at the other end of the bench.

"Good morning," responded Sebastian and continued reading.

The future famous author could not find a way to begin, and so he sat silently until he saw that the character was getting ready to leave.

"Don't go away, I have something important to tell you."

Sebastian turned pale and breathed nervously: "Me? You are sure it's me?"

Bartolo smiled: "Aren't you Sebastian?"

"Damn it," thought the main character, "he knows about the drug dealing; otherwise how would he know my alias?"

"Fine," said Sebastian, "but let's not talk here. Follow me."

They walked together, turned down the alley and arrived at the wooden house the author knew so well. They were in exactly the same place in which the meetings had taken place. All was quiet; there were no signs of anyone around. Because of this, no one heard Bartolo scream as the dagger penetrated him several times right around his heart.

The Forbidden Street

Pompeyo del Valle
Translated by Sabina Lask-Spinac

*For Pili (ladies first) and for Carlos Fernández,
beneath the Mexican sky.*

In a café on the Place St. Michel de Paris, the taciturn old emigrant from a small Spanish American nation listens skeptically to the details concerning the political and social situation of his country, from which he has been absent for more than twenty years. The tales told by some young men recently arrived in the metropolis, with minds set to study if not to achieve glory, seem incredible to him. One of these tales makes him uncomfortably warm in a particular way: The Commander who has converted the little tropical republic into a private hacienda has a mistress whom he honors with a regular visit every Friday, since, besides being methodical, he is also very superstitious. During his whole visit—from four in the afternoon until seven in the evening, not one minute more or less—the traffic of vehicles and passersby is categorically forbidden to enter the street where his mistress lives. Moreover, all the houses in the neighborhood must have their doors and windows completely shut. Violators of this law suffer a terrible punishment: They are served as food to the diabolical horses of the dictator.

Bartolo Gris—for this is our disbelieving man's name—forgetful of the story, decides one day to take a brief vacation in his native land because he feels vaguely nostalgic. Since he has no relatives in the capital—where he has stopped in order to travel inland later on to his tiny province—he has taken lodging in a hotel and struggles to get used to the alien atmosphere that has surrounded him from the moment he descended from the plane at the primitive airport. He takes a cold shower, drinks an invigorating glass of whiskey and soda at the bar, and goes out, relaxed now, for a walk in the city at one of whose secondary schools he had received his baccalaureate and was even the captain of the basketball team.

Our man and the hours ramble on. Without realizing it—his mind is preoccupied with memories—he has entered the forbidden street. Everything there is tranquil, solitary, as if petrified; not a leaf moves. Bartolo Gris shrugs his shoulders and begins to whistle softly like one who is afraid or who doesn't know what to do with himself. Suddenly the feeble whistle freezes on his lips as swiftly, silently, a black carriage drawn by six horses, also black, bursts in, as though it weren't touching the paved surface. The coachman abandons his seat and opens the right door of the vehicle. From inside appears first a hand whose ring finger flaunts a ring mounted with an enormous purple stone; next appears the colossal foot of a male goat, projecting a long shadow on the ground that rises along the high walls to blend with the ragged blood-rimmed clouds. It is the national shadow, the gigantic shadow of the absolute master of that feudal fiefdom lying among blue mountains and rivers full of somnambulant fish.

The eyes of the great and powerful lord survey the lone, dusty street and discover the heedless one, who remains immobile, watching from below a fish market sign. In the all-embracing pupils light up two red dots of anger that seem to take on an independent life, like two spherical animals, and Bartolo Gris soon finds himself floating, levitated, jolted in the electric air. His clothes become loose, immense, like black prairies where frenzied horses grapple with brimstone dragons, and he watches in anguish the green color that is covering his skin, his hands, his fingers. He remembers past nights on the French Riviera and sweats and smiles and sighs, pained and afflicted by *saudade,* or nostalgia, as they say in Brazil. He also thinks of billiards, one of his favorite pastimes. In his imagination he sees the smooth marble spheres rolling over the soft plush and sinking into the leather pockets after caroming around at jaunty angles. His legs no longer have the strength to support him. They fold under him like fragile fibers, letting him fall heavily, converted into a heap of fresh hay inside an impeccably cut English suit.

The coachman gathers the sheaf of damp and shiny grass and offers it to one of the horses that draw the carriage of the supreme commander of the forces of land, sea, and air and the president-for-life of the republic.

The Absent One Inside

José Roberto Cea
Translated by Elizabeth Gamble Miller

*T*hey say I'm tormenting them purely for pleasure because I'm stuck on myself, sadistic. If they only knew the truth, the real truth, such an idea would never occur to them. But the communication between us is so poor that no matter how much we try, we're apparently not prepared to find out about everything. I realize my sister goes to extreme measures to make me happy, so does my mother, but that isn't enough, for they don't understand the rest, they think I'm the kind of man who doesn't know how to get along by himself. Their attitudes are understandable: they don't want the neighbors to gossip and to think I'm something extraordinary. No doubt I will be, but to achieve greatness I have to cover lots and lots of ground, something they don't understand, they think it's fine for me to continue doing what I am. They think it's enough to give me security and peace of mind. My lot is to do something hard, extremely hard! That's the way it is! . . . To each his own. It was my father's lot, for instance, to have to brag on me in front of his friends, there's no way to change that. My mother's, to be afraid, the way she always has been. My sister's, the one who doesn't really know who she is, what to do, how to behave, except to spy on me and look for ways to help me; but with her way of talking in metaphors, especially about my work, it's hard for her to communicate. The other relatives are shadows, silence, impenetrable darkness, a wall. We're all at the mercy of changing winds and each of us is looking for salvation. Each one of us is trying to find his own way out, not someone else's . . .*

Then I came in and I asked him what he was doing. He answered that he was meditating. "You seem odd," I insisted; but he told me again that he was just meditating and not to worry. I know he realized he hadn't convinced me, but he continued his posture, without attaching much importance to my presence. I tried to bring the question up again. I recalled the sentence . . . No one knew to whom it was directed, but he kept it mentally alive, and close to him. It was then he came up with the notion of collecting butterflies. He made magnificent collections of them. His pleasure was in displaying them. At first it was difficult for us to live in that atmosphere, but simply because he was there with us we became accustomed to it. Besides, he didn't bother anyone with it, butterflies are so beautiful, so easy to care for, take so little space, and, in addition, they have other charms too lengthy to enumerate. On the other hand, if he were to collect fish, it would cause us numerous problems. Fish, out of water, have eyes like little boys who are lost, and then the water misses them and unleashes tears like a forsaken little girl. That's enough to make anybody sad, to cast him into a deep, soul-shattering depression. That being the case, I advised him to collect birds, but we immediately realized the inconvenience; you know, cages would have to be different styles so the surroundings wouldn't be monotonous; besides you would have to concoct receptacles in which to keep the warbling of the birds. In view of those problems, he decided in favor of butterflies, and he got beautiful specimens that were admired by every-one. There wasn't a soul in the region who didn't talk about them wherever he went. What we didn't know was how he found those beauties; but there they were, increasingly fantastic, extraordinary, unique. The whole house was immersed in his undertaking, no one was unaware of his activities. Even when he was out, his atmosphere remained behind. We waited expectantly for his comings and goings ; it excited us to think he would return with new finds. The family didn't let themselves think about where it would all end . . . Often I thought it was a fairytale, a dream, an Irish folk tale . . . Because even he would occasionally come upon us like a little butterfly . . .

At first we were afraid, especially with the boy being at the dreamy age, when so much turmoil could hurt him. "He might go crazy on you," people were saying. "That boy is at an age to be watched." "Having big dreams like that is bad, very bad." Hearing all these opinions upset me. It's that it's so easy to be taken by surprise, and since all of us at home were so afraid, it was an unhappy state of affairs.

I was an easy prey to anxiety. To pull free of its quicksand I went to Mother; she was in the same state. There were two of us now, anxious females, two of us lost in lengthy labyrinths never before traveled. No one talked about this for fear of being made fun of, despite the fact that at home we had come to a blind alley and were in the depths of unspeakable despair. It was enough to see the worry reflected in each other's eyes, the yearning to be out of the situation . . .

When he heard the sentence, he was absent from us for days. He looked at us blankly. We told ourselves that he must understand and so it was. One morning he came to me and told me what he had decided to do. It was then we discussed possible occupations and what kind was most appropriate for the situation. After much discussion he decided in favor of the butterflies.

At home we tiptoed through the halls; for one reason or another we were afraid he might have left one of his beauties somewhere and we might step on it. It was torture to live in that house, but his family had to help in some way, we were the only ones who could understand the situation.

He continued collecting butterflies; it was his only interest; we encouraged him to continue. It was important for him to accomplish his work, as he would frequently say.

We didn't become aware of his situation directly from him, but from his music teacher. I have the scene indelibly engraved in my memory of when his teacher came to the house to inform us of his discovery: "Madam," he said to my mother, "your son is precocious, a true artist, I would even go so far as to say a genius." My mother was frightened, and I was too; we immediately called my father at his office. "But, dear," he responded, " that doesn't mean he's crazy, rest assured it's a good thing for us, we can be very proud of him, that's the only way for our lineage to be perpetuated." "But . . ." whimpered my mother. "No buts about it, woman, calm down, I'll be right there," responded my father. "What! What did you say? Why an artist is an artist here or wherever . . . Don't insist on his being crazy, the crazy ones are those who think an artist is crazy . . . Calm down; I'll be right there and I'll talk with the teacher." And he cut the connection. My mother, trying to calm down, continued her conversation with the music teacher and the math teacher who was with him; as for me, that companionship seemed odd, suspect, since art and mathematics . . . They say so many things! . . . But here were these two teachers declaring the same thing: "The boy is precocious, approaching genius, we can say." At home we were really afraid; only my father remained strong, I guess it was worth something to have studied in Europe. He urged us to be calm, assuring us that he would prove that our fears and near panic were all because of something that wasn't really important . . .

The neighborhood is waiting to see what happens. Having a genius in a home like ours and in our circumstances isn't an everyday, commonplace occurrence. From one minute to the next the situation tenses up, puts our nerves on edge, makes us take leave of our senses, and there he is, as if there were nothing out of the ordinary. A loaded atmosphere, and him, nonchalant, always self-assured and busy about his task, without deviating an inch from the path he's traced out. That's his lot, he says. He has an iron will that's terrifying! . . . In some ways he and I are like the Arabs at the store on the corner. In the afternoons, when the sun comes through the window, the Arab sits in his old chair with the deerskin throw and begins to sing in Arabic, a nostalgic, extremely beautiful, old song, but a song of loss. An aimless love song. A song of blind return to the homeland . . . When he has sung it many times, he begins to drowse with the song on his lips . . . and he sings it in his dreams. Suddenly he wakes up and begins crying. He cries a lot and says he's been abandoned in the desert, says it in Arabic, then repeats it in our language, more or less intelligibly. The rest I know from his wife, who is saving money to return to their land with her husband. "He does nothing but sing or recall memories, then he cries, that's the way he dilutes his desperation, his dissatisfaction, his yearning for the lost valley, he tells me. He isn't doing anything really serious about returning to our land. He's not even happy about Yasser Arafat, who is doing everything for us." When she finishes, she starts crying too. "To get up our strength and keep on struggling," she adds, "to really return . . ." To the faraway land that they only see in their dreams, that is only good for helping them remember, to have nostalgia as a salvation, a handhold to keep on struggling, to sing and continue crying . . . It is possible that that land of the Arab storekeepers is not as beautiful as ours, but their great nostalgia has beautified it to such an extent that, when they get there, if they do, they may not like it and will return in order to continue dreaming . . . "Each arrival is a beginning," says my father, then he adds, "and to search is not to escape; to desire is not to get out by running away . . . Each dream is part of a reality we lack." My father knows what he's talking about, which gives us confidence and prevents our suffering too much; although there are difficult moments, these then pass and everything returns to its customary rhythm.

One morning, he returned from his wanderings with a beautiful specimen, he ran straight to me to show it off. It was supremely beautiful. It transported me to lands I had dreamed of. He seemed pleased, but then he began to find fault with it. I scolded him for his attitude, but he immediately found a new imperfection, and finally left it abandoned, defenseless. From that moment on he sank into a state of depression and nothing about his collection satisfied him. He spent long hours closed up inside his room examining the specimens. When he came out he was obviously tired, as if he had walked a long way. Those days were terrible for us, even my father lost his habitual composure at times. My brother was, as at first, absent from us, as if the sentence bothered him again. We all tried to help him feel better, to satisfy his least desire, but he was simply lost, withdrawn, absent from us. Suddenly, the butterflies no longer gave him any satisfaction, but he didn't dare destroy his collections, for they tied him to something. He was suffering and that made us suffer too. Again our home was a pit of anxiety, a labyrinth, a desert, and my brother was the light, the mystery, the savior, who held the key to peace and happiness. But it was necessary to suffer and wait. To wait and suffer. Meanwhile we needed to help him find himself, to find his new path. "What path?" he asked, and frankly we didn't know what path it was or why we called it that. But somewhere distant, down deep, between dream and vigil, we sensed a discovery that would make the walls disappear; for my brother, from one minute to the next, would show us the key to the way out . . .

Our suffering has been lengthy but doubtless his is more acute, since he's both victim and victimizer, even if he does say his phantoms are different. And perhaps they are, because his confinement to bed and then to a wheelchair has changed everything for us, so my mother says. Father goes on being imperturbable, asking all of us to hope; of course, he has always given us hope, he has since the first moment of the misfortune and it's because of him we do not falter nor will we ever weaken in our search to better my brother's life. We deserve it, he deserves it . . .

Restless

David Escobar Galindo
Translated by Elizabeth Gamble Miller

To Jeannette.

Through one of the picture windows one afternoon, he saw that magnificent buck crossing in the distance, taller and more handsome than any he had seen before in his lengthy life. The deer paused for a long while, as if just discovering the world, and then went deep into the swamp, which was now a prisoner of the shadows. On the following day, carrying all the necessary trappings and strategies, he went out to hunt it. He was joined by some of his more skillful servants, with whom he had realized great deeds while on interminable journeys that left them covered in dust, bathed in sour sweat, and spattered with the blood of diverse beings, their eyes gleaming all the while with a mixture of ferocity, fatigue, and victory.

They rode for two days through the woods searching for the superb specimen. Not even a trace. He encountered abundant game, but he had no desire to kill any other animal, and, looking angry and disheveled, he returned without any game at all.

Some time later, on another afternoon, the buck again appeared at the edge of the swamp; and, digging his nails into the stone, he observed it from the picture window. A satisfying moan simmered in his chest as he called his helpers, urging them to come that very instant. Offering no objections, they rushed to prepare an immediate campaign. They noted his quick breathing, denoting determination, and the kind of tragic expression that firmly set his jaws. His bronze skin, moist from aggressive feelings, bruised the bluish air of the exhausted season.

For days and days they traveled. Perhaps in a circle. The servants and their horses could no longer stand on their feet. They were gasping for breath as if they were dying. He left them in a clearing and went on his way. In the swamp night and day are not very different. Nowhere was there a trace of the animal. Only the usual trusting, defenseless sort came out to meet him. He kept on moving. His clothes were falling to shreds. His face was purple and bruised. A piercing ray shot out from his eyes. And then, in a small clearing, he saw it. At ten, at twenty, at thirty paces. Resplendent, stately, almost human. Visibly shaking, he prepared the bow and shot the arrow, which hit the buck in the forehead. The animal didn't move, but blood began covering its head. In one quick leap it disappeared into the thicket. He touched his forehead, in an anxious gesture, and found only sweat mixed with dirt. A painful fury made him weep in broken whimpers. For in some dark zone of his mind the certainty had begun to form that the deer was none other than himself, and that the will and hand in pursuit—attributed to himself—were but the incomparable reaches of divine grace, searching for him through the swamps of memory and of dream.

The Raccoons

Jorge Kattán Zablah
Translated by Elizabeth Gamble Miller

"**G**et up, man! Don't be a lazy bum! Go see if those damned raccoons came back last night!" Hortense said that morning to her husband.

Hearing his wife's voice, Venancio jumped out of bed and ran to the window of his humble dwelling. He pushed aside the curtain and confirmed that the raccoons had returned, leaving the usual destruction behind.

The little house of Venancio Canjura, located on the outskirts of Cojontepeque, was one of the most admired in that region: neatly whitewashed, with a roof free of holes and a garden with roses and very green grass, which made its owner very proud. And that grass was precisely where the raccoons had been up to their tricks for several years. The first time the devilish animals came to Venancio's garden, they dug a ditch, rather deep and several yards long. On the following day, Venancio and his wife filled in the ditch very carefully; but during the night the infamous animals returned and opened it up again. From that time on, the raccoons never ceased punishing the Canjuras with their nocturnal presence. For the couple it all came down to repairing in the morning what had been destroyed the previous night.

At first Venancio held the hope that one day the undesirable visitors would fail to come, but as the situation continued, he began frantically to imagine a thousand ways to prevent their opening up that ditch again.

In "The Patriot," the cantina of Don Saturnino Aguado, Venancio's friends, also great friends of Bacchus, hadn't the slightest idea of what was happening at the Canjura house. That miserable Canjura never would tell his troubles, so how could they? Not even if they had been fortune-tellers!

The topic of the day's conversation between Don Satu's customers was a political matter that worried everyone, except Venancio, who forced himself to feign interest in his comrades' chatter.

"Looks like Gen'ral Protanola's government is 'bout to collapse," said one.

"You're gonna see how my good ole Comandante lines him up 'fore ya kin count one two three," added another.

And each one gave his opinion about the political crisis that was approaching.

"They sayin' Comandante Zapiola's closin' in on the capital."

"I sure's heck hope he does, so's to end all this thievin'!"

"Yeah, thattud be solid! So's they'd stop grabbin' with thur hands full what belongs to poor folk!"

"They been tellin' me the Comandante's got more'n a thousan' men armed to the teeth!"

"God grant it, Brother!"

During these conversations, Venancio, with a distracted expression, showed no inclination to participate. His thoughts were on another place, not very far from the cantina. His garden, the ditch, those raccoons that were making his life miserable. Politics was the least thing bothering him. "Slaves like us are only good for fattnin' up the rich guys," Venancio had said on more than one occasion. The only thing that mattered to him now was that the animals stop digging the ditch and that they go to Cochinchina to try somebody else's patience.

Once Venancio tried to poison the raccoons. He ground up some bottles and put all the pulverized glass into some beef. Then he filled in the ditch and on top he placed the bait.

The Canjuras were very pleased. They even celebrated beforehand, by drinking a bottle of brandy.

"Now we'll see the end to our troubles!" said Venancio.

"God grant it. I got a lot of faith in Saint Quickness," replied his wife.

Immediately they were beset by a long silence. There was no joy on either face as the two of them began thinking the same thing: "What if the poison didn't work?" Both of them turned pale, and they went to bed with an uneasy feeling.

At daybreak, Venancio heard the usual litany:

"Get up, man! Don't be a bum! Go see if those damned things came back last night!"

Almost automatically, Venancio jumped out of bed and ran toward the window. He pulled back the curtain and, in great consternation, saw that the raccoons had dug out the ditch again, leaving the meat intact.

His worries in tow, Venancio arrived at Don Satu's cantina to down
a few slugs of firewater. Drinking the first glass of brandy, he noticed
right off that his buddies were talking about the same subject as on the
other day:

"Now Gen'ral Portanola's gonna fall on his ass."

"I'd like to see the same thing dished out to him as to that bunch of
thieves 'round 'im."

"Let those no-goods bleed."

While his friends talked about the attacks against the government
people and their desire to see them bleed, Venancio, drink in hand, was
thinking something similar. He wanted to go on the attack and to see the
blood of his sneaky enemies flow, those raccoons.

When he got home, he was wearing a big smile on his face. He thought
he had conceived of a brilliant plan. He had decided to stay home from
work for a few days in order to be able to spend his entire time looking
for a way to trap the obnoxious little beasts.

With some rusty wire and the help of some pliers, he built something
that looked like a rat trap, but enormous in size, about fifty times larger.
"Any bugger lands in this trap—raccoon sacked . . . neck hacked!" So
reasoned the desperate inventor.

Once he had filled the ditch, he set up his contraption and went to tell
Hortense:

"Woman! I've got the trap ready! It's a whizbanger!"

"I seen it through the winda," she answered. "Those sonsabitches
won't get out of that!"

That night they went to bed feeling very good. They were convinced
the raccoons would reap their reward very soon.

"Get up, man! Go see if they fell in the trap now!!" said Hortense the
following day.

And once more, mechanically, Venancio sat up, then shot over to the
window. He observed shortly, to his horror, that the destructive animals
had tossed the trap aside and dug out the confounded ditch again.

Hortense, when she was informed of the fact, pulled her hair and burst
out crying.

"Don't worry, woman!" her husband said to console her. "Tonight
I'm gonna finish off those pesky bastards! . . . You'll see. I'm gonna blow
'em away with my *compadre* Ruperto's double-barreled shotgun."

When it began to get late, Venancio sat down on a stool, holding the
shotgun, and started waiting for the invaders. About midnight he began
to yawn, and the raccoons still showed no signs of life. "There's a full
moon and they can't get by me," mulled the hunter. Suddenly, in less
time than it takes a frog to wink, he was sound asleep. He awakened

sometime later only to realize his efforts had been in vain. There was the ditch again.

There had been a time when Venancio and Hortense's lives were very different. In their home they used to discuss many things: relatives, harvests, sicknesses, rabbits, lambs . . . But not now! The raccoons were absorbing everything around them and their calvary lasted twenty-four hours a day:

"Will they be back tonight?"

"How come those beasts have it in fur us?"

"What time you think they came last night?"

"When are they gonna stop hittin' us?"

"How many you s'pose came last night?"

"If they came yestiday, they'll sure as heck be back today."

"Why don't they go do somebody else in?"

"It's 'nuf to drive ya crazy!"

"They oughta go over to my *compadre* Ruperto's and make thur ditch!"

"All I want is fur them to leave us be!"

"That's what I say!"

"I gotta see Don Indalecio," Venancio said to himself, in his agonizing frustration.

After having heard Venancio out, Don Indalecio Barrientos, the celebrated town witch doctor and extremely wise arbitrator for offenses, pronounced:

"Look here! Ya git some burro piss off a widowed burro that hadn't ate and sprinkle it all over the ditch. An' ya got it!"

And that was what the worried Venancio did. But the raccoons kept on frequenting his garden without showing the least respect for those blessed urine specimens.

"There's only one way left. Don Agustín will get me out of this mess," reflected Venancio.

Don Agustín Garfio, ex-priest, who, according to the viper tongues of the district, had been excommunicated because of the sexual gluttony he gave free run to, after listening sympathetically to the sufferings of Venancio, said to him while he also handed him some papers:

"Listen well, my son! Here I give you Saint Lucifer of the Countryside's prayer for mercy. Put it under your pillow and, after about three days, the raccoons will cease to bother you."

But, in spite of the good intentions of the ex-priest, the miraculous prayer failed to render good results, which left the Canjuras immersed in the most frightful anguish.

During that time, Venancio didn't even go down to the cantina; he had concentrated on his own problems so much that his misfortune was consuming his life. But, one Saturday afternoon, he decided to take a little turn about the establishment of Don Satu to "wash out his mouth," as the ill-fated man used to say.

As he approached the cantina, he heard a great racket. At first he thought his friends had gotten into a knock-down-drag-out from being drunk; but then, as he went into the place, he saw that everyone was hugging and letting out wild joyful howls. When the noise diminished a little, he found out what was happening;

"Great! They blown off the Gen'ral's head!"

"And they say none of his *compadres* got out with thur hides!"

"They also sayin' when the Comandante and his *compadres* rode into town it was just like in the movies."

"They say they's sword-whupped one of Don Satu's women friends. And she bein' pregnant!"

"That's revolution fur ya. Good folks allus taken the rap for them sinners."

One of the ones there celebrating the fall of the general, when he perceived that Venancio didn't seem to be participating in the festivities, spoke to him this way:

"Hey, Don Vena! Seems like you're not too hot on the Comandante winnin'. Could it be you're on th'other side?"

Venancio, remaining calm, answered without beating around the bush:

"Politics's not for the poor. We're law abidin' folks. We make a livin' workin', sweatin'.

"You mean, Don Vena, the Gen'ral wadn't no thief?"

"You, Don Arnulfo"—for that's what that bad friend's name was—" didn't understand me right. The Gen'ral was not only a thief. He was a big thief! A robber!"

"Don't you think Comandante Zapiola is gonna be better?"

"No one who's mixed up in politics can be honest," answered Venancio directly. "Maybe he's not as big a thief. But that's a horse of a different color."

"What's really a fact is that you're a sonovabigbitch! A sevenmonther from the prick!" the importuner suddenly burst out as he pulled out his machete.

Fortunately, Don Saturnino intervened and didn't allow the matter to go further.

On the way home, with the incident in the cantina totally forgotten, Venancio's suffering over the raccoons, which even during that dangerous altercation had not ceased paining him, increased in intensity, to the degree that it didn't let him sleep at all that night.

But the passing of time works true miracles. Almost inadvertently Venancio and Hortense acquired a certain stoicism, gradually becoming accustomed to the unfair task of having to fill in the ditch every morning. But of course, always with the hope that one day the aforementioned animals would leave them in peace.

"Get up, man! Don't be a lazy bum! Go see if they came last night!" Hortense said one morning to her husband.

Venancio, as always, jumped immediately out of his bed and flew over to the window. Pushing the curtain to one side, he contemplated something for which he was not prepared. In disbelief he rubbed his eyes to assure himself that he wasn't seeing visions. But no. He had really seen it. There was no ditch. The raccoons, for the first time in so many years, had taken pity on the Canjuras. They had left them alone.

The house of Venancio and Hortense was full of joy that day. They celebrated like they used to do on very special occasions—with abundant brandy. She even smoked a big cigar. Suddenly, in the middle of the celebration, Hortense blurted out a question.

"And what if they come tonight?"

"Don't say that, woman, it'll bring bad luck!"

But that night the raccoons didn't appear in the garden. Nor did they the following night or ever again. Later, the Canjuras found out that a hunter, with better luck than Venancio, had trapped them all in their den and had exterminated them.

Before long, the Canjuras were overcome by a chronic melancholy. And understandably so, because the continual uncertainty about whether the raccoons would dig out the ditch had been their only spiritual nourishment for years. They hadn't realized that those animals of the devil controlled their brains and souls. And now that it was definite that the raccoons would never return, what did the Canjuras have left? How would they fill that vacuum? What would they now have to sustain them?

As was to be expected, they aged overnight, and within a few days, while working in their garden very close to where the raccoons had been digging before, they were surprised by death.

That Confounded Year . . . !

Hugo Lindo
Translated by Elizabeth Gamble Miller

We can't move around.
The air is so heavy we can't breathe.

We are hungry, but talking about it doesn't help at all. We can't even yell now. We don't have strength enough to complain or room enough to scream.

And I'm the one to blame.

Not the only one, of course; but the one to be directly blamed, the one who brought into the world all those who must share this horrible responsibility—my children, grandchildren, great-grandchildren—who have carried this destructive task of preservation to a greater and greater perfection.

We can scarcely move, a little to the left, another little bit to the right. My neighbor's sweat has an acrid odor. Ours does too, no doubt.

This must be what used to be called death throes. I wonder if they lasted this long. For days and days and more and more days.

We are all waiting.

But, can I really be thought to blame? I don't know. I can't think clearly. After all, to a certain degree, I was forced to do what I did.

I should add that I didn't initiate the research. Hardly. Other scientists preceded me and laid the foundation for the whole process. My first misfortune was that I hit the mark, and the second was that I had the offspring I did.

Before, when there were still libraries because there was still space to keep books and other things, you would have found my name in any encyclopedia, as the winner of the Asimov Prize for Medicine and Physiology for 2142. But, later, with what the ecologist-economists came up calling "space per capita," this was naturally reduced to extremely restricted perimeters. We were forced to get rid of books and laboratories, vehicles, anything that occupied the few cubic yards available for each human being.

Beside me, here, is my mother; a discernible presence exuding a hint of fermented wood.

She might also be considered partially responsible, not just because she bore me but also because she got me involved in solving the multiple equation of cancers.

Already some viruses had been discovered through the ultramicroscope. Others still retained their terrible secrets. And despite the many volumes, the data, the essays, and opinions treating the subject, the fact is we knew little, very little about the disease.

We are hungry.

In regard to hunger, it seems humanity has always had some information.

Our hunger, however, is different. We don't eat, that's true. We don't even take any vitamins or any of what we used to consider the normal store of drugs in a home in the twenty-first century. But from the time a child is born he is given "Multiple Food Depot." Rather, from the time a child used to be born. No one is born now. How could you have children in this demographic concentration so reminiscent of bacteria cultures? No one is born.

No one dies.

Mea culpa.

I had been involved in that kind of research for several years already. Practically from the time I graduated from the university with my title of Doctor of Mammary Gland Carcinoma in Mestiza Women.

My great-grandfather, who was also a doctor, although with much less specialization, as was typical of his time, would have been amazed at the mind-boggling amount of mathematics we had to learn and the operation of those unforgettable devices (which eventually occupied very little space, but even so had to be disposed of) by means of which, through almost instantaneous electronic computations, we succeeded in deciphering entire chains of ARN.

I say that I was already involved in the matter, under the tutelage of Dr. Strimberg, when I contracted a very painful viral pneumonia. With Dr. Strimberg's single application of Omnimicina penetrating ointment, the pain disappeared by the following day and I could continue my work.

Then, Ellen—who, incidentally, has stayed close to me—came down with a fulminant intestinal infection. I cured her, with similar applications of Omnimicina.

Omnimicina! Good heavens!

I still remember well the very lengthy catalog of diseases we had to learn in the first two years of Medicine and Physiology before narrowing down to a specialization. It was an almost superhuman effort to do so, and not because of the Greek or Latin names that were almost always in combination, but because of the enormous number of somatic, psychic, or psychosomatic imbalances.

Afterward, as everyone knows, diseases were classified as I have just indicated. Later, it was discovered that there was only one illness, the psychosomatic, which assumed an infinite variety of forms and intensities, but which basically responded to three types of medication.

Then came Omnimicina.

It became unnecessary then to catalog diseases or to indicate separate treatments. Omnimicina and all was well!

On the other hand, we had to study mathematics.

That permitted us to know the precise composition of each nucleic acid and each protein and to know where we were to apply the scalpel. The scalpel, figuratively speaking, since we had transcended that primitive stage of inserting a knife into a man's body. No. It was only a matter of changing the placement of a nitrogen atom, placing one of carbon in the appropriate place . . . To accomplish that we had the biological computers of the brilliant Dementhel!

I was meditating over the biochemical composition of a cancer serum when Orlando the cardiologist came in. The only cardiologist among my children and one of the few, the very few, among my numerous offspring. Because soon they became unnecessary.

"Papa, may I speak with you?"

I gave him an appointment for the following day.

All of us have always been like that. When we do something we devote our entire energies to it. We don't let our minds wander and we don't let anyone else distract us. I was working on that serum. Nothing else could claim my attention at that moment.

On the following day at the appointed time, I was struck by the fact that Orlando turned up with Recius, another of my children, an electronic engineer. Recius didn't have an audience with me. But I tolerated it, provided he didn't speak.

Orlando explained his plan:

"Recius has already developed to an advanced state various devices of electromagnetic detection, suitable for diverse technical applications; many of them for use in the telecommunications industry, in every aspect of the term: holography, teletrivision, aviation, cosmic leap, instantradio, etc."

"Cut it short, son, I already know that."

"Well all right: we have decided to join forces. Between his engineering and my cardiology . . ."

He then proposed exactly what I had foreseen.

So now we would have at our disposal a mechanical contraption capable of pumping a human body's entire blood supply forever, with a minimum expenditure of energy.

And it frightened me.

I didn't say anything, but it frightened me.

It is true, of course, that we doctors should do everything in our power to preserve the health and lives of human beings. I undertook the fight against cancer. Orlando and Recius, together, fought against heart problems. Recius, by himself, against accidents. And Leonard, the biocriminologist, against tendencies, whether inherited or acquired, to engage in war, violence, and crime. And Antígona against hunger and aging.

A moment would come when . . .

And of course, the moment did come.

We are like that. Something is either done perfectly, or not at all.

My mother was walking in my direction.

She wore a crestfallen expression. She had a greenish skin color.

"Son: I want you, as a doctor, to see this . . ."

And she, a Mestiza, showed me her left breast. A little tumor the size of a pea could be clearly discerned.

Some specialists still resorted to the scalpel in spite of the fact of its nonacceptance by a sensitive public. I was against it. As long as there was any other recourse, I would continue preventing the procedure . . .

It was only natural for me to devote my future efforts more intensively to the problems that I had delineated some time previously.

The Asimov Prize of the year 2142 represented the culmination of those efforts. And the other culminating fact was that my mother is still alive.

If this is living.

Let's establish, where appropriate, a degree of blame. I don't reject my own. Nor do I defend my children. But neither do I want to feel or believe that I am solely responsible. Because, for one thing, it wouldn't be fair.

My memory retains some of the data from the statistics that had to be burned to make room for people. I'm going to attempt to bring that information into clearer focus to clarify things.

At the end of the twentieth century, the "demographic explosion" was already being felt; its pace was accelerated by geometric progression: more inhabitants, more children, more inhabitants, more children . . . Planet saturation was calculated for the year 2300. I'm rounding off the numbers.

Why did the saturation come earlier?

The demographers hadn't made a mistake in calculations, since even then there were already calculators and electronic computers of great precision and amazing speed.

What caused the miscalculation was the existence of this cursed family that hadn't been taken into account, couldn't have been taken into account.

My family.

Which begins with me, really, because although there were doctors, lawyers, and engineers among my ancestors, there were no researchers or inventors.

Besides, the available records say one thing very clearly: this chain of deoxyribonucleic acid that characterizes us begins with me. And, unfortunately, it's inevitably inherited.

Do you suppose I'm to blame for that?

I was reared in the midst of a home that was more or less traditional, one of the last middle-class homes left from that period when children didn't ask for an audience with their parents but went directly to them without preliminaries, when there was a kind of indecent social promiscuity.

And that type of society inculcated ancestor worship.

Therefore, I was brought up to love my mother.

And when she said she had that tiny lump in her breast, my reaction was not only that of a specialist but that of a good son, twentieth-century style. I applied myself more energetically to the biogenetic research I was involved in and solved the many problems regarding cancer all at once. Preventative and curative aspects. That was my prize in the fatal year of 2142.

It is entirely possible that a portion of my blame should also be attributed to the familial social environment in which I spent my first years.

And there is yet a slimmer thread. Now that I remember it, there is one detail, apparently of little significance, that with the course of the years registered considerable importance.

Because it wasn't at all unusual for a test tube to be of poor quality, or for the glass to break for no apparent reason. Perhaps I wouldn't even remember the incident if it hadn't been that . . .

Let me take it a bit slower: I was saying that the demographers, in making their calculations, didn't take into account the future existence of this family that, biologically, begins with me.

Neither did they foresee what Dr. Strimberg, my teacher, called graphically "the reversion of the capsule."

I will first explain this phenomenon, before relating the other events.

The capsule matter was as follows: since a little after 1900, various contraceptive pills have been in production that were of sufficient efficacy while women consumed them. But, as soon as they, for any reason, stopped downing them, nature took a peculiar revenge: it increased their reproductive possibilities and caused them to have double, triple, multiple deliveries.

Organizations conscious of the impending problem, which in fact was already beginning to be a reality, campaigned for what came to be called "responsible paternity," which on many occasions should have been called "responsible maternity." Let no one bring into the world more children than those he will be able to feed, dress, house, and educate! Their arguments were in a certain sense moral; but they conflicted with the ethical and religious convictions of many people. For that reason, perhaps, they placed emphasis on statistics. I remember having read in a book—I will always yearn for the time when there was room for a book!—that about 1970 the world had 3,632 million inhabitants; that toward '75, it was expected to have more than 4,000 million; and toward '80, 4,500 million. Conservatively calculating, the author came to the conclusion that the world population doubled every fifty years, and that, consequently, by the year 2310 there would be more than one inhabitant per square yard. So, in the year 2360, we would be about like we are now.

But the scientific arguments and, particularly, the statistics didn't impress the great masses.

On the other hand, religious and moral entities talked about the limitation of birth as an attempt against life; that the one yet to be born is already a living being, even when it has not become independant of maternal anatomy. And they offered damnation to the rule breakers. This last turned out to be more powerful than the syllogisms.

So that was how the "reversion of the capsule" was produced.

Because, although both groups intensified their propaganda, for every supporter attracted by the organization to limit births, the religious entity gained three or four.

If these three or four new supporters had been among those who hadn't used contraceptive methods, probably the statistical curve would have turned out to be more precise, and preventative measures would have been duly accomplished. But for the most part it was a question of women who had taken contraceptives, and the result was a proliferation of twins and triplets, which produced a tremendous geometric progression. That is what Dr. Strimberg called "reversion." Others, less scientific or more passionate, called the phenomenon "vengeance" or "the revenge of the pill."

Since, after all, both the mysteries of cancer and those of heredity and fertility were to be found in nucleic acids, Dr. Strimberg said to me:

"Dr. Harbis, what would you think of taking advantage of the research being done at present and trying to find an antidote for the problem of reversion . . . something that will make it impossible?"

"The reversion of reversion?"

"Right: the reversion of reversion."

"Do you think it's a viable project?"

"Is anything impossible? Might not these phenomena all be within the same protein stock?"

As usual, he was completely right.

I still had a lot of middle-class education in me, and my thinking was that before speaking on a subject—and, more important, before working on one—many moral questions needed to be considered before making the decision pro or con. Frequently the opposing sides seemed equally convincing to me. There were times when both of them seemed terribly immoral.

Since I'm not an expert on those questions, I decided to ask my wife what she thought. Ellen reacted emotionally. In part, because of her very-twentieth-century femininity, in part, because she herself—and, naturally, me!—had been a victim of the reversion. No one is unaware that we have a number of children, and that they came into the world in threes if not in fours. And the most important ones arrived after my accident with the test tube, because for Ellen the reversion was now simply irreversible.

Nor is it unknown to anyone that Orlando, Recius, Leonard, and Antígona were born within exactly twenty-three minutes of each other, in the order just given.

I repeat, Ellen reacted emotionally.

"Do it, do it, please! Now not for my sake but for the multitude of females who are victims of the 'revenge of the pill.'"

"The 'reversion of the capsule,' dear."

"Whatever you like. The victims are my concern, not the words, and this indecent way of giving birth like dogs to quantities of wailing, half-blind pups."

"But you have no reason to complain . . ."

Actually, although the supergeniuses of the family hadn't been born yet, we already had some fifteen or twenty offspring. I don't remember exactly . . . because I never even succeeded in learning all their names.

I wasn't mistaken in thinking this research could be carried out in conjunction with that related to cancer, as not only did it not interfere, but it turned out to be complementary.

I don't know if it could be considered biochemistry or engineering. The calculations that had to be done! How can we place this oxydril here without disrupting the balance of the molecule? What should the temperature be at a given moment, and how much should it be lowered, and within what fraction of a second? . . . Those who have worked on these things know the mental concentration they require.

Never have I spoken badly of Dr. Strimberg; I owe much of my scientific formation to him and I've admired him all my life. He was one of the last to die, and the mere fact that he's dead evokes respect and envy. But nothing prevents my saying that one of his not very commendable little habits was that of surprising you.

He would slip in and, with his rubber-soled shoes, not even his footsteps could be heard. And suddenly, with an imposing, booming voice he would speak:

"What are you busy with now, Dr. Harbis?"

I was so immersed in my observations and quandaries that it was like being catapulted into a devilish mental parabola. Something like the sensation one has when trying to go down a step that isn't there. And I gave a start, which made the test tube vibrate violently in my hands. It broke. I was cut by it slightly, an imperceptible wound, on the thumb of my right hand, and into the cut flowed that greenish liquid that . . .

Why continue?

It's a well-known story how all these poor devils are stretched out on the ground next to one another and another and another, semibreathing, semisleeping, semialive in this infernal heap and with no escape.

I was inoculated with the tiniest bit of the greenish liquid and it modified my genes and all this molecular chain that turned me and all my children, grandchildren, and great-grandchildren into supergeniuses, horrible monsters of an intelligence inevitably transmissible for centuries . . .

For centuries and centuries?

No longer.

Before, in order to procreate, a man and woman had to lie together. Nowadays human beings are all lying down, men and women tumbled together, heaped up like bananas put out to dry in the sun. And that way, precisely because of lying so pressed together, no procreation is now possible.

That will put an end—I hope—to this confounded heredity.

Orlando, Recius, Leonard, and Antígona, were born a year after the accident.

Wouldn't the test tube factory that put such fragile tubes on the market possibly bear responsibility, at least partially? Or, perhaps, Dr. Strimberg, who startled me so with his abruptness?

I never achieved the reversion of the reversion.
Or the revenge of the revenge, as Ellen calls it.
After the small accident, I didn't try to investigate the matter further; I devoted my time totally to the cancerous mammary gland of my mother, a Mestiza. The results, you now know. There she is, frequently muttering and cursing such a long, boring, sterile life. A sterile life! Despite her present descendants who number more than a million people!

Leonard Harbis followed my own steps in genetic research, but to other ends: to apply them to the aggressive tendencies of man. To his formula, synthetically called LH-999, one may credit the fact that wars have ended and that, gradually, individual squabbles began to disappear. He began by administering LH-999 in psychiatric hospitals, then in jails and, with its efficacy proved and its lack of secondary effects, it was adopted as obligatory in schools, army camps, universities, etc.
Between Orlando and Recius, the tiny, cheap, perpetually efficient cardioelectron became fully developed.
Recius alone, as an engineer, perfected detectors and reactors that prevented car and plane crashes, engine fires, ship collisions.
We already had Omnimicina.
It was then that Antígona had just carried things to an extreme.
Women, as you know, have always been women. It is precluded that not even the most demanding academic education ever succeeded in divesting them of a certain indefinable, capricious pleasantness, a certain way, sometimes surer than logic, to confront events so as to conceal day-to-day reality with a kind of poetic film.
By then we were already living in narrow cubicles and those of us who had had a freer childhood and youth were not acclimating to such circumstances. But she and her lover found it natural. When they came in from their activities, they had to get into a cage with each other and their children in common, into such a reduced space that it was impossible to hide a sign of fatigue, a bad body odor, or an impatient gesture.
In that cubicle, because it was scarcely a sheet wide, there was a mirror. And one morning, when everyone had already left and she was alone, Antígona looked at herself in the mirror.
Being a woman, she quickly detected some insignificant little wrinkles beginning to appear at the corners of her eyes. At that very moment, and

perhaps by coincidence, the last four sets of twins in one of the contiguous dungeons were crying. There was no need to ask why: Antígona had attended them more than once, as their doctor, and she knew hunger was the children's problem. "Denutrition" was the scientific name. But it was hunger. Plain and simple.

And those little lines and that crying forced my daughter to change the direction of her activities.

In the future, her time was devoted to fighting those two scourges of humanity: the aging process menacing it and the hunger gripping thousands and thousands of parasites of this ill-fated planet.

Unfortunately, she was victorious.

Hunger, we do have. But not denutrition. Damn that Multiple Food Depot that keeps us alive, half alive, while hunger diabolically envelops our bodies and souls!

End result: no one dies from old age. Or cancer. Or hunger. Or violence. Or from an accident. Or a heart attack.

Here we are, tossed in a heap next to one another and another and another and another . . .

And it all began with me.

In that confounded year of 2142, when I received the Asimov Prize.

Cards

Ricardo Lindo
Translated by Elizabeth Gamble Miller

A mermaid hung out her single stocking to dry.
Sadly, seriously, the fishermen repeated an ancient song.

The mermaid, fragrant with cinnamon, was warm and restless. A fisherman of the Bronze Age set his bronze eyes on the naked mermaid. But the mermaid loved a sailor who was young and strong beneath the sun storms. The sailor was sixteen, taciturn, and blond, and he loved the shadows of tobacco smoke above the tables in the afternoon. When he was aroused, not only his member but his entire heavy body would contradict the laws of gravity and remain inches above the ground. The lily skin of the mermaid fit him closely like matter to form, as advised by Aristotle. They made love amid the planks at the dock upon canvases stained with tar.

The bronze fisherman exuded a repressed bitterness. One time he saw them in their dock hideaway, repeating the movement of the waves, and he dreamed of committing murder, using a knife with an emerald encrusted handle. Thick, green drops of rust stained the pupils of the bronze fisherman.

The age-old story of unrequited love.

Among the barrels at the tavern where the seamen usually gathered at noon to watch the dust dancing on the sun rays, again and again the fisherman found the young sailor with a demeanor of triumphant indifference. Thus do those protected by hidden constellations and crowned by beautiful, banal, lofty winds tend to act.

When the sailor had his arm tattooed with a mermaid beside an anchor, the Bronze Age fisherman understood his rival was claiming a title that should now in fact have belonged to him.

The small mermaid realized the feelings she was stirring. In the presence of others, she blatantly flirted with the fisherman. With her squirrel eyes she teased him to the point of exasperation, and even let her breasts be touched by his large, callused hands. But it never went any further. The fisherman accepted the situation, comforted just by seeing her. His unattainable desire turned to something close to love, so much so that he no longer visited other mermaids.

The sailor chose to ignore the matter, which was even more disagreeable to the fisherman. He seemed to hear his name among other sounds and followed by laughter. He wasn't far from the truth.

The bronze fisherman often contemplated a day when the sailor would depart, leaving behind the weak and disconsolate mermaid, who would fall into his arms. The scene was enacted again and again while he was waiting for the fish.

But although the sailor watched his companions leave, and even though he was beginning to tire of the mermaid, he never followed them. The lethargy of summer left him moored there.

The bronze fisherman grew silent like a tree. Once again he thought of the mermaid as he gathered in his fish, as silent as himself, and also made of bronze. He seemed to be an ascetic of the seas who, though unable to believe in God, continued to pray from excessive habit and to fill an aimless life with futile acts.

The Circle

José María Méndez
Translated by Elizabeth Gamble Miller

Here we are, Pedro, Alberto, Eduardo, and I. Pedro is still young, I notice, too young for his age, and he doesn't drink. None of us is drinking. That's strange. Inveterate drinkers, and now all of us abstaining. I am still marveling at how young Pedro is. He looks like he's twenty. Why, he's at least forty-five. He's talking like in the old days, when we were freshmen at the university.

"We've got to organize a blood brotherhood. First, to sign the pact we'll open our veins and keep them open long enough to fill an ink well. We'll write the first manifesto in blood, an oath of revenge."

Pedro used to talk to us like that whenever the subject of the missing bodies came up: the story of our friends who disappeared after the jailings and the shootings in the demonstrations. We knew the truth even though we had no way to prove it, and their names weren't on the official lists of the captured. We knew they had been buried, but not in cemeteries, or had been burned or thrown out of planes into the ocean. But we always rejected Pedro's remarks in an effort to cool his guerrilla fever. The death of one man, whoever he is, solves nothing. We'll never be able to organize a force strong enough to confront the government; every attempt to do so brings greater repression, increases tyranny, provokes greater injustice for the helpless people we're fighting for.

Now no one speaks up to contradict him. We behave in a most unlikely manner, just like understanding older brothers. I think either the years have made us more tolerant, or else nothing matters to us now.

As usual Eduardo brings up the subject of music.

"I look over the gallery of musicians," he says, "and I find very few frauds. On the other hand they are numerous among writers and painters. Why is that?"

"Do you still play the guitar?"

"All the time."

He reaches out to take a guitar down from the wall and plays something by Albéniz. He has changed his style; it's more profound, more expressive. I would say it's somewhat alien to the composer.

"Also," he continues, "I play the violin and saxophone and the concertina."

And he takes each of those instruments down in turn and plays them, interpreting several unfamiliar compositions. So unfamiliar to me that I don't even try to guess who composed them, notwithstanding my vast knowledge of musical matters and my extraordinary ear, which always permits me to name the composer correctly when I hear a musical piece for the first time. "Is it possible," I wonder, "that despite being Eduardo's friend for so many years, all my life, I didn't know that besides the guitar he also plays the violin, the concertina, and the saxophone?" I finally decide I have a questionable memory; it's a faculty that will deteriorate with time.

Alberto was always impudent and shifty; his physical appearance reflected it. But now his face has changed. His sly look has become direct, his laugh, ironic and irritating before, is now charming, his unruly hair has been tamed. His voice doesn't ring sharp and false, but deep and sincere. He talks to us in a most unexpected manner.

"I don't think you can divide men into good and bad. As a matter of fact, even though we were given reasoning powers, we are essentially animals. The mass of humanity is controlled by instinct and chance. Education modifies the inherited biological structure very little. Very few people have the ability to control instinct or the force of events, or can clear the obstacles civilization has been constructing in its effort to degrade us. They are the prophets, the saints, and the philosophers, individuals born with the attributes of sensitivity, intelligence, and willpower; and knowing they have these gifts, they cultivate them. As you know, I've just been stumbling along, dimly illuminated by the scant light inside of me."

"What is going on here?" I wonder. "Have we gotten completely turned around?" And I don't understand the situation until I wake up. I've been dreaming. And all the characters in my dream are my old friends, friends who have already died.

Now here is Francisco, the one who sneezes constantly; Federico, the weight lifter; my uncle Roberto, and me. The picture is somewhat incomprehensible because we are sitting around a table in a bar and Uncle Roberto repeatedly used to swear he would never take a drink, or

set his foot in "one of those dumps." Nevertheless, here he is, with us.
I would have liked to throw it back at him, make him eat his words. But
I couldn't. In the first place, there was a reverential fear; in the second
place, I didn't know what kind of drinks they sold in this bar or what we
had been served. It was probably alcohol, but it could be something else.
To become enlightened, I brought the glass up to try it. That didn't help
at all. The contents had an indefinable taste that was totally new to my
palate.

Uncle Roberto's insolent manner and demeanor had diminished
considerably. He was saying:

"We all assume poses. Worse than assuming them is being controlled
by them. When we adopt a pose, we don't realize we're imposing a
narrow mold upon ourselves that continually makes its impression on
our personalitities, on our souls. When we try to break out of that mold,
we are no longer capable of doing so. It's as if we had placed ourselves
inside a suit of armor."

Federico said:

"One can always get out."

I thought: now that idiot has stuck in his two cents. Now he's going
to say you have to be a man of strength to break through the armor and
that no armor exists that he can't break out of. But he didn't say that; he
simply added:

"You, yourself, Uncle Roberto, broke out."

Uncle Roberto closed the dialogue.

"You have understood me, Federico."

"Wow," I said to myself, "this is something, my arrogant Uncle
Roberto has turned humble, and the imbecile Federico has become
understanding."

I looked over at Francisco; he had always been selfish. He used to say,
"Your worst enemy is the one you've helped. Giving alms contributes to
the creation of a society of beggars." Now he added a third voice to the
conversation. "It is possible to break out," he said. "As for myself, being
greedy, as with all the sins we commit when we're young, used to be
comfortable, almost biologically satisfying. But in time it turned against
me. I was stingy with myself. You have to be careful; almost everything
in life boomerangs."

"Wow!" I thought. "The whole world is topsy-turvy, turned wrong
side out like a sock." And my mind became so jumbled with ideas that
I sensed impending insanity. Within ten minutes I had recovered my
composure, when I became completely awake. Again I had dreamed, and
the people in my dream were dead, and they had been for a long time.

Now it happens regularly. I get together with relatives or friends every
evening. But during the dream I discover they've died. This is frighten-

ing. When my wife sees me wake up sweating and disoriented, she tries to dispel the effect of the bad dreams, telling me I shouldn't worry, that it has nothing to do with the illness that plagues me, my headaches, my hands shaking, the convulsions.

This time we are inside a gray room, enclosed in opaque glass walls. There are more than fifteen of us. A slightly reddish light glows, flickering. We are sitting around an enormous rectangular table. Some get up; others come in. Each one, before sitting down, comes over to me, slaps me on the shoulder or shakes my hand. The cordial gestures are accompanied by an enigmatic smile that upsets me. It's disconcerting until I finally decipher the meaning. Eventually I come to understand: I really am with them; I have definitively joined the circle.

To Tell the Story

Alfonso Quijada Urías
Translated by Elizabeth Gamble Miller

The shadow from the pilaster supporting the southwest corner of the roof of the house in front developed later than usual. Only now the sun was beginning to shoot out weak, fleeting rays. Through the banister's heavy railings, discolored by time and by the rains, paraded other shadows beyond the now familiar ones. To those familiar silhouettes were added others, distinguished by their novel apparel. Extraordinary—you might say —considering the usual. Especially for someone who for many months has been observing at that hour the first movements of the day. For the substance of dream becomes fragile and frightening as the years advance. So dawn and the calm offered by the first light are anxiously anticipated. Light that uncovers spaces: walkways, a succession of portals, grated windows, rooms, columns, little puddles, movie billboards like black stripes projected against the daylight of the street.

In confusion they mill about. A ruckus is brewing on the corner with people who begin to run and yell, waving their hands and charging about the vendor's empty cold-drink stands. From the center of the square the crowd sometimes shifts to the middle of the thoroughfare to see close up, to satisfy their curiosity. Only a few minutes before, the first mortar shells were heard. One at the police station. Another at the guard house. The "kids" had come down, cautious silent shadows of a night that was disappearing with the dawn's first light and crowing cocks. Stationed in key places, the majority of them waited until the commandos in charge of assaulting the police and guard stations fulfilled their missions. Apparently there was little resistance. The Commander of the Guard was out whoring. The attack surprised him at Juana Puñales' brothel.

And there, right in the middle of the street, displayed in his underwear, was the little man standing along with the rest of the prisoners.

People didn't know what the explosions were at that early hour, whether it was the work of God, the Devil, or the "kids." The bang, bang, bang of guerrilla shots scattered in all directions. People later ran pell-mell, but at first they slipped along stealthily, like dancers. Tiptoeing on the pavement. The sidewalks. In front of the posters advertising the movie. Under the lighted letters. Beside the line of newspapers. Crossing the streets. In the same direction. Through a narrow street with tall houses. Until they reached a passageway between two tall buildings with faded, wrinkled walls, covered with greasy stains and the remains of political tracts that had been glued on and torn off. The water and the sun plus the children's scribblings made a mural with a wrinkled surface thick with scraps of letters. Numbers. Yellowed candidates' faces. Grotesque. Phallic drawings. Phrases. They finally came to a major esplanade where there were more people. Children playing. Behind them a string of mountains like udders. Bloated. Another blob of people on the patio at the mayor's house. And another below the church atrium. Everywhere. "The kids have taken over the town," they were saying. Always in an impersonal tone.

There were many young people (girls among them) looking too young to have ever fired a gun. But you had to see them. They had undoubtedly crossed the river, judging by their shoes covered with mud and gravel. Townspeople began to emerge much later. Responding to the noise and to the silence itself that had preceded the uproar. Some came out of necessity. Others spurred by curiosity. So the tumult gradually grew. Finally they were in full view from head to foot. From head to foot. All their garb. Not noteworthy for being exotic, but for its lamentable state: shoes worn out, pants "larger than the deceased," and especially the weapons, old, repaired or patched up with some truck part appropriated by an ingenious mechanic. People were coming out of all the corners—more and more people. The whole town became a party. The "demoted" were the target for sarcastic jibes. Ogres and wolves under the power of Tom Thumbs and Little Red Riding Hoods. "The kids have taken over the town," they are saying.

People coming from the market brought bread, flowers, empanadas, coffee, sweets, for the "kids." "'Terrorists,' *La Prensa* says," said the bus dispatcher. "And who believes *La Prensa* at this stage," he answered himself. The students came, wreaking havoc as always, producing turmoil. Girls—as at a party—made up, dressed up. "It looks like a carnival," said the Berlin Bar's fat man.

In a matter of hours—that seemed centuries—love pacts were sealed. New dreams devised. New alliances. Many woke from a long stupor. Others died, when they looked in the mirror. However, it was well understood that "that" couldn't last. There was a sense of danger. A nauseating (although distant) odor hung in the air. It clung to the houses and the streets. There were rumors. Warnings. Sounds like stones being pummeled down a rampaging river. The "kids" sensed that the town was in danger of becoming a trap. And, in anticipation, they undertook (with provisions and hostages) their return. While they were so engaged, the bells of the Church of Our Lady rang out and the echo was lost in the hubbub of the people. "They say the kids have taken over the town," everyone is saying.

Then, they looked up. And erupted into confusion. Running down the street. Looking for a place to hide. Thousands of people like ants trying to find an anthill.

"The Germans are coming," one little boy told another, while they were running down the street.

"Don't be a dummy," the other said, as if playing at war, "those aren't Germans; they're Americans and now you're gonna see, they're gonna drop the atom bomb on us."

Just then the helicopters (three of them) flew over the city. Dropping gradually lower and lower, almost scraping the roofs, the treetops. Disappearing between the towers and appearing by surprise at the height of the palm trees.

The bombs began to fall, one after the other. One after the other. Another. There was a tremendous roar. A bomb fell on the bell tower. The vibration traveled from house to house. In one fell swoop the windows slammed shut, dropping out pieces of glass; inside, no plate, glass, mirror, or frame was left intact. Roaring along its twisted path: chairs, balconies, rubble walls, posts, antennas, refrigerators, chests. Another bomb broke the plumbing's black framework; disconnected fragments still sticking to the walls emptied out a grimy rusty liquid. A dirty mixture into the streets.

Inside the houses people continued running, surrounded by voices, screams, and crying children. Stunned by the bombing, they ran among smoldering clothing and cadavers. Amid medicinal salves, bottles of oil, juices, sauces, macaroni, clams. Each one as if fleeing its container. People were still running. They would squat under the eaves, in a corner, then continue, senselessly, running on top of broken glass, pieces of iron, bricks.

Not a stone was left atop another.

Through the banister's heavy railings were silhouettes of other shadows. Images ripped open. Dead, wounded, rubble. The dead. Difficult to count. There were so many. And there would have been more if "the kids" hadn't gotten fired up. If I am alive, it's by pure miracle. Perhaps. Possibly. To tell the story.

The Suicide of Chamiabak

Napoleón Rodríguez Ruiz
Translated by Elizabeth Gamble Miller

In the Chimintal tribe some of the men were very old. They had come from unknown regions to settle there, possibly attracted by the cool waters of the Paxaco River winding alongside the tribal lands. At ten in the morning, as if by chronometer, the old men placed their stools in a line along the river bank and began sitting and watching the interminable flow of the waters. They didn't talk. They didn't comment on anything. They simply contemplated with distant eyes, perhaps the water, perhaps the land stretching out before them, wildly lush on the other side of the river. Or perhaps the birds. Or maybe the history in their thoughts. What is certain is that every day they were there. At twelve noon, also as if by chronometer, all of them rose to their feet as a single man, each picked up his respective stool and went into his own hut not to appear again until the following day. The village was large in size and the tribe large in numbers. Toward the north side was the Barrio of the Young, boys and girls who made love, had children, and devoted their time to hunting and working the land. Every Monday each old man's hut was provided with a week's necessities. His children, grandchildren, great-grandchildren, great-great-grandchildren, and so on, an unbroken series of generations accomplished this. Every two hundred years one of the old men was found dead on his sleeping mat. Dead because he was dead, with no explicable reason for it. They would bury him with great ceremony and would say "until we meet you again" because they were sure they would see him again before long. Since a hut, a stool and a sleeping mat were left unoccupied, a replacement was chosen from among those living in the Barrio of the Young who were getting to be about a hundred years old. Selection was made by drawing lots.

Toward the south rose the barrio called "The Resurrected," where lived the dead who, having now tripled in age after a hundred lunar years floating about the atmosphere, fell to earth with their lineal, almost transparent bodies. Renewing their custom of sitting by the river, they left their huts on bright moonlit nights and sat in a line squatting on their heels at the edge of the stream to listen to the song of the waters and converse with the gods. At daybreak they returned when dawn was just touching the horizon.

The group of Living Ancients constituted the Supreme Tribal Council, which decided important matters. And the group of Resurrected Ancients formed the Supreme Appellate Council, which decided the same matters as a last recourse.

But the truth was that the government of the tribe was administrated by a single man. That man's name was Chamiabak, and he was the oldest in the tribe. He had attained three hundred years of age. Three hundred years of two hundred sixty days according to the native calendar. He was wise, just, and strong. His subjects said that he had attained immortality, and, with it, had assured the eternal happiness of the tribe. He had never suffered from any illness and, as he was ancient, he could be taken for one of the gods who presided over temple sacrifices. When he was asleep he looked placid and serene, like a sleeping saint. He scarcely ate anything. He lived off fruit and honey. The tribe venerated him like a god. All their destinies were in his hands.

The Indians, being accustomed generation after generation to seeing Chamiabak alive, no longer worried about his safety. They were sure he was immortal. Therefore, he couldn't be subject to any danger. The gods had conceded him immortality and, with it, continuous health.

They couldn't even remotely imagine that he could die.

But Chamiabak the wise, Chamiabak the just, Chamiabak the healthy and favorite of the gods, did know he could die. He knew his life depended upon that of an animal. Chamiabak the master nonetheless had a superior: his guardian animal, his *nahual*. His *nahual* was an old lion, who had lived so long that he lost his mane, and his body was slick like the skin of a squash. No one knew the age of that ancient governor of the jungle. He had taken possession of the mountains centuries and centuries before. And he governed the jungle with a firm hand and kindly understanding. All the animals and all men respected him. But no one ever knew he had the privilege of being Chamiabak's *nahual*. He, on the other hand, had known it from childhood. It was during a dream, the dream of an Indian child, that he found himself lost in the mountains of Chukuláj. He was intently looking for a way out when, suddenly, he heard the howling of wild beasts in different languages and dialects. Protected by the underbrush, he cautiously approached the place the voices were coming from. And like a miracle he saw that all the jungle animals had gathered in a wide clearing bordered by a charming little stream. It was a day of Kiéj, which is a good day, when the souls of the ancestors are full of goodwill and are receptive to the pleas of mortals. At that moment, the Governor of the Jungle was speaking, a very nice lion, with very yellow, round eyes like sunflowers. And he was saying: "This afternoon we are gathered here to make the distribution of the *nahuals* to the children of the Chimintal tribe. So listen well and engrave upon your memories the name of the one that corresponds to you. You, Yellow Deer, one and only of your kind, you will be the *nahual* of . . ." And he continued the interminable, monotonous distribution until the child, who was now beginning to be bored, was surprised to hear the governor saying: "You, young lion, who are white as milk, you there next to the blue jaguar, will be the *nahual* of the child called Chamiabak, who will live while you live and who is called to be the wisest man of the tribe." And with that he ended his distribution.

The child, fearful of being discovered, quickly ran away, but unluckily he became entangled in some bamboo and fell to the ground. With the fall he awakened from his dream, but remaining in his mind, tattooed as if in high relief, was the white shape of the lion beside the blue jaguar.

And he always sensed the echoing voice of the Governor of the Jungle pounding into his brain the name of his *nahual*.

Later, when an adult, and very wise, he would often run into the lion. Coming almost up to him, the lion would show no ferocity at all. On the contrary, he moved his head with such grace that he almost seemed to smile at him. Chamiabak also smiled and he found he could roar to greet the lion in his own language.

Chamiabak the just, Chamiabak, the wise, the immortal Chamiabak knew that he had to die. Lately the idea of death had been chasing him like a desperate hound. His sleep was restless. He no longer looked like a sleeping saint when he dreamed, but like a mass of bones and nerves that intermittently jerked, stirred by the wind of death.

Worried and restless, one day he went over to the zone of the Resurrected to consult with the eldest of them. When he arrived, all the polycentenarians were in a conference. They were discussing the necessity of changing their hour for visiting the river.

Precisely the one whom Chamiabak had come to consult was saying, "We can't change it; we can't change it. Let's not forget that we have returned from the Kingdom of the Shadows, and therefore the Shadows are ready to help us. Furthermore, we belong to them. At night, we hear the voices of all those who have not yet returned. At night, the waters sing before the moon and the air is filled with ultraterrestrial melodies. Yes, Brothers, we belong to the Shadows and . . ." he interrupted himself at that moment because Chamiabak came in. And, addressing him, he said, "Come in, O wise and immortal Chamiabak, welcome to this valley where time has stopped and flesh has lost its reign."

Everyone turned toward the recent arrival and greeted him very reverently.

"I regret having interrupted your meeting," said Chamiabak, "but a matter of the utmost importance brings me to see your superior. And since what I plan to discuss is not a secret, I will do so before you. So, O Chief Supreme of the Valley of the Resurrected, I want to declare to you the reason for my concern and my anxiety so you may give me advice. All in the Valley of the Living believe me to be immortal, but I know that I am not, in spite of the fact that I now have three hundred years behind me, years of two hundred sixty days, as is our division of time; and for many days I have felt a death wind at my back. I have often dreamed that my guardian *nahual* has been destroyed and that, as a result, I have stopped existing.

"Dying doesn't frighten me, but my tribe will suffer many calamities without me. Peace will be destroyed and the war between brothers will resume and dye the waters of the river red. I ask you, therefore, O You from the Shadows, to tell me if my death will come soon."

The Superior of the Resurrected thought carefully. And directing an inquisitive look at the others, he said: "Chamiabak, my wise friend, I have no power to predict the time of death. I have come from the Shadows, it is true, I have passed through the dark Valley of Death and after wandering through blazing atmospheres, immortality has been conceded to me. But only the gods can say when a man is to die. The dreams you have had and your presentiments, O just Chamiabak, are of great import, but to know if those presentiments are to be fulfilled soon, there is only one path, Chamiabak: go deep into the jungle, search until you find the old lion that is your *nahual*. And if you see he is sick or sad, then you should prepare to die. Because the gods have instituted the *nahual* and it is hard to imagine a sick or sad lion unless death is close."

"I will go, I will go, O One from the Shadows, tomorrow precisely, I will search until I find the Governor of the Deep Jungle."

"Go in peace!" all the Resurrected said to him in a chorus.

On the following morning, Chamiabak tossed a full honeycomb and many fruits into his deerskin bag, arranged his bow and arrows, and assuring himself that these were covered with sufficient poison, he took the mountain path. His sadness and concern never left him for a moment. The song of the morning birds that had always caused a sweet troubling of his spirit now tasted of a funeral dirge. The wind moaning in the thick underbrush sounded like a raging storm. The screeching of the owl, echoing from the depths of the dark ravines, was translating his own thoughts: "You will die! You will die! You will die!," and suddenly, the whole jungle filled with strange cries and every voice resounded, pounding inside his head. Then he remembered clearly his dream as an Indian child, when, lost in the jungle, he came upon a gathering of animals who were designating a *nahual* for each of the children of the tribe. He remembered the lion white as milk and the blue jaguar beside him. The memory brought tears to his tired eyes and he yearned for those happy days when the blood of his youth boiled in his veins like a miraculous liquor.

In thinking and remembering, he failed to notice how late it was getting in the day. When he realized it, he stopped beside a little stream, ate a little honey and drank some water, scooping it up in the hollow of his hands.

He had walked a long way. No doubt he was in the heart of the deep jungle. The day was advancing toward nightfall. Chamiabak was conscious of the fact that it would be impossible to return. And, suddenly, he stopped moving and meditating and said aloud: "Return! Who said I am to return? Soon night will come and multiply all the shadows. And I will only be one of them. I will be blind, and for me light will come to an end, the jungle's thousands of arms will squeeze my blood and soul from me, and I will sleep forever."

A roar that shook the mountain made his ancient three-hundred-year-old body creak. And immediately thereafter, he heard the noise of a struggle, like bodies tumbling down a ravine. He walked as fast as he could travel and when he came to a clearing in the woods he found, miraculously as in his dreams, the same inlet that he had come upon when as a child he dreamed he was lost in the jungle. And there, beside the little stream that might be singing or might be crying, a fight between giants was taking place: a death struggle between a jaguar and a lion. And Chamiabak, stunned and pale, let out a cry that seemed to emerge from the very heart of the jungle: "O, Gods, O, Souls of the Dead, it is the old white lion and the blue jaguar that are fighting! O, Jaguar of the Devils, why have you rebelled against your sovereign, how do you dare put your filthy, callous, butcher's paw on the venerable head of the Governor of the Jungle?"

The fight continued. The end result was clear. The young, yet seasoned, blue jaguar, doubtless a descendant of the one that Chamiabak saw in his dream, was stronger and more wily. He had already repeatedly defeated the old lion, who had found defending his authority and his empire to be increasingly difficult.

Chamiabak didn't hesitate for a minute. He placed the arrow in his bow. Aiming carefully and confidently, for he had always been the best archer in the tribe, he waited for the right moment, and vehemently let his arrow fly. At that precise instant, the old lion, making a supreme effort, gripped the spirited blue jaguar between his claws. As a result Chamiabak's poison dart pierced the head of the old lion, whose body at an earlier time had been as white as milk, and now was as slick as the skin of a squash.

As if electrocuted he fell, and the blue jaguar leaped upon him and tore off the now dead skin of the Governor of the Jungle. Chamiabak felt the arrow in his own heart and fell dying. But, from farther away than life and from closer than death, his arm appeared tense on the bow and he shot at the blue jaguar and it also fell, stretched at the feet of the *nahual* of Chamiabak.

Gloria Lara

Mario Cajina-Vega
Translated by Don D. Wilson

The funeral ceremony in the church could well have been happening before a civil divorce proceeding in court, thought Gloria Lara.

". . . sins of the world," the parish priest was sing-songing with grand resonance.

The ministerial voice drew itself out in tremolos that wanted to be chords, the chords climbed ritually among the incense, the incense circled the commonplace cupola and then descended like a tomb of prayers and murmurings to settle on a coffin that was no longer of this world.

Heat. The flower wreaths are also dying and their quicker agony consists of softly wasting away, odor by odor, until they infuse the naves with sickly fragrances. Weakness of the stems? Premature decay inside the coffin?

"I'm very sorry."

"Our condolences."

The voices fell like black-bordered cards.

Other expressions, much longer, sounded and passed by like a discreet funeral procession.

"We came as soon as we could."

"We're here to be with you."

The wooden benches were exactly like the kneeling desks in school. Likewise, wear and tear had lent them an old waxen finish. From their niches, with limestone halos, some statues perpetuate the tortured imperfection of mestizo saints. Votive offerings, flickering lamps, trembling garlands. In the chapel of the Spanish nuns the statues were purer, idealized through a celestial allegory. In the modesty of that enclosure, Innocence raised her prayers again, even though the girls, in class or during secret conversations in the dormitory afterward, might confide little sins to each other, stirred up by curiosity, spurred on by puberty. Adolescent, unsure of themselves, living through a scarcely involuntary passage, would they perhaps be sins, venial sin, mortal sin, those secrets about the shape of their legs or jokes about the uncurved flatness of the Mother Superior? Little notes from friends, kept and reread persistently, spoke of kisses and amorous idylls, of romantic scenes in Sunday movie shows, and of the trifles (sports, diversions, letters: "My cousin Gloria Lara is a poem") that are the same in all boarding schools. She always smelled of caramel and of novels; meanwhile ranch vacations came or unhurried, formal visits to the capital on a train as slow as time.

The priest, fifteen years later, finished. His arms raised the metallic hyssop, the chasuble slipped around like a final golden radiance, and a responsory of last waters sprinkled flowers, coffin, parishioners, in an ample liquid blessing. Gloria Lara went out by herself. To provincial courtesy, composed of neighbors and community, solitude has no meaning; the privileges of grief do not include it. It will always be interpreted as madness or bad manners, if not perhaps as downright disdain. Would they say now that she seemed crazy?

The price of her solitude came from the past. If the ultimate immolation, that which frees us exhausted in grief, were not penetrating her limbs, overwhelmed by the fatigue of an endless mass for the dead, she would be able to contemplate that ephemeral, artificial reality with sarcasm: a routine that has more of social ceremony than of religious resolution. Wakes, condolences, sorrows; the swift, ceremonious parade always prolonging itself in everlasting succession, going around endlessly through a ritual of customs, customs, customs. There she would be, in the middle of her stay, between tedious, tiring visits, presiding at the end of a betrothal or the start of adultery.

"Don't cry, don't be so distressed, for the love of God."

She walked, like the beauty of an elegy, through the atrium of the church. The sun fits the lead-colored flagstones to her steps. A sudden sweat chokes her. It was the foreseeable immediate outcome of the weather, but she felt it as the first chill of a flesh whose anguish, deliberately postponed, no longer is going to dissolve into convulsions or shudders. When her thirty-year-old body, despairingly besieged by desire, solicited passion, consolation, sensuality, she would have only sheets around her. Whiteness of passive contact. Indifference. Coarse clothing that divests her of all sensation.

Before, at least, there used to be the living together, the daily excitement. Quarrels, fights, incidents, flowed toward the natural channel where happiness and distress, disillusion and nostalgia are neutralized.

An unaccustomed breeze, bathing her with its rapid turns, snatches her mantilla. She runs to recapture it and a little picture flies from her missal. Another burial, now almost forgotten. All her blood pressure reflects, with consternation, the saying of Thomas à Kempis, printed with the utmost credibility: "Flesh, not angel."

She opened the car door and seated herself, suffering the humiliation of this memory. She did not ask herself if humiliation represented the highest fee of Christianity, the humbling before God, or a virtual human aberration that tends to deny itself in nothingness. "Flesh, not angel" . . . Years ago Kempis, through a poet, changed into Teilhard de Chardin, and Gloria Lara was captivated and heeded the music of love, touching her in all her youth.

A pure voice sounded . . . The memory of Gloria on reliving words and minutes burnishes a golden ornament carefully treasured.

Pure and young. "The salvation of the body, as for the rest: theology." Laughter, natural and free. The ascetic and the visionary, with sisterly phrases skipping over centuries and convents, united in a single Catholic and inexorable definition.

Now grown through time, in the complete mastery of her dreams, Gloria Lara still listened to the same voice, which had turned ironic, brightened by an almost metaphysical happiness, proclaim: "Let's bow to Brother Body! Long live blessed matter!" And she was free, free from the acerbic disapproval of those who respect a faith without favors, singing: "The Church is not so concerned for the soul's salvation; that is more or less certain in the mysterious hands of God and of his invocable mercy; now the Church is interested in saving the flesh."

"To think," Gloria said to herself, "that a worm destroys us."

She put the card in the book and closed it; the vision of the past collapsed, now without a future.

As if to smooth her own confusion, she retouched her hairdo in front of the mirror. Her looks restored her, a smile halfway between grace and corruption, made transparent in the glass. She seems not to respond to that image; or perhaps—she thinks—this new countenance is her truth: features from which the hauteur and the beauty were departing, leaving only the first bitter warp.

"Desolate?" ask her astonished eyes. "I give up," confesses the dry mouth.

Starting the small Volvo, she drove cautiously toward the highway, negotiating streets dotted by houses of only one story. On one of the

corners, with the high, wide construction characteristic of boarding
schools, she saw her first school. There, perhaps, she had been placed like
a girl for whom love was as disappointing as the uniforms of that time.

The Volvo ran on, the road ahead. The shadows come on softly, falling
from a colorless sky, and the landscape begins to melt away.

In the confusion of dusk a half-cold drizzle fell incessantly. The
country of rain! She would not return to this humid attraction that
dispels a temperature too intense. She remembered the weather and the
seasons. The copious rainy season of the tropics. Morning is an eyelid
that keeps sewing its rainy threads, and they quiver, the hours, in
corridors of pots of roses. Domestic, guardian life. Everything is born and
reborn as plant rhythms. The vespertine twilight approaches with the
smoothness and softness of a nature made of petals. There is no violence,
other than the boisterous storm in which thunder and lightning scratch
each other like wild cats. Afterward, everything is reduced to gentle
waters. Yes, infancy, adolescence, youth, in places like this they identi-
fied happiness with dreams, forgetfulness with resignation. One day one
passes from innocence to trivial idleness, and the province insensitively
tells of the general calamity. Without mortifying, one's sensibility
became molded to the city map. Which were the conversations that
Gloria Lara would consider final? The years don't erase themselves; they
are voices, voices that suffering keeps latent. Love, with its beautiful,
mystic language?

"In a city of twenty-five thousand inhabitants one cannot tell the
truth; it is preferable to live it in realization of one's self." He never could
tell the truth about those twenty-five thousand inhabitants who, perhaps for that reason, turned into a walking lie for both.

Ten years of alcoholism humiliated her love of yesterday in Gloria
Lara's heart.

The cleansing breezes started a mechanical rhythm. If she could
disperse with air brushes all the particulars that criss-cross a forehead,
in this way clearing off the crust of aches, afflictions, regrets . . . She
trembled before the linking of another foreboding. The urgent questions
of her flesh, broken into promise after promise of love-unions, could no
longer be answered with innocence, either. During whole years her
senses had awaited complete possession. She wanted a surrender that
was given in delight in order to receive touches of harmony, far from
sterility, far from frustration, the full human fruit for the unique flavor
and natural sense of the beautiful. Free and fruitful purity in the carnal
consensuality of creative pleasures. There the prophet's presence did not
disappear. She intuited that vague, imprecise, but promising spiritual

sphere where the ideas or traditions of a religion too compromised with temporal situations are dissipated to be replaced by the primitive vision of a clear, renascent faith, eager for the new luminosity and the whole cosmos.

She felt that her youth had been humiliating. She had experimented only with herself, testing a clinical act with the docilities of a patient.

Her angry foot punishes the accelerator and the car skids swiftly toward the ditch. She manages to control it; she rests her head on her hands, which opened and closed on the wheel, repeating to herself that she is still thirty, but her sex felt its solitude as the worst persecution.

They kept coming closer, the lights of Managua, depicted and erased on the glass. The drizzle lessened. The road becomes a boulevard here, and on both sides modern developments parade by, contrasting with the small cabins of farmers. A procession of commercial signs vulgarized the view of the mountains and the lake, raising billboards high against a twilight almost lakelike. She maneuvered up to begin the circling ascent toward the Loma de Tiscapa. The American embassy first, then, at the bottom, the citadel of the Dictatorship where the waters of the small lake of Tiscapa, mysterious and off-limits, forbid access. The gentle hill done with, the Volvo descended toward Managua.

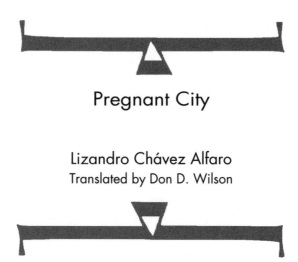

Pregnant City

Lizandro Chávez Alfaro
Translated by Don D. Wilson

His four girls were making a racket in the backseat of the car. The rearview mirror gave him an instantaneous picture of long curls and toys. With her legs tucked in on the front seat, his wife was dozing. What Dr. Barquero reproached himself about was so brief and far away that he had no way of retaining it in his memory. A bird does not retain the vague irregularities it flies over. From the self-confident posture in which he was used to driving, he saw below the exquisitely neat furrows of another tobacco field, spread out on life-giving land. Hollow, the little valley repeated the greens and blacks in welcoming stripes that he'd seen and would see every year, traveling to his family home.

To his right, surrounded by light, issued a group of children—students in bright reddish uniforms, like eruptions from the clayey slope that supported that curve of the roadway. Barquero ended up capturing them from behind in the rearview mirror, smaller and smaller in the act of disappearing within the curve. He allowed the image but not the warning of invasion. Three, four children walking along gossiping, farther and farther away by dint of the expansive glass. Irresponsibility, this was the descriptive term for that happily multiplied presence. Five other children trotting along made incomprehensible signals from a ditch, maybe goodbyes, that he did not want to answer now nor before, in this or any other situation, avoiding the risk of endorsing the great offense, even if only by omission.

In the clarity of his duties, Barquero saw himself happily armed with a scalpel that would always do what was needed to close off ways to excess: tiny cuts that some day, in the end, would amount to miles of quick sutures and only one scar, hardly visible, but effective in its services. He believed that giving license to proliferation, not raising his well-honed obstacles against it, was to descend to a realm ruled by glands.

He held a part of his senses set on redrawing curves with the wheels of the car, and the other part, vaguely annoyed by the materializing of the wandering population, radiated outward from audacity to fallacy. He was thinking that every species cries forth its ravager, and that man, solitary in his sovereignty, would have to provoke in himself his own ravaging. For want of general calamities, he would have to hold back the emissions from his organ. Once again Barquero made fine balances between plagues, wars, hunger, and sterilization programs, some required by the exact nature of the system, others offered by intelligence. His ultimate assurance in the face of the teeming menace: if the triumph of the species over the ancient calamities had framed this new demographic calamity, the species itself would have to dismantle it.

He had no room in himself for despair, much less for horror. Enough for him a calm devotion to statistical prognostications and the will to answer them in proportion to his half-secret apostleship, because of which he sometimes had to execute quick maneuvers on the sly in the red mudhole of an open abdomen. Directed into a double professional pathway, that of the flourishing clinic and that of the dispensary strategically established in a district of the capital, he did his duty in every way one could wish. In one he earned legitimate money, and in the other he conformed to the oath, with his special addition: a sterile organ is worth a hundred. He was bent on persuading, but in the presence of seeming defeats he showed impeccable resources of deception, and the free operation (the name the patient tended to give it did not matter) inexorably took in the generous bandage or a gash in the genesis. For an occasionally inconvenient reaction, he also had a repertory of replies garnished with patience.

Corina, his oldest daughter, gripped his shoulders, shocked by the sight of a buzzard flying with a dead snake in its beak. The bird crossed the road and lost itself in the gulch, while Barquero went on teaching a principal concept of ecology. He bent back an arm to touch his daughter's hair, at his shoulder. He turned back to see the light mounted on vast, verdant ridges. The breeze touched an ear, like an endless, warm tongue. Below, to his left, was a constellation of round rocks, very white, perfect between the pasture that held them and the sun that bathed them. When he felt the mortal disobedience of the machinery that he had had under his control a second before, he checked a cry; he freed it, once in flight, writhing in the effort to catch it all in the enormous instant: the little bodies hurled from horror to horror, his wife's waking scream, God's providence, Lucas's hands tuned to the blackness and the hardness of his tools, the deepest cleft of the error, which? where? enlarged while he was falling, scraping, he reviewed his sins, on earth, in heaven, beaten by the brutal spoon that held him back, on the other side of a trick that lost its name and regained and lost it in the silence of the next bounce, curved silence inhabited by a surgeon's gestures, old or new, by mirrors of intended voices: a small mirror for his ungraspable daughters, for his reddening wife; a filthy mirror for Lucas, manipulator of nuts and tie rods; a round mirror for the sum of his plans, loudly smashed in the last impact against the rocks.

Lucas dragged a piece of cardboard infinitely soiled from grease. Despising anything finer than his clumsy shoes soaked with oil, he kicked at the edge of the cardboard to finish putting it under the next car.

He began his workday just past nine, still with no wish to open up the transmission where, by his prognosis, the breakdown was. After drinking coffee, he stood quietly, sucking his decayed teeth, gazing at a wall, far away from the underhanded protests that Chabela, his wife, took to the kitchen, crushed by the scorn that sprang from him, fell on her, ugly and bristling. By shouting, he drove his youngest children to the other end of the lot that framed his workshop: a large shed, a leafy *ceiba* tree, and heaps of iron parts covered with grease or with rust.

Standing beside the car awaiting repair, he looked at his children making balls of dirt; he saw them make innocent trifles within the larger filth, where he wavered between the futility of having begotten them and the impossibility of repeating it. Seven children of the great itch; pushed blindly into and out from the very belly of the repulsive, bawling face that turned sour there in the dampness of the kitchen. Some at work, others in school or at play, as if poorly fastened to his pain at having yielded to the glib-tongued attacks from the mouth of that little doctor whose eyes would soon be fermenting in the craws of buzzards.

He flopped down on his back to go underneath the chassis covered by dust and flattened masses of dry mud. There, in the opacity of his domain, with one arm he repeated the very familiar operation of loosening nuts, with a gaze that traversed the heavy sky where a mechanic does and undoes, guesses right or is mistaken, the absolute lord of systems composed of an exact number of pieces subject to his will, knowing that when pressures and tensions were increased or decreased, he was tinkering with the life of the machine as well as whoever entrusted himself to it. At his age of thirty, two-thirds of it lived with some car part or other in his hand, Lucas noted the authority gathered in his calluses, and he nourished his bitterness by comparing it to a surgeon's power: valve by valve, kneecap by kneecap. Four nuts ill-placed on the braces of a front axle, they would probably suffice to cause some friend to pass by his shop and idly show him the day's paper, announcing that now he had one customer fewer: Dr. Barquero, dead in an auto accident from losing control of his car.

Upon his chest black drops fell dripping from the open differential. He felt some teeth made useless through wear, half-hidden in grease. Thus he imagined his own parts ruined by the operation: incomplete, cold, greasy, thrown on the ground by his corrupted will. He could repair those meshings and see them turn again. But Barquero had put his hand on his whole life, ahead and behind, with no one to give him help. *The thing is very superficial, Lucas,* he said, when he already had him under local anesthesia, pieces of advice and surgical skills, stretched out as he was now, mouth up, thorough in the useless observation of steel parts attached to other pieces of steel. *You'll see what a fine life you'll have, Lucas.*

He had walked out of the dispensary with nothing lacking in the firm setting down of his feet, but with the first doubt taking hold on the inside, like a little unreachable patch. Angled playfully at the matter, he promised himself to make up for any passing bother when, his wounds healed, he would engage in the endless intercourse that a man free of the menace of pregnancy ought to deserve. On his way from the dispensary to the local bar, the most suitable spot for the celebration, he was elaborating seductive projects. To every desirable female, he paid a wink in advance, a smiling sample of the bellyful they might be given later on.

With the first swallows, he leaned over the sad puddle that was his inability to communicate what he was celebrating; neither to cry it out nor to whisper it, by its name and with its signs. He knew that not even in the most secluded place would he dare to pronounce Dr. Barquero's key word: sterilized. *Well, Lucas, that fact is going to be a matter of pride for a responsible person like you.* But now in the bar, he understood that word in the same way that the rest would understand it. Steeped in brandy, the start of melancholy was yielding place to the advantages of his new condition, repeated in the guise of successive drinks. Ritually, the spree led to a bordello full of gaiety from its center to its borders of green plastic curtains, swelled by the lake breeze, unmoved before the noise. Lucas started a raffle in which he would be the prize. He dealt out among the women little paper pieces torn from a newspaper's edge, swearing that for the magical number he had fried coco plums, bananas in milk, roasted star apples, and a whole new repertory of obscene delights created for the consecration of the lucky one. He exchanged pinches for pats, poured out money to the jukebox, but never so drunk as to forget his recent wounds. Beyond the noise and the dizziness a horrible event was taking place, that beneath the mask of Lucas there lived the first night of an ugly prostitute overwhelmed by her bloody days, a desolate young woman, a crazy person, in the best of circumstances. Nothing prevented him from crossing through the interior curtain of the bordello with any of the women in front of him, and thrusting himself into her trap in the first wretched bed, and dying with his sutures burst. Nothing, at least, of what he knew under the name of fear. There were other things, impassable, new and strange imbroglios between him and everything around him. A flood of tears seized him, spent from suffering such surprise, elbows on a table. It was a flood from a fallen head, hanging in half phrases and sounds that burst through bubbles of confirmed masculine drivel; pure anguish collected on that common ground where the entire sex has been accumulating its reasons for supremacy.

His friends pretended ignorance of his fall, or they concealed it by shouting immersed in the general hubbub. From some forgotten mouth came the predictable insult. Lucas rushed impetuously upon the first one who refused to face him, tearfully angry and followed by his people ready for a fight. Striking and struck, he kept himself on the crest of the fight, upset by the relief offered with regard for his still warm wounds, a man's wounds, he told himself.

He spent the following two weeks glued to his tools, riveting an armor made of motors and auto bodies. Between his weekdays of fifteen to eighteen hours of work, there intervened only dreams excreted with contempt and with contempt forgotten. He awoke at dawn with his muscles irritated by a vigor that was also fuel for his suspicions. He felt that it, a new force or spirit of progress, was the disguise of a death or of many deaths twisted into some part of his integrity. He was glimpsed outside his shop, grazing meekly, more animal than ever, but not enough to keep him from claiming his equality with them. Seven children were enough, yes, that was understood, even regretted in the moment of concession to Barquero, but that corrosive dripping remained of not knowing what in hell had been taken from him forever. Maybe his only access to consummation. Maybe his insatiable way of sovereign imposition.

There was no lessening of his virility; he continued getting erections in the frame of the conjugal bed, indifferent to the mute petitions of Chabela, but greeting the morning air with a hardness rising at the least stimulus. His organ had lost the name of genital, although not the force nor the size of its muscular obedience. In the darkness, grazing the limits of rebelliousness, Chabela would move a trembling side closer, or with a certain audacity, she would let some absent-minded fingers rest on the hairiness of his legs. Lucas remained unmoved, his back rooted to misgiving. The night that he finally agreed to give something to the wife who filled the bed with insinuations, he had another pair of surprises, resolved in a single discharge of rage. It happened that at the end of his exertion a slight dryness awaited him, the revelation of the robbery committed in his fountainhead. Afterward, when he talked of where and how he had slain the danger of any more children, Chabela sat up looking at him tentatively and then, smothering herself in clothes, became an irresolute fountain of noises, neither happy nor unhappy. Again Lucas remained in the midst of what was not knowable, moved along his whole length by the vibration that the woman transmitted to the bed. Such indignation grew in him at the supposition that Chabela was giving him in this way a dubious and convulsive consent, as well as at the suspicion that submissively she was blaming him beneath the shell of her laughter. For his eardrums stretched tight by suspicion it was too much celebration of the end of misfortune, too much censure of himself: the problem itself rejected by blows with the hands, by roughly shoving, until he had pulled her out of the room and spanked her upon the rusty pieces of steel.

Determined to reacknowledge the forms that the world was taking outside his shop, one afternoon he shaved himself, seated in front of the side mirror of a small van, while Chabela carried water from the only faucet to the bath made of boards and car-body parts. He bathed, slowly showering himself with gourds full of water, aware of the black lather that ran down from his ankles, channeled by staggered fragments of brick tile, as if it might be there where the antidote to a buried fear of going out could be fermenting. Whatever the way, he left, true to his glossiest halo. The farther he got away from the shop, the more he seesawed between indolence and challenge, with his hands still kept in his pockets, advancing unhurriedly from the dirt roads to the privilege of pavements.

He halted on the corner by a movie house displaying the burst of colors projected by letters and faces of neon. Nothing stood in the way of the further progress of his sortie, except a secret reckoning of bellies that came pursuing him in his shadow. Planted in the midst of the hubbub on the corner, he was taken by surprise at the novelty, which struck his whole body: a pregnant woman passed, almost pushing him off the sidewalk; she was most dignified in the task of carrying that precious belly, with the fabric of her dress molded to the extensive upper curve and the rest molded to the air, stretched out in vertical folds, like a semicircular curtain that jubilantly awaits the stage hand's action so that the show can open. And this precious flowered, jiggling belly was only the banner of the crowd that he had all along been counting without wishing to accept it: a new presence, seen again rather than remembered. Bellies in quantities never before seen. It seemed a general pregnancy, convened for marking his passage, everyone passing each other in the streets, emerging from doors and windows; round bellies, some full, others small; walking and sedentary, proud or embarrassed: all of them palpitating eggs incorporated into the breathing of the city.

The burden of the discovery benumbed him standing there. He spat his rage out the corner of his mouth, without energy to enter the movie house and lose himself in the showing of three films offered for one price.

Holed up in his shop, he was cleaning the narrowest ducts of a carburetor by dint of his lungs when Dr. Barquero appeared, along with the quietness of the Ford Galaxie that he was driving. He saw him get out, cool. His mouth, pressed against an orifice, continued blowing forcefully. Barquero had come prepared to devote another apostolic moment to his sterilized health and to trust his mechanical skills once more. Pouring out the usual palaver, he asked for a careful checkup of his car, on the eve of a trip. Lucas smiled gratefully, when he already knew what parts to touch, already imagined from what side of the highway the annihilation of his annihilator would come.

Without fail, the neighbor came, provided with the newspaper, asking if he knew yet who had died. Lucas stretched his limbs beneath the car under repair, crawled out with all the tools. From the ground he looked up at the face of the neighbor so high above. After a noisy snort, a worn-out blinking, he had nothing to add to the news.

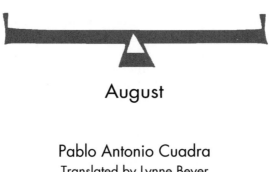

August

Pablo Antonio Cuadra
Translated by Lynne Beyer

*To Javier, the smallest and most
enthusiastic reader of this story.*

Palo Alto—"the frontier of forsakenness," the old-timers say—the last open plain before the great mystery: beyond, the jungle raises its curtain of giant clumsy trees, damp, tenebrous greenness clinging to the mud, a solid front against wind and sun—the angry, impotent, livid, sun that day after day attacks and retreats, spat upon by toads, harassed by predatory birds.

We stand at the frontier of silence. The afternoon plays its final blues on the savanna, on a small gray sky clearly reflected in each muddy footprint of Villagra's horse. We've come this way many times. Never any farther. Never to the snake-infested badlands where lumbermen and root-gatherers in rubber capes harvest misty legends, or scream in the distance, never to return. "This is where the cowhand's business ends," says Villagra, pointing to the last section of the plains. "A horse is for the open sky."

We have been talking along the way. Son and grandson of cowhands, Villagra son of Villagras, Nicanor had had enough of the Institute of Granada and returned to the plains. "The history of the country!" he says mockingly. And he recites passages of texts he learned at school, ending with: "My grandfather and my papa walked through history shouldering a rifle! They were always wanting to drag me off my horse to hear their stories!"

He's ten years older than I. "I was born during the revolution against
Zelaya, you during the Mena war." He tied his memories to events the
way he tied his horse to fence posts. His mother marked history by
pregnancies. "When Concha's belly was big as the sky . . ." Still more
dramatic, his grandmother buried sons at the foot of each historical
event. "When they killed my Bernabé in '93," or "I lost Genaro during
the war against the Yankees."

The sounds of the jungle suddenly stop. Thousands of insects, thousands of wings, antennas, stingers suspend their up-to-now incessant
labor: I know that silence!

"Look!"

Nicanor Villagra gets down from his horse. "This time he didn't even
wait until dark!"

He stoops to examine the tracks. My dog follows behind, whimpering
and pitiful, dodging deep muddy spots and stopping to rest on *zacate*
plants, his tongue dirty and drooling. He whines when he smells the
tracks. "He's pissing," I say. Villagra shoves him aside. He's mean to the
dog, says he's a mutt because he comes from the city. He bends to
measure the trace of the enemy, a paw print.

"The history of the country!" he says again. The print is shallow but
rough; heavy but light; agile—a mark of fury gouged into the earth: the
paw! I know that trembling in my horse's ears. The paw! Stamp of the
brute-king who exacts his tribute of fear, subjecting all flesh to his
nocturnal rule.

"This is the history of the country!" Villagra spits and points to the
spot on the ground with the end of his whip. History, as always,
impressed in mud and blood.

"He's seven years old," he says. I keep silent. The paw! Whose was it
during those seven long obsessive years? Twice Nicanor was called to
revolution and twice he returned, on foot, because the movement had
collapsed. So he came back to the "frontier of forsakenness," to reread
the death toll: the devoured calf, the colt chased and sacrificed almost at
the front door of the hacienda: the cow struck without warning by a
savage bite in her swollen udder. And always, the paw print: wide, not
too deep, but rough; heavy, but at the same time light; and always the
same depressing silence, a denunciation.

"Shut that dog up! I'll have to beat him."

"Here are some coyote tracks," I say.

"He's going toward Palo Alto," says Villagra, without hearing me,
pulling his hat down angrily over his eyebrows. We continue bent over,
along the muddy plain, in harmonious and supple stride, as if we were
watching the progress of a birth. Here the crazy tracks take a turn and
escape—the deep shell of the print converges with the bourgeois gait of

the wild pig. The deer are leaping: the fine member sunk in slender, springlike haunches, ready for the stampede. They all make way, all give in to incontestable power: the plain a plush carpet for the rampant monarch.

My dog, following behind, begins to whine again. Not the constant, pitiful cry of a dog in pain, but a prolonged whimper, starting low and rising to the high pitch that communicates fear. The sound streaks blackly across the afternoon. I quiet him down.

The moon rises smoky over the steaming depths of the jungle, its milky clarity paling, making for a deep, anemic twilight.

"It's moving between two lights," says Villagra, halting the horse for a moment. For the first time, he smiles. He turns to face the jungle behind us, staining the horizon between moon and plain. He breaks the stock of the rifle, blows forcefully down the barrel like someone venting into it the spirit of devastation, puts in two new shells and closes the rifle.

"Let's go!" Then we see the long line of cowhands, silhouetted along the horizon, shouting as they come. Villagra raises himself in the stirrups.

"Sons of bitches! They shout at everything!"

I still can't make out the distant shouting, but I can see the graceful movements of their horses. One of the men waves his hat, his voice growing louder as he nears, until the word strikes, etching into the shield of the stony moon: "Jaguar." Again and again, backward and forward, the cry fills the plain with the dreaded feudal name: "Jaguar."

Villagra wants to quiet them, but they begin again, pointing to the west, "The jaguar's attacking the Palo Alto corral!"

There's a pained look on his face as he pulls his horse up short. He turns to me like someone citing a witness. "It's Palo Alto!" His childhood corral, with its savanna sky supported by the highest tree, the *guanacaste*, that sheltered parrots, magpies, morning *guises*, other migratory birds. The tree filled with sounds of birthing cattle, wild horses. The white-horned "Lily," ancient mother, just recently gone. And the dark, ever-mooing "Widow," sacrificed, perhaps, in blind cruelty; the noble cows that lent the hacienda its prestige and monetary value, those of the Palo Alto corral, guarded by Clarín, the surly bull, your favorite, your bull that you trained to hunt jaguars: so he's there— let's see! I read it in your eyes, Villagra, and you read rebellion in my heart, too. Now!

"Take that dog and keep a watch from the scrub patch where the *pijules* nest," he shouts to the *sabaneros*. Then, with his gun hand he signals: "Forward!" a gesture of attack, rebellion, war—against you, treacherous, august power.

We start to gallop.

Manuelita, Virginia (named after my grandmother, "the blessed señora," Villagra called her), and Nicanor were the last three of the twelve children. Nicanor was destined for the city, mathematics, and letters. But he was bored to death cooped up within four walls, propped up at a stationary desk. He got through the primary grades, turned eighteen, and fled the Institute to join his first revolution.

My parents stopped him just in time. He was dragging a long Mauser and stuffing cookies into his ammunition pouch while he waited for the troop train at the Granada station. They brought him back to the hacienda, where old Villagra greeted him with a tamarind branch and scorched his back with it.

"Now that you've refused to be a gentleman, you're going to have to be tough. Here in Chontales we need men!"

Manuelita and Virginia cried. Nonetheless they got him up at dawn to join three cowhands bound for Palo Alto—the Frontier of Forsakenness, as the old-timers called it—where the old cattle grazed. The last savanna reserved exclusively for breeding; endpoint of history, where December wept upon the almost primordial hides of great-grandmother cows who died throughout the year giving birth to the wild race in freedom and in mud. No more diminutives, no more sonny boy, no more *cumiche*. But that's what he wanted, what he'd yearned for when his eyes were focused on a grammar book.

(We are galloping along.)

This is what he dreamed of as he drank in, paragraph by paragraph, the bitter brew of "the history of the country." The jungle lay behind, the backbone of the Republic. The obscure origins of the tribe, from time to time lost sight of, with the onset of revolution, with the arrival of troops emerging from the jungle, slaughtering cattle as they came. It was out of this exalted landscape, the damp, tenebrous green, that generals appeared—mud-men, dark as the song of the Lion-Bird, poisoned by snakes, silently and unsung, their names uttered by death again and again. There, in the presence of the great mystery that long-ago morning, the horse had set upon the coyote at top speed, whinnying as he came and mimicked by parrots and macaws in the greenish-red clamor of dawn. The coyote, startled, flung himself into the bramble thicket, indecisive, preferring not to flee, slyly considering whether this persecution was worth the trouble of moving on in his state of tiredness, or whether it was better to use a little stratagem and hide in the thicket—or then again, whether it was better after all to flee. So he wavered. Then his alert nose caught a scent and he wavered, and Nicanor had no time to free his machete before he saw, rising from the tall grass and needles, the shining spotted powerful jaguar. Not a sound. A solid lightning bolt with tense haunches. It sprang, silently, powerfully, from the ground, hung for a moment over the tallest grass and disappeared. The skin shone in the light, and for a long time seemed to stop in midair, lustrous as a robust, shining tree-trunk tossed up into the air, but tossed transformed, solidified as pure impulse, allowing no extraneous line or other foreign stain to take away from the potent, clean, solitary leap. Nicanor reined in his horse. It was his hand that pulled hard on the reins even as his eye retained the silent, muscular, electric bolt. The horse stopped cold and sank his hooves in at the edge of the thicket, trembling but stilled; agitated, yet contained, awaiting orders from his human counterpart that would relieve his fear and perplexity. But Nicanor let down the blinders, tied the reins tightly to the saddlehorn, and dismounted. It was a matter of seconds. In the wake of the great leap he had heard an opaque, mortal sound. He cut a path with his machete through the briars, grass, and myrtle. The coyote, now far away, looked with curiosity in Nicanor's direction. His heart had told him, and there she was: fallen, her chest open, suffocating in the roil of her own blood, the great rolling eyes watching Nicanor, watching his arrival with profound anguish and almost human tenderness in the glassy pupil: The Widow, the one he'd milked as a child. There, on the black cow's pale udders, he had learned to press his fingers smoothly, firmly, drawing out the fine stream of milk. The cow lay on her side, moving, struggling desperately to open her hind legs and get to her feet. On seeing Nicanor, she turned again and raised her head, but the effort caused a bubble of blood to spring from her torn chest. Nicanor flung himself upon her. She was giving birth: between her hind legs was a small, blind animal struggling for life. The mother was trying to send it forth, but each effort diminished her own life, warm and dulled by the savage bite. The paw, too, had left its mark—a deep, possessive print in the mud. Nicanor applied pressure to The Widow's veins and arteries to slow her death. He hugged her chest.

"Come on, girl! Slow. Slow!"

She drew breath and stirred her head, striking the ground with her horn, struggling for what was now beyond her reach, gulping at life and pushing it out from deep within. But the blood gushed furiously from her neck, spilling over Nicanor's hands, soaking his arms and chest.

"Easy, girl!"

In the eyes of the mother both dying and giving birth, a blue light sank, pale and heartrending, like a painfully intimate twilight. She opened her mouth to bawl, but her rough, dry tongue dangled helplessly and her breathing could only drag up a hoarse murmur.

"Widow! Widow!" Nicanor shouted into her ear. Her eyes, when they opened again, had a desperate new brilliance. With all her might, she drew breath, sounding like a terrible bellows, like a terrestrial abysmal wind that completely drained nature of its last reserve. She pressed against her womb—tensely, brutally, pushing from her depths. Then she finally raised her head and tried to see the life that was issuing from her womb, but a frozen shadow penetrated deep into her eyes and her head suddenly fell lifeless to the ground. Nicanor ran to the little calf, half-buried in the dark well of her sex. Blood flowed on the ground. He tugged at the suffocating little creature, pulled hard until he felt something give way, and it emerged, supple, oily, elastic. He broke the sac, cut the umbilical cord, slapped him nervously on the lungs and then paternally cleaned his nose with the edge of his shirt. He saw the tender, startled eyes clumsily deciphering the light, and thought he heard a faint, almost celestial bleating—a bleating that golden orioles and herons would carry over the misty Eastern hills.

(We are galloping.)

Villagra and the calf were almost one, both raised at Virginia's petticoats, encouraged to be gentle, domestic, and good-tempered. Nicanor carried him around day after day until, "That's it, little bull," he had to stop for fear of getting a hernia. Once he'd gotten bigger, the household disasters that he caused began to multiply, along with Manuelita's complaints. He came into the house like a dog, chewing and dirtying clothes on the line, knocking over furniture and breaking dishes, completely unaware of his size or strength.

One afternoon, he tried to thank grandmother for a pinch of salt that he'd licked voraciously from her shaking hand. In an exaggerated gesture of affection, he pushed her over backward. It proved to be a fatal fall. The night of the wake, old Villagra pronounced the sentence—with the whole family's approval, except for Nicanor and Virginia, who didn't dare protest—"That animal has got to be castrated and put out to pasture." Andrés Villagra, the eldest of the six brothers, had just arrived from Juigalpa for the funeral. He took it a step further: "A farm animal raised in the house is no good in the house and useless on the farm." The ranch workers, listening as they drank their brandied coffee beneath the great summer moon, made fun of the little bull. They relished seeing him stripped of his privileges and once again restored to his place among the humble. But then out came Nicanor, speaking in angry low tones, close to their faces.

"Anyone who touches this animal will deal with me." Then the son of The Widow bellowed. He was tied to a post, and he roared with the force of a bull—bellowed, leaving his youth behind, taking the leap toward the loneliness and power of the male, assuming the haughty position of the stud bull, tearing the night to shreds, and throwing open its dark gates in his call to the herd and to a freedom he recognized as his, in the fresh torrent of sex and horns. Someone said: "He has the father's powerful voice." And Nicanor named him; from that night on he was called "Clarín."

The name went back to the first cattle, distinguished by their daring, chosen to defend the borders of the hacienda—soldiers who fought the jaguar to defend the boundaries: that's what Nicanor Villagra meant: Tigerbull, Clarín the bull!

He brought him to Laguna Seca on the other side of the river, near Palo Alto, where wild ducks flying overhead gave forth startled quacks on the rare occasions men appeared. Sometimes the herd, in times of drought, leapt over the gully that enclosed it and found itself enveloped in a grassy silence. It was a melancholy spot, but here the heir to power would live out his exile, and in exile he would be trained to conquer. His tutor taught him how to charge. He taught him to foam with rage at the sight of a jaguar skin, to defend his rights and the territory of his corral. Nicanor was something of a mystery to the other inhabitants of the plain. History is nebulous, and he was at the intrepid age: at night he would cross the plain of San José to sneak a visit with Isaura Gadea—the Villagras and Gadeas were enemies—and in the morning he took off at top speed, with a jaguar skin tied to his saddle horn. When Clarín turned four, Nicanor took him to the Palo Alto corral. The cows, aloof but curious, watched him advance, young and powerful, with his red-painted horns, following like a dog behind Nicanor. But the old bull—Cantaclaro of Palo Alto—looked up uneasily.

He backed up, roaring, shaggy, tearing into the earth, throwing dust over his back. "This is your moment," Nicanor touched Clarín's testicles with the whip. "Either you nail him in the corral, or I cut your balls off." He let out a yell, mounted his horse, and without looking back he took off for the ranch.

Some time after noon, old Villagra and the *sabaneros* who were tending the calves saw Cantaclaro come running at top speed, battered and bleeding. Disconcerted, they watched in silence as the nervous, heavy stud bull circled around in the corral. "It has to be the jaguar," said the camp chief. Old Villagra ran to get his rifle. The other herdsmen let the calves loose and ran to their horses, shouting for Nicanor, who rode behind them, pale but happy. When they reached Palo Alto single file, they saw Clarín grazing, still excited alongside his new herd. The *sabaneros* burst out laughing. "Whose bull is this?" asked Old Villagra, but his question was simply meant to break the silence and vent his fury. His old cattleman's eye had already recognized The Widow's son. "Whose bull is this?" he shouted, looking askance at Nicanor.

"Now you can see," said Nicanor—"if I had obeyed you out of sentiment, look what would have been lost!"

Clarín raised his head, looked at them proudly, and pawed at the conquered ground. Then his roar resounded through the cloud of dust-penetrating, imperious, raising echoes far away at the jungle's dark borders, beyond the Frontier of Forsakenness.

"Let's leave the horses here," Nicanor says.

We tie the two colts to a small *jícaro* tree, lower their blinders, and take off our spurs.

Nicanor, bending down, studies the tiger's tracks. "We're right on his heels!" he exclaims. The grass is scarcely beginning to spring back from under the sharp, oppressive, and at the same time light, almost airy paw print of the jaguar. We hear a roar from the bull. Crouched down, stealthy as criminals, we abandon the direction of the tracks to get to a *nancite* tree with low branches covered with thorns that scratch our hands. The afternoon light is dimming more rapidly than we can travel, and leaving behind an ashen gray day—it's as if all the colors of the plain and sky have turned to marble. Nicanor slings his lasso over a branch and gives me his hand, and then before my eyes, the savanna draws itself up into a circle, with its proud *guanacaste*—the Palo Alto—holding up the old discolored sky as if it were a tent. The panicked cattle spin and turn, tracing orbits of mud and trampled grass. They try clumsily to produce a solid mass. They break formation, try again. A cow jumps out to push her calf along, bumps into another, starts to charge at her companion, turns to join her, and circles around again. All this commotion makes for a protective circle, tight, solid, unified. The bull directs, punishing delinquents, charging angrily at slow ones, with baying and butting of horns forming the protective circle, the sacred wheel, until he suddenly stops, cutting a black silhouette against the twilight, his head high, tense, ears pricked up. We stand up quietly in the branches. Nicanor slowly raises the rifle to the level of my eyes, just as a honey-colored cow jumps out from the bramble thicket. The bull has roared again and the cow runs toward him, nervously looking back. Behind her, a newborn calf caked with dirt takes a few quick shaky steps and falls. The cow hears the bull's hoarse, peremptory bellow and the calf's weak, supplicant bawling. She falters, turns back nervously and helps the calf, pushing it gently with her horn, but the grass behind her is parted, not by the breeze but by an obscure menace that makes not so much as a whisper, and in utter silence, an unnatural, faintly disquieting trembling that startles the cow. A bird passing overhead screeches and turns, alarmed in its flight. The cow hesitates again, looks around, shakes her head as if trying to rid herself of a pesky fly, goes a few steps, trying to get the calf to follow, but the inexperienced and clumsy little animal stays put, bleating. Then I exclaim, "Nicanor!" and he sees it too: pulling himself over the low ground, slowly, believing himself still hidden when in fact his bright spotted back is partly exposed. He drags himself along, his front paws moving in a swimming motion, while his hind paws seem to measure the exact angle of the muscle he will use to spring; the supple, elastic tail sways like a pendulum, marking time in gold and shadow—a calculated fleeting instant.

"History's repeating itself. History's repeating itself," I think I hear the murmuring of Nicanor's voice, and his angry hand pressed to the firearm is also mine, aiming, sighting on the slinking bundle that is moving again now, tensing and bending its supple force, preparing for a leap. "Now! Now, Nicanor!" I say, believing myself to be shouting, when actually I've only murmured an ineffectual broken phrase, and then we see the bull charge furiously. What I mean is, I see a sudden streak of volcanic rage surge forth, and hear his hooves pounding the mud, and echoes of his fury tear the air. But the jaguar, simultaneously, soundlessly, leaps in an arc and lands on the calf, and we hear the sound of bones cracking. And on top of that blow, comes the lightning-bolt paw. *Arriba!* Instantly he leaps again, growling, the huge body extended, gleaming as if the skin were nailed to the sky—and his legs and paws spread wide, with claws that could snag the wind. He turns and bends in midair, hurls himself farther without even touching down, while the bull turns, off balance, confused, stops in the mud, roars in indignation, turns again, and charges with his useless horns at the shadow, which leaps and flees. And leaps again. And silence.

Nicanor lowers his gun, furious.

"We lost him!" I say.

"Son of a bitch!" he shouts. "Son of a bitch!"

The silence of defeat embitters the sky like the mouth of someone betrayed. I try to force my eyes to pierce the violet ambiguity of the plain. Nothing stirs! Not even that shamed black statue that is the bull. Not even the circle of cattle, paralyzed with fear. Not a tree. Not the wind. Only there, slight convulsions move what's left of the little calf, lying in its faint, innocent blood, reduced by death and twilight, as if invisible ants were slowly carrying it toward the earth's dark womb.

"Let's go," says Villagra. He can't bear defeat. He jumps down from the tree and I follow. We hear the distant cries of the cowhands. Cries. Far-off cries, "son-of-a-bitching" the jaguar. Maybe it is fleeing.

"It must have leapt from the thicket," I think aloud.

I look for the bull in the gathering darkness. Clarín is moving back slowly without moving his head. Then his hoof touches the blood of the calf, and he pauses. He sniffs, raises his head in an almost human movement of denunciation and bellows, a mournful bellow—but at the same time savage—which the cattle take up in chorus, stirring, raising dark echoes throughout the night.

Oh, black beacon! Where else has this fatal chorus wrung my heart? I think of long-ago nights, ashen mothers circling the sunburnt walls with laments.

"Look! Look!" Villagra says into my ear in a tight voice, raising his gun. I search anxiously among the shadows. The bull's roaring stops. He moves nervously, charges his flock authoritatively and does a turn around it, forcing the cattle to draw together more compactly. The timorous, obedient cattle reconstruct the wheel of the roundup, flashing horns, and guarding the timid, fearfully bleating calves in the center behind their rumps.

"Where?" I ask. I open my eyes wide, but uselessly, as the night devours every form.

"Where?"

Villagra brings his face close and points toward the marshy flats. Yes! I see! A round shadow. It's coming back! Oh, God, give me the eyes of the country folk, clear and sure. Free me of this imaginative, distracted reader's eye. The jaguar *is* there! We scramble up the tree again. There he is. We can hear him now, far off, sowing fear with his cry from behind the brambles. But there he is, not merely reaching, but surging out of the night, as if he were pulling the jungle behind him, with its humid, sluggish twilight stealing over the plain; no longer hidden but domineering, hidden in himself but manifest as his crime, determined to advance toward the bloody meat.

"Get him! Get him!" I want to say, shouting silently. No! Don't think. Look!

This time Clarín distrusts blind rage. He only smolders like coal burning underground: he advances slowly, cautiously, head down, making an arc with his powerful neck and low horns, as if his main concern were to plow the soil.

The jaguar hesitates. His eyes, cold as stars in the gaseous gray month of August, are forced to look twice at this new planet, this slow black force with which he is about to clash. But he pauses, comprehending the extraordinary power that will set the stakes.

Oh, Clarín, our own rage! Forward!

The jaguar crouches. A flash of moonlight bounces off his fatefully brilliant teeth, menacingly bared—the beast invested with his cruel trademarks, power of eyetooth and silver light that dances on his spotted tunic, tyrannical and bloody. He crouches lower, clinging to his own shadow, hiding within himself. He pulls himself along, preparing for a low attack to the neck. I can hear his snarl, filled with spit and loathing. But the bull advances. And keeps coming.

Now! That's it! That does it! He charges. Gores it. Attacks. Slams. Collides. We hear a cry. He's got him! Go! The entire plain, the centuries-old hacienda—everything is on the table. Now! Now! Go, boy! Go, Clarín-bull, go! (Is this me? Who? My soul is screaming, and the cattle are moaning miles away, echoing your screams, Villagra, yours and mine!) Charge! Charge, with your ten generations bellowing. Again, boy, sink your horns in to the hilt, hit him, knock the jaguar down, overtake him, charge, kill!

But he jumps, all bloodied. Oh, moon! The jaguar is hurt! He falls down, and Clarín gets him again. Don't give up, Clarín! And the jaguar falls, limps, gives the cow a swipe with his paw, kills her—the murderer!—once more he kills, and oh, the explosion! We hear, we hear only the impact, the angry snort of rage—hear only the body once again being gored, and his scream—and then I see the unappeased head pressing, raising up, picking up the cat and throwing it and dragging it and crushing it against our tree, and then the sound of the body being disemboweled and the scream of pain, and once again, against the shaking tree, and the sound of the guts being squeezed once again, and now the breath only expels blood, and once again. No! The rage will never die. He strikes, and strikes again. Villagra's hand is on my arm like a vise. Below, almost at our feet, the fury repeats its crazy blind blow, reducing the enemy to dust, its memory to dust—as he drags him, still charging at his remains, bellowing over them—and again buries the insatiable horn in the corpse.

It seems endless. He retreats and with fiery eyes, surveys his surroundings, north, south, east; then, sniffing, turns, transfixing the vanquished, bloody, monstrous corpse. Each blow a number on the death toll, citing the crime and its revenge: for Azabache, flower of San Miguel; for sweet Ursulo; for you, Golondrina; for Griselda and Lily, the sweet Lily of the white horns; for the renowned Scion of La Luna; for Rosa; for Palangana; for the delicate, ravaged Queen of Soroncontil; for you, lastly, the unknown, nameless victim.

The cattle send up a wall of cries, and we're shouting to the stars. Nicanor embraces me, delirious, jumping down from the tree:

"Ballsy boy!" he shouts, dragging his gun along the ground.

"You're crazy, Villagra, no!"

He doesn't hear me. He approaches the bull, trembling with excitement.

"Clarín, boy!"

"That bull is still mad, Villagra!"

"Villagra!" But he doesn't hear me.

"Clarín. Clarín, boy."

He goes slowly toward him. He calls to him, and two blood-filled eyes stare back.

"Villagra, you lunatic! Villagra!"

The bull lowers his head. He stomps the dense bloody soil with a hoof. He moves back.

"Clarín! Clarín! Boy!"

I shout: "Don't go near him, Villagra! Careful!"

But he goes ahead, talking as he nears, his voice just a murmur.

"Clarín: you acted like a man! Clarín!"

"This is my signature!" he shouts to me, raising his fist to the moon, as the bull, suddenly docile, bends his head down childishly, to accept a kiss on the forehead.

The House

Horacio Peña
Translated by Leland H. Chambers

They spent their whole lives saving to buy the house. Buying it became an obsession for the whole family. No one talked about buying a house; instead they always said "the house," as if it were a person, a beloved being, alive. Overnight it managed to be built in our hearts, and each one began to do without even very small things. Penny by penny the walls were gradually put up, the bricks, doors, and windows were put in, penny by penny; over the days, the years, the house was built and taken possession of a little at a time, and there it was, though we didn't see it nor was anyone residing in it, something invisible that filled time, space, memory, life, and death.

Every two or three months when the money was counted that had been saved in an old wooden box, the whole family got together to do the accounts, and Grandma took the tiny key for unlocking the treasure and the bottom appeared with a few coins scattered here and there, and they were taken out, with those of similar value and size stacked together because it was easier to count them that way, and besides, when they were brought together that way they resembled tiny pillars, the columns upon which the roof would be placed, the dream would come true. All that in a solemn ceremony. Since the previous night we had been talking about opening the box, about how we were going to see how much it held. And I dreamed about those stories my grandmother used to tell me in which a boy discovered a coffer in the heart of the forest with an immense treasure of coins, cups, vessels of gold, a treasure that made the whole family happy because the father would no longer have to go into the forest to cut wood nor would the mother have to get up before sunup to wash or iron, and everyone would eat well, the table would be heavy with fruits, soup, good food, and a lot of it, all kinds of things: Beowulf in the cave, defeating Grendel forever. And the following morning, very early, the key was brought, the box was taken out and removed to a little room where we all made a circle while Grandma inserted the key and raised the lid and the few, tiny coins would all appear before our eyes. And after counting them, doing some calculations concerning how much we had and how much we needed, and closing the little box and putting it back in the same place, empty now, while the money saved in it was moved to another place. And that's the way it went on for months and months, years and years, until every one of us was getting older, but always with the hope of possessing something of our own.

Grandma's hair became white and her face began to be filled with wrinkles; little by little she was losing her quickness of movement and her body was becoming weak, but she never lost the shine in her eyes, those eyes that gave life to her whole body and, I would say, to all the family's dreams as well, because behind her eyes burned a great will, firm and tenacious, a will of iron that never flagged for even a moment, that had made her daughters and grandchild lead decent lives within their poverty. Those eyes were the columns, the foundations of the house, and Grandma was its cornerstone. And Mother and Aunt were coming to realize more bitterly what time is, and what the dream was that seemed as though it would never come true. They saved wherever they could, and even where they couldn't. It became more difficult for them to buy a new dress, meals were rationed and planned very carefully so as not to waste a single cent, and of course all those things that people who have money used to do and still do, such as vacations, get-togethers, parties, we never got into such things, either before or after the house entered the hearts of the whole family.

Life became harsher for Grandma, Mama, and Aunt, who made sacrifices in hundreds of things in order to make that golden dream come true. They no longer wanted to walk from one place to another carrying their small bundles of clothing, moving them in wagons or handcarts when we changed from one house to the next—or rather, from one room to the next—when the owner would take a notion to raise the rent to a point that was beyond the family's resources, beyond what we were able to pay; when the owner, with a degree of avarice and voracity he would never lose but that would grow greater with every passing day (and especially with all that has happened lately, the ruining of the city), when he would inform us that the room was really quite cheap and that there were others able to pay more than we could, and in spite of our entreaties and our pleas that we couldn't go that high but perhaps we might a little less, he would shout mercilessly, "This is final!"

In those days, Aunt and Grandma and Mama all worked outside the home selling fabrics in an establishment run by some Jews, and every afternoon they would go out with me to look through the poorest districts, the ones farthest out from the city, for a room where we could take our few, poor things. That tour would begin about one or two in the afternoon, with our inquiring where we might find an empty house or even a room that wouldn't be very expensive because we couldn't pay very much; there were only four of us, three women and myself, just a boy in those days, a child already embittered, born old, filled with a hatred, that has always been increasing, that never ceases to grow, and proud of this hatred which is a hatred of all these things that produce misery and injustice, of a country in which I hope not to die, and Grandma or perhaps my aunt saying that they wouldn't have any problems with us, that we didn't make any noise, and that the rent money was already put aside, for we were poor but the first thing always was to save up for the price of the house.

It was a lengthy pilgrimage through district after filthy district, looking at shacks with dirt floors, the kind you have to toss water on to keep the dust from being stirred up—but it always rises anyway: a fine dust, nearly invisible, that gets into your eyes, your throat, all the pores of your skin, that suffocates little children and makes them cough, get sick, and eventually kills them. Districts like this can still be seen both inside and outside the city: shanty towns, slums. Because today there is more death and misery than ever.

Going up and down every street until we came upon a room we could afford and arranged things with the landlord, always in fear that the next day or even the very same day some other person might come looking for a room and offer more than we had and the owner would give it to him despite the fact that he had promised it to us, despite the fact that we had given him our rent money in advance, because when we arrived pushing a handcart with our bundles he would tell us he had already rented it to someone else, and now the problem was much bigger because we would have to return with our cart to the old place and face the landlord there with his shouting and his demands, shaking his fist but finally, confronted with Grandma's tears, granting us like a god a "day of grace" during which we would have to find another room.

But all this was going to come to an end with our own house, even though it might be tiny and very simple, because the important thing was to have it, something of one's own, that you knew belonged to you, and that with time would gradually be improved on and fixed up, would be painted the way you wanted without being afraid that the owner would come and throw us out saying that the room was too cheap and that he wanted to raise the rent higher, that if we were able to pay we could stay and if not we would have to leave—without fear and trembling in the face of the rich people's greed, landlords who charge a fortune for a room where there are no facilities for anyone, a tiny little room where you can't even breathe, a "little egg," as Grandma would say, as she keeps on saying, but this is an unknown language for them, though they know perfectly well how people live in these rooms and that they are exploiting them.

All this would come to an end with our own house. It would be small but I knew that Mama, Grandma, and Aunt would always keep it shining, clean, and pleasant. I had never gone into those mansions of the rich, though I could imagine how they were inside, where everyone had their own rooms and you didn't have to stand in line to take a bath or take care of your necessities and where everyone would be able to turn the handle without having to go out to the outhouse, and you wouldn't have to stand in line to get water from the well, and the house would be a big one, without rats emerging from the cracks at night, from every hole, without insects or cockroaches coming out of every single corner and keeping everyone from sleeping, flying around, buzzing past your face, humming near you the whole night through so that you were only hoping for daylight to free yourself from that nightmare that you knew would start all over again the following night. Every night.

And day by day this house gradually turned into something that would not allow us to rest; we were always talking about it, about how it would be arranged, where the old chairs would be placed, and the table. And always the sacrifice, more sacrifices than before, more hard work than before, all aimed toward that house that already had a name and a history. I saw how my mother, my grandma, and my aunt saved penny upon penny, how they denied themselves hundreds of things, yet they never stinted on me, they really didn't, for I went on living just the same as always: with something new to wear during Holy Week, some toy for Christmas. But I made my contributions too, without their knowing it, to that house that filled all their hearts; I deprived myself of sweets and caramels, certain things that they would offer me and that I would reject happily, alleging that I didn't feel like it, that the sweets gave me a stomachache; and they believed this and little by little they ceased buying sweets and caramels altogether.

And our going somewhere to have a sherbet disappeared too. To one of those places like "Verdi's" or "The Golden Ant," which were the "in" places at that time, where the rich kids got together along with their parents every Saturday or Sunday in the afternoon, or on holidays; those spots where it was like entering an enchanted garden, a palace filled with magicians, magic, an incredible place where they served enormous bowls of sherbet of every color and size, pink, brown, yellow, orange sherbets. You'd sit down at your little table, clapping your hand partly to get some service and partly so that everyone would see that you were there too, and always, then as now, children worse off than we were would appear, devouring those bowls of sherbet with their eyes, sherbet topped with cookies like flags flying high above an enchanted castle, approaching the tables where I was, momentarily turned into a lucky little boy in front of my big sherbet bowl.

But later on, when the idea of having our own house had gained sway over dreams and miseries, I never went to those places anymore because I knew that everyone else was sacrificing in order to buy the house and I too ought to put my grain of sand into this house that was now a beautiful obsession for Mama, Grandma, and Aunt, who would get together every two or three months to count up the money saved during that time, and I was happy and proud to watch them at it because I knew that my sweets and caramels were among the pennies they had collected, the sherbets that I had not eaten in those places that have disappeared now, although the hungry children have not, in fact they are even more numerous, and I have ceased to be a child like they are, and I see them again but with hungrier faces, I see them clustered around those places that have sprung up after everything that has happened, that is, the destruction of the city, places still more elegant, with air conditioning, with carpets, because the country now has more money than ever, although misery and hunger are now harsher than ever, and a house to live in, a room to die in, is impossible to obtain despite all the money that has come here, a country where the pets of the rich live better than the poor:

the elegant spinster ladies
feed their smooth-haired fox-terriers
plums, raisins, and ices

and there go the waitresses, the same as always, running them out, getting them out of there so they won't be a bother with their hunger and their hands held out asking for something to eat, so they won't pester those of us who are seated, but the children furtively return when there is no longer anyone at the tables, they come back in and collect the leftovers in pieces of newspaper or in paper napkins, as if they were thieves, those hungry faces, those sourly empty eyes

of children looking at the desserts,
the apple turnovers, the
vanilla and chocolate sherbets

those hungry faces picking up a piece of bread, a fistful of rice, but someday thorns will emerge from their hands,

thorns filled with the fury of their innocence,
thorns that later on will be like whips,
like handfuls of rocks thrown by angels
with dirty faces.

And occasionally Mama and Aunt would give up. There were days when their faces turned gloomy after counting the money, and defeat was seen on their faces because the money, the coins, were not enough and they thought it was better to abandon the idea of the house and buy food and clothing—but then they would find themselves again, listening to Grandma: there she was, raising her hands, moving her arms, defying and defiant, giving encouragement like a general haranguing his occasionally faltering troops—that's the way Grandma was, all of that and much more than that: straight and erect, who for a long time now had been the pillar on which the house was raised, the cornerstone of all our dreams.

There she was, crossing her arms, covering herself, covering all of us with words, while I watched and watched her from my corner, with pinched heart and dry lips, mouth tense—my whole body was tense—a knot in my throat and my eyes filled with tears and sobbing that wanted to come forth but that didn't come forth, a sob like the sound of ocean surf on the verge of exploding, of breaking up, but without weeping, without giving any sign of my presence, making enormous efforts to hold back my crying so they wouldn't know I was there, but hearing and watching my grandma and then my mother and my aunt as they picked up the money, put it away, and—with more confidence now—told Grandma they would keep on going.

When I started working, in all kinds of strange jobs, unusual jobs, among people that weren't and still aren't interested in those things—I was a traveling book salesman—the dream of buying the house became a little less distant.

We were able to save a little more, but now Grandma was extremely tired. On her return from selling something or from making a few small purchases, she would look quite ill, terribly fatigued. That was when she would sit down on her big wooden chair to think that perhaps now the fairytale dream was about to come true. And Mother and Aunt also were aging, overpowered by time and misery and the anguish of the years, but finally they could see that the dream begun so long ago was closer, one could almost touch it, the house at last! where youth and happiness had been left behind, where we were going to live with the memory of the sacrifices that had been made.

Mama had seen a house that she liked, that everyone liked, and that we could buy, "put a down payment on" as they say, and afterward we would continue paying on it every month for a year or two; a used house, fairly old, but one that I knew would take on new life under the care and love of us all. So we bought the house and afterward we continued the payments for several months until it was ours, and we moved into it with all our things and spent several days cleaning it up, washing it, arranging it, placing tables and chairs the best way possible so it would look its nicest; Grandma no longer got around with that grace and agility that she used to know but, seated on her big wooden chair, she would tell us how it would be best, although from time to time she would get up and take a turn around the living room, touching the rocking chairs gently, running a hand over the table with a smile that lighted up the farthest corner of the house, that filled my whole life. The dream that had been born one morning or perhaps some afternoon on a dusty street, with the whole neighborhood shouting, the confusion, in the middle of my bitter childhood, though occasionally filled with an immense joy—sorrow and joy over things that others could not comprehend, things lived, felt: a joy and a sorrow that I would never exchange for anything with anyone.

Now we were here, in the long-dreamed-of house that filled the lives of my grandma, my mother, my aunt—an incredible house, an impossibility that had actually come about.

I remember the first night we slept in it. We spent hours and hours talking, about the past, about all the misery that lay behind it, and when night came, when it was almost midnight, Grandma turned out the light and everyone went to bed after the excitement and the joy and the weariness, but I remained in the living room, sitting in Grandma's chair, and fell asleep.

Grandma didn't enjoy the house for long, she died three or four years afterward without my being able to give her everything I had wanted for her, to cover her with gold from head to foot, to cover her with all those lovely things she had never had, to spare her the work she continued to do until a few days before she fell gravely ill, for she would always get up before sunup and begin to get ready for the day's work, the long, endless day.

I could never give her those things that other elderly women like her had, elderly women who were the grandmothers in the homes of the rich, good clothes, outings, security, and a tranquil existence, but I did as much as I could to alleviate her poverty, always hating everyone, hating the country, the people, the system in which I continue to live.

And years after Grandma's death—I wasn't able to see her die, for, like Ulysses under the curse, I was traveling around from island to island—there came the destruction of the city. With the earthquake came hunger, pillage. We, like everyone else, fled from the disaster.

But after a week we began to go back to the house every day to see how it had fared or to see what was left, nothing or almost nothing. It was still there, still standing, but empty, filled with dust, in ruins, in the middle of a silent street, of a whole city filled with silence. What we had been unable to take with us because of our haste and fear was ravaged, stolen, and only the house remained.

We would go every day to look at it, to see if it was still there, to see if they had stolen the doors yet, the windows, the washstand, the bricks. We went out very early toward what remained of the city, and on turning the corner we would see it. Sometimes we went in, shoving aside stones, boards, tiles that had fallen, but other times we remained in the street, gazing at how little time the dream had lasted. At first it was safe from the attack, from the fury, but then little by little it lost everything that had made it what it was, because for us the house wasn't something inanimate, something dead: it was our own lives, Grandma's life and death, and we talked about the house, about her, as if she were another beloved being.

One morning we went to see it as usual, and even before we came around the corner something told my mother that the death of the house had commenced.

It was totally bare, with none of its doors; that's the way its death began, those were the first things taken from it, the first things they deprived it of; they had stripped it of its doors, wrenched them off and pulled the hinges right out, leaving the doorframes splintered and injured. Mama cried right there for a long time and said that this was the end, the end of the house, of the city. And on our return she was crying too, but saying that maybe they would just take the doors, that maybe they would leave the rest alone.

And the following day the windows disappeared, window frames that had been painted in a green color, a light green; and so day by day, every time we went back we saw less of it, we encountered only debris and more debris; the bricks gradually disappeared in this way, the faucets, the washstand, a wooden partition wall, the clotheslines, the locks, everything was disappearing, dying, until one day we went and there was nothing left.

It was a slow death that no one could put a stop to. Tooth and nail, things had been torn from the house as if it had been an enemy. The bricks in the kitchen, which were the only things to have been saved, together with a small window screen, also disappeared finally, and the only thing left was the walls imprisoning the silence and the memories and my mother's sobbing.

And one more time we went just to see it, perhaps to remember; we hadn't intended to go there exactly but to somewhere else around there, and Mama said we should go by, and already before we turned the corner we could hear the sounds of tractors. We were just in time to see the last wall coming down in the midst of the dust and pieces of board, and now nothing at all remained of it but the flat ground, like a burning plain in which our memories, my grandmother's life and death, were in flames, a house built along the whole length of our anguish, now leveled, a house that became lost in my childhood and the lives of all of us. Nothing more.

On the Stench of Corpses

Sergio Ramírez
Translated by Don D. Wilson

Funeral march music playing at daybreak through all the city byways and the murmuring of the people who traveled the dark streets, praying in chorus to be guided to the churches that were tolling their bells, announced that the mother of His Excellency had died in the palace.

The republic was engulfed in sorrow, and a sea of flags waved at half-mast during all the days the corpse dressed in angel's clothing was paraded in a glass coffin through the city streets, without anyone exactly speaking of her burial. Until His Excellency announced she would never be buried, indeed, would remain at his side as always, always accompanying him at ceremonies, at audiences, at receptions, at parades of the military, and at all governmental affairs whatsoever.

At first it seemed easy for the chambermaids to dress the dead body for each occasion and to seat it appropriately propped at the right hand of His Excellency—but before long the stench was terrible, for the embalming procedures were still very precarious in the republic.

At the elegant banquets the ladies choked back their vomit for fear of offending the Dictator, who impassively followed with his head the measures of the chamber music that cheered the meals, and the gentlemen, according to the palace custom, offered the old woman the best bites from their plates. The ambassadors were always obliged to kiss her hand, although upon taking her jeweled fingers they were left with greenish particles of skin between theirs.

The matron, with a veil over her face, tranquilly assisted in the process of her decay, oblivious to the poisoning of the air, reclining on her golden throne, listening with her unyielding ear to the pastoral conversation of the Archbishop and the compliments of the French ambassador.

The day came when the maids applied rouge directly upon the fleshless cheekbones and covered her discolored and dried-up hair with a gilded wig, leaving her stiff arms in a gesture of perpetual greeting.

By the time the empty clangor sounded again in every church to announce the death of the republic's First Lady, the ministers, ambassadors, and the other dignitaries were perfectly used to the smell of the carcass and to the worms that crawled calmly around their dishes and climbed up their wineglasses.

In the Midst of the Downpour
They Took Away My Cousin

Mario Santos
Translated by Don D. Wilson

I am in front of the neighborhood bakery. I wish I could throw stones at the windows and puncture the bicycle tires, and for that I have three nails in my pocket. Throwing rocks at toads has sharpened my aim. Any toad whatever scares my mom and to touch them gives her shudders. She has seen me chasing crickets and said to be careful about killing any cricket because it is a sin and as punishment I could turn as small as a cricket when I die. I don't kill them but catch them and put them in a cardboard box I have smuggled under my bed, and they spend all the cold night squeaking. I think the souls who pay their penalties in hell complain the same way. The crickets' singing drives my mom crazy. With dislike and disgust I watch the baker, who looks like a hairless monkey, all covered with flour.

And I remember with pain that that old baker was hanging on my cousin's every step. From dawn until night lost itself in all its mysterious voices. Night seems to me like an abyss of thoughts. I love the night and I dream a lot about the moon. When the patrol car drove up with that abrupt manner, the old man appeared with another man and pretended in every way not to notice the scandal that my cousin's arrest was causing.

Days before, two young men had appeared at my house and chatted with my cousin under the shade of the guava tree on the patio and their voices could not be heard. Their hands almost spoke. When they left, my cousin told them: "We'll be seeing each other. Remember, there is much dark business in this, and there are no options."

With this weather, you can't play as you want to. The ground stays sheer mud. But what I like is to get all of my body into the mud. My cousin told me once, when my mom was scolding me because I went around as filthy as the very earth: "It's a mistake to say you're as filthy as the very earth. You must realize that it's not the earth that makes you filthy." On Sundays when I come from Mass with the other kids, we start to play marbles behind the church, and that is when I am in the puddle smearing my arms and my face with mud. Ha, but then my mom clears the mud away from my body by slapping me! According to her, winter is not very likeable. But she rejoices to see the madonna lilies blooming on the patio. My mom says the rainbow colors are the colors of world peace. The rainbow rays light up the facets of the leaves of the alligator pear and the other trees that make up a little jungle of leaves and flowers on the patio in back of the mechanic's shop.

In that little grove, at twilight, my cousin used to meet the woman from the grocery. I was the go-between for the little love notes. He has two coffee-colored eyes as large as a cow's and stares so forcefully that you believe he can read the mind of others.

All the women ran out to the street.

My cousin Humberto was pulled out of the bathroom and dragged to the door, covered from the rear with rifles and pistols. At first the women shouted. They upset the streets with a valiant uproar. They were armed with frying pans and clubs and dared the policemen to release my cousin. But the police leveled their machine guns. At the instant they put my cousin into the jeep, the downpour broke out and the women fell silent and, drenched, went back to their houses. Their husbands stuck out their heads and looked on, barechested. They were apparently afraid of going into the street and they hid in the half-open doors. Fearless under the rain and on a courageous impulse I clenched two rocks in my hands. But the strength and determination to throw them at the policemen deserted me.

They were building the stalls in the church plaza and there was as much dust as salt in the sea. That day, in the midst of a cloud of dust, my cousin first arrived at our house. I saw him go in and I had great luck at marbles that day.

My mom called my name from our rooms and ordered me to wash my hands. When I returned to the dining room she told me, "He's your cousin Humberto, son of your Uncle Camilo. From now on he's going to live with us." That noon we ate spiced iguana meat. At night we went to the stalls and he bought me everything I asked for. We were watching roulette when Xiomara kissed me on the cheeks and asked who I was walking around with. I told her with my cousin Humberto, and he began to flirt with her. As the days passed, she fell madly in love with him. There came a time when Humberto hardly left the house and something was always needing to be put in order there, and he took care of the wood and swept the patio. One noon three men with unfamiliar faces arrived to eat at the house and they talked with him while they ate. The three men changed my cousin. That afternoon he did not go out to paint a sidewalk landscape and to teach me to sketch. He never again painted the girls going to school nor the horse-drawn cart nor the big, yellow corner grocery. My mom says my cousin is an artist with the brush and that it is inherited from my grandfather, who died wanting to paint walls with his hands full of paint.

He became quieter and started to spend much time in bed reading the books those men had left him. With that change I lost the desire of getting to go meet my dad which he had promised me even if my mom got angry with him.

I think the moans I heard last night at bedtime were my mom's, who was crying without tears for my cousin's absence and how much we will miss him.

I also think she was wrong when she said to her friends that her brother Camilo and the nephews thought themselves better than us. Because my cousins were studying at a parochial school and my uncle was an agent for a foreign company for electrical appliances. And he was ashamed of us in that we earned our daily living and my necessities for school with this simple and cheerful selling of food.

Nevertheless, Humberto was not ashamed of poverty nor of our humble way of knowing how to work to live. He painted the table and chairs. Without Humberto now, the house has returned to its old smell of food and burnt grease and the warmth of the coming and going of my mom and her speedy making of the meals after coming from the store at seven in the morning and mixing up a *tiste* for me and my two rolls with butter, and now she has pants and a shirt ready for me and quickly I go to school with her blessing and her kiss on my forehead.

The passing cars are dripping with water.

It seems that in the center of the city it is drizzling. The coal dealer comes down with his damp clothes and pushcart covered with a burlap coffee bag protecting the remnants of coal. My mom is the first customer of this man. He says good morning to her.

Xiomara is standing, leaning against the wall of her house.

I look at her as at a sad little statue like those my cousin sketches.

One senses jasmine and gladiolus perfume when one looks at her face. She has fixed her nostalgic eyes on me. I am struck with admiration for some time by her legs, which look the color of a ripe mango. Her dress is short, and the wind lifts it up to the edge of her buttocks covered with black panties trimmed with red, her favorite colors. She lives in the middle of the block on the same side as my house. Her dad is a shopkeeper and he is a friend of my mom and not her lover. On that brick sidewalk, Xiomara walks the neighborhood every afternoon flirting with my cousin. Her long, black hair is like the cane flower; it is always playing with the weather. Since they took Humberto, she seems like a wilted begonia. Her stares are long and heavy, as though something were pressing on her heart, and she does not let herself laugh with the easy and carefree laughter of before. Her laughter used to be like the little doves of Saint Nicholas. She knew my cousin didn't have a job, and he used to sketch her just as she stands this very moment, leaning against the jasmine-shaded wall.

She used to send him cigars and call him "the philosopher-painter without hope in history." I was always running after her skirts and kissing her legs as if she were my mom when we go to bed and she runs her hands over my body and nestles at my side and we press together chest to chest until we fall asleep.

I heard the moans and supposed it was grief for my cousin, and because I'm easily made sad I cried a little quietly as the toads and the frogs cry when they feel the ache from the stones. I wasn't sure whether the reality of my feelings or the moans of my mom were for the misery of my cousin. Humberto used to sleep on the other bed and had made a paper screen with newspapers and magazines to separate the bedrooms. Night after night my mom thought me asleep and would get up on tiptoe or slip away to sit on my cousin's bed, and all night they'd talk and talk so agreeably and gently that I was gradually lulled to sleep by the braided rope of their voices. One night I stayed awake. The moon was entering through the window overhead. I was counting the stars in the night and my cousin was telling my mom that the police patrol had invaded the house, and they found five pistols and six ammunition boxes and they dragged away my other cousin, Sebastian, pushing and kicking him. My Uncle Camilo had not come home that night to sleep and they hadn't even an inkling of his whereabouts. But he had seen everything from the house across the street, where they had hidden him on finding out about the accusation. Their house stayed in the hands of the agents. I realized why Humberto had come with only the clothing he had on, and the tailor who owed my mom a meal made him two pairs of pants. I also heard when he said the baker was the plain-clothes agent for the police here in this district.

The Castilian pigeons are flying like little angels in a juicy feast of sweet agitation below the sky's brilliance. I feel the sweetness in the bills of the pigeons, and it is like the feeling of eating mango syrup around Holy Week.

I am in front of the bad, fat, loathsome man's house in our neighborhood. The urge keeps pressing me to break his windows. No one around here buys his bread or considers the jukeboxes that he rents out for parties. He has his customers, but far from here. I would feel like a real man if I could find my Uncle Camilo and tell him of the vulgar, evil arrest of Humberto, and maybe he could find some way that my cousin could return to the house and take me to the movies and tell me when he is going to take me to meet my dad and talk through the nights with my mom while I dream about the moon, and then I would have more things to tell. It's enough for my mind to observe or sense something and then it is never forgotten.

The water was falling like a river. Humberto raised his face, full of anger and gray as the feathers of the pigeons. His goodbye to me was a clenching of his teeth and a nod of his rain-soaked head. I threw myself at his waist and didn't want to let him go, but a policeman forced me away like the donkey he was, and he heaved me like a rag doll into the ditch where the swift water was washing along all the local garbage. My mom stared right through everything in front of her, keeping her eyes wide open in spite of the water coming down, and with her hands thrust into her apron she was squeezing it between her legs. The police left in the midst of the downpour. The driver honked his jeep horn four times and the baker who was watching everything from behind his glass window began to laugh and with a black umbrella and a stump of a broom came out to the street to sweep away a dead cat that would not let the current in the ditch run free.

Francisco

Fernando Silva
Translated by Lynne Beyer

He opened the door and saw that it was pitch dark outside. No moon, and not a single light on in the other houses, just several bonfires glowing in the grass.

"It's going to rain," the man said. "This heat comes with rain." He turned and went back in.

"It's not that late yet," he thought, as he went to bed. He passed a hand over his sweaty chest and rubbed his shinbones.

"I'm scared," he said to himself. "Yes, scared . . . I've never gotten mixed up in anything like this before. But here it is already, so what can you do?"

Later he lay staring into the dark, his mind spinning scenes as if he were thumbing through an old magazine . . . and so he saw himself working at the customs office when he had lived at the harbor. Then he'd worked as a porter and, when he was needed, filled in as engineman on the small tug that transferred heavy loads to the other docks. How well he remembered those days—more than anything, the heat and summer sun. He had loved the heat and the scorching sun beating on the wharves, and the splatter of water when the ropes were pulled up between the blackened planks of the old dock. The sweat that dripped from his chest now reminded him of those days when he was asked to work the launches and came home exhausted, flinging himself down on the sand by the storeroom to enjoy the afternoon breeze off the lake, his eyes burning with the splendid light, as he awaited the sound of the gong and the fat woman's cry at the other end of the alley.

"Lunch time . . . lunch time!" And when he got up—"It feels like I'm there right now," he said to himself—the outline of this body would remain, drawn in sweat on the planks: his back, the circle formed by his hair, two large spots for his shoulders, and his arms alongside the body . . . "and I'm scared," he said to himself again.

"But there's nothing to fear! Let's see," he thought, raising himself and lifting his head. He got up and sat on the edge of the cot.

"I'll just go over what I have to do," and he began: "First, I wait for the call . . . three times. I'll hear a stone fall on the roof three times. Since my house is the first as you go up the hill, that means," he reasoned, "they'll be coming from below. When the last stone falls, I wait, count slowly to 180—which is three minutes. That's how long they say it'll take them to cross the patio. I hope they come alongside the *resedo* trees.

"That's what I told the doctor," he recalled. "Why did I get myself into this!" Then he began again: "OK, then I open the door just a crack and wait to one side. A man should appear.

"'What time is it?' he'll ask, and I'll answer, 'It's only 11 o'clock.' He'll say, 'That would be right, because today is May 11th.' That's the code. I have to have my knife ready . . . 'Because at any moment you may have to use it and run,' the doctor tells me." And he wondered again, "Could I kill someone?" and his response was: "Well, what I'd really do is slam the door on him."

"Next," he said, "I take them to the spot. The main thing is to get them by the guardhouse. It'd be safer to go in the dark. I know there's only one guard there—one poor, sick guard. I already talked with him yesterday, as I explained to the doctor. But just to avoid any mishap, it'd be better to pass behind the guardbox and turn to the right until we get to the fence by the pond. They'll bring the rifles in burlap bags, and one of the boys will carry the machine guns. When we get into the brush, I'll be in charge. I figure it'll take three days to get down to the coast, to Punta del Coral. We'll spot the boat with the doctor's binoculars. We'll spend a whole day unloading the arms, and then another day waiting for another group to pick them up. Then they'll take them as far as the pigsties, and we'll return by the same path or else continue on—who knows?"

It was pitch dark. "Everything is going fine. Up to now I've completed every task they gave me. But I'm scared, of nothing, and of everything. 'The heart is faithful,' my friend Trinidad used to say—and the poor slob died from a gunshot," he smiled, and exclaimed, "Strange world."

He sat in a corner of the house and looked intently at the six young men stretched out on the floor.

"Who are they?" he wondered. "Who could be the father of that one? Or that one sitting against the wall? They seem to come from good families, and they talk like educated people. There's nothing more to do," he said. "These boys are brave." He thought a moment. "I wonder if they are. You have to be brave to get mixed up in all this . . . Am I brave?" he asked himself.

"Listen, friend," one of the group began, dragging himself over to the side where the man was.

"Umm hmm?" the man answered.

"You know the place pretty well, don't you?"

"Yes," answered the man, and his next thought was: "Why did he ask me that?" Another of the youths drew near.

"How many will there be at the guardhouse?" he asked.

"One," said the man.

"Oh, good," said the boy. "That one we'll knock off."

"Shit!" he said to himself. "Would this kid be capable of killing a poor, sick guard?"

"There's only one guard there," he explained, "a poor, sick guard," he added.

The boy didn't hear. They were standing all together now, discussing something in low voices.

"What heat," said one, getting up, and turning toward the man. He asked, "Can't we open that window?"

"Wouldn't that be dangerous?" the other asked.

"They're nervous," thought the man. "They're scared like me." He smiled. "It's OK, I'll open that window." And leaning against one of the ceiling beams for leverage, he pushed open the window toward the outside. He sat down again in his corner and returned to his thoughts.

"Who are they?" He was distracted for a moment, and then took it up again. "My son could be like them. One of them could be my son. The tall thin one with the cap in his hand I don't like. The other, short one, seems like he's not worth much." A flash of lightning sent a burst of brilliance in the window and for an instant illuminated the faces of the youths.

"The one on the right," he decided, "that one I like. Short, dark, heavy-set, with short curly hair: that's how my son would be," he said to himself with satisfaction. And studying the boy he'd chosen in the dark, he went on: "He's the only one who hasn't spoken. He hasn't asked me any questions. He must be cool and calm like me—and brave." He nodded twice and smiled. "Good kid," he went on. "My son would be like that, no more and no less . . . Why don't I have a son, my God! What would his name be? I would've called him Francisco, after my uncle who brought me up. My uncle would have been delighted with Francisco the rebel. My uncle, the old-style conservative—stubborn as a mule," and he smiled. "That's what I'll call him: Francisco." He raised himself up a bit to get comfortable. "I feel like getting up and giving that boy a hug."

Time passed. The tallest of the boys rose, took out his fluorescent watch and read it, shading it with his hand. "Just fifteen minutes to go," he told his companions, who were suddenly nervous. "Listen!" he turned to the man, "Fifteen minutes to go!"

"OK." The man got up.

"You'll be the last to go," said the boy. "Wait till I give you the signal."

"OK," the man replied.

The minutes passed. The tall boy noted each one on his watch.

"OK, this is it!" he said gravely, and raising a hand, he added: "Like we all agreed." He went to the door and slipped out sideways.

They all went out. The man heard the loose sound of their steps amid the rubbish, and then the far-off splash of something falling into the water. The sound was repeated several times.

"They're getting into the boat," he said to himself. He waited. In a while, he heard a whistle. "The signal," he said. He went out quickly and closed the door without making a sound, and then he moved along with his body bent over.

They were all there in the boat, as well as two new ones wearing ponchos. He recognized one of them and said, "Good evening, Doctor."

The other clapped him on the shoulder. Then the two strangers also got into the boat, while the man stood in the water holding it still. He guided the boat away from shore and pointed it out toward the open water. Once in the boat, he searched for Francisco. "Where would he be?" he wondered. "I wish he were here next to me. I'd never have let myself be far from my son."

"Don't move around," he told the others, in a clear voice. "Don't knock the oars against the boat. Save your breath and row hard—slowly but hard," he advised them. Where could Francisco be? Another lightning flash spread over the sky, and he could see that the boy was up front. "That's good," he thought. "This makes it seem like we're going hunting. Francisco's up front with a rifle. I'm running the boat, so I'll be able to see him. The kid's smart—he's quiet, but he doesn't miss a thing. What a good shot my son would be! Why don't I have a son, for the love of God?"

Going along in silence, they heard the water splashing in the dark.

"This fucker is heavy," said one.

"Shh." The ones in front silenced him.

Several long shadows passed over their heads. The man crouched down, rowing hard. By instinct, he adjusted the direction of the boat, raised his body slightly, panting now and then.

"How are we doing for time?" asked one of the boys.

"We're on time," another answered.

They followed the river. Rain was sounding heavily in the scrub forest. The lightning bolts came from far away, cracking in the sky like whiplashes. No one spoke—they floated along like shadows.

Time passed. The rain that fell now was a cold drizzle.

"There it is," announced the man, "in that clearing to the left."

"Aha!" they responded.

"We'll row in among some *guabos* right along the shore," said the man, "under the branches, where its darker. Then we'll get out single file, and follow the shore to our right. The thing is to keep to one side of the guardhouse, so no one sees us."

"Everyone got it?" asked the boy.

"Yes," they all responded.

The boat slid in beneath the boughs of a tree.

"Keep down," said the man. They all huddled together, and soon the boat was jammed like a nail among the tree roots.

"Start getting out," the man ordered.

"You know the plan!" said the tall boy.

One by one the boys got out of the boat, sounding off:

"Careful!"

"Watch it!"

"Now!"

"Let's go!"

"Next!"

"Hurry!"

"Their voices sound strange," thought the man. "They sound empty, weak—these boys sound dead."

The man got out at last, tied up the boat to one of the knots on the tree trunk and emerged, almost getting himself garroted by a branch. He pushed himself, rocking back and forth like a monkey, until he reached the spongy humid ground. He followed behind the others, hidden in the shadows of the tree trunks.

"I have such an urge to shout: 'Francisco! Come over here with me. Don't you see I know this place well—careful, kid, careful, you're going to get a thorn in your heel.' I'm scared for this kid," he thought.

The group advanced, covering a good bit of ground. One of the boys carried the machine gun under his arm. Another two stopped to set the sack of rifles down on the ground, and immediately began to pull out and distribute the arms.

"Does Francisco have his rifle?" he wondered. "I can't see Francisco. What's happened to him? It'd be just like him to walk around there unarmed. We have no idea what could happen here—who knows! At this slope we were going to stop and someone was going to go out and reconnoiter. We have to be careful. If they discover us, it's going to be dangerous getting through the clearing by the pond."

"Let's go! Let's go!" someone said.

"Who's that giving orders?" the man wondered. "Shit! That's crazy! That's not the plan!" He asked again, "Who gave that order?"

"Come on, let's go," the others said, running one after the other as far as the clearing next to the pond. "Get down!" one of them said, and they flung themselves face down on the ground and lay still.

"What could have happened?" the man wondered, not moving from his spot. No one drew breath—it was so quiet you could hear a pin drop.

"What's that noise?" the man wondered, pricking up his sharp ear. It sounded as if someone had stayed behind and was walking up on tiptoe . . . "Could it be Francisco?" he pondered, worried. He cocked his ear again. "Yes, someone's coming . . . how strange, and I can't see a thing. Something moved there, behind those vines. I can't shout from where I am . . . Maybe it's an animal—there are lots of foxes around here. What should I do? The closest to me is the tall one, but I shouldn't get up." He moved a little to one side and raised his head—how strange! He turned quickly, and at the same instant, from the heavy underbrush came flashes like lightning, and screams—human screams, animal screams . . . and then he saw no more. He heard a cry above him, and threw himself headfirst onto some boards. He turned and felt something like a bite in his shoulder, and a splash of earth all over his face.

His thoughts were vacant as he crawled and crawled, until his face burned against the grass. He called up another burst of energy until he felt himself plunge into the water . . . "OK now," he thought, as he hid himself among the reeds. It hurt when he felt his shoulder, which was bleeding. His arm hung down alongside his body. He touched his hand— "Like a rag," he thought, sobbing, and ducked under for a moment. He rested a while and then drew the other hand out from under him to secure himself among the reeds. "I can't take this shoulder," he said. He stopped his leg from floating, turning a little on one side, and held still.

He heard voices and footsteps from where he had come. He positioned himself and waited, stretched out in the water, trying to catch his breath.

"It's the police," he thought. "We were sold out—they were waiting for us." He moved out of the reeds, let his body go slack, and went under for a while. Then he floated for a minute more, and raising his head, heard a cry quite close to him: "Bring a light! A light!"

He ducked down again and waited. He remained in the same position until he heard someone approach, pause, take a few steps, and then turn back.

"Someone's there," he thought. "It looks like they're crouched down or hiding. I can hear his breathing from here. Maybe it's Francisco," he thought, and a chill passed over him. "Francisco," he repeated—"it's my son trying to reach the bank . . . my son!" he repeated, in a turbulence of pain and fear. "Maybe he's hurt and looking for help—" his heart pounded inside his soaked chest.

Then he raised his head and saw the boots. "It's him," he said, feeling as though he'd suffocate. Then he stretched up as much as he could, raising himself up on his bloody shoulder, until . . . a lightning flash from over there: "Francisco!" he cried, horrified, and now he could no longer support himself. He let go of the reeds that held him up and fell into the water, face to the sky. There was just one flash and the sound of the discharge.

A policeman ran up and another came to the bank and lit up the pond with his spotlight.

The yellow light shone on the water, where a patch of blood extended toward the shore in the muddy whirlpools caused by the sinking body.

The policeman withdrew the light from the pond and shined it on the traitor's face: first the heavy boots were seen, then the pistol dangling from his sweaty shirt, and finally the face.

"Put out that light," said the other, turning away.

"Fine." And the policeman turned it off.

Rite

Luis Bolaños Ugalde
Translated by Charles Philip Thomas

The spider of shadow keeps weaving its web.
No longer can I distinguish your female form. I keep following you, slowly, from a distance, without your seeing me. Following the reflection of your footsteps on the last rain-covered streets. Following the dissolving twilight that is you, the echo of you that escapes me and is lost to me in the dark thresholds of the houses.

You've gone without me, without saying anything, without looking up. Everything was so brief, so intense and without direction. Maybe you wanted to stop me and say something; maybe I already refused to understand you. There was a change, a struggle of silences, deep, fearful, and smothering. At the end you got up without making any noise and went out into the thin afternoon air.

The town was calm, stifled perhaps by our own silence. Swallows were flitting about in the transparent breeze. The nearby trees were becoming more and more shadowy and blurred, farther away. I tried to call you and I couldn't. The fear of losing you destroyed my words. And I followed your footsteps already covered by the dust on the road. The last houses have remained behind, entangled in their own honeysuckle, lost under the moss of their tiled roofs, surrounded by green translucence. We keep climbing toward the east, I don't know where exactly. I feel that a murmur of hidden water is following us on tiptoe. Every now and then a cold damp voice whispers that makes me shiver.

I'm afraid of losing sight of you
You have disappeared in the light and shade of the moment

You don't exist now
I'm following another unknown woman
Now you lie down smothered in leaves, shadows and wings.

And I see you again in the pale afternoon light with your body covered over with branches and moss tossed by the wind. Is it you? If I could only see your eyes. If I were only certain that these confused tracks I'm following are yours. Don't hide, let me speak to you, rest on the edge of the path. I run and I get closer, I'm reaching you, I want to shout but I can't. And you feel me, you hear my breathing that gets closer to you and you run even harder, toward the top, I don't know where exactly. You're escaping me, you lose me among the gigantic trees and green-tinged spider webs. You stop, you go on, you get farther away. The path climbs with you, rough and tumultuous, all the way to the top. And then you run headlong among the ash-colored *guarumo* trees and frightened birds.

There, in the distance, a clearing opens up. I see you run with your hair and voice to the winds and you finally stop in front of the three ramshackle houses lost in the bluish fog of an empty plaza. You hesitate and then you throw yourself into the darkness, calling. I hear the sound of three doors that open and close at the same time. But I don't see you enter any of them. You disappear, dissolve in the darkness, become transparent.

From the other side of the plaza I contemplate the shacks for a moment. The dust-filled air of the late afternoon reflects in the broken windows. Old ferns and extinguished lamps are hanging in the corridors. There is a wicker chair in the corner. I cross the plaza and the street, shouting your name, and a pack of hidden dogs answer me. I stop and wait for a long time. The dogs finally go away, pushing unseen branches aside. And they change into echoes. And the echoes into crickets.

I get a grip on myself and I go closer. I knock on the center door and it comes down on me, falling to pieces. A rusty and moth-eaten scream is heard. Your voice. No, it's not you, I'm forgetting. You're not in this house although you're in all of them. Then I hear another voice, slow and timorous, an old woman's voice that seems to come from far away, beyond that vaporous white dress that loses its shape in the copper-colored dust that is still vibrating in the air:

". . . *granary* . . ."

It was probably a little later at night when I found your bed. It was over a wet and clayey ground, in the midst of some old millstones, rickety carts, and sacks of corn. The moonlight shone through the cracks of a roof battered by the rains, and it traced strange designs like a musical staff over your body. I closed my eyes and again remembered your beautiful face, your sleepy tranquil eyes, your lovely white nose, your always moist lips.

Here you are now, in your pine box, with your eyelids half opened and your purple-colored neck, at the foot of this dark man who looks at me from his iridescent pupils and smiles at me with long elegant teeth in which the sheen of my own is reflected.

I kneel down. The man squats, sinks his still shaking fingers into the soft white earth and offers me a handful. I take the clay in my hands and put it over your unmoving face. I run the clay over the landscape of your face, I feel your perfect nose, the sockets of your eyes, your cheekbones. I caress the cold of your cheeks and the silence of your mouth with my muddy fingernails.

Do you remember that amber afternoon
in which the water under the bridge surprised us
and laughing you said that the rain
was making boats over the river
and I put my hand on your face
because I wanted to trap your smile that way?

That was how I learned your face by heart with my fingertips. You had a small mole on your right eyelid that could scarcely be felt and when you laughed two pools of shadow were opened up in your cheeks. The blue line of a trembling vein was joined to your neck and scaled it, dividing you. Now I want to reconstruct your face from memory, give life to the clay with my hands, to again feel the murmur of blood in your flowery skin.

My fingers have slowly modeled the learned features. Your confident breasts, your skin like cashew, your mysterious teeth.

Now the bank is drying
upon waking you will find the same face
that the water was reflecting
below the bridge that afternoon.

With my index finger and the thumb of my right hand, I take the still-soft edge of the mask and, in one movement, I unveil you. Eyes open to the breeze, deep as wells. Long nightlike eyelashes. Under a sallow skin full of wrinkles the bones of your skull stand out.

The Path of the Wind

Alfonso Chase
Translated by Charles Philip Thomas

To Olga de Echandi.

I know I have to follow the path of the wind.
—Yolanda Oreamuno

And we began the trip in the morning: me, my father, and my brothers. My mother stayed at home. And the trees spread out, green and tall, with immense flowers and crowned by clouds. And we began the trip, all of us full of sadness for having left behind what we had and not knowing what was going to belong to us. And the skies were opening up, and looking upward you got dizzy and the sounds of the carts clattering over the town's paving stones and it was all being left behind, lost in the distance, and I could only remember my cousin's scarves, and my mother's. And I was riding on the top of the cart, with my toy soldiers and straw dolls and the book of old stamps and my hands in my lap, and my sparkling eyes devouring the countryside, pale at the beginning, but more restored perhaps as soon as I finally got used to the movement of the cart and to everyone's silence.

And the trip began in the morning and the hours were long and the days rolled into one and rain didn't fall and the nights were the same as days because of the monotonous sound of the insects, because of the wild craziness of the cicadas, and because of the joy of our running into Luis Esteban Curti, who on the way would keep telling us about talking plants, trees that rose off the ground, and golden eggs sometimes to be found in the corral. And we continued onward to the north and me always in the top part, or feeling the rays of the sun and the moon, and grabbing flowers by just reaching out my hand, listening to what the man was saying to us and thinking about the hot coffee and the mint and the corn fritters, about the sound that the water made on the roof, about those foggy early mornings, about the fact that I'm always awake or I sleep, occasionally, in my father's arms, or near our new friend, who would whistle at night and calm the insect noise with his voice, or prepare us lotions against bites and aromatic smoke from leaves to frighten off the wild animals. And the trip went on and on and there weren't any houses along the road, and we drank water that fell from the sky, boiled in large tubs, and we ate greens or fruit, like birds. And dawn fell on all our eyes and afternoon was at hand, held back by a few words from Luis Esteban, and my father feeling jealous of my affection for the new friend and my brothers envying the conversations that they couldn't have and the hand games that he taught me and the sounds that he could make by whistling and the herbs that I began to collect. And my friend now slept near me and at night I would feel it when he would get up and walk among the trees and if I stayed awake I could hear him talk with the forest animals. And our arrival at where we were going was being delayed and the days got mislaid and my friend taught me tricks and new words and sounds to practice with my lips, and body exercises to make my chest grow, make my waist thinner, and increase the size of my arms, and to raise my arms high up with my fingers completely flexed and to sit down rapidly and blend into the trees and speak with the animals and I began to feel that my father was enjoying scolding me and that my brothers were not giving me enough food, or they were getting on my nerves over Luis Esteban, and he would say nothing and only look at them with his clear, frightened eyes, and we would go to bathe in the river, my friend and I, naked and happy, while my brothers would grumble and my father, very pensive, would beat the oxen with his whip.

And the trip continued and my pants got smaller and the nights began to be different from the days, and the darkness was becoming accustomed to my eyes seeing farther than the shadows and my brothers were looking at me with hatred and my father with indifference, and I understood that there was nothing between us any longer and that the beginning of the trip was only a distant memory, lost between the roof tiles of the house and the distance between them and the sky. And one day my brothers said that they had seen Luis Esteban taking a bath and that he had a tail, and that he lived for hours and hours under the water, submerged in search of something but they didn't know what it was, and my father asked me if my friend had a tail and I told him no, and he said how did I know and I answered that we took baths together. And the trip continued on a road full of trees that fell from the sky and water that appeared by merely touching the rocks, and my brothers were afraid of me and they were saying so to my father who didn't say anything, but I knew that he was also afraid of my hands but most of all of my eyes. Luis Esteban would disappear at night and he found us later, in the morning, some miles farther on, fresh and happy, as if being born from the grass and trees. I was able to do many things now with my body: twist it until I made myself like an arch, my arms were strong and I could walk on my hands, in the trees I could walk like the monkeys and naked I could encircle my body with my legs until I touched my back with my feet. And the trip went on and on as if we were going in circles and every day I learned something from my friend, and we slept together, as if to protect ourselves, and I realized that I was getting farther and farther from my brothers and my father and they insisted that my friend had a tail and they spoke among themselves and would murmur like rats smelling garbage and they said that during the night birds and lights would flutter near our mats and all of us would be tense and now we weren't speaking to each other and we almost didn't look at each other and now for me there was no longer a trip or trees and I was just going along looking at the sky and one night I realized that I was alone and I woke up completely and heard noises and screams in the forest and when I saw his body beaten to a pulp I cried bitterly and my brothers washed the clubs in the nearby water and my father didn't say anything and the following day the stuff broke out all over my oldest brother and they began to rot, one after the other, and my father was afraid and killed the oxen and there they were, everyone rotting away except my father and I wasn't saying anything because I couldn't speak and I felt as if I didn't have anything in my body now and they would not die from their putrefaction and they smelled horrible and people who arrived covered their noses and near the river, dry now, they erected a cross like those from Caravaca, and women came who went to bed with my brothers, covering their noses. And children were born and adobe houses were built and I continued wandering at night through the town and nobody said anything to me, but everyone crossed themselves and the nights came and went and I was still living on the top of the cart, with my tin soldiers and my straw animals until I began to do handsprings and sleight-of-hand tricks and spread out the cards like Luis Esteban did, and I went from plaza to plaza moving away from everyone and I'm telling you all this, my friend, on this trip where we've met each other, it's the same one that Luis Esteban Curti told me, one starless night, when I was a boy like you are now, and making the trip in the same way you are now: perched on the top of the cart and between the tin soldiers and the plastic figurines, with pockets full of cookies and books and the night outside. As if it belonged to us.

Burned Soldiers

José Ricardo Chaves
Translated by Leland H. Chambers

Que tu brilles, terme pur de ma course!
—Valéry, "Fragments du Narcisse"

Narciso knew that he could not fail. The lives of many men depended on the success of his action, he thought, so that if he were to give himself the luxury of being unsuccessful and in that way allow a victory to the enemy, it would be only a symbolic victory, so to speak, which in just a few days would be changed around into a defeat. But it was not for that reason, for those few hours of the adversary's triumph—at the cost of the extermination of his companions—that it ceased to affect him psychically. The big, old hacienda house where the invaders were concentrated was the focus of his anxiety, of that heroic rage of one who must prevail. The defeat of that handful of men, Narciso's commando group, would be translated into a step forward for the opponents, the mercenaries. The liberation of that hacienda, the destruction of the arsenal that was there in the white house of wood and brick, had priority. The bursts of fire from the machine guns had quieted the birds with iridescent plumage that, hours before, at dawn, had been chirping and singing in those tropical trees surrounding the house and that stretched to the north through the jungle, miles of heat, mosquitoes, and a sticky dampness, the sweat of interminable lifetimes in search of the enemy, with weariness accumulating day by day, with the fear of being ambushed and themselves becoming the fallen.

Nonetheless the fear was not so strong as to hold Narciso back. The conviction that History was his tutor offered him an antidote that was enough to control his fear of death. The feeling of being right constituted a cooling balm for that always open wound—the consciousness that at any moment he might stop thinking, feeling, running, shooting, to become merely a part of the landscape, a body tossed out in this damp jungle that so rapidly putrefies corpses and swells them with pus and fetid odors.

Narciso had almost managed to reach the big house. He only needed to crouch down and slip past the unprotected shed and blow up the arsenal. A few seconds more and he would at least manage to get to the mansion. And he made it. He himself couldn't believe it. But the work was not finished yet. He would doubtless have to kill a few more and fix it so the place would be blown to smithereens and he could get out alive. He was sure to be lucky. In an upsurge of optimism, in the midst of that very serious situation, of bursts of gunfire that cut through the wood like a saw, of the utmost nervous tension, he thought of her, of his wife, Jacinta, and he saw her far away, grieving, but he tried not to see her any longer, and so returned to his fear, the expectation, and suddenly he felt a trembling in his legs, an abrupt nausea that threatened to make him vomit, all of which notwithstanding didn't prevent him from shooting in all directions, up, down, right, left, in a kind of death rattle that made him want to throw out into the world this terror that was lacerating him so thoroughly.

He had seen his enemy, or rather, a shadow, a bulk that he intuited as such. That was what he shot at. He didn't hear a groan but on the other hand he did hear shouts of warning and footsteps on the wood floor. He had only a few seconds before firing back and surely dying. Suddenly a roar was heard that seemed to pulverize everything, Narciso included, and then came the heat, the collapse, the fire. Everything that had not caved in was very soon consumed by the conflagration that followed the explosion. Stunned for several seconds down in the rubble, with fire in his clothing and on his skin, but moved by an animal's primary biological terror, Narciso succeeded in getting up very painfully, though he was rapidly being consumed, and ran outside despite the bullets that might reach him there: a rapid death, not the pyre.

He thought he perceived the other, someone he surely would have had to kill or who must have shot at Narciso, also getting up, like him, from amid the burning wood and pieces of the partition wall, and also like him with his face nearly veiled by the fire. The two human torches ran through the field looking for a merciful bullet or the water of the puddles in which the mosquitoes were reproducing, WATER!, yes, WATER!, something that would pacify this pain. As if guided by a single instinct for survival, the bodies succeeded in reaching the dock and falling into the river, from which they were rescued by some of those on Narciso's side. The mission was brought to a successful ending, since the enemy base had been destroyed. Even the body count had turned out in their favor: fourteen of the opponents to three from the army. Several wounded, and among those the two burned men. What they pulled from the water were two pieces of flesh, two twisting masses from which any personal trait had disappeared. Nose, lips, cheeks, all this and more had become mixed together indistinctly, eliminating any peculiar mark. The uniforms, totally consumed, did not allow them to distinguish which was which, and the only thing that was known for sure was that one of the burned men was Narciso. But which one? It was a matter of some interest to know which was the hero and which the traitor.

The two bodies were of like stature and similar complexion. Nothing allowed them to be distinguished. It wasn't long before a helicopter took them to a hospital in which they were both taken care of without the least delay. No one thought they would be able to survive in such a condition, but they made it nonetheless. Little by little, in the face of the physicians' disbelief, the bodies began to recuperate, the wounds to heal over, like two fleshy swamp plants that refused to die, though not without consequences. The bodies were unable to speak, to see, perhaps even to hear, and they depended completely on the others to be moved around and transferred from place to place. Stretched out on makeshift beds, they needed someone else's help to be fed. From their mouths surged moans, grunts, but no words.

The attempts to distinguish between the hero and the traitor were useless. Those animated dolls seemed not to allow such a thing. Gradually they recovered certain movements, to extend their arms, to sit up, but they never ceased to be marionettes guided by an external will. A Jewish nurse who followed the whole process of slow and double recovery was unable to avoid seeing in the two bodies a kind of wretched sham, frustrated *golems* in which the divine breath would no longer shine.

One morning a woman arrived at the hospital. She gave her name as Jacinta and said that she had come for Narciso. After weeks of uncertainty she had learned that he was there. She had had to wander through many offices and past a great number of little windows before finding this out, just as she had to do all over again later on in order to get permission to visit. She said she was Narciso's woman, not his wife. Accompanied by a doctor and two officers, Jacinta was taken before the two bodies, of which one might say at that moment, were it not for their breathing, that they were dead, so pronounced was their immobility and their inattention to this world. After a few minutes the woman began to cry, unable to tell which of them was Narciso, but declaring just the same that he was here in this room, that she felt him, that he was one of them but she didn't know which. In actuality what she felt was that Narciso was in both bodies, separated, divided, but she didn't say this for fear of being considered a lunatic. Instead she proposed the idea of taking the two bodies home for a while while she figured out who was who.

The idea did not displease the doctors, overloaded as they were with the sick and the wounded, though it bothered the military officials a little since it meant that a prisoner of war would leave their custody. Nevertheless they ended by accepting it, since the state of both men was so nonfunctional that it would never allow them to take flight or anything like that. Meanwhile, they would celebrate the heroism of the soldier with a parade through the streets of the small city, so full of military cloaks with political insignias and legends, with the faces of revolutionary demigods. Since the hero's identity was unclear, both blind, deaf bodies were put on show, propped up by soldiers before the bustle of the crowd, in a horse-drawn carriage and accompanied by the sounds from a band of musicians. Jacinta felt proud of Narciso. For the first time, she kissed the two faceless faces, those fistfuls of twisted flesh and eyes whose gaze was absent. "Narciso," she said, and kissed one of them. "Narciso," she repeated, and kissed the other.

The two men were transferred to Jacinta's house. She tended to them as if they were children, solicitous in all the details of cleanliness, clothing, and food, which she prepared in a very personal way and put directly into their mouths. Strange expressions sketched themselves on their faces, which were interpreted by Jacinta as smiles. This filled her with satisfaction. The tenderness that invaded her at times was shaken by the idea of finally discovering which of them was Narciso. This perturbed her exceedingly, since if it was really true that she loved him, she was also certain that she had become very fond of both bodies. In reality, for her they were nothing but Narciso himself, her very beloved, twice over. Breaking with either one of them was to eliminate half of her love. Considerations of an ideological kind, the patriotic aspects, carried no weight in Jacinta's soul. She had suffered enough during the days Narciso was at the warfront and after the explosion, when she knew nothing of his whereabouts. No. She would never be separated from him again: from them. It was better, she said, to have a surplus of Narciso than that a single piece of him should be missing.

Jacinta recalled Narciso's taste for smoking black cigars. So she bought a box of them and one afternoon she lit one and placed it in that mockery of a mouth, in that living orifice, and the bluish smoke began to inundate the room. She did the same with the other man, who also smoked. From that day on, Jacinta would light a pair of cigars at sunset and put them in the mouths of her puppets and she would laugh with them, each in his own rocking chair; sometimes she caressed the tufts of hair that grew from their skulls like islands in an archipelago, and she would watch the sun go down and become hidden from that blueness which the twilight rays were washing in shady hues.

Without realizing it, Jacinta was gradually growing fonder of one of the men, the one that made more grimaces, the one that smiled more, she said. When she washed him, her hands were not stingy with caresses, and that was why when she was washing him one morning she discovered, not without surprise, that his deformed flesh still reacted, and on gazing at that erect mushroom she had thought forever withered, she left the room fearfully. That night (and other nights) this image would come back into her mind and bring on a powerful inner ardor. That was how her passion, which at the outset she felt distributed equitably, gradually slipped little by little toward one of the men, even though both were still Narciso.

Nevertheless, the excluded one was not unaware of the change. It is not that he suffered any bad treatment. No, of course not. Jacinta continued being lavish in her attentions toward both of them, but it was only with the one that she felt this strange electricity which bothered her so, though in a fashion that never ceased to be agreeable. The other one, with a kind of vegetable sensitivity, gradually gesticulated less and less and spent many hours curled up on his bed, like a sick bird. It was only when several days had passed that Jacinta began to worry, but the process seemed irreversible: grief, increasing. He did not smoke anymore at sunset.

The puppet's grief was soon Jacinta's grief as well. The only thing that revived her was the other's gesturing, his timid movements like a large baby's. "Narciso is healing," she thought, and was unable to avoid pouncing on him and lighting a cigar. The very morning that dawned with one of puppets dead, the grieving one, the other began to stutter something that seemed like words. Once more a great grief was being compensated by a great joy. While she was weeping, Jacinta laughed, too. She didn't move the dead one from his bed. She approached the stammering one and as she embraced him she called him "Narciso, Narciso." Her happiness caused her to break out in bursts of nervous laughter, and while she held the gesturing one up in a grotesque dance she felt once again that flesh growing against her own, and for the first time the puppet uttered some clear words: "I'm not Narciso."

At that moment, Jacinta heard another voice, not the one she was expecting, not the one she had so often dreamed of hearing. She stopped holding up the body, which fell heavily to the floor. Beyond it, on top of the other bed, the other body remained rolled up into a ball. Several hours went by before Jacinta was able to say anything, so disturbed was she.

Notwithstanding, the light of the setting sun seemed to make her calmer. Then she placed the two men, not without effort, in their rocking chairs. After that she sprinkled gasoline in all the rooms of the house, over the furniture, in the corners. With a match she lit the fire at the opposite end from where the puppets were. Then she ran back and sat down in the third rocking chair, midway between the mute one and the stammerer, the still one and the gesturing one, the living and the dead. Before the fire reached her the smoke did, and there was the sunset behind the picture window, and Jacinta waited for the end, the blue fire and warm smoke coming closer, while she heard the dull, shaky voice saying, over and over again, as if in a song being sung by a retarded child, "I'm not Narciso, I'm not Narciso."

Funeral Rites in Summer

Carlos Cortés
Translated by Pamela Carmell

He was in the coffin and his head looked like a hog's head. Huge and pale pink and swollen. In each nostril there was a cotton plug. I saw just his head. Somebody from the funeral party was taking pictures. Magmarión's testicles were enormously large and they had gotten stuck in the bathtub drain. Africa hadn't heard his shouts. Magmarión was at the beach house where Africa had made and had birthed all her offspring and kinfolk. The beach house was made of fired clay and Africa was a woman darkened by the sea of years. She wasn't a frivolous woman. Her first son, Magmarión's, was named Monday. Africa was a dark woman, a foil for the blond streaks and blond lights of a dawn in bed. Her mane was chestnut-streaked, a zig-zag of color falling somewhere between honey and stirred-up straw. It wasn't red, except suddenly, abruptly, between twilight and the gallop of the fireflies that crossed the sky like lightning wrapped around her collar once or twice. Hers was a bronzed whiteness. Magmarión loved her with a crazy passion. I met her very briefly, but that one time was enough.

Africa had a collection of anacondas in her house. Milky Way was the best cerastes of all. Her horns were silvery and very pointed, despite the summer pruning. Africa, dressed in bright white and stockings, looked like another wall of breaking waves brimming over with memory and the absence of a satisfied solitude, conquered again in bed. I looked at the sea in her eyes. Bahía Blanca, in twilight by now, was a cliff full of lights. At that time, I lived in the south, next to the docks of Almirante and Port Armuelles. In those days my father worked at the Chiriquí Land Company, and we crossed the inland sea to meet Magmarión and Africa.

On the trip, we took along as provisions a complement of books by Plutarch and Volney, *Amazing Detectives*, and *Look*. My father's erudition was dense. We unpacked in the rain and slept that dawn in the sawmill. I was still trembling all over when Africa woke us the next morning. The talk was that the blond woman would breakfast on coffee and bone marrow. My memory is like plaster, lapis lazuli, stucco. It is like an old cerebral mausoleum. Everything is stored there, intact and in place, but the incantations are missing to decerebralize the chambers of that dusty whiteness, the slits in the light and time, in the fog of antiquity.

My father got off the mare. We understood that dawn serenity very well. Africa was walking around dressed in trousers. She led us to the porch and from there to the parlor. Piled up on both sides of the bookcase were fish, small lizards, transparent insects, and books in German, Africa's native language. I felt dwarfed in the midst of that natatorial activity in the rain with day just coming on. We swam toward the living room and we felt we were going right into the wolf's mouth. My God, we were still just entering the corridors of the dawn. I let my mind ramble in lapses, feigned attacks, and catacombs. We went in and swam against the gulf current. Because of that, we made very slow progress in questioning Africa and her servants. In the living room was Magmarión, untouched and exquisitely white, dead. Outside, an ocean of rain boiled around our mounts and our gear.

Papa was and will always be a butcher and that's why they called on him. We moved in unison, like twins, in cream-colored shirts and felt top hats on our heads. Anyway, I was wearing long sleeves to protect against the blood. In the past year, although not every day, I had practiced my carving skills along the rocky edge of the Bahía Blanca, before the deluge. In the confusion back home, I had gone into my grandparents' closet, and they gave me a sheet and several shirts for the days and open countryside to come. That night and dawn when we arrived in Almirante, crossing the open mouth of Port Armuelles all the way to the delta of Chiriquí and the broad velvet beaches of Terciopelo and Punta Catedral, I said a prayer to my Guardian Angel, my sweet companion. We crossed at intervals. Walking to New Castle, I counted thirty-three houses along the way. After the trip, there was the matter of finding Milky Way and Magmarión and his offspring. Papa looked over his armory and found their blades intact and their balance unswerving. Nothing was amiss. Papa dressed several times and the third time he took off his shirt and stood there, naked from the navel up. Without a single excessive gesture nor a single abrupt movement, he split Magmarión's khaki shirt, which we then tossed in the trash. We didn't want to leave any evidence. Papa always thought about human foibles. We were sure we would find a wound or find him in the state of decomposition that lands someone in court. But there was nothing like that. Magmarión was a mountain of a man, a fort. "That's what happens to people as crude as he was," said Gabino, my papa. "That's what happens to people, to houses, to the countryside, to the living and the dead, friend and foe. You'd better get used to the truth of the lie."

Following Africa's directions, we tried to get Magmarión's body out of the swamp and, as my father said, eventually to disembowel it. Time was hounding us, and the rain too. There was a lot of water in the house and drop by drop the living room was turning into a rotting mess everywhere. When I got to the body, Papa's hands were already stained. There wouldn't be anything for me to do, but I wanted to get my hands dirty too. The first thing I noticed were Magmarión's long, yellow toenails and the soles of his feet that looked like giant, olive-colored tamales. He was a great big son-of-a-bitch, I said to myself.

Then Papa began. Magmarión's mouth could have swallowed Papa's whole body. The anaconda submerges herself in the soft flesh, but nothing else. Then she comes up, no longer submerged all the way, and stays there chewing on the small intestines. Digestively and ceremoniously, the cerastes swallows the organs that contain death. I talk to her, no one else notices, and our breathing meets, her mouth and mine. Papa isn't completely finished. The carcass doesn't resist because Africa, knowing about Magmarión's deeds and his evil ways, uses ointments for just that reason. Then they bring us some tin cans that had had lard in them where the salty, stringy innards of Magmarión the Good will be deposited for eternity. So the lard cans will be holding more lard, then.

There weren't a lot of widows during the summer ceremonies, but Africa has kept on in watchful mourning and follows Papa's knife strokes with inverse precision. The anaconda has done its savage work. Papa studies me triply hard, I'm sure, and I nod because you can't waste a minute on things like these. Pestilence gets spread around with the rain. I look at my hands and they are filthy, but my father's will be even more stained from the sin of inserting his hands into the body. Soiled by cleanliness. At noon the moon comes up and the drizzle covers us all, but it is very cold. Father goes on cutting and cutting, with no one's help. Africa is still standing like a widow and mother. I take over weighing the pieces and keeping the cats away, but it's a hard job. Finally, Papa takes out the shrunken liver and I see that the legend is true, that Magmarión spent his life drinking. I heft the liver in my hand and the cat wants the prize for himself. I splash behind him. I'm sure everyone has noticed. The women want a piece of Magmarión's liver and they snatch it away and the guts roll around in the mud. The cat and his pals grab and lap up what they can. I get there to recover what few humors remain. I put them in the can of rancid lard and close it, disgusted. The revelry has quieted down. Africa covers her face with her hands for the first time when Papa holds up Magmarión's still warm heart. It's a miracle but Africa is a wizard of miracles. Papa passes it over to me and I measure the muscle with my fists, but it has already lost its color from coming in contact with the cold sea air. There are just a few chambers to check over and to fill up with ointment. When asked, the old women bring thread to close up and they pour salt all over. I bump into the mourners. Papa has disappeared and has gone way down into Magmarión's now clean body. When he comes out, he has a gold key for Africa, a legacy from extinct gods. Papa plugs up the mouth and lays several coins on the spectral sockets. Night enters the room and candles appear too. The light is faint and I try not to fall on top of the dead man. For the first time, Papa is mopping off the sweat with his dirty hands. Finally, there are the gigantic testicles to be gathered up and divided among Africa and Magmarión's sons, as it is written. But that will be done after the funeral. For now the cadaver shines in the light of the bonfires on the beach and the downpour has calmed down. The anacondas are in a frenzy and Africa calms them with her nails, flatulence, and animal fat. Papa is paid with the last measure of deference: Magmarión's silver palate and some gold teeth that Papa extracted. Papa now fills Magmarión's mouth with linen and cotton. Then he leaves the stitching to me. I tug on the thread to find the perfect one, because the mouth has become fetid and stiff. No one helps me. I feel terror in my icy hands. In the shadow of the ceremony I see the shadowy markings on his cranium, the ossifying of his breath. The body moves and even tries to get up, but it's just my hands, trembling and fighting against the shadows. The water has stopped falling; what's more, the twilight is worthy of the gods.

The funeral will be at nightfall and in silence, so that no one will learn the exact grave site. Africa designates two or three young sons to die with their father. Others take off running and disappear. The widows grow black before the whitewashed pale of the walls. Magmarión is finally ready for death's wood frame. Papa returns with yards of straw, the finishing touches for the small coffin. The body has been reduced to just under five feet. The embalmer's strategy. I endure the smell and the nausea while I adjust by hand an old tooth that has fallen from the procession. Because I drew the thread too tight, Magmarión's pleasant expression stands out from the shadows to curse us. Few things remain. Africa embraces her living sons and the living mausoleum walks toward the waters. The beach is empty and white. Some fireflies and two men, their mouths covered, show up at the fire. I have lost track of time, but it is night. The sun has gone down. Papa wipes off his body in the milky foam of the balsam. Behind us stands the echoless cliff. The throng of widows has sacrificed an anaconda, but Africa doesn't say anything. We circle round the oily depths of the lagoon. By day, the boas and I will swim through these pools in search of a catch, but now the funeral procession, like a sacred crocodile, follows the wake of light on the water. The heat burns us. I feel the suffocating and electrified breeze. I blink and tears stream down my face but Papa doesn't take notice of it. I see his face and it looks carved in ivory from the effect of the sun. He is visibly tired but satisfied, reflecting on his triumph before the worms. Africa now invokes all Magmarión's ancestors. It is the high point complete with fireworks. One or two fiery blasts streak the space. Black butterflies flutter around at the bottom of the burial mound. No one is sobbing. The silence covers us, while, little by little, the funeral ropes sink the lifeless body of Magmarión into the pus of the earth.

The Trunk

Fabián Dobles
Translated by Leland H. Chambers

They didn't have to knock down the door of his hut. He never bothered to put up the bar. He lived with his dog who was so old he only barked sitting down, lived amid his patches of corn, yucca, and banana, amid the grunting of a few pigs and the warmth of a couple of cows who gave birth every year just so the jaguar would have some more calves to devour.

"Did you want something, amigos?"

"Stand up. You're under arrest!" The soldier with the narrow brow was threatening him.

"So that's what it is. And may I ask how come?"

"Orders from above," said the guard with the bulging eyes.

"Oh, shit. And they let the three of you come for just one man!"

With some cord they tied him to a post outside and began to search through everything. They turned his meager belongings inside out, his big sleeping mat, the roofing thatch, some old letters they found in an earthenware jug and kept; and when they came to the trunk squatting in a corner beneath a frayed throw and asked him for the key, the man, shrugging his shoulders, said from where he was standing still tied up that he had lost it years ago.

"We're gonna to have to take it with us anyway, but it's so heavy."

It really was heavy, heavy as seven devils. Then they untied the prisoner to help them carry it out to the old gun carriage that had wandered up to his hut so long ago. Afterward they made him hitch up his oxen and go with them to where their military jeep was waiting.

Little by little he was leaving the mountains behind, the clearing where he worked without fences, without anyone looking over his shoulder, or anything else.

The third soldier, the one who was missing an ear, thought they'd never had any dealings with a more courageous farmer.

He sat down and placed his hat between his feet. Facing him at the desk was the major, who had just finished speaking. Beside him were the guards, and a secretary with a typewriter.

He glanced at the clear sky for a few moments, then at the walls, finally at the military nose in front of him. His fifty years of sturdy bones sat erect on the chair and his hands were resting on his thighs, long and thin as poles.

"Your name?" said the major.

"Gervasio González, sir."

"Second name?"

"Isn't any. I don't need one."

"ID card?"

"Don't have that neither. That's the truth, sir."

"The charge is smuggling, but you already know that we're after something else."

"Whatever you say, sir. All I do is take care of my farm and try to stay alive."

"Hmm . . . farming . . ."

"Sir," the man with the narrow brow put in, "maybe the body of the deceased is in the trunk."

"And if it's worth as much as it weighs, it's gotta be worth a fortune," said the one-eared one.

"Shall we open it up?"

"Oh, yes. Go ahead, boys."

And they went at it with hammers.

And started taking things out. First, an axe. Gervasio's eyes shone; his mouth tightened.

"That was Feliciano's, my oldest son. He'd be about thirty now—" and his toes were twitching down below. "You can't trust a falling tree, everyone knows that, don't they sir? He got crushed by one."

"What's this other thing?"

The soldiers were unfolding it.

"Turn it so I can see it . . . Oh, yeah, Lucinda's First Communion veil. Some guy made a fool of her, it was Mr. Foster, he was the boss at the lumber export company, and she ended up on the streets."

When the major saw what came next he shivered and his nose grew sharper.

"Oh yeah, what you're looking at there's a little skull. Just what it looks like. I dug it up to keep it because I loved her so much. She was the youngest, her name was Angel."

"And this apron?"

"Who else? That was my wife's. She finally passed away from nursing the little one that died. Never went without it." And his Adam's apple jerked up and down within his lean, stringy neck.

"Didn't you find any newpapers, magazines? Just that garbage?" the major asked the guards.

"No, we looked all through it."

"I have reports that this man is going around making an ass of himself and putting ideas into the farmers' heads . . . We already found that out."

Meanwhile the one whose eyes seemed to be bursting out of their sockets pulled one more thing out of the trunk.

"Major, sir, look what it was that weighed so much."

Which gave a rusty clinking as it curled up on the ground.

"Chains?"

"Made of iron, there they are, sir, real thick ones. The lumber company left 'em behind, out in the forest," and the farmer's eyes softened somewhat as he explained, all his bones and the tendons of his face growing taut: "I tossed 'em in the bottom of the trunk, threw my memories on top, and dropped the key in the river. Those're the fucking chains that weigh us down, that's the truth, sir . . . Ignorance, poverty . . . The day we shake them off . . ."

"Quiet! You have no respect for authority! Secretary, get all this stuff back in the trunk and write out the complaint for the judge. Right now!"

"The crime, sir?"

"Preaching revolution. Didn't you hear it?"

Floral Caper

Carmen Naranjo
Translated by Charles Philip Thomas

Flowers and flowers and more flowers, he had to place them on the floor of the corridors, in the kitchen, in the bathroom, because the dining room, the living room, and the entrance hall in front could no longer take any more baskets, vases, bouquets that didn't have vases, the receptacles were filled up and the neighbors said thank you and thank you but it was enough with the eighteen arrangements that he had palmed off on them. The door knocker never quit and here you go, is there a wedding?, and now someone is knocking again, but they can knock till they die, there isn't room for any more.

Faced with each one of the first hundred bouquets he impatiently wondered why, there was no reason, he was an unknown, a newcomer without status, a person who nowhere else had received even a simple welcome, save for the anonymous impersonal, ragingly cold ones on the streets and in the airports. He argued the impossibility of it all, but that vanished in the face of the perfect coincidence of the name and the address. But so many, so many flowers, not even possible for his funeral, he had fingers to spare when he counted his few friends spread out in time and distance, none of whom had the means to buy flowers, nor the mind to do it, and there was also the fact that they did not know about that hidden hatred, so intimate, of the petals, the aromas, the corollas, the declaiming beauty of the roses, of the gladioli, of the tulips, of the violets, of the wildflowers in the fields, because he would shut his eyes in the presence of gardens, he would flee from comparisons with the fragrance and grace of those inanimate things that in cowardly ways soften the hard, deformed, and sickening face that underlies everything.

To hell with the flowers but they were there, where they neither fit
nor were wanted, in spite of that so secret eagerness for welcomes, for
warmth, a simple point of support and nothing more. He was drowning,
the asthma, the sneezes, the knowledge that the air was escaping, they
were stealing it from him, besides inundating him, throwing him out of
his house with more contemptuousness than the distrust he was always
running into because he had his eyes open too wide, or he wasn't the
gracious type, or they didn't give him time to retouch the photographs
that the others made of him. Never, that's the reproach, never the
affirmation, neither the I nor the you in relief. Actually, it's already late,
an afternoon of flowers that he doesn't understand and that perseverance
in knocking at the door to saturate him with garbage and more garbage,
because that's what they are after all, garbage of frivolous adornments,
of undefined messages, the language of queers, symbols of cowardice,
and the amusement of hypocritical show-offs. Also a passport, because
they're never cheap, they're always expensive, flowers aren't just given
away, ordinary ones were never sent, it's a matter of the special ones and
afterward come the accept-me, the invoices for the favor, the keep-me-
in-mind.

Fury set the flowers alight, and their colors became an extravagance
of noisy swelling in paints and aromas, until reaching the blast of
greatest aesthetic quality with the natural overflow of a humid splendor,
undeniable, perfumed, in keeping with the roundness that the absolute
generosity of a perfect fruit acquires, the child, the fingernail, the bullet,
the skeleton, and even more beautiful because the withering will have
a rhythm of withdrawal in the obvious conundrum implied by the
expressive, bountiful beauty that used to be.

Invasion, that was all, a planned invasion of his ridiculous property,
completely someone else's or simply rented, whatever you want to call
it, because his space was a transparent thing that belonged to him insofar
as it didn't belong to others, like a sign impossible to draw because it had
a color not foreseen in the whole spectrum, or because one has not
understood a signal that is common to the others, or because everything
was filled and surpassed like an entire being that wanted to make itself
comfortable with his name and a vague legacy of half-formed thoughts
that can't be written and communicated since they're incomplete, and
that is his only legitimacy, his absolute identification of inconclusive
permanency.

Perhaps at the beginning surprise overtook his own confirmations,
but now that there were so many and people were continuing to knock
on the door, they were getting in his way more and more, they begrudged
him his own little space, now the problem of time had already resolved
it with a certain ease: it was a matter of being born every day, of going

without breakfast the lactation of bad memories, to have the midday orgy with the musculature of complete lasciviousness in order to abuse an organization put to the service of the glandular ceremony, then to arrive in late afternoon with that agony which gives the sensation of having cut off its own wings for a flight that behind the illusion of the trip had only a catastrophic goal, and then to enter into the night with the baggage of death that envelops an orphaned Our Father and a feather-brained Hail Mary, in order to dig into the insomnia and say to himself without hope, I'm awake in a sleeping world in the face of the moon's changing humor, of the graveyard traveler of the stars, and of the somnambulant path of rotund suns over the shoulder of an unfortunate man with an inconsolable pity for himself and a frightful fear of discovering his poverty without a possible magic mirror that would smile when he smiles and laugh when he laughs.

But the flowers could be something worse, melted caramels to kill the recipe of cream and sugar, chocolate and vanilla, or small bubbles without much vitality, or packages in ribbons and bows for a noise of broken glass, or marijuana smoke that the others are happily inhaling, or litanies of consolation in front of closed doors with banquet echoes, or anonymous Christs who exalt the ordinariness of suffering. However, they were just flowers and flowers, with their tranquil perfumes and their beautiful petals ready to symbolize everything false, everything eternally false, everything validly false.

When he realized the punishment, he made a barricade in the street with roses and carnations to the fore, white lilies and tulips on the flanks, and a lot of daisies signaling the transporting from one side to the other of the baskets, arrangements, and bouquets with gladioli and broken-off irises. Not one flower remained in the house, all of them outside in the middle of the street, together with the last deliveries made by the devoted messengers, totally convinced that they had seen insanity flower. Afterward he slept very tranquilly, like the characters in short stories sleep, without knowing if they brush their teeth, use pajamas, go to bed in a bed, lean back in a corner, if they tell stories before going to bed or fall asleep right away because the verb is magic.

The following morning he received a medal with three suns adorning a single sunflower of a certain size, on behalf of the grateful citizenry for that incalculable effort of beautifying the street. Besides, a decree signed by the governor in recognition of his initiative, an order to have his photograph taken of him smiling, from mid-breast up, that would be placed in the pavilion of notables, and an invitation to lecture on flowers in the place designated for city festivals.

Oh, the flowers, the flowers, the blessed flowers, those country elves, that explosion of happiness, that unequaled generosity of the earth, that game of love for which they love you so much, a little, or not at all.

When the invoices arrived with the evidence of his own orders, his own requests, his own doing, he smiled to himself with the exactness of an open rose. After many days it wilted; maybe he confided too much in the splendor, for it always ends up lasting only for a while, perhaps a very little while.

Disobedience

Julieta Pinto
Translated by Charles Philip Thomas

She waited all month for the signal that she wasn't pregnant. She drank cup after cup of camomile and sour cane, all alone she lifted the heavy stone for grinding corn when she could never get up enough energy to move it on other occasions. She swept the house twice a day and then she sprinkled water that she had brought in an empty lard can so heavy that when she climbed the hill she felt her arms would fall off. The damp dirt floor didn't let the dust escape but she continued in her zeal to rub the table and the chairs as if instead of dust she sought to strip away the color of the wood.

The children were amazed by such activity and took advantage by climbing on her shoulders and playing horsey-back while shouting to her "Giddyap, giddyap, horsey, faster, run and we'll give you a sugar cube!" After several races she would fall on the cool grass, damp from sweat and her cheeks burning. They laughed and tickled her until they were able to get her on her feet and continue the game. Porfirio said nothing. He watched her out of the corner of his eye like a child who has done something bad and doesn't dare to look you in the eye. One day when she came in with the youngest children hanging on and her face as flushed as the wildflowers that the oldest girl was carrying, he dared to say, "You're going to miscarry, Paula." She looked at him with such severity that he lowered his eyes and didn't dare say anything else.

The first month passed, then the second, and she cried bitterly from the fear that had turned into certainty. Since that night she had continued to sleep with the children and he hadn't dared to say anything. After two months she returned to his bed and told him that she was sure she was going to have a baby and hadn't been able to get rid of it. Her voice was so distressed that it spread to him, and he cursed the drinks he had had on Good Friday.

It had been his brother-in-law Ernesto's fault. He was buying milk at the Ledezma's dairy when Ernesto whispered in his ear: "Follow me, old man, and you won't regret it." He forgot that Paula needed milk right away to make bread and followed him.

In the cool spring in back of the house, Ernesto had a small hogskin sack and several bottles of clear liquid. "Take a drink, you're my *compadre*, and we ain't never celebrated being friends." At the sight of the bottles he forgot that it was Good Friday, that he had to return home soon, and wiping his mouth with the back of his hand he raised the bottle.

His eyes filled with tears and he controlled an urge to cough. "This is strong stuff." "D'ya think I was gonna give you any old shit? Have another, that's what you're my *compadre* for." The second drink tasted better, his throat was used to it and it didn't burn as much. The third time he didn't wipe his mouth with the back of his hand but eagerly took the bottle and downed two swigs in a row. "Keep that bottle, I've got more." He couldn't stop until suddenly instead of one Toño he saw two, the spring began to toss around as if it had turned into a snake with scales of foam, and the bottle escaped from his hands and he couldn't manage to stop it. Ernesto broke out in loud laughter and he thought that he should be the offended one. Little by little he stood up, frightened by not being able to catch his balance when the trees began to spin all around. The footpath to the house was moving back and forth, and when he went to take a step he slipped and fell on the side of the road. With eyes wide open so as not to crash against the crazed trees, he continued to advance step by step, while his body lurched from side to side. He discovered that he was walking in the darkness, a darkness that had calmed the trees and hidden the path. It was only the rocks that, like the crumbs of bread in the story that his wife would tell to the kids, led him to a river. As if in a dream he remembered that this was the river where his wife did the wash and if he climbed the hill he would get home. The hill had become so steep that he had to climb it on his hands and knees. He slipped often and lost the progress he had made. He had the urge to go to sleep on the bank of the river, but the desire to be with his wife gave him the strength to continue his climb. A mouthful of fresh air hit him when he was finally able to stand at the top of the hill, and he made out his house a few yards away with the candles already out. His wife was sleeping but he knew how to wake her up, he was sure that afterward she would thank him for it. He arrived staggering in the room and his hands groped her warm body. He took off his clothing with great difficulty and climbed into the bed. "Damn bastard, where did you go, all afternoon I waited for the milk and you never came back. Of course from the smell of your breath now I know what you did." Her voice was soft, almost a whisper so as not to wake the children. He didn't answer but his hands searched for the body that slipped away from him. He didn't understand the words that begged him to leave her in peace because it was Good Friday. The priest had said from the pulpit that during Holy Week they ought to hold off relations between husband and wife, above all on Good Friday, because they might give birth to a monster. On that day God was dead and the devil would make them bear his children. He paid no attention, otherwise why else had he climbed the hill? And by force he satisfied his desire. The following day his wife spoke to him only to say that if she was pregnant and she had a devil it was all his fault. He didn't dare defend himself, his only excuse being that the drinks had made him forget it was Good Friday. "I told you, I told you so many times but you were too drunk and didn't hear me." And she ran crying from the room.

The months kept going by and her belly kept growing. From the third month she began to feel movement and it frightened her. "You see, I've got something strange inside, none of the other little ones moved so soon." "Maybe he'll be stronger than the others." "Of course he ought to be strong, if he's the son of you know who." The pains began in the fourth month, she felt like two hands had opened her hips and left her without air, that they were pushing into her stomach and squeezing her liver and kidneys.

He took her to the doctor, and he found nothing out of the ordinary. She didn't dare tell him about Good Friday because in the city they didn't believe in such things and, least of all, the doctors. She asked him if it wouldn't be better if they took out the baby and the doctor looked at her severely: "Why didn't you think about that before letting yourself become pregnant? An abortion in this month would be fatal." The return trip tired her so much that the following day she wasn't able to get up. Porfirio brought his sister to do the work and the little ones kept getting into the room every second as if they wanted to convince themselves that their mother was in bed.

Paula began to lose the color that had always shone on her cheeks, she ate little, and her eyes sank into two dark circles. "I know that it's devouring me," she told him one night, and when he saw her enormous stomach, he believed it. Several times he thought about bringing in a midwife to remove it, but the doctor's words stopped him.

He didn't take any pleasure in his work. Whichever child appeared he supposed it was bringing news that Paula was worse, that the pains had increased, perhaps that she had died. He didn't greet Ernesto anymore because of the involvement he had in the matter and he even dared to go to church on Sunday with the kids to see if God would forgive him. He hadn't gone back to church since his wedding day. His father had said that that was women's business and so he had believed it. When he returned he was surprised at the face of the Virgin, so beautiful that he contemplated her through the whole Mass. They must have brought in the new figure three years ago when they built the new bell tower. No matter how much Paula insisted that he help in the afternoons on the construction of the towers where they were going to put the bells, he had been foolish and had gone to the general store to play dice. Now he repented; probably such an unfortunate thing wouldn't have happened to him if he had helped.

The last month, Paula couldn't move from a chair. The weight of her stomach was so great that she fell forward if she stood on her feet. Her husband helped her from the bed to the chair, and her sister-in-law had to stay with them until the child was to be born.

She never called it "child," nor even knitted a pair of socks for it. She had told Porfirio that she ought to drown it the moment it was born, that was the only way she could free herself of it. He agreed so as not to contradict her, but he wasn't as sure as she was.

He was cutting a field of chili peppers when they arrived to warn him that Paula's pains had started and that he had to go for the midwife. In his hurry he left the machete in the pasture and took off as fast as he could. He found the old woman ready with the basket of instruments, and he wasn't surprised to hear her say that she expected it today. Paula was screaming when they arrived, and it frightened him to see her neck and face so swollen. Her stomach was moving around as if there were quarreling dogs inside and she screamed with each movement.

"He is going to be a feisty child," the woman said while she put on the water to boil and heated the scissors in the candle flame.

"He's going to be as strong as his father." He was so frightened that he didn't pay any attention to her. He couldn't take his eyes off that moving belly for an instant, and he imagined that below the white skin something black and hairy was struggling with itself. He began to sweat, more from fear than the heat, although the closed room had turned the atmosphere into something unbearable.

"It's so big, it's gonna be real hard for you," the old woman said while she wiped up the sweat with a cloth. "Clench your teeth and push." She tied a thick strap to both sides of the bed while she said, "This is gonna help you push better." The groans had changed into hoarse bellows that increased in intensity. The old woman bent down and stood up satisfied. "Now there's the head, it's a matter of minutes."

He had to sit down in a chair because his trembling legs didn't allow him to stand; his teeth began to chatter against each other without his being able to stop it.

"Don't push, don't push," the old woman shouted. "It's so big it's dangerous if you go too fast." A sad cry filled the room. Paula opened her eyes, and she extended her arms to receive the two fat, white babies that she snuggled tenderly to her breast.

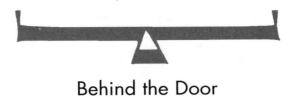

Behind the Door

Uriel Quesada
Translated by Leland H. Chambers

How pretend to be calm? I don't understand anything, I have no idea what the devil I'm doing here! Explain it to me clearly and slowly. I've never been so lost. For the first time I come into this place and those white clouds of gas have me all confused. I'm more worried, though, about the fact that I can't see you. I can guess your presence behind the curtain, but you give the impression of lacking both face and body. However, that's impossible. What could this gas be? Look here, I also feel as though I exist and yet I don't. I hear my voice, but I seem not to exist. I try to look at my arms and legs but I can't break the illusion produced by this gas. Where is it coming from? What kind of establishment is this? It's possible for my memory to fail me. Sometimes they tell me at the office that I'm absentminded. But I can give you the complete facts: "José Luis Figueroa. August 2, 1962. Graduated with honors in Accounting, presently working as an assistant in a publishing concern." Does that seem correct to you? How do you know so much about me? Surely the people in the office must have brought you all this stuff. What more do you want to know? What I did during the last hours? That's really difficult. A Thursday at work doesn't especially produce events to remember. Although . . . yes, there were three things that vaguely come to mind. First, the oppressive heat all day long. Second, the director told us the reports were urgent and we decided to work overtime. Third, some joker knocked at the door, I opened it, and no one was there. If you want me to talk about that I'll be glad to, although I don't understand why you are so interested in such a puerile event.

It happened this way. We were in the office (the door was closed to the public, we had taken off our coats and ties, shirts were unbuttoned, the women had the fans turned up to the max), and the bell was ringing insistently. The receptionist had gone, so I offered to open. There was no one on the other side of the door. I was going to close it when I noticed some strange things: a dog ran out of the narrow street that separates our building from the house across the way, and some kids came after it. At the other end, near the front door to the house, our neighbors were gesticulating. I don't know them very well, and I didn't think they were looking for me, so I shut the door and went back to work. No, wait, something else happened: something like fireworks going off. Since this isn't the month for celebrating anything, I thought, "Those are gunshots."

But that's ridiculous. Who would be shooting in the middle of a street lined with decent houses, on a Thursday, at five o'clock in the afternoon, with so much light? I heard the explosions, closed the door, and came back in. The people were working away without any problems and I convinced myself that my conclusions were foolishness. I finished up a small detail before leaving for home.

But I didn't leave. That's strange. It wasn't my day for going to see my girlfriend, and it wasn't the right time of day to run errands. Now that I stop to think about it, I didn't even finish my work. Plus, now I realize that my companions weren't very calm. There was a moment of shouting, but I didn't shout, I couldn't. It seems to me, though, their shouts were on my behalf . . . but there was no reason for them to be shouting unless something might have occurred and the shouting had something to do with my part in the occurrence.

Now that I think of it, I went back into our building, but not into the back. I didn't get past the lobby, and they all came out there shouting. Now I remember, they were talking about shots, about an armed robber. So then it wasn't fireworks I heard at first, I wasn't mistaken. Let me put the facts together: our building is always in the shade, the only way to know if there is light is by going out and crossing to the other side of the street. See? That's how I found out it was a sunny afternoon, that was how I was able to see the people who were gesticulating so clearly. I must have been so scared by the gunshots that in a couple of jumps I reached the entrance and slammed the door. Now I remember the dry jolt on the wood, and that's why they all came running from the back and asked, "Was that a gunshot, José Luis?" A little after that, when they were trying to get me up, someone explained, "It was a stray bullet . . ." Get me up? Yes, that's true, now I get it, that detail had escaped from my memory until just now. How do you explain that? The only way is this:

I heard the shot (or shots), I retreated quickly—I remember I stepped backward—I must have bumped into the table with the magazines because I fell on my back and it struck me.

That dry sound was not the door but the table at the moment it shattered. That's why all my friends came, the neighbors, the police, and the nurses, and like an extended echo I heard the explanation, it was a stray bullet, José Luis, it was a stray bullet, Judge. It was a very strong blow, it almost knocked me out completely. I saw everything in a constant coming and going, a lot of sentences I didn't manage to understand. I do remember that Anita held my head on her lap while I was covering my stomach because I felt hot and . . . my skin was in shreds . . . . But now I see it all clearly: I went out to the street at the moment of the shots, the stray bullet was not an anecdote nor a distant peril, it was close, so close that it managed to reach me, shoving me backward. Anita told me, as a consolation, "There was a burglar in the house opposite, when they discovered him someone knocked at your door looking for help, and that's when he started shooting." That was why the dog and the kids were running. When I went out they tried to warn me with their gestures not to, but I exposed myself, and a stray bullet got to some of my organs and . . . The police came. Anita was crying hysterically, the rest of my companions were looking at each other with long faces . . . The ambulance arrived but they didn't pick me up, they just covered my face with a piece of cloth. Anita was talking with someone they called "Judge." They ran a piece of chalk around me. When they got me up no one bothered to give me blood or oxygen. I ended up in the back end of a very dark van, wrapped in a bag.

But I still wasn't in any condition to understand. I assumed that I would wake up in the hospital, surrounded by Anita and the rest of my friends, my parents . . . But here I am, and you aren't answering. Have I remembered everything well enough? Because if that's the case, explain to me what I'm doing in this place, why didn't they take me to the hospital? Tell me what happened to my body, what am I doing here, what am I now?

The Back Rooms

Marco Retana
Translated by Charles Philip Thomas

To Manolo Jiménez, creator of fantasies.

On the eighth day of the month, she castrates the pig and the braying ox, and on the twelfth, the patient mules. On the twentieth, during the long days, she begets a wise and good son.
—Hesiod

They had to be born there. It was natural for them to be born there, they had even prepared the room for them, from the moment when the old lady felt the pain and advised Lola, the official midwife. Someone remembers that her aunt said: "We have to make the room ready for the stupid one." And the room was readied, following an old custom in the town: at the back of the house, a square room, without any window, with only one door, a cedarwood door—if at all possible—securely nailed on a cross of the same kind of wood, and fitted into its slot like the door to a fortress was an enormous crossbar—on the outside—double door latches and a combination lock.

"It's better to get it ready right now than to run around later." And the order was respected without the least discussion. The experience of the town. . . .

It had been a lot of work for Fortunata to get pregnant. When she married Belarmino, the people who had always been like that asserted that nothing would come out of the marriage. Maybe some thought nothing good. Others simply said that nothing at all would. And they left it at that.

Actually, now three years had gone by, and there was nothing noticeable about Fortunata's belly. What the people didn't know, nor will they ever know, were Belarmino's series of trips with his wife to Cartago, to ask the Virgin de los Angeles on their knees for the miracle of a child; they went to Escazú also, where Petronila the witch still lived, now with the prestige of having been at the convention of witches in Colombia, from which she returned with a Hindu who spent the days on the patio of the house, legs spread apart by his corpulence, examining the enigma of the blackbird's song.

If we give heed to the people, we should applaud the just foresight of the aunt, for when she ordered the room built, it wasn't known that Fortunata had gotten pregnant. Examples of not-so-fortunate children were abundant around there: Maco, who masturbated in the church atrium on Thursday afternoons, when the Sisters of Mary were attending their meetings; Cornelio, who made love to the calves in Melitón's pasture; Chepita, who the young men lay down with in the cow dung or on the anthills, because she liked it better that way; Carmen, whom the young kids called the witch—whose witchcraft roamed along other paths—and who always went around without any inner accoutrements, gizmos that she never knew in her whole life. The witch would lift up her dress in front of the schoolchildren whom she would pursue and show off the black fright she had had since she was fourteen. And Lilo's sons, a total of fifteen, of whom five survived, with horse faces; and Justiniana's children, four of them, one with a quarter additional coccyx, whose pants would be pulled down in the pasture in order to see the appendage, and to whom they gave the nickname "Little Tail" and who also wandered around the devil knows where, living off his anatomy with a Salvadoran circus; another, with exaggerated "urinary" parts as the priest would say, and it was sworn to around there that he would fill a woman six times over, like the "bitch dog" Gueisa, his companion from his running around at the La Tolima hacienda; a third one became a priest. Finally, there was the smiling Fortunata, who came to get married to Belarmino when she was already close to thirty, and who had spent the past two decades as a woman receiving nocturnal male visitors through the windows that always remained open on the hot nights that extended from January to December.

My town was interesting.

When Belarmino realized that it was impossible for him to procreate and fulfill the commandment from the Bible, he made use of all the means that the Christian religion allowed him: visits to Cartago, novenas to Saint Gerard, Trisagions to Saint Caralampio, rosaries to

Saint Jude, the patron of lost causes—he used to say. Since on the biblical side nothing worked, he tried the fortune-tellers, teachers, and professors of divinity and humanities who in those days had grown rampant in his native town. He didn't find anything. Then he got himself some secret texts, whose origin we are unable to discover, books in whose pages he intended to find the reason for his inability. Belarmino was not worried about whether what came would be good or bad, according to the experiences that we've already described. His virility was in doubt, and everyone recognized it, given the procreative possibilities of Fortunata, her wide thighs and splendid breasts inherited from a mother who nursed four children, and there could have been twenty, had it not been that the impregnating male died crushed by a tree the afternoon when Justiniana had prepared him a soup of *quelitas* and *chuchecas*, of recognized aphrodisiac value. It was he, Belarmino, the people were pointing at. And that was bad.

Certainly, as we have said, this proliferation of children in the town wasn't of the best specimens. Now there wasn't a single home that wouldn't have had to build, let's say not just one, but several rooms in back. Innocents, most of them, that's true; but disgraceful things in the end, which had to be hidden but not for what the people would probably say, since no one could say much, but rather for the itch to believe that nothing had happened there. And thus Lelo spent twenty years with a pacifier stuck in his mouth, and Lalo arrived at school with a skin of transparent color, and with that color he was placed in the kitchen to wash utensils, and with the same color he was taken to the Paupers Cemetery one morning when the sun also wielded its own transparencies. Lulo was brimming over with strength and vitality. "What the hell did it do for him?" the father said, and when he got to be sixteen years old he went to a cabaret to move his bulging muscles and to play house with the queers from the city. But, since it was necessary to recover something for the labors on the coffee plantations, and as every once in a while someone would get all the way through school, the parents risked their all so that new children would be born, and it is possible that this was the reason that impelled Belarmino to search through the pages of medieval texts looking for the medical miracle that would permit him an offspring and affirm himself as a man.

One day, after hundreds of pages of strange readings, Belarmino ran into what would be his salvation. A *Brief Manual on Medicine*, in whose chapter 20 was described a "remedy for married men so they can have children, and can do their conjugal duty," set him on the road to the paternal bliss he had been searching for the past three years. The manual said, give or take a word here and there,

> from the beginning of the cure, take a half-ounce of this potion when you want to go to bed to sleep, and drink about four ounces of good wine. Eat a half a pound of good shelled almonds, three ounces of shelled fresh piñon nuts, two ounces of meat from near the kidneys or loins of small lizardlike animals called Skinks, three ounces from the base of the testicles from a dog and a vixen, very well done, seeds from a caterpillar, two ounces, long pimiento peppers and Cardamom seeds, three drams of each, some white honey. Grind all the ingredients mentioned and mix them with the honey, and put the mixture on medium live coals in order to make the white potion, and in the dessert mix two drams of spices from Diamoscho, and drink it every night, as I said. Each night when you go to bed anoint your genitals (which are your testicles and member) with this hot liquid and cover them with a hot hand towel.

I don't even have to tell you Belarmino's delight upon finding this treatise, nor how many benedictions and prayers he said for the soul of Fray Agustín Farfán, the author of this miraculous recipe.

He still hadn't tried it but he didn't doubt its efficacy.

The only problem with the treatise that had reached Belarmino's hands through the centuries was that he was not clear about the meaning of certain words whose ancient etymology was impossible for his intelligence to understand. Piñons, Skinks, Cardamom, and Diamoscho sank in the void of Belarmino's empty head. Not so with some of the other things that his good mind recognized, and for those he couldn't find, he could find a substitute. Instead of a good wine, smuggled brandy, that was it, like a flash. The good Belarmino assumed that the lizardlike animals must have been the variety of lizard that was so abundant near the coffee plantations, and from then on there wasn't one of the little creatures with a head, from which the meat "near the kidneys" was not removed; castrated dogs showed up around town, which witnesses ascribed to one of the many devils who had made life hell in the neighborhood of San Rafael. And since foxes eat chickens, everyone was grateful to Belarmino when it was discovered that his forays through the coffee and banana plantations were eliminating the last remnants of that nocturnal canine. Into the grocery stores came pepper, the pepper that Belarmino was buying by the pound; whatever herbs had fame for their aphrodisiac powers were ending up in the pot—substitute for Cardamom and Diamoscho—and honey began to be scarce in the area. When the brew was ready he began to drink it. The first few nights he was at the point of losing his intestines when they gave back the mixture that his stomach refused to accept; but since the will is stronger than nature, the day came when the suspicious waters were tasting wonderful. And since he believed that the more he took of the mixture, the better were the possibilities of a pregnancy, then he would take double the recommended dosage, besides his two or three drinks of contraband brandy, and so on for a space of two months.

One night he called Fortunata and told her the secret. Then they prepared for the acid test. Fortunata believed it wise for her to drink at least half a glass of the medicine, beside several glasses of brandy. Belarmino doubled his portion that night, and five times the mat shook with the vigor of the new macho man.

Because there was inbreeding; because there were curses that a priest had blurted out many years ago, when witches were plentiful in the town, and they wanted to throw in his face all kinds of filthy things; because of the diseases that were never cured and therefore the women were being born with goiters or prone to the sins of the flesh, since through the flesh was where evil crept in; "because you all are living in mortal sin, because the devil settled in this town thousands of years ago and you haven't fought to expel him. You shall all go to hell, following the path the damned one marked out for you . . ." said the Spanish priest whom the archbishop had sent during Holy Week.

Be that as it may, Fortunata became pregnant. Two months along she was seized by an attack of listlessness; what screams, what vomiting, what runs; chills and cramps; spasms, diarrhea, and colic; her teeth fell out and the varicose veins that had appeared in the first month burst. He fed her fox meat, snake, lizards, and toad; and there was no creeping or climbing animal that Belarmino did not disembowel between his disgust and his cursing; a bottle of brandy every day, that's what the old lady gargled—she says for the pain— until the delivery time arrived, and then there were two of them. From the beginning it was noted that the pair would go into the back room. Two white bellies; four pink eyes, like rabbits. Even the sunlight bothered them. They were left there. There they are. He and she.

Now many years have passed. There were several Belarminos. So the "Manual" made its mark, and Fray Agustín must be very satisfied. In reality, nine months after the twins were born, Fortunata was preparing for a new adventure. This time he was born throwing a tantrum, reddened, with a brutish face that no one denied him. When he grew up, he went into politics. One day he sold his heritage and became a legislator. The fourth child remained forty days dead in the old lady's uterus, until the forty-first; when nobody could stand the woman's presence, it came out in pieces there by the Jorco River. Fortunata returned home, and devoted herself to housework. Twins returned with the fifth and sixth. They were wrapped in the umbilical cord when they were born, and they were buried like that in a box that was painted white. The seventh was lost in the water. When the ninth month was approaching, Fortunata's water broke, and the following day her belly deflated. For the eighth she suffered more. She felt some sharp pains in her stomach, and the kicks wouldn't let her sleep. At birth he weighed fourteen pounds, he had three teeth. "I'm not surprised," said Fortunata, and he measured thirty-two inches long; one extra finger on each hand, which totaled up to twenty-two fingers and toes, and a half-moon-shaped birthmark on the left side of his face. "The eclipse," said his aunt. "This fucker will be a bad seed." And the right testicle was three times larger than the left one. There weren't any comments about this detail. Finally, though it was well past time for the menopause, Fortunata got pregnant again; but like someone who no longer wanted any more, she departed upon giving birth. The child was born the color of eggplant, and Fortunata considered her labor in the world to be over. "Now she will return," the Hindu from Escazú told Belarmino, "now she will return, and possibly reincarnate as a mule."

Many years have passed now. There in the room at the back is the little couple. If you were to make an appearance through a crack in time, you would see them, all pinkish with their little frightened rabbit eyes. Sometimes she is below, sometimes on top. That's the way they sleep, tired, satisfied.

Metaphors

Samuel Rovinski
Translated by Charles Philip Thomas

"*Intoxicating as Mahler's music in a warm meadow full of primulas and butterflies, of girls dressed in white, protecting themselves from the sun with colored parasols, a large table loaded down with bright colored fruit, wine, and candies, the intoxicated buzzing flies and mosquitoes, children playing games, the murmur of the river, the whisper of the wind through the branches of the willows and the spruces, and a couple lying down on the grass, making love,*" he thought about her upon seeing her come nearer, smiling.

The emotion had chilled him with the excess of metaphors, and he cursed his habit of transforming feelings into images. But she returned the smile, and he dried his trembling hand on his pants before taking her genteel hand in his, her skin *like that of a recently cut fig from the garden of a powerful caliph, prohibited to foreign eyes, guarded by one hundred eunuchs, on a suffocating summer afternoon, the sensual song of the captive princess who is burning with desire for love and dying for his kisses, with Rimsky-Korsakoff music.*

The handshake was cordial, like the smile, but her hand evaded his desire to hold it forever. She said a couple of trite sentences to him and continued on her way to the buffet table, to talk with the others. The sensation of abandonment derived from the failure of the encounter, which he had sought with such eagerness, made his spirits fall, plunging him into an immense unpleasantness, *like that of a modern Werther, loathing the worldly fickleness, dying of unrequited love, the black-birds of melancholy striking his heart, while the chords of Sibelius's "Vals Triste" dispense the tones of profound sorrow to his pain.*

While he served himself a shrimp canapé and a glass of white Rhine wine, he thought that the metaphor was very apt and he followed in the steps of the beautiful one, who was working her way enchantingly among the guests at the cocktail party.

He was jealous of all those men who managed to keep her amused with ingenious sentences and make her laugh, showing her smiling teeth *like pearls set in the halo of an angel, the serene progression of her smile in the melody of a celestial harp, maybe the Summer in the "Four Seasons" by Vivaldi, and that undulating movement of her hair to show her delicate face, with a coquettish gesture, like the fluttering of a nocturnal butterfly,* while he had to be happy with admiring her from a distance, in the hope of another opportunity to approach her, a hope that each time became more difficult *because of the insurmountable wall of misunderstanding.*

He continued with a ham sandwich and then filled his hand with cheese rosettes and goose-liver paté, foreseeing the difficulty of returning to the table as he was being pushed away by the wave of table companions who pressed against him in order to get him to abandon his spot.

The artistic atmosphere comforted his soul. He felt very good conversing with the important people in the country. It was the propitious occasion to display knowledge and sensitivity, praising some and vilifying those who deviated from his perception of art. Over the years the idea of mastering the norms of quality that turned the young artists onto *"the path of the sublime"* gave him a sense for words, which he could emphasize with gracious worldly gestures. He disdained contrary opinions from those who forged their criteria in books without *"possessing an innate sensitivity."* He felt as though the world had been outlined for him by means of immutable rules, and he was fulfilling the all-important role of preserving the plan. In this manner, his life was passing imperturbably. Until the beautiful girl appeared and disturbed his feelings with a new emotion, unexpected at his mature age, when one believes oneself to have seen and experienced the greatest secrets of passion.

He wanted to dazzle her with his judgments on art, seduce her with the authority of his knowledge, and see her tremble with emotion, *like a little fawn captured in the net of the clever hunter.* He would invite her to his studio to show her his work, his books, and his collection of autographs of famous people. On a summer afternoon, *the colored clouds from the sunset, sifted by the windows in the studio, would impregnate the atmosphere with a hot sensuality that favored the meeting of the lovers, as in a Moravia novel. From the garden, the hypnotic emanations from the queens of the night, blanketed by the shadow of the fiery flowering cedars, would mix with the solemn, deep, and virile tones of Dvorak's "Concerto for Cello." That afternoon she would fall submissively into his arms, after swearing eternal love for him. She would be his beloved, the object of his devotion and the model for all his works.* He thought all that upon seeing her looking over the sculptures and studying them carefully.

He was undecided. He didn't dare approach her. But at that moment she was alone and he wouldn't find a better opportunity for his intentions. He hurriedly swallowed the sandwich and went toward her, after quickly cleaning his lips with a napkin.

"Excuse me for interrupting you. I was admiring your way of studying the sculpture. Do you like it?"

She looked at him with curiosity and returned a smile full of sympathy.

"I don't know if it's important whether I like it or not."

He took the reply as an indication of ignorance of the meaning of art, but it was an honest attitude. He felt more attracted to her because *her beauty was complemented by innocence, purity, by primitive contemplation of an art object, like one of Maillol's* Bathers, *by her chaste expression sensually accentuated in some ways free of complexity and with the vigor of adolescence. He had a yen to see her, her beautiful image crystallized someday in one of the gardens of the Tuileries, exposed to the adoration of the passersby who would be thankful for their discovery.* He looked at her in ecstasy and said to her in a fatherly way:

"It's very important, Señorita. To find pleasure in a work of art is the first step to the knowledge of values."

"I know that. However, I believe that it's not as important as the intrinsic values of the sculpture. One should like that which is beautiful and makes one feel good. If that's a value, this sculpture isn't worth anything. It's a repulsive extravagance. However, it has the dramatic aspiration of providing a tremendous impact of horror in our soul. If Rodin were looking to restore the stylistic integrity of sculpture, which had been lost since Michelangelo, as Herbert Read makes one see it, certain contemporary sculptors, like the author of this extravagance, consider that the effect of terror on the soul of the spectator, by means of ugliness, can be as sublime as a work of Michelangelo. But the effect of terror is not sufficient, and the other characteristics of a good sculpture should be present. Taken in this way, I can give you my opinion."

Horrified by the wisdom emanating from the beautiful woman, whom he had believed to be pure in her innocence, he scarcely was able to babble:

"Yes, please; give me your opinion."

The beautiful woman half-closed her eyelids in an effort to concentrate that made him fancy her *as a modern Athena scattering the riches of wisdom over the land*. And, almost without breathing, she said, "'L'art s'insere a mi-chemin entre la connaissance scientifique et la pensée mythique ou magique,' Lévi-Strauss tells us; that is to say, art is halfway between scientific knowledge and mythical or magic thought. And he says, further on, that to know the real object in its totality we have the tendency to operate from its parts. The resistance that is raised against us is compensated for through dividing it. So you see, this sculpture barely approaches art. And do you know why?"

At that moment he lamented his ignorance of French, and cursed himself for not having ever read Lévi-Strauss. It was *like seeing yourself trapped in a whirlwind, without the means to defend yourself, a Tristan lost in the forest of storms, getting further away from Isolde and his hopes of finding the Holy Grail dashed*.

Stunned, he scarcely managed to say, "No, I don't know."

With that same sympathetic smile, the beautiful woman took him by the arm to make him walk around the sculpture, pointing out the defects to him with the poise of a master teacher:

"This writhing is not a projection from the artist's terrified soul, rather, it is a pose, a pedantic attitude. Do you see the contortion at the base and the metal scaling?"

He nodded like a robot, without daring to refute her. Each sentence removed a stone from the building of his artistic beliefs. She made him seem stupid, prematurely aged, *like the dawn disintegrating in the splendor of the morning. He was a doll in her perfect hands, a defenseless little child listening to the Delphic Oracle.*

The beautiful woman continued as if it were the most natural thing in the world:

"The sculptor must have seen it in some catalog of revolutionary works and copied it; not by conviction, rather, I repeat again, by affectation. Where are the elements that should provoke panic in us from the ugliness? As Herbert Read says, the whole conception of tragedy is based on the recognition of the shadow in our souls, the dark powers of hate and aggression. But in tragedy, in its classic form, these dark powers are redeemed by heroism, and the soul is purged of its mistakes. One can still find catharsis in the terrible realism of *The Crucifixion* by Grünewald or in Goya's *Disasters of War*. But there is no Goya nor Grünewald in this metal sculpture. It doesn't produce catharsis but rather mortification. Doesn't it seem like that to you?"

Yes, it did seem like that to him but it didn't seem like that to him. In reality, he was totally confused. He looked into her eyes timidly and answered in a broken voice:

"Well, I like it."

The beautiful woman returned a burning stare of sympathy that barely hid her compassion. She discreetly moved away from him, wielding an intelligent excuse, and went toward a group of young people, who received her with great demonstrations of affection.

He was totally destroyed and made no effort to hold her back. What for, if the art lesson had been like a strong slap in the face? What hurt him most was not having had arguments at hand to refute her. He was beginning to be overcome by shame and frustration. Why didn't he react when faced with that Gorgon? Why did he let himself be hypnotized so innocently? *Like Theseus, armed with strength and astuteness, he should have eliminated the Minotaur, found the exit from the labyrinth, and subdued the beautiful woman with a brilliant speech, full of dazzling metaphors, with tones of Strauss's "Transfiguration."*

He looked hatefully at the sculpture. The twisted base and the metal plating were the artist's pose. There isn't any authenticity. Everything was false, mediocre, deceiving. Where could one find the soul of the matter? It was *like a cry of affirmation from a lie spreading throughout a cave of zombies, the grimace of a bat, the dark night of the wolves.*

He broke out in a cold sweat. He felt ill. He seemed to be in the middle of a nightmare, where all those people who were laughing, talking, drinking wine, and devouring sandwiches were making fun of him. Certainly the beautiful woman was spreading it around, what had happened, and from that moment on his reputation would be destroyed.

His anguish took over when he remembered the critical praise he had bestowed on the sculptor. Surely, the beautiful woman would talk about him in a derogatory manner, hiding it under a mask of sympathetic gestures. He was like the king, naked in front of the court and the people.

Convinced that nothing more was holding him at the party, he hurried out through the people and went home without saying goodbye to the sculptor.

That night, the perfumes from the garden and the blue magic of the moon soothed his pain. The white petals from the queen-of-the-night were swayed by the hot wind, which excited the corollas, making them spread their hypnotic influence. The garden was populated with playful elves, enchanting dryads, little pages in small carriages, and thousands and thousands of characters becoming intoxicated with the music of Mendelssohn's "Midsummer Night's Dream."

Perhaps he could have reconciled with the beautiful woman, if the images of *The Crucifixion* and the *Disasters of War* had not appeared in his memory, to transform the peace and harmony of his existence into a constant nightmare.

The Face

Victoria Urbano
Translated by Sylvia Schulter

Slowly, I shut my eyes and felt the euphoric sensation of sleep. I do not know how long I slept. Maybe for many hours, or perhaps for only a few intense and refreshing minutes brought on by my weariness. Then, as I turned over, I saw its face. It was a clean, fresh-looking face, with firm skin, and a smiling expression, although, truthfully, the smile was divined rather in the eyes than by the mouth. It seemed strange to me, but I stretched my arm out to touch that person who was looking at me from so close. My arm spanned a much greater distance than there appeared to be between its face and mine, and still it was out of my reach. Frightened, I sat up. The bedroom was dark and I realized then it was only a dream. I switched on the light and looked for the alarm clock I had put into the nightstand drawer. It was an unusual looking clock, one I'd purchased in Berne. A small figure characteristic of that city's fountains was drawn on each of the numbers. Thinking I must still be dreaming, I rubbed my eyes because the clock was different. There were no drawings or numbers on its face. It was a completely blank face, with two hands and a second hand that were motionless. I got up. The pink slippers were at the foot of the bed. I raised the blinds and looked out the window that faced the garden. The modest dawn had yet to reveal itself and the birds were silent. I slipped a robe over my shoulders and made my way to the bathroom. I put toothpaste on the toothbrush and switched on the light so that I could, as usual, look at myself in the mirror as I brushed my teeth. The mirror was there, but my face was not reflected in it. I rinsed my mouth and imagined my teeth very white and shiny. I went to the kitchen to prepare myself a cup of coffee. I set the water to boil and opened the refrigerator to take out the orange juice. On top of the refrigerator was a kitchen clock. It was not ticking. I had probably forgotten to wind it, and as I turned on the light to do so, I realized that its face did not have any numbers on it either.

The kitchen had four windows that faced an enormous garden filled with fruit trees and magnolias. While I looked at the clock, my back to the windows, I had a strange desire to turn around and look toward them. For a fraction of a second I remembered the stories of Job's wife and the wife of Orpheus, in which curiosity was harshly punished. What should I do? Cunningly, I chose to employ deception. I would not turn my head just to ease my curiosity. Instead I would wait until the moment when, to get the bread out, I should be forced to go near one of the windows, under which the breadbox was located. And that is how it happened.

Dry toast, to keep from getting fat. Oh misery! What would I do with the temptation of apple turnovers?

The curtains moved and then I raised my eyes. Outside the window I saw the same face as in the dream. It was smiling at me placidly.

The smell of coffee . . . what a marvelous aroma! How stupid people are who drink tea in the morning! There truly are many simple things in life that give us happiness. Don't anyone try to take the pleasure of hot coffee away from me!

I sat down at the table and, as I brought the cup of coffee to my lips, my eye fell on the other two windows that faced me. No need to say it. There it was. A familiar face with reddened eyelids, just as when soap gets into them when you wash your face.

Where have I seen that face before? The expression is so familiar to me . . . Well, it could be a face from one of Botticelli's paintings . . . Yes! When one has seen so many paintings in the museums of the world, there comes a time when it is difficult to differentiate the painted images from the memories that other human beings have engraved in us throughout our life.

The face is there, smiling at me placidly. Its eyebrows were elegant, and it had blond hair.

If we imagine all the faces and gestures that have been shown to us ever since we first saw the first one from over the edge of the crib—strangers, friends, and families—we would more than likely create a terrifying picture . . . Who could it be?

I decided to open the patio door and offer it a cup of coffee. I took the saucer from the cupboard and poured the hot drink. I took the chain off the door, pushed open the screen that is used in tropical climates to allow the breeze in without also letting in the mosquitoes or other insects, and, going out, I headed for the person who was looking at me. This time it smiled at me with its mouth as well and, in a natural and familiar manner, started to reach for the cup of coffee I was offering. As I extended my arm, the cup hit an invisible window and fell broken to the ground.

It must be the breeze, which has stiffened with daybreak. How frightening it would be to live, without knowing it, in a world enclosed by walls and ceilings of glass! The air glistens with the light! Why don't I get up early every morning?

Something seemed strange to me. Of course, I was distracted while contemplating the daybreak and, for an instant, oblivious to the strangeness surrounding me: the fact that, as the cup fell and shattered, it had made no noise. I returned to the kitchen to get the broom and dustpan. What a shame to break such a nice cup! I had bought it in Belgium when visiting Bruges for the first time . . . How nice it is to travel and buy something from each place as a souvenir! Oh well . . . When I went out, broom in hand, there was no evidence on the ground of anything having broken.

The big magnolia trees. Their blooms are like porcelain. How many years have they been in my backyard? These trees have existed since the Cretaceous era. They have been familiar with the night and the dawn for 170 million years! They are almost eternal trees!

My mind wandered toward the magnolia trees, and while watching a lovely bird that suddenly perched on a branch in plain view of my eyes, I forgot about the image that was haunting me like a memory. I made my way toward the middle of the yard and thought how wonderful to have one's own garden, isolated from the world by walls made of undulating branches. I looked up and the sky was blue, with some clouds that surprised me by their stillness.

I've seen clouds like that. Where? Certainly, I remember! I see it again! It is the painting of Prince Baltasar Carlos on horseback, painted by Velázquez! No, that sky was more blue and the clouds were thicker and darker. How silly of me! I should not compare them by their color, but by their motionlessness. Now that I think of it, Velázquez captured an instant of the sky, and although clouds cannot move in a painting, the painter gave the impression of movement by means of the horses' raised hoofs. Thus we can imagine that when the animal lowers them, the clouds will also have changed. But the clouds over my yard are not moving at all!

The bird had a proud crest; I saw it rise when the bird delivered its morning warbling. But oddly enough I did not hear its song! Cautiously, I went toward the tree and the cardinal did not move as I approached. Erroneously, I thought I would be able to touch it simply by reaching out my hand. I tried it even as I thought of it, and was puzzled by my discovery: tree and bird were out of my reach behind a glass wall that was invisible to the eye, but smooth and hard against my fingertips.

Run your hand over an invisible surface that encloses us. Run it slowly. Feel against the palm the surface of the hardened water. The surface of the still air. The surface of a tear hard as ice and widely broadened out. Run your hand over it and feel the crystalline anguish. That which you cannot see but know is there.

I did not want to scream. I looked at my feet and saw the slippers were not damp, as they normally were with the dew from the grass. I bent down to touch it and felt it was fresh but dry. I went toward the plum trees, wanting to lean against one of them, but my shoulders met only with the hardness of an invisible wall.

A prisoner. Is this how a bad memory feels, perhaps? My God, what a deception! Who is talking about bad memories? My life has always been pleasant. I was always given affection during infancy. As a child I had a dog who taught me the meaning of friendship. I had more than enough joys as an adolescent and later . . . Oh, life, love, and fortune have treated me so well! Who is talking about bad memories?

I decided to knock on that apparent wall with my knuckles. Nothing! Not a single sound, and still the obstacle was there. That was when I began to worry. Would the rest of my property be fenced in? Running both hands along the wall, I walked around every perimeter that belonged to me and convinced myself that I was, in fact, a prisoner. I pounded anew until my knuckles hurt.

Knock, knock! How terrible the feeling of oblivion! I look in through a window that, strangely enough, does not have any curtains. My whole family is in there, together and happy. And here I am, outside, where not a single soul is to be found. Knock, knock! No one even hears my anguish! I now see my mother's face. She is the only one who notices my absence, like that small empty feeling in your heart. She comes to the window, resting her forehead on the glass, and I smile at her, feeling my anxiety loosening its hold on me. But no, my mother does not see me. Could she be blind? Could she have lost her sight? No, I see the memory in the pupil of her eye. Her pupil is the mirror of my life. Mother! Mother! Why can you not hear me?

Everything is useless. Useless and incomprehensible. If the circumstances in which I found myself had been the result of a nightmare, I was certain I should have been awakened by now. But there was something that I could not have dreamed: the pleasant taste of the coffee! Then, what should I do? I headed toward the house and there, sitting next to the screen, I saw the hatchet the gardener used to cut the branches. I took it and with determination I struck at the invisible wall, hoping to shatter it into a thousand pieces.

Oblivion has no blood. You can't kill oblivion. I look for its heart but it does not make a sound. It is a clock without eyes, without ticking. It does not see or hear us. Nevertheless, we remember it always.

To have a hatchet in your hand and strike against the impossible is as absurd as screaming in a vacuum, where no sound echoes. I soon realized this and dropped the weapon, with a gesture of defeated resistance. I went inside and sat down next to one of the side windows where I could see the abundant hydrangeas and rosebushes whose blooms have given my eyes so much pleasure. I put my forehead on the palm of my hand and, for an instant, exhaustion seemed to plunge me into sleep.

Memory's veins are navigable rivers and dream is a boat. When one remembers, one thinks or dreams. What emerges first, the image or the word? If I say "boat," I immediately think of Gil Vicente, and his trilogy takes me to beaches that are nothing but solitude. That is what memories are: faces that appear from the other side of the invisible wall.

But no, I did not sleep. I laid my head against the tall back of the Spanish armchair where I was sitting and turned to look, as I have many times before, at the rosebushes. Outside, on the ledge of the window, a fearless green lizard was sunbathing its prehistoric beauty. Amid the clumps of hydrangeas was a nest of lizards. It was common to see them climbing up or clinging to the window screens, or stretched out on the ledge during the warm hours of the day. But the slightest noise against the glass would send them running to their hiding places. As I watched, I smiled because a memory came to mind.

I can no longer remember when. It was a beautiful cage that I had, as small as a tea box, but with no detail missing. Its bars where made of very thin sticks and it had a door that opened vertically, an exact replica of the cages used by lion hunters. Only this one was a small cricket cage made—where else?—in Japan. I had been sleeping and awoke to see a beautiful lizard the color of grass that had entered the room and was resting, clutching the curtain. To see it and to think about my cage were all one. I got up and cautiously moved the opened cage toward it, and then I touched its tail. The lizard entered the cage and became a prisoner. With mixed emotions, dominated by joy at my cleverness, I put it on top of a table and began to observe it. Clutching the bars, it looked for an escape, climbing up and down and, like a prisoner in anguish, sticking its head through the tiny wicker bars, its body unable to pass through. All of a sudden, it stood motionless and it seemed to me its tiny eyes were crying. Then it was I who felt anguish over having locked it up. I ran to the garden and set it free.

It occurred to me to tap on the glass of the window to scare the lizard now sunbathing. But it did not move. Could it be dead? No, I could see its heartbeat beneath the green skin. Then I remembered that none of my taps had made any noise. The best thing was for me to get dressed and go out.

How I like the smell of soap. How I like the smell of water. Water smells like clean skin.

I could not see myself in any of the mirrors, but I knew myself well. I was as old as my memory, and I was as tall as I wanted to be.

I put on a cheerful looking day dress and went out feeling quite good.

At first, the street looked familiar, but after walking for a while, I saw that there was no road traffic. Could I be in Cologne and have forgotten? The street I was thinking of in Cologne was called Hohe Street, and it was a pleasure to walk along it. Oh, how well I remember the beautiful shop windows!

I want that small crystal crocodile. I'll hold it in my hand. I long to see how its scales shine in the sun.

No, it was not Hohe Street in Cologne, nor Florida Street in Buenos Aires. On those streets, even when there is no road traffic there are still so many people that one can hardly get by. No, the street I was walking on was deserted. It was not even a street, but a wide avenue with three lanes. Why was I taking the middle one?

I feel as light as an illusion, with no years or sorrows. I am as old as my memory. My memory is a wide avenue of solitude.

Suddenly, down the left lane I saw several people approaching. Their faces were familiar to me. I wanted to talk to them but they did not stop. They did not even look at me as they went by. I cried out a name. Nothing!

Silence has no language, it has no cry, it has no voice.

My mother went past also. She had aged a lot. She stopped and looked at me. She looked at me! I was merely a memory in the pupil of her eye!

Memory has no language, it has no cry, it has no voice.

I ran toward her. It was vital that she see me, that she talk to me, that she say my name. But how horrible! An invisible glass wall was separating us, and my mother continued on her way, taking her memory of me with her.

Anguish has no language, it has no cry, it has no voice.

At the end of the avenue I kept walking down, yes, there at the end, like a setting sun, the face was smiling at me.

Death has no language, it has no cry, it has no voice.

The Sweetheart of the Spirits

Lucas Bárcena
Translated by Leland H. Chambers

The call is urgent, pressing: "Agua! Aguaaa!"

One's gaze immediately searches for the tower of smoke that indicates catastrophe, but in vain. There is no fire, and no one is dying of thirst. From beneath the bower of branches a girl comes running, hair uncombed, the pieces of a rag doll trailing behind her.

"I'm coming, I'm coming, Aunty."

"Where you go so I can't never find you when I need you?"

"I was looking at the little pigs the sow had, Aunty. There are three of them, and one of them is dying."

Her aunt waits for the girl to come closer to her on the little crudely made balcony, and when she gets there, she grabs her by the ears and continues to scold:

"Must be why your mama ran off and left you when you were tiny because she must have known you wouldn't never be nothing but a nuisance. You act like you gonna to spend your whole life around the pig pens or out in the woods like the animals . . ."

The girl says nothing. She opens her eyes wider, with an expression of mystery, of interrogation. She has already heard those same expressions several times but they don't mean anything to her, and she would like to understand them. But she soon forgets, and starts to play once more.

It was some time ago that Paco and Martin lost their way in the Huile mountains. The boys were walking along without going anywhere in particular, until they found that daylight was on the verge of ending. At first they took it as a joke because it didn't seem possible they could get lost in this region where they had been born. But when they thought they were finally coming out on the road, they discovered they were back at the very point they had started out from, swaying down the same path. Through the leafy branches a chorus of birds and monkeys followed them as if mocking them. Soon night came, and then they had to camp out beneath the trees. They were filled with weariness and ravaged by thirst. But sleep conquered them quickly. In the light of the new day, they once more began their search for the lost paths and those that led to water.

What kind of spell had fallen over the countryside, where not even a single spring was to be seen?

When the day was pretty well along, something like a shout came down from the top of a small knoll. Guided by the sound, they went up toward the top, and then down on the other side. Simultaneously, with a voice that seemed rather like a moan, the singsong message of a small stream reached them. They ran to slake their thirst, and after drinking, their astonished eyes contemplated the tiny body of a pretty little girl seated crying on the bank. Her eyes were expressive, and her skin white. Beside her appeared the remnants of some food, perhaps of fruit. The boys spoke to her, and spoke to her again, without receiving any reply. The little girl only looked at them, as if frightened.

They waited a long time to see if the mother of the child would appear. Nothing. After several hours they began the return with their precious charge. When they reached the village there was joy over their return and puzzlement over the little girl. Teams were immediately formed to go in search of her mother. Nothing.

In those impoverished huts, the little girl continued thus to grow under the care of compassionate hands. They called her Agua by name, which means "water." And because of the circumstances under which she was discovered, no name was more appropriate. But little by little she went from hand to hand, changing "aunties." It seemed as though none felt comfortable when they had her in their keeping. Because no one could manage to prevent her from escaping sometimes and staying out in strange places for an hour or more, at the end of which she would return carrying unusual flowers and fruits whose origin she could not explain. All kinds of conjectures were offered regarding where she had come from, and it was even said that when the little girl didn't go out in the forest, the flowers and fruits would appear, carefully placed at the door of her hut by the first light of dawn, and that in the mornings she would cheerfully collect them.

It was then that they began to call her "the sweetheart of the spirits."

The farm workers would encounter her seated by the side of the road with an absorbed look as if in the midst of a long wait, her gilded curls falling down into her eyes, a smile on her lips, and her hands crossed one over the other.

They were now quite accustomed to seeing her this way, and it gave them joy to encounter her, a pleasure to their eyes. Her voice, clear and cheerful, was caressing at the same time.

She did not seem to fall in love, and if she had it would have been a mysterious love, the love of an ideal, of a rite, of something unknown.

She wandered alone, and alone she talked. Occasionally, like the saint from Assisi, she called the birds and the rocks her brothers . . .

The heat is a spider's web stretched out over the forests on all sides. It has been three days without raining, and months, it seems, since the last real rain. There is a strange worry among the villagers, a concern that they futilely attempt to conceal. It has been three days too since Agua disappeared.

She has spent five years there now, and the last time they saw her she had been coming down from the hills with her clothes all wet and her hands filled with ferns and twigs. The villagers talked about this more than the business of the drought.

"She didn't come home this afternoon," her "aunty" said. "But her dolls and that little mirror, they're still here. Long as she didn't take 'em with her, that means she gonna come back."

"I ain't seen her on the road neither, not yesterday nor the day before. Most always she sits on the same rock," someone else said. "Or else on the bank by that stream she takes a dip in sometimes."

Isn't it strange about this little girl whom no one really wanted, and yet whose absence is such a concern that no one can disguise it? Aren't there lots of hard-working girls in the village, and good ones, too?

The questions are posed secretly, and none is given a sincere reply.

It isn't known who initiated the search overnight, but soon the woods are gradually filled with shouts.

"Aguaaa!"

"Aguaaaaa!"

Every meadow, every bit of flat ground is gone over, all the dark ravines are scoured, rocks lifted up, even the tops of the trees are searched. Once more the birds and monkeys take up their duets from their leafy branches. Afterward the village remains as if deserted, and the first shadows stifle the final shout:

"Aguaaaaa!"

Little by little a fine rain began to fall, to the accompaniment of a bolt or two of lightning. And it spread gradually. By midnight the nearby streams were swelling and creeping up and touching the white cane doors of the huts with a discreet, liquid knock.

There was fear. Disturbances. But nothing happened because the village was perched on a hillock and the water could not rise so high.

On the following day, by the threshold of every door were traces of slender footsteps, formed by tiny feet like those of delicate children.

And Agua never returned.

The Horse in the Glassware Shop

Ricardo J. Bermúdez
Translated by Leland H. Chambers

It had been just like all the other days. Well, not exactly, not for someone who observes things closely. Things manifest different peculiarities of agreement according to the analytical capacity of whoever is observing them. That's why I say it was just like the others. I'm a simple person with a few personal obsessions. So simple am I, or so superficial, that I don't grasp the differences right away. For me, two drops of water are just like the third one. The sea is an infinite number of drops of water. Human beings are a human sea, and all alike, only some are more alike than others.

As I pointed out, it had been a day just like all other days. The sun rose through the gateway of the horizon where it rises every day. It was the kind of light that shook up the birds and forced them to sing just as has been going on ever since I remember. A light that warmed the beds of sleepers and made them waken the way they do every day. The city grew crowded with the same old eagerness and murmuring as always. The bold were running after their shadows and those who were calmer followed after their dreams.

Then I said that things could not go on being the way they were. One thinks he has a certain individuality when he repeats what others have said. Besides, I was constantly playing with the idea that it is our enthusiasm that changes their monotonous uniformity, our disposition not to fall into the snares set out every minute by routine habit. I had heard this once, and it occurred to me to repeat it now. For me the day was just like all previous ones; nonetheless, I proclaimed that things

could not go on being the way they were. So I don't know if I said it in
the spirit of prophecy or of protest. Sometimes we need to break up our
tedium however we can.

The priest crossed himself when he heard me say it. For him at that
critical moment I was nothing less than a saint, an authentic, enlightened holy man. Without a doubt God was making revelations through
my mouth and a new messiah was at the point of reappearing on earth.
To change things is the same as shining a new light on the Gospels:
tightening the wire where the tightrope artist performs circus stunts.
Before he went off I heard him offer blessings on the prophets because
they arrive first at the festival of transformations.

The politician did not miss the opportunity to pay heed to that
business about things changing. With his left hand he made an approving
gesture. Had he been dressed as a priest, I would have sworn that he made
the sign of the cross over himself, too. Wearing a habit changes a man so
much. His eyes shone greedily because I had just given him a good slogan.
To change the world is to convert those who receive things into those
who grant them. He embraced me strongly and went running off to the
party offices.

As on other mornings, people were pouring into the market. The
fishermen had already come back with their baskets filled with the fruits
of the sea. The butchers and the vegetable vendors had also gotten there
early, and they were in a cheerful frame of mind. Sales were marvelous.
Everyone seemed to proclaim the joy of being alive. Housewives were
chatting spiritedly and none showed any resentment over their husbands' conduct. The general accord was so remarkable that the policemen looked like thieves and the thieves like policemen.

I was thinking that things couldn't go on being the way they were any
longer. This had occurred to me (or I had recalled hearing it said by
someone else) while I was shaving. Every time I shave I cut myself
alongside my mouth. Even though I change hands or razors, when I shave
I cut myself. Anyone who sees blood in the mirror early in the morning
can't be calm for the rest of the day. Something is badly wrong when
there are faces without wounds and visages loaded with scars. I wasn't
sure if it was better for all the faces to show scars or for none to have
wounds.

According to the newspapers things were progressing marvelously
well. The headlines all seemed written by a single person. The editorial
in the most respectable paper argued for the necessity of building
mechanical escalators to reach the top of Mt. Everest. This omen filled
me with doubts: it supported my idea that things could not continue
being the way they were, but the coincidence turned out to be merely
formal. For them the important thing was the mechanical escalators. For

me, that the policemen cease to look like thieves and the thieves like policemen.

As I went past the glassware shop, the horse was grazing quietly next door. Since I was a boy I had seen it there, growing and getting fat. The glassware shop too had become larger and stocked with novelties. They were side by side, as always. Their habitual proximity had rendered them almost indistinguishable. We couldn't tell if the horse was an emblem of the glassware shop or the shop the most unusual shelter of the horse. When it comes right down to it, reality is what the senses perceive, as well as, sometimes, what the sensed phenomena do not conceal.

In the park the light pretended to be a naked queen. Borne by the wind, it moved over the grass, and the palm trees danced with it. Groups of children were running after butterflies and learning to discover themselves by pursuing flowers with wings. Sweethearts got together in the shadow of the colonial cupolas. Disheartened passersby noticed none of this on their way to the tax collectors' offices. Neither did the lottery ticket vendors, nor the fortune hunters who were pursuing them through the streets. I insisted on affirming that things could not go on being what they were.

In the afternoon the students planned a protest. After a few minutes they changed their minds and decided to go swimming at the beach. The men from the union hiring hall had also arranged to get together and march. At five its leaders went off to the cantinas. Eight cartloads of rocks and two hundred soldiers were left waiting in vain. As the secretaries returned to their homes, I observed the punctual return of the swallows. The city lights came on every time the twilight extinguished one of its lamps. The day had been just like the others, but despite my growing obsession, I was convinced that the night would be that way as well.

At dawn I dreamed that the horse had gotten into the glassware shop. At first, that image did not engender any disturbing feeling at all. It constituted the subconscious's way of reacting in the face of my conviction that things couldn't go on being the way they were. I couldn't imagine how the horse had managed to get through the door of the shop. Nor if it might have done so through one of its windows. Probably it was over the roof or by means of a tunnel. Those details were of no importance when compared to the fact that one statuette—but only one—was discovered crushed beneath its hooves.

There the horse was, turned into an example of the fact that brute force can act without creating havoc. In its new surroundings that specter constituted something like astuteness sublimated and carried to the most subtle extremes. Against all likelihood, the horse was suddenly inside the the glassware shop. What was surprising in this situation was that happy show of daring and dexterity. The proud culmination of reality transferred to the plane of the unbelievable. The triumph of the astonishing and the defeat of the habitual and orderly procedure of things.

When I started to shave I was still submerged in the traces of the persistent dream. The vision of the horse in the glassware shop was still splendidly in my consciousness. I might have remained in that state of dullness if it were not for the usual cut next to my mouth. Then I woke up completely. Despite the blood the mirror also picked up my complacency due to the hallucination that was finally fading away. Still I managed to perceive the straggling image of the equine head next to some flickering candelabras. Afterward the shouting of the peddlers and the murmuring of the devout turned aside the last vestiges of the annoying monstrosity.

The temperature of the air was the same as I had felt yesterday in my clothing, briefcase, and glasses. As happened every morning I set out for the university. At the first intersection the shoeshine boys were polishing the same old shoes as ever. The stores opened their doors and buyers were preparing to pursue the acquisition of their innumerable provisions. The invariable servant was beating the rug thrown over the balcony railing. The same old cat still savored its usual snack and the flock of sparrows had already forgotten the last three of their babies that would never learn to fly.

Encouraged by the dream, I came back to my belief that things could not go on being what they were. In a notebook inside my briefcase I kept a helpful sentence that proclaimed this to be the only world possible. I also carried a manual of probabilities and an engraving of Archimedes in the act of placing his lever. We all have our preferred amulets as close to hand as possible. The streetcar went by me like an undesirable, obstinate pachyderm. Inevitably I associated it with my grandmother's missing blouses. Perhaps things did change if one survived their deaths and resurrections.

At the university the rules seemed to have changed. The small knots of people were denser and a larger number of hands were hammering a counterpoint against each other. Academic speculation had disappeared, and its place was occupied by a sort of witches' council. That's the way I understood it as I made my way among the comments of the scientific sect to which I belonged. Everything indicated that the phenomenon had occurred just as I myself had dreamt it before awakening. Something incredible from a mathematical point of view, from a physical, juridical, and even religious point of view. Something that left the learned teachers and their students in a state of absolute perplexity.

It was the hardy drinkers from the union hall who had noticed the event. Along about two in the morning and in company with some students who had joined with them. They were coming back singing the Internationale, once the stock of rum had been exhausted within a radius of two leagues surrounding the monument to the Martyrs of October. At first they couldn't believe it. They thought it was a phenomenon of the dawn brought on by the rapid cooling of alcoholic gases. Afterward they managed to verify that it wasn't a mirage caused by a reflection from the moon. Nor the simple desire that something unusual would happen to justify the tardiness of their return to their homes.

Like a sly god the horse was found within the glassware shop. Head, trunk, and four legs standing out over a throng of grayish phosphorescences. Only one statuette had been crushed in the nocturnal assault, and not even the most astute night watchmen had managed to notice it. This was doubtless the work of an intelligent horse. That's what the most intoxicated ones thought. And since no one was sober, there was no opposition. From that moment was born the legend that this was an intelligent horse. In all the history of horses in glassware shops, none had managed to do it with such dexterity and such a minimum of lament-worthy breakage.

People couldn't believe what the newspapers, radio, and television were relating. Later there were two hundred soldiers to prevent those people from getting close to the glassware shop. They were the same ones who had waited in vain the previous afternoon for the clash with the workers. It doesn't make any difference how or when it happens, in the long run the soldiers and the workers always clash: workers dressed as soldiers and workers dressed as workers. Perhaps when the soldiers and workers are just men, there won't be any occasion for clashing. Then there won't be any reason why things should be different, either. Horses wouldn't have to get themselves into glassware shops so the world will seem different.

We discussed this at the university while the workers and students were fraternizing with the soldiers. Unforeseen events tend to make people's behavior more uniform. The stupendous event of the horse in the glassware shop was forcing them to forget their differences. The stupor of the novelty capitivated their attention. But the equine magic didn't turn out to be strong enough to daze everyone. Scientific reflection was opposed to accepting the extraordinariness of an event that was perfectly probable. If the horse had been born and bred up in the vicinity of the glassware shop, the natural thing was that it should end up inside it. The surprising thing would have been for the glassware shop to have gone out and charmed the horse into bondage.

After three days I began to believe that it really had been the glassware shop that had enthralled the horse. There was no clear evidence that this species of glass spiderweb had trapped it like a bumblebee buzzing around it. But the flasks and jars and glasses and lamps do have an ineffable attraction. The inadequate eye of the animal perceives the glitter of the objects and not their significations. It is we who do not allow ourselves to be seduced in every circumstance by their splendor. The horse simply had a propensity toward the hundreds of luminous winking signals emanating from the glad eyes in the glassware shop. From this point of view, the glassware shop constituted its logical destiny and inevitable prison.

This time I was sure I had not heard from someone else that the glassware shop had taken possession of the horse. It was a different thought from that which had led me to believe that things couldn't go on being the way they were. The idea was born out of the suspicion that the horse had been seized by the glassware shop. I confirmed it the first time there was a clearing in the crowd and I got to look the horse in the face. His mien was that of a prisoner. The many offerings he received reaffirmed my idea. A few hours after the event his situation had turned intolerable. His most vehement admirers even went so far as to say that it would cause the mute to speak and the lame to walk.

Some recalled having always seen the horse next to the glassware shop. Others that the horse and the glassware shop had been born simultaneously. That's what was said by the old men, taking on an importance they no longer had since the law of obligatory retirement. They said that when the horse was born the glassware shop was established. They also mentioned some venerable progenitors: a mare and a merchant, both of them magic, whose traces were lost in time. The two of them had grown like two parallel lines. So close were they that a third group of commentators never noticed that the horse and the glassware shop were two completely different entities.

All those days the exploits of the horse were the only things talked about. For many, they were worthy of being sung by epic poets. Nothing seemed to diminish the dimensions of his heroic figure. Not the thousands of glasses that were being destroyed little by little. Not the fetid piles of manure into which he was transforming the abundant fodder they served him. Not even the blue flies that swung back and forth around him and that thereby became sacred. As sacred as the hairs from his tail and the ticks that certain merchants managed stealthily to put on sale.

All in all, together with the fact that he was visibly getting fatter, the horse was not happy. This opinion I put forth at the university. Several colleagues disagreed because the important thing was to ensure his meals every day. The fact that his corpulence restricted his freedom of movement didn't matter. Or that he was in the glassware shop and it was impossible now for him to get out of it. To run through the fields after the mares. To romp on the grass after the rain had soaked his back. To change trees in accord with the rhythm of the sun and the moon passing over his head and would pass again so many other times.

But my convictions are something else again, and they have their reason for being. For me, no horse exists that would voluntarily exchange its freedom for a ration of alfalfa and a sack of corn. Therefore I had believed and continued to believe that the glassware shop snared him. It's certain that the shop had not moved from its site. That it was there in the same spot as always. As everything is, in hopes that the enthusiasm of human beings will change them. Thus it was natural for the most obese of my colleagues to conclude that the horse had entered the glassware shop and not the glassware shop into the horse.

The things that surround us constantly tend to resemble us. Their secret aspiration is to stop being inert and immobile. To mount by those rungs that certain oriental religions mention. To change themselves into beings. Our aim at the same time is not to allow ourselves to be seduced by them. Not to fall into their snares that range from the sirens' song to the fires they kindle in our minds. Not to barter away our freedom just to transform ourselves into things. Not to barter it away in spite of the fodder and sacks and statuettes and thrones and palaces and empires that we might manage to receive for it.

Not even the intelligent horse in the glassware shop knows this. Neither do the obese students at the university. Still less the multitudes defenseless against the glitter of the unforeseen. I assumed this when I said that things couldn't go on being the way they were. Now I know that the only things that change are those that we change. It happens when we defend what we are. When we reject being simply things. The dream of the horse awakened me from my dream. I understood the senselessness of change for the sake of change. The ineffectiveness of subtle appearances. The terror of mere substitution. The threat of playing with enervating mirages.

The days have ceased being the same for the careful observer that I now am. Ever since the horse got into the glassware shop they are worse. Worse because many believe that these have been better days. Such an illusion in reality makes them worse. The horse and the glassware shop no longer exist for me. They exist like spectacles at the fair. As triumphs of deformity. As symbols of the absurd. The sudden metamorphosis of the horse has not managed to change the order of things. Neither will his truculent and pernicious final deification.

What people say or fail to say in order to justify their fears does not bother me. The days continue to be insufferable and the conformity is of such magnitude that with impunity the policemen still look like thieves and the thieves like policemen. The priest crossed himself again when he saw me. On this occasion because he read my thoughts. The politician also insisted on waving a greeting with his left hand. It was an uncertain greeting that might have remained unnoticed. Nothing more opportune than ambiguity when the bulging eyes of the censors were spying through the window. He seemed to want to tell me this. Then he crossed the street toward the glassware shop at a run in order to fondle the lustrous tail of the horse for the thousandth time.

Love Is Spelled with a "G"

Rosa María Britton
Translated by Leland H. Chambers

Bad luck has been my steady company since the day I was born. Actually, it was a long time before that, because I never would have chosen the parents I've got if fate had given me the opportunity. I would have chosen them rich, white, and above all, a long way away from this place. My Aunt Elida, who lives with a drunken husband and has scads of kids no good for anything, is always saying (when she's in the mood to give advice) that you make your own luck. I always had my doubts in this respect, but what else could I do but pay attention to her and try every way I could to make myself a special kind of good luck, for me alone? I might have been able to resign myself to existing and getting along just like all my relatives. Starting with my sisters: some of them were kept women, the others in bad marriages, all with mediocre jobs, surrounded by sniffling, bad-mannered little brats who are all going to end up getting in trouble. I don't see any of my nephews in an important job; the only thing they're ever going to do well is kick a beanbag around in the streets and skip school. Whenever I see them around here I'm embarrassed for them to always call me "Aunty, Aunty," in front of my friends from the office. They're always so filthy. I was aware of the odd look Laura Requena gave me when I explained how they belonged to a very dear servant of my mother's and so they always called me "Aunty" out of affection. That Laura! Just because she's the daughter of some Spaniards, she's really so conceited. And she doesn't even have noble blood! Her father's nothing but an ordinary furniture man, but since they've got money she thinks she's the queen bee. She really gets me down. Though no one would think so, to see us going around together all the time. But that's the way life is. Friendship with her is just useful. Period. I've had to put up with her airs, but someday, someday when I reach what I want in life, I'm going to tell her off. For the time being I have to bear with her, because she is the only one of my friends who's got what it takes to help me meet that someone again who I've been waiting for so impatiently and who's going to get me out of all this. The biggest problem in my life has always been my family. They're nearly all of them dark. And all of them, without a single exception, are poor and stupid, which is the worst thing. I think it wouldn't make any difference for me if I were like them, but destiny played a nice little dirty trick on me there, because I was born light, with my hair a little wavy (with some blond tones) but with a good straightener anyone would take it for naturally straight hair. How did that happen? No one knows, though I suspect my mother knows very well and doesn't dare to confess it. She talks about a distant uncle who was blond just like me, but frankly I really doubt it. There's something fishy about that story, but no one is going to commit themselves, much less my mother, respectable widow that she is. She sells eggs and lottery tickets in the market. My *official* father—although, I repeat, I really doubt it—was from Darien. He died years ago, when I was a little girl, but I remember him very well: a dark man, with shining eyes and the smell of brandy always on his breath. There are seven of us kids; only the oldest was a boy, the rest were girls, and as I said before, either they've all married badly or someone's keeping them, and they are all dark, without exception. Since I'm the youngest and blond besides, I was always my mother's favorite, she never got tired of singing the praises of my golden skin and eyes that are a kind of greenish color going on gray that make me very attractive, especially when I've got make-up on. My sisters all went to public school, but me, they sent me to The Immaculate Conception of Mary, at a great sacrifice, as my mother has let me know her whole life long. Not The Immaculate Conception of Mary where the rich girls go, the white girls, but the business school, the one by Herrera Park, where the daughters of well-to-do families used to go, and the daughters that rich people had on the side. In my homeroom there were three like that, and they were so stuck up you wouldn't believe. So now I see them, they've got everything, and one of them is even a member of the Union Club and all that, because her mother married her "beloved" after his wife died. That's what I call having good luck . . .

We lived on Fourteenth Street West, the "Street of Slippers," so-called because the women all go around that way, behind a grating where my older sister would spend the whole day hustling every man that went down the street, while Mama worked in the market from daybreak on. It never occurred to me to bring any of my girlfriends home from school.

Why not? So they could see my fat sister Clothilde leaning against the grating with her tits almost hanging out, her conked hair never combed, always laughing fit to be tied with anyone who went by? She's already got seven kids, and every one of them from a different father. Now and then she dares to come and ask me to lend her some money, and there's no way to make her understand that I don't want anything to do with her . . . Stupid: she takes the cake. I always tried to better myself. In grammar school I was the best student in the class. I studied hard, because I had a feeling that would be the only door that would open to let me out of here. I was in love with gringos ever since I had the use of my brains. My sister Maritza used to say I lived just to go to the movies, and in that I give her credit where credit is due. I used to save my last cent to go to some theater on weekends to dream in the darkness, enjoying those blond, beautiful people who live in big houses, with several luxury cars, and no financial problems, dancing and singing even to make love . . . I longed to meet a man like that someday, tall, white, muscular, far away, a long way away from the grating on Fourteenth Street and the Quintero *negras*, as they called my sisters. A lot of times, after getting out of school I went on foot as far as the main avenue, near the Cinco de Mayo Plaza, just to see them go past, with their uniforms so nice, those handsome men, exactly like in the pictures. One of my uncles saw me down there and told my mother, which got me a good scolding because—get this— she said there were a lot of drunken, impertinent gringos around there. As if I didn't see enough drunks on Fourteenth Street, and they were black and ugly, that's even worse! When I was fifteen we found out that a girl who lived nearby had married one of those Americans and went to live in the United States. The wedding took place in the Canal Zone, with the groom in dress uniform, and his companions made a court of honor with their swords and everything, just like a picture with Tyrone Power. The bride's mother brought the photos so we could see them and told my mother that she hadn't allowed most of her family go to the wedding, so as not to embarrass her daughter.

"We have to make the race better," she repeated as she related the details, and my mother agreed with her so earnestly that right then and there I was convinced that *my* father hadn't come from Darien, not a bit, and that my color hadn't been the result of any accident in bed. That day I decided to snag myself a gringo, too, no matter what it took. The image of that neighborhood acquaintance surrounded by beautiful people brought me to the conviction that I could do the same if I put my mind to it.

All the way through high school I spent a lot of time studying English. I never missed an American film, and I made a big effort not to read the subtitles in Spanish. I'd buy magazines that I would read paragraph by paragraph, dictionary in hand. I graduated with the highest marks in the school, and I got the reputation in the neighborhood for being conceited because I wouldn't have anything to do with anyone there. My sister Clothilde went away to live in the Juan Díaz district with a man a lot older than she was, and that was a relief for everyone because my other sisters, even though they were dark, were at least very respectable, they all had boyfriends, and Clothilde's affairs made it hard for them because she didn't hide from anybody what she had a yen for. She had three of her children there at home, still unmarried, even before she went to live with that man.

I got a job right away. Blond, nicely dressed, passable English, Palmer handwriting, a hundred and eighty words a minute on the typewriter with no mistakes, a faultless Gregg shorthand. I passed the exam way above the other applicants, although at the last minute I had my doubts if they would take me because some of them came directly from the other Immaculate Conception of Mary, with "important family" stamped right on their faces. With the address I gave them on Fourteenth Street I couldn't hide my family no matter how much I tried to. A nervous shiver ran down my spine when the Head of Personnel asked me again if that was my whole address, a little put off that I didn't have a telephone where he could call me.

"I'm an orphan," I lied for the first time. "My uncles that brought me up moved to Chiriquí. Right now I'm staying over at the house of some people I know, but I'm looking for an apartment."

My family was really pleased when they found out about my job at the bank, my mother especially, and she gave the news to all her customers at the market even though I begged her not to. Poor woman, that's the way she is. I've always loved her a lot, but how it bothers me that tendency of hers to exaggerate things! Everything she talks about. So what, who cares how many eggs she sells every week, or who her important customers are, or how many times she's won at the lottery? And that mania she has for talking about her grandchildren, even Clothilde's seven bastards. People ask questions and she just answers any old way. She always goes around bragging, my Blondie does this, my Blondie does that, as if her other daughters didn't even exist. That must be the reason for making the race better. . . .

It doesn't bother me when they call me Blondie, that way I stick out from the rest of the neighbors. But at the bank I told them my nickname was Kary, with a K, that's an exotic, elegant letter that I always wrote very stylishly, and with the "y" at the end to be different from all the other girls in this country whose real name is María Caridad. Cari, that's the way they write their nickname, it's just not an elegant name; it's much too common.

From the first I felt happy at the bank, with the air-conditioning and that smell of new and unusual things. After a few months I got to be secretary to one of the assistant managers, because I took pains with my work. Nobody did it better than I did. I spent almost my last penny on dressing nicely so I could create the image of a girl who works just because she wants to, not from necessity. But the truth is, all of us at home were working, some as teachers, others clerking in stores and things like that. My salary wasn't needed, but it wasn't much, anyway. Mama never left her spot at the market, for it brought in good money, you have to say that for her. With all her seventy years she's still there, day after day. I would have liked to move out somewhere by myself, but the money didn't catch up with me. I had to endure living in that house on Fourteenth Street, sleeping on a sofa in the room with my sisters. I never let anybody from work go home with me. To cover up where I lived I would catch a bus as if I were going to Bella Vista and then get off a long way from there to transfer. What a face that Laura Requena would have shown if she ever found out where I lived; she put on such airs because her family had a house in Bella Vista near the swimming pool. I had some would-be suitors, both in the neighborhood and at the bank. The ones in the neighborhood I never even turned around to look at, they were just lazybones, half vagrants, always standing around on the corners approaching every woman that went by. I confess that at the bank I almost let myself be tempted by a very nice boy in Accounting. He began by inviting me to go out a few times, and I kept saying no, but then he insisted so much that I gave in. We went one Sunday to the dance at the Balboa Gardens. I preferred to meet him at the door, with the excuse that my mother was a little sick and wouldn't allow me to go out with anyone. What bothered me most was that he started right away to treat me as if we were already engaged or something like that; he'd dance very close up and he wouldn't take his arm from around my shoulders when we went back to the table. His sister came too, with her husband, he was a dark-skinned guy who worked in the Canal Zone, and right then my enthusiasm about Arturo was over and done with. I got rid of that group as soon as I could and only let him accompany me to where I caught the Bella Vista bus. I was determined he was not going to carry on anymore with me. A long time afterward he married one of the cashiers in the bank and they even invited me to the wedding, and that's how I found out he came from a family just like mine: poor and ignorant. When I think what I saved myself from!

I started going into the Canal Zone with Laura Requena and another girl, looking for gringos. Of course, we never expressed it this way, but all three of us knew pretty well what we were up to. A cousin of Laura's who worked in Balboa invited us to have lunch one day at the whites'

Club House. My heart leaped in pure emotion when I went in there for the first time. I didn't have eyes enough to gaze at all the soldiers, all so neat in their khaki and olive-colored uniforms. They all looked like movie actors! We managed to get a few friendships going, but naturally we made it ever so clear that we weren't going to sleep with anybody; Laury, Edy, and Kary, we were Panamanian girls from good families.

It was at a party in the Officers' Club at Amador where I met Jerry White. I don't recall who introduced us, but right then I realized that that fellow could be the man of my life. He was an awfully poor dancer, stepping all over me, apologizing every time and then coming right back and doing it again. A tall man, a lot taller than I was, with somewhat harsh features, a complexion made all red by the heat, with his hair cut short in a military cut. He came from a small town in Ohio, and the only thing he talked about with any kind of animation was about the day he'd go back there, a long way from this infernal country that was always too humid, too hot, and full of mosquitoes. Ohio! That night I savored that name until I went to sleep. A place that was just about like a paradise on earth. A man like I'd dreamed about and prayed for! I was never what we'd call religious, not even in school where the nuns injected you with religion in a hypodermic needle. But when I met Jerry, my Gringo with a capital G, unmarried and looking for a decent woman, I promised novenas and masses if this all turned out. We went out several times, simply as friends, either to the movies or else to dance at one of the clubs in the Zone, with Laury or Edy (her name was Edilma and we decided to change it to something more up to date) going along with us so the man wouldn't get the idea that I was just any old girl whatever. He thought my accent was cute, so I exaggerated it and made faces like a Latin American señorita, but naturally from a very good family. We almost always met after work somewhere in the Zone, and I fixed it so that everyone believed the story that my mother was too strict and wouldn't let me go out with men even when my girlfriends went along, and that was why he couldn't accompany me home. The first time I dared to go out alone with Jerry was on a Saturday. Up till now our intimacies had been restricted to walking hand in hand or perhaps a quick kiss from time to time in the darkness of some dancehall, because at a fixed time I would rush out to catch the Bella Vista bus, under the pretext that my elderly mother was waiting for me anxiously. No intimacies! Laura, who is not stupid, said it quite clearly: "You don't want to give your little finger to these gringos because if you do they'll grab you by the arm and later on they won't respect you."

Jerry invited me to the beach at Amador without my girlfriends, and he stressed it two or three times to be sure I had understood. In reality the idea wasn't very exciting to me. The sun has the habit of bringing out the race in you, and besides, I didn't want to get my straightened hair wet for anything in the world because then anyone would realize that I had been ironing it straight. But he insisted so much that there was no way out, and so I went, with a Jantzen bathing suit that cost me a pile of money on Madurito Street. He was waiting for me right on time at the gate to the base, accompanied by another American couple that he wanted to introduce to me.

"This is Kary, my sweetheart. The only souvenir I want to take back from Panama."

He let it drop just like that, in a casual way, like Americans do sometimes. I could have died right there. My heart was beating so hard I couldn't even catch the names of his friends, who were smiling and congratulating us as if they were already witnessing the ceremony. We went to the beach and I went in swimming without caring about the sun or the hair-straightener, since my Jerry from Ohio wasn't up on those details. In the water I let him kiss me and touch me everywhere, and he put his fingers inside me down there. What a look of surprise on his face when he realized that I really was a "señorita." It seems to me, without being conceited, that if he wasn't already completely convinced, that day he decided for certain.

"Just let my family find out that I've met a natural blond in the tropics," he said to me later.

I looked at him a little frightened, thinking that he was probably dropping me a hint, but that wasn't it. Jerry just couldn't imagine the Street of Slippers, not even for a moment, nor my sister Clothilde, nor the eggs-and-lottery-ticket stall in the market. We talked everything out that day; they were transferring him to the United States in three months and he had decided to leave the army after that.

"Trouble is starting in Korea," he informed me, "and I don't want any part of that business. We didn't just get out of one war to get into another. I've had enough with what I've seen. I only saw the end of it in the Pacific, but I've had enough of the army. I prefer to go back to Ohio to work in my father's plumbing business. You're going to like Canton. It's a quiet place where nothing ever happens."

From that day on, Ohio turned into an earthly paradise where I would have an enormous house, with dogs, cars, air-conditioning in summer and good heating in wintertime, and above all, no Clothilde, no gratings, no lottery on Sundays. And when I got there I'd never, never look back again. As soon as I boarded the airplane, they were never going to know anything more about me. I was a little sorry for my mother, but right away she understood my desire to make the race better. A gringo! Her daughter María Caridad had snagged a gringo! She couldn't help it: she told all her customers and all the neighbors about it. I had the feeling of their hatred-filled looks on the back of my neck when I went to work early in the morning. We had decided to get married in a month, just a civil ceremony for now, because, since Jerry was a Protestant and I was a Catholic, we were going to wait a tactful amount of time for the religious ceremony, which would take place in Canton, attended by his numerous family, since I was nearly an orphan. Laury and Edy were dying of envy, I know, but as far as I was concerned I couldn't care less. The atmosphere around the house turned dark, strained. My sisters almost weren't speaking to me at all, because they'd found out about this phantom sweetheart they had never seen.

"Be careful, then, don't jump backward," Maritza said mocking, one night before going to sleep, referring to the possiblity of having dark-skinned kids because of my family.

"Let Blondie alone," my mother came out to defend me, for she was the only one who understood the situation. "Get yourself to Ohio, you don't have any future here. Everything is better in the United States, absolutely everything. It's just like in the Canal Zone there: orderly, clean, with those commissaries chockfull of good things. They don't have any cockroaches there, no scorpions, and everybody goes around in their cars."

We continued to go out, all our plans made now, and the days passed with an exasperatingly slow pace. Jerry had me get a passport, and at the American Consulate when I went to apply for the visa, I put "white" alongside the little box that indicated race. The official didn't show the least surprise, which filled me with pride. Jerry's friends were going to give us a small reception the day of the civil ceremony, which would take place at the courthouse in Balboa. They thought I didn't have any family in the capital, just a sick mother for whom it would be impossible to attend the ceremony. I only invited Laury and Edy so that they would stand up with me. At home the only one who knew I was getting married was my mother, who agreed with me to keep it secret from the rest of the family so as not to upset them. Poor Mama, she knew all about that business of making the race better.

The day before the wedding we went to the Kirkpatricks' house to help arrange things for the party. They lived in one of those homes near Corozal, in a place called Los Ríos, which most resembled a clearing scratched out of the forest that starts right there. While I was talking with Carol, the men took charge of moving the furniture to make room on the back terrace where the party would take place. I saw Jerry pick up one end of the wicker sofa and Carol's husband the other end, and I heard Jerry's scream when the snake sank its teeth into him. Tom Kirkpatrick took off with a machete after the animal that was sliding rapidly toward the patio. Afterward they told us at the hospital that it was a *verrugosa*, a very poisonous kind of snake that apparently had coiled up beneath the sofa. They couldn't save Jerry, because there's no antidote for that poison. Later on the Kirkpatricks took it on themselves to let me know the day and hour when the army sent Jerry White's body back to Canton, Ohio, in a metal coffin, so his family could bury him. I shed enough tears to fill three oceans. For Jerry, for me, and above all for Canton, Ohio, which I would never have the chance to get acquainted with.

I'm still here on Fourteenth Street, with my passport ready, working at the bank with Laury, because Edy's already got her gringo and is living in Nashville, Tennessee. Since I'm older now, I can't give myself the luxury of waiting much longer. I've had several North American friends, but unfortunately either they were married or their enthusiasm didn't last. But I can't get discouraged. Someday I am going to get married to a gringo who will take me away to live in the United States, and they are never going to hear from me again on Fourteenth Street West, I can tell you that.

The Woman

Enrique Chuez
Translated by Leland H. Chambers

First was the short path through the yellow patch of corn up to the door. When her grandmother died, a dimension of everyday life went with her. Everything that the body of the old woman aroused in the meaning of her young life faded away. So that she would forget her grief her father bought her a doll to substitute for the one who had died, the one who had forsaken her.

The men went down with the coffin, which hid, for a moment, the patch of corn where the tassels were beginning to flower. She played with the doll and without telling anyone she gave it the name of her dead grandmother. She made it some little suits from the clothing left by the deceased. It had that fragrance of old camphor.

Time restructured itself once more, became whole without the presence of the old woman who quickly disappeared from her memory, leaving behind the vague feeling of a toothless voice and some frail hands. Days became themselves again, and people were the same.

Then everything was getting ready, coming together so that moment would arise when the old man should come down the path. He stopped before the door, wary of entering, and said good morning in a lukewarm way. Her father addressed him with sugary submissiveness and there, at the death of the recent days, they talked about the land and the corn. His father opened his mouth with a smile like a pocket until the old man's hand reached out and deposited the money in the light of the dead year, that tranquil, pastoral December. Then, after he went away, the months passed.

The doll continued to fill her life, her little games. There were certain obstructions that revolved around the river, the corn for the hens, the work of pounding the rice, the rain showers. Suddenly one day the old man appeared again. He emerged from the countryside and walked up the path. Her father nervously turned here and there several times before approaching him. Now standing before him he spoke to him with his mouth, with his hand, with his eyes.

Then the old man talked and talked, calmly. She saw in her father's eyes the lifeless shine with which he had gazed at the cornstalks withered by the drought and with which, day after day, he had prayed to the image of the Nazarene on the calendar. She also found herself filled with the look that came from the cold eyes of the old man. After that the path got used to the swaying gait that brought her candies and crackers, after which the skinny hands tried to feel her thighs with rough caresses. Meanwhile, the days hung outside like bags of fiery lead and the cornstalks bent their dried bodies down before her father, who contemplated them sadly.

That time when the old man came. When once he had gotten inside the hut, he gradually swelled larger and larger while her father was reducing in size, moving his hands like a spider. The old man's words emerged and humbled the other words rolling around over the bare floor of the hut. From time to time the old man's gaze sought her out and would get underneath her bodice, her white bodice. Then he said something to her father who looked at her in horror while frantically shaking his head in refusal. The old man put his face closer toward her father, letting his voice fall hard and slow over him. The time went by, and her mother did not return from doing the wash in the river. Her father began to weep and got smaller and smaller until he disappeared. The old man's body filled the hut entirely and his hands sought her, trying to take her clothes off first with coddling and petting and then with violence. She resisted, panic possessing her, when he came near her mouth in order to kiss her. She called her father who did not exist and continued calling for him with her eyes when the old man covered her mouth so she wouldn't scream. Afterward came the pain, the terrible fear, and the long dream into which she fled to hide herself.

When she opened her eyes the old man was no longer there, and an anemic breeze reached her from the mountains. Ordinary things changed their meaning and their familiarity. Her father was a shadow with muffled gestures, a blurred face. Her mother made another shadow, useless, hateful.

After awhile the old man appeared again. The shadow of her father disappeared; and by the door, through the doorway, the skeletonlike cornstalks stood sending their images in beneath the summer light. A violent shudder ran through her body with the memory of the pain that the old man had caused to be born in her flesh. She tried to get away but his hands held her back, and a scream left her mouth when they threw her down on the earth. Then she heard her father's yell. She saw the disturbed face of the old man above her and she also saw it when he looked toward the light in the doorway and said, No, friend, while getting to his feet and hastily buttoning his fly. She also looked toward the doorway and saw the rifle pointing at the old man. Behind the little, cold hole was the face of her father. It was a different face: the face he had had when taking those coins and going off toward town, that he had when he returned with the doll he gave her while caressing her hair.

At the same time she heard the explosion throughout the hut. The old man lifted his hand toward his forehead where blood was dripping toward her from a hole. Her father drew near her while she backed away in fear and pushed away the hand that sought her hair in order to leave a caress.

The old man's body, twisting in convulsions, was flung down on the red earth, the fly he hadn't had time to close still open. The wound continued to force his blood out into the afternoon where, after it had spread itself around, the earth eagerly drank it in through some cracks.

Her father said to her with a hoarse voice, Forgive, forgive me, for the love of God, daughter. I never wanted to do it. Then he brought the rifle barrel to his temple and right beside her she heard the second explosion. The impact of the bullet so very close to her splashed blood on her face. Other faces, among them her mother's, appeared at the threshold and they poured forth screams and cries as she saw their arms reaching toward her.

Afterward there was a silence of many days of sun and rain and long hours of loneliness. The face of her mother hovered over her the whole time. The eyes of that face looked at her and spoke to her, seeking that pain, that grief which emanated from her and walled her off from the day and from the summers.

Thus she allowed herself to grow without saying anything.

When she was fifteen, her breasts pushed out in front of her as if showing her a road right in front of her eyes. She felt herself prepared to confront whatever there was beyond the dead cornstalks and the still-intact path. She made a bundle of her few dresses, put on an old hat to protect herself from the sun and, barefoot, without looking at her mother's picture, went down toward the town.

She had to live far away from her memories.

She still had her life ahead of her.

The Chameleon
Claudio de Castro
Translated by Leland H. Chambers

I used to turn myself into anything, that's what chameleons are for.
Coarse earth, either dry or damp, and fertilized.
Air. Water. Ice. A cat, a lizard. A toad or pigeon. I was
always changing. That's why I took several passports with
me. The same name and date of birth along but different
faces. I made a living by making things out of myself. No
matter where we visited I always made a great impression.
Children would become delirious. They would scream enthusiastically. Women would faint. Old folks grew pale and crossed
themselves. People were amused. Scientists were astonished,
kept taking notes constantly, and drew a lot of diagrams and
abstract formulas that I never ever managed to understand.
And sometimes—this is what pleased me most of all—stories would come out in the papers praising my ephemeral art. But there were skeptics, incredulous folk, the kind
who, when they get inside the tent and see the transforma-
tion, start whispering and making sour faces, grumbling about
the money they invested and looking inquisitively around for
any sort of mirror, string, pulley, or other machine that would
show the secret of the trick. A friend whose name was Octavio
helped me. He traveled with me and held the curious
at a distance; he kept the marks from taking pictures
and the high-and-mighty from coming close enough
to touch me. He would sell the tickets at the door
and also keep the books. And he's the only one
who knew precisely what we brought in, how
much we'd made. He'd pack up the tent and take
it down again whenever we went to another carnival. In exchange I taught him some interesting tricks
so that someday and on his own hook he could set up
his own show. He was a good student. Nonetheless,
sometimes he was a little careless. He liked to showoff
what he knew. That's the way it is. And
the way it was. Until the night when he
completely neglected me. I had changed myself to cool grass, tall and lovely, when an
impudent fool came up without his noticing it;
he simply crossed the safety line and with those
grotesquely heavy paws of his reached out and pulled
a fistful of grass. It was too late, of course, though Octavio
shoved him away and threw him from the tent so roughly that
he smashed his face upon the ground. I shuddered and bent
completely over, just like a sea of wheat ears hit by a hurricane.
I became a human being again, screaming in pain. Those who
were present confirmed that there were no pulleys or mirrors or
any cheap tricks. And the grass still clutched in the hand of that
wretch was also transformed into a portion of my flesh, since what he
had wrenched away was my eyeballs. Now Octavio has to be my cane.

Family Photograph

Ernesto Endara
Translated by Leland H. Chambers

(A portion of a rather long letter to my son in which I tell him about things that otherwise he would learn in a distorted fashion, like that business of when the family decided to have itself photographed.)

Now I know that you wouldn't take it this way, but I really felt ashamed in those days when I was more or less the same age as you are now ... You're going to be eleven this December, aren't you? In those days your grandfather's wife couldn't stand me and your grandmother's husband only put up with me because he was very much in love with my mother. More children were born from each of those new marriages. At the time we had the photograph taken they were so little that they hadn't yet developed that unhappy human capacity for hatred and rancor, so therefore I think that your half-uncles, that is, my half-brothers, never thought the whole thing very important. Now I understand that our lives used to be so full of inhibitions—we were so conventional! Notice that nowadays we don't have those problems since you get along so well with my other children and your new stepmother, and I, as you've noticed, feel such a great tenderness for your mother's new daughter, and I believe that if your new stepfather were a tiny bit less jealous I'd get along very well with him. Ah, but in those days we needed human warmth so much! That's why there were so many comings and goings, so many violent secret meetings sprinkled with weeping, so many pleas and so much stamping of feet, before the family jointly decided to go to the photographer's. Is there any self-respecting family perhaps that does not have a family picture in their album?

I recall that the first big problem that came up was, who was going to have the sublime job of focusing and capturing us for eternity? It was decided that the photographer should be blind, discreet, and competent.

At length we found one, recommended by Carluncho, who himself was just starting with the camera at that time and already showing great promise, but of course he couldn't do the work since for us he suffered from a serious problem: good eyesight. The one Carluncho recommended lived in an upper room behind the "93" Cantina where it opens out on the Rochet patio. Not only did he live there, but that's where he did his business—that is, that's where his studio was.

And we all went, nor does it need to be said that we each went alone, by ourselves. It was important for people not to find out. You know how we Panamanians are, and in those days it was worse since we were so uncertain whether to go on being a little town and keep on observing the siesta or whether to ascend to the rank of city and take the leap. Hidden behind a billboard that said, "Sabino Knows How to Paint," I saw them all go past. My stepmother was the only one who was uncertain about finding the address—and she also had the disadvantage of carrying her youngest child in her arms—since, being a gringo, she couldn't tell which was the studio on whose stairway were registered the numbers on her slip of paper. I quickly followed her up the stairs. We were all there.

The photographer, who was blind because of an accident and not from birth, had by this time become accustomed to his obligatory shadows. His studio was always dark, since he never turned on the lights—except to take the pictures—or pulled back the heavy curtains that remained forever closed. Perhaps he did this so that his friends or customers would not feel any kind of advantage over him, or perhaps so he would pay less for the electricity, although in those days the "fuel clause" had not yet been invented. What made the biggest impression on me was his way of getting about, like an old cat, and his lightless eyes which in the tenuous clarity that entered through the doorway seemed like two little bronze balls that had been submerged in the ocean for a long time. With some ceremony, he was accommodating us one by one, indicating where we were to put our feet so as not to trip over the extension wires or the lamps.

He seated the older ones each in an armchair, placing the children alongside their respective mothers. Naturally I was to be in the center, for which I felt very important. When he turned on the lights, very powerful ones, we all were dazzled momentarily. The photographer gentleman, very understanding, waited a few minutes until our pupils became accustomed to that radiant brightness, and then he dived beneath some black sheets that hung down from the contrivance and was adjusting I don't know how many things for minutes that seemed like an eternity to us. At length he emerged, upset and trembling a little.

He explained to us simply that with his eyesight gone he took so long because he had to search by feel for the little numbers that adjusted the distance and the lens opening—at least that is what it seemed to me he was trying to explain. Very kindly he asked if we were ready. My father, my stepmother, like me and my four half-brothers and -sisters, answered affirmatively.

But my stepfather had a coughing fit, and the ribbon my mother used for pulling her hair back fell off. We had to wait. And it was a good thing this happened, because a few seconds later a terrible sneeze burst forth from out of me and totally messed up the blond ringlets of my half sister on my father's side. The photographer made use of the situation to warn us, in his voice that also sounded like that of an old cat, that we should try to keep our eyes fully open during the whole process.

Finally we were ready.

To actually snap the picture was a very simple thing; it didn't take any time at all.

It seemed absurd to me that when we left we should have to go out separately once again, because I thought that the photograph would have brought us together in some loving, magic way, once and for all.

It really disappointed me that it wasn't that way.

Some days later they entrusted me with the delicate mission of going to pick up that memorable photograph. The hope of that beautiful plate bringing us together was born anew in me. The blind man received me in the midst of his tranquil penumbra, handed me an envelope, and I paid him. On going out into the street I opened the envelope and took out the prints, enjoying in anticipation that image of the family united forever. What a blow! The photographs were all just one big black splotch. I went back up the stairs once more and with tearful eyes I reproached the blind man, thinking that it was a cruel joke or that he wanted to rob me. But he excused himself smoothly—his excuse didn't seem very technical to me—he said that surely the reason the prints hadn't turned out was that a smile was missing.

Nonetheless, since he returned the money to me, I went away whistling a tune . . .

Gloria Wouldn't Wait

Jaime García Saucedo
Translated by Leland H. Chambers

For Jarl Babot.

S he used to write poems and then forget, she would forget everything, she would bleed her heart dry and leave it by the side of the road like an empty pail; she would go on without turning her face. The world was filled with us. We were young and our enthusiasm turned like a rose in the winds above the rim of the pitcher of happiness. And she would tell me always to find something, it didn't make any difference what it was, but above all, to find something and learn to settle accounts, to empty the pitcher and fill it up again and so on forever. Thirst never ends. I was so disconcerting, and she was so wise. I will never forget our warm, frequent get-togethers in that coffee joint. We would talk about literature. Gloria, sensitive and lucid, exceptionally endowed with a beautiful modesty, was very understanding of my painful agony over wanting to be a writer. She convinced me that the theme always came before the form, and that the characters could annihilate the author.

As the permanent prisoner of my tortures, I queried her until weariness set in. I wanted to pick her brain dry, down to the core. Gloria had been successful as a poet but her greatness was not for this people; foreigners who were unaware of the way she drank her coffee or how she applied her lipstick had discovered and loved her better than we ourselves. There is still so much to say about Gloria. That she was unique? This could be repeated until one wearied of it. That she was mine! Well, this is something only I could feel, as warm and vital as the sun's light in the room where I spent most of my days. Those long walks through the labyrinthine avenues of plastic and rubbish in the enormous city were like a sort of ritual that was engraved on my heart. Gloria was sick. I never found out if she was conscious of her premature end, but her agony was useful to me (how frightful!). I only needed to see her suffer. Cancer is implacable. And I began to write my novel, my great novel.

Gloria could wait a little longer. The dragonfly shouldn't get too close to the light, its wings could burn too quickly. And I was determined to move ahead. I was ready to suffer for her, to utilize her as my favorite character. Her fatalism, ever more entwined within the skin of silence, turned incomprehensible to me. My twilight thirst was bringing forth cold tears. And I loved the infinite solitude that in my room provided me with the pleasure of exorcising the cancerous demon transformed into an ideal character. It was a preparation for the offering of the supreme testimony. I would be immensely famous, like Flaubert, or Dumas. Gloria was Emma, Marguerite, whoever . . .

Bitter is the parting when the memory falls apart. Gloria was fading away, but she would be able to wait. My great work was not finished. And I was pouring my whole self into it, just as she begged me to do. All my trembling, my phantoms, this whole stupid life came forth in torrents. At times I thought I was Gloria, and on numerous occasions it wasn't she but I who suffered the fatigue and the shudders of death lying in wait; and I wanted to die, to speak to the wind like a madman interpreting an ancient book, to be alone, absolutely alone night and day, like an irresponsible corpse. Gloria, my unfortunate archetype, was leaving me for the clarity of darkness. The novel was coming to a close.

A writer ought not feel shame for his pathos. Before she died in September, I read her the manuscript. Gloria listened with the voluptuousness of a stiff rag doll, sweet and bitter. I saw her as a wrinkled fragment of life, a bare, tired tree who still was able to smile. She told me that art was more powerful than reality. She revealed to me her secret imperfections, recondite defects, and failures. I understood then that she had always been deceiving me. This Gloria of defeat had no part in my novel, and I asked her, begged her, to wait a little longer. I had to do the whole thing over, but she could no longer offer me anything, and turned into a thousand unsuccessful pages lying in my lap.

I had failed. I realized that the novel was nothing more than a tedious bauble of exquisite words. Disillusioned, to recover my lost inspiration I began to look for Gloria in other women. Melancholy and grief would never again be as genuine as then. I was no longer the same. I imagined I had lived for a century. The world turned hostile, exasperating, repugnant. I had thought I was God. Too late I found out that He does not write fiction. I had been too imperfect to realize that.

Duplications

Enrique Jaramillo Levi
Translated by Leland H. Chambers

It's not the first time the man passes in front of her. In actuality she has seen him at least three times, hovering around, since parking the Mustang close to the gray van she has been ordered to keep watch on. After following Li Peng all morning, who very strangely looks exactly like the man who has just gotten to the corner, who is lingering there looking at her, and who now is beginning to walk toward her again, the woman seated in the Mustang is waiting for him to emerge from the embassy. It's been more than twenty minutes since she saw him go in through the main door. The guard must have recognized him immediately, because he at once made a gesture with his head and stepped to one side. Li Peng did not look behind him as she had expected. If he had any suspicion that perhaps they were following him, he gave no sign of it.

When the man who has been looking at her gets close to the Mustang, he bends his head down to speak to her, something that surprises her greatly. It has been a sudden movement, and the woman doesn't manage to get her hand into her purse where she keeps her pistol. Both look silently at each other. Though still incredulous, she is able to confirm then that she is dealing with the real Li Peng, although this cannot be, since the latter has still not come out of the embassy. Nevertheless it is he. At least, their features are markedly similar, the same baldness, identical nervous tic in the left eye, same skin with signs of some long-ago pockmarks. And he keeps looking at her fixedly, with a seriousness that recalls the thoroughness with which she had days ago studied the enlarged photograph of the man whom she would have to follow around everywhere until further orders. But no, it can't be. She recalls perfectly that it was the very moment when Li Peng entered the embassy that she had noticed this other man for the first time (the one who was now asking her respectfully, "Aren't you Señora Torres, of F.I.B.R.A.?") who has been watching her insistently from the corner and who looks so much like the other one.

"I believe you're making a mistake, sir. I'm Señorita Corrales, a schoolteacher. I don't know the person you mention."

"But you are identical to the woman who spent the entire morning following the man who went into the embassy a little while ago."

"I don't know what you're talking about, and I repeat that I don't know any Señora Torres."

She doesn't understand how this man can know that she has been following Li Peng and yet be confused about her name. She has an urge to confess to him that, yes, she has spent the morning tailing the other man, although she is not Señora Torres, and also that she finds an unusual likeness between Li Peng and him. But the hand of her interlocutor has already thrust itself in through the car window and is opening the purse that is on her thighs. He is pointing her own pistol at her now, and with a gesture he motions for her to slide over to one side. The man opens the car door then and seats himself beside her.

They remain in silence for some minutes. Señorita Corrales begins to think that this man in reality has to be the very Li Peng whom she has been following. Perhaps she only got mixed up on seeing the other person enter the building. Her angle of vision at that moment didn't permit her to be absolutely certain. Perhaps her eyes had wandered away from the true Li Peng for the fraction of a second it took for the boy on the bicycle to go past. Yes, now she recalled that detail. And immediately she must have set her eyes upon that someone dressed in similar fashion who was approaching the guard. Which brings her to realize that she has been discovered.

She tells herself she is lost, but at that moment both see Li Peng emerge from the embassy. He walks right in front of the Mustang and when he fixes his harsh gaze upon her eyes, which are watching him perplexedly, the woman confirms that it is simply a matter of his having a face identical to that of the man who is continuing to point the pistol at her and who now is smiling for the first time.

"He's identical to you!" she exclaims, frightened, unable to hold herself back.

"It is I, my dear Señora Torres," he says, preserving the rigidity of his smile.

When the shot comes, the woman realizes that the pistol still has the silencer on it that she herself had put on this morning, and she thinks that in some way she must really be Señora Torres, so that the true

Señorita Corrales would logically be that woman exactly like her who is now getting out of the other Mustang parked on the other side of the gray van, the one who is hurrying her step so as not to lose sight of that other Li Peng now going around the corner, giving up his gray van, knowing himself followed and being the owner of a face that is the faithful copy of the one owned by the man who was seated there when he shot her but isn't any longer as she falls into the space that he had occupied.

Señor Noboa

Raúl Leis
Translated by Leland H. Chambers

For Ernesto Cardenal.

S eñor Noboa is the owner of half a province. During the last fifty years he had extended the lands inherited from his father by squeezing small landholders so they would sell him their small properties for a pittance. This was also how the large properties he inherited had come into being.

Of the many things that Señor Noboa possesses, the most valuable is the banana tree. In association with a foreign company, his lands are covered with green-gold stalks and clusters that are watered by the sweat of thousands of laborers, who never earn more than ninety dollars a month.

Once a year Señor Noboa personally tours his lands, atop his white horse and sweating heavy streams beneath his Panama hat. None of his banana camps fails to receive a visit from the lord and master. On that day, the only one all year long, something out of the ordinary happens. The peons turn their backs and refuse to look him in the face, because the legend has gone around that every time Señor Noboa visits those places a laborer dies of some illness or accident.

They all remember when three years ago a machine shredded the hands of the Chinaman Ramírez, and he died with the blood spurting from his wounds while he got paler and paler until he was white as a piece of paper. Or good old Sebastian, who was hit by a lung problem that finished him off before you could say boo. And Rafael? he got sick and died from the insecticides they used on the young banana sprouts. Not to speak of Matías, he was surprised by a coral snake in a clearing and that was it for him in spite of all the spells and invocations offered by Domingo the *curandero*, who traced the sign of the cross all over him in saliva and dark tobacco.

So that is why the people don't want to look Señor Noboa in the face, because they think it is the only way to avoid the evil spell the boss carries around with him. Señor Noboa is quite familiar with the legend that time has woven around him, and he enjoys it fully. It fascinates him to be able to instill that double fear. On the one hand, to be the omnipotent buyer/owner of all that effort of sweatsoaked labor that topples the banana stalks with lightning blows from sharpened machetes; and, on the other hand, to possess this supernatural power of causing death with the same ease as one snuffs out a candle. But he knows that his only real power is the first. The second has come about only as the result of stringing together a fortuitous series of accidents linked to the natural risks of the job like little chains of thread crocheted by a dressmaker's hands.

He spurs his horse and reaches the last of the camps, where the foreman greets him while looking only in the direction of Señor Noboa's mud-caked boots.

"So this is the troublemakers' camp," the master says to himself, and brings to mind the several attempts at strikes that have taken place around this place throughout the year. "No one is looking at me."

And he laughs inwardly, convinced that his legendary power is a potent ingredient for thoroughly crushing those who question his authority by alleging salary or health claims.

Hundreds of laborers are gathered around him with their eyes set on the clouds, the dirt, or the greenness of the forest. Without dismounting, Señor Noboa lets loose on a tirade in a stentorian voice. Right to the heart of the matter. No beating around the bush. Puts them in their place. Sets the example. Threatens. Warns. A pause to wipe off the sweat.

Without looking at him, a group of peons pulls on a rope. A woven grass mat that faces the master falls, exposing a large mirror to view. Señor Noboa stares at himself in it, full length, on horseback, face to face. And Señor Noboa sees Señor Noboa as he falls from his horse. As he shudders with strange convulsions. As his face grows purple, his hands twitch. As he dies with all his might, as his mouth fills with ants. While the *curandero* Domingo vainly outlines cross after cross in saliva and dark tobacco all over the body of Señor Noboa.

The Village Virgin

Bertalicia Peralta
Translated by Leland H. Chambers

Alexis, Alex, Alejandrito, brother of mine, I am trying, I am doing everything possible, doing what I can, doing my part, as you say, I talk with everyone, I go everywhere, I dress like people who come from good families, talk, laugh, argue, give my opinion, drink cocktails, smoke, read, write, I get exhausted, believe me, I do my utmost never-endingly in the café until midnight, sunk in a cup of coffee, reading all the dumb news published daily in the newspapers, about President Johnson's stupid claims, the student strikes in Rio de Janeiro, in Buenos Aires, Charles de Gaulle's trips, the numbers in the lottery, the bombing in Vietnam, the hard time they gave Frank Sinatra in Mexico, I chat with Luisa, she asks me for a cigarette, then some matches, and then she begins to talk and her words, her sentences gradually open a way over the tables and the warmth heats up even more, I watch her lips move, opening and shutting in an intermittent gymnastic display that more than one athlete would envy, and then Henry doubtless will drop by with his adjustable pants and his thin, fine hands that seem to be trying to take flight toward the skies, pigeons, little pigeons white and beautiful flapping in the air, and he'll probably start babbling away to Luisa and then he'll ask me, "How've you been today, old man?" and I'll probably answer him, "Like shit," just to go along with the general tone, though things have actually been going along just as always and I don't have any reason to be annoyed, to the contrary, the landlady forgot to collect from me, and the doctor invited me to lunch so I didn't even have to put out for lunch. Ah, Alejandrito, if you could only see how I'm vegetating in this village! I'm wasting away, I swear it, it's not that I'm putting on airs, it's just, well, that one knows that in another city one has a certain value, in a city, a real city I mean, well, one could be something, work, fight, in short, one could live, what the hell, like God said: full steam ahead! But damned if the people here aren't satisfied that this place is really something! They even get hostile if you say anything to the contrary, and they're capable of hanging you just like during the Inquisition. Only yesterday Luisa got all worked up and we went to the movies and saw *Love on a Pillow*, a color film with Brigitte Bardot, but what music, brother, I really loved it, you know how I get with music, I didn't even want to move a muscle, not even to breathe, so that every heartbeat would bend to the rhythm and movement of that music. When we came out we were walking along, taking in the breezes a little—you should see how sticky the heat is here—with Luisa sweet and chattering along as always, practically hanging on my shoulder, we got to the open-air café on the jetty, and suddenly there I saw her, wearing her black sweater with little gray knots sticking out, hair cut straight across the forehead, gaze lifted out over the world as if ready to take in everything in front of her. I followed her look and steeped myself in the contemplation of the city by night, excuse me, I meant village, and now it didn't seem so detestable; an interminable procession of diminutive lights swayed above the water's surface, gently, so gently that I began mentally to hum a tune from my infancy and without realizing it was suddenly back to my origins, my brothers and sisters, the schoolroom with its dark wood floors and high windows, teacher with her black hair and marvelous mouth, the round, plump letters, wide-lined notebooks, my evening punishments and recreations, my longing to be a writer and be famous, and I felt sad and I gazed at her as if begging her for something, I don't know what, but I needed to be in her sway at that moment, her smile, her hands that she was pressing one against the other, surely fleeing from some imaginary chill, or perhaps a real one. I waited patiently until several friends arrived and then I was able to get up and go over toward her without Luisa noticing.

"May I?" I said, with a gesture as if to sit down. She looked at me indifferently, and I felt that something was breaking up within me, something from that childhood so slightly recovered a while before. Suddenly I felt like an imbecile, without knowing what to say. She lowered her head, put her thin lips to the straws, and sucked gently while raising her black eyes toward me beneath her lightly arched eyebrows, a silent interrogation, and I smiled at her, still searching around in my brain for some explanation, some word, a single logical reason for having gone up to someone I didn't know. Among decent people this is a boldness, of course, but at that moment I wasn't inclined toward rules of decency. I lit a cigarette and then after a pause that seemed very long and difficult, she whispered, in a voice that seemed like a leaf come loose in April, "It would be a pleasure."

Oh, Alex, never in my life have I been so in love. All at once I had fallen in love, it was the classic love-at-first-glance, I'm certain of it. Don't make fun, you know I don't believe in that either, but I swear to you that I loved her from that very moment. She listened to me with her sea-wet gaze, her closed hands, and I talked a lot, on and on like I hadn't talked to anyone for a long time, I told her about my unfinished paintings, my failed lawyer's career, the house where I used to live, that I was fed up, yes, that was the truth, fed up with all these people, I told her about you, Alex, about our house with the huge mango trees in the patio, about how nice it was on Sundays when they gave us money for the offering at church and we spent it for "mafa" and coconut sweets, I told her about my hopes to be a writer, my sheets of paper trapped in my room underneath the portable typewriter, I asked her to let me show her my poems, to let me invite her to my house. She laughed and I felt like crying from joy, I was breathing fast, and I looked at the sky, happily. I wasn't aware when Luisa and the others got up until they were right next to me.

"Oh, excuse me," I said with all naturalness, "let me present Señorita . . ." and I sharpened my ears so as to catch her name in the breeze: "Stella," she said, and brushed me with her arm as she rose. She made a move to pay, but I refused and begged her to let me charge it to our account. She said goodbye and left.

Now I am searching for my virgin, Alex, I can't stop thinking of her. Luisa asked me who she was and I told her it was a childhood friend I hadn't seen in a long time, but she didn't believe me. She got a little cooler and more independent after she noticed a drawing of a virgin with her gaze lifted and hair cut straight across the forehead, and another of a virgin in a black sweater with the little gray knots, and another of a virgin with hands pressed together as if protecting herself against a kind of cold that does not exist here, and I'm working hard, really hard, and I'm happy and every evening I walk around in my village, without losing heart, looking for my virgin with the black eyes and a voice that seems like a leaf come loose in April.

Alexis, Alex, Alejandrito, brother of mine, it's really nice that the city is so small, tiny, like a village, with a hill of streets running up it that you can cover completely without tiring, where you can come to a halt at one point and make it all out, and you can even shout at it at the top of your voice from the jetty opposite Ancón Hill, or go up to the Bridge of the Americas during the day and whistle: and everyone will hear me, every resident will know that I'm looking for Stella, and even though Luisa doesn't talk to me anymore and is leaving, I know that I'll find her, really, I am certain of it.

Our Boss

Dimas Lidio Pitty
Translated by Leland H. Chambers

When he arrives at the office, everyone observes him intently. The women because he is elegantly dressed and is right around the age when one's temples start to gray, and that is when people say that men are inclined to deceive their wives; and the men, because they secretly envy him his ties, always matching his suits and in tune with the prevailing times. So that his arrival gives rise to a general expectation in the department, and this reaches its climax when he says good morning in a voice that is well modulated, crystal clear, as if it had received a gentle brushing at the same time as his teeth.

"Words seem as if they were made for his mouth," one woman remarked, at the pinnacle of ecstasy. "I would give anything to have a husband like that."

After soaking up the unanimous admiration, our department head spends a few minutes bringing himself up to date on what has happened before 10:30, his usual time of arrival. Next he dictates a memo and talks on the telephone with several persons—other department heads, friends (he is in the habit of calling his wife to ask her if she has slept well), perhaps the minister, or in special situations, the president himself. Immediately after this he goes to the food bar and requests a glass of fruit juice.

On his return he converses with the minister's secretary and sometimes with the associate minister. Along the way he greets the public relations director. Because it would be good, of course, for the improvements he has introduced to the advantage of public administration and the benefit of the country to become known.

Returning to his office, he signs the memo previously dictated and orders it sent off. Then he lights up one of his imported cigarettes (extra long, with a deluxe cigarette holder), and his face takes on dimensions of greatness. If we weren't familiar with his virtues, his sensitivity, his grace, his gift with people, if we had not been aware of the aroma of his exclusive cologne every morning, we would say he is not human, he must be divine. One has only to see the impeccable cut of his suits, the fine quality of his shoes.

But the most extraordinary thing, the quality that wins him the goodwill and appreciation of all, is that in spite of his illustrious family background, which might well have caused him to display some vanity, he is neither arrogant nor supersensitive. On the contrary, we can approach him to discuss any matter whatsoever with the absolute assurance of being listened to.

It is true, however, that at times, when we explain the problems about accounts payable or the imbalance occurring in specific items among the tax deposits, he permits his mind to wander, contemplating his Dunhill lighter and putting on a dreamy air that reminds one of Mastroianni. But none of this is of any importance. When one thinks of his many virtues, what can this small defect signify?

Since we are quite aware of his merits and know the importance of his emotional balance, we almost always avoid embarrassing him with annoying matters. At all cost we try to shunt aside any difficulties for him. That is why the functioning of the department falls back on us, principally on the slight figure of the assistant head, a small man of humble background, discreet and retiring, but extremely competent.

The truth is, to say it once and for all, we cheerfully take all the work on ourselves so that our boss can attend to his friends or concentrate on some special affair. For he is a man with a great many obligations, being constantly besieged by receptions, board meetings, seminars, and the like. Besides, we understand very well that for a person of his stature it must be terribly disagreeable and bothersome to have to busy himself with details.

On the other hand, and this is something that fills us with pride, confidentially, we have found out that he was named to this position so that the country might be honored to have a man of his lineage in this post. And there are those who say that his appointment here is in line with the larger aim of familiarizing him with financial matters, because he is destined for very high posts indeed.

Now, the crowning moment for the boss comes, it's really sublime, when we gather in his office, set apart with big glass partitions and curtains, to tell him some joke. Surrounded by everyone then, he seems like a general in the midst of his troops, or perhaps a leader idolized by his people.

You ought to see him laughing. His delight is so contagious that we all get simply euphoric and we even forget our own penury, our misfortunes. And if one of the girls gets a little too enthusiastic and seats herself on his desk, he never shows any annoyance, on the contrary he gives her a hug and laughs all the harder. Really, he is incomparable. No other department of the ministry can boast of a boss such as he. And he possesses such aplomb that only on one occasion did we ever see him in a state of confusion.

That day a taxpayer came in to request certain information of capital importance for the proper functioning of his business. As is usual in those cases, the one to provide him with it was the department head, and so to him the man was directed.

The man, who was quite pleasant, to be sure, spent a long while explaining what he was looking for, but the boss, who happened to be wearing his most beautiful tie that day, did not understand. Finally, the man began to sweat and got all green and purple in the face; he said just to forget the whole matter, for he had realized that it was not so vital after all.

Right afterward, suddenly putting on the most cheerful bearing in the world, the man offered to tell him a joke. The boss, who adores jokes of every color and tone, from the purest to the purplest, accepted, very pleased, and in another demonstration of his benevolence, his eagerness to mix with his subordinates, called us in to hear it, too.

"Once there was a really dense fellow," the man said, "and they gave him this riddle: Put in a circle the stupidest, sorriest excuse for a living creature there is. It's not a rat, not a hyena, not a centaur, it's not a frog. So what is it? Just step in front of a mirror and it'll tell you."

When he finished speaking, he looked fixedly at the boss and asked him if he had understood it.

"No," the boss answered, jovially and amused, "I don't understand anything."

"That son of a bitch didn't either," the man said. "Look, here's a mirror."

Then he glanced around at all of us with a strange expression on his face and departed without even saying goodbye. The boss, for his part, took up the mirror, his brow furrowed, and examined it attentively as if hoping to extract the key to the riddle from it.

Now the most extraordinary thing, we'll never forget it, is that—and this trait without a doubt confirms his illustrious origin and his education abroad—despite the painful mental effort he was putting forth, he never ceased to caress that most elegant and expensive of his neckties.

Games

Pedro Rivera
Translated by Leland H. Chambers

"Juan, Carlos, get in the house."

The shadows incised in the plateau announce the collapse of night-fall over the little village. The adobe hovels, unsymmetrical and scattered about, grow silent in withdrawal. Dogs are barking, horses are neighing, cicadas dominate the immense mist, the horizon of sound.

The boys don't answer. They are playing a game of catch-me-if-you-can, putting on a show of pitiless fighting all over the dream stage, in the dampness of the earth.

"Juan! Carlos! Are you deaf or just playing dumb? Darn it, I'm going to take the whip to you, then you'll see. I'm not responsible if you make me do that. You need the patience of a saint to handle stubborn kids."

The boys approach. Aunt Paulina stands in the doorway, and her eyes focus on all the recent dirt on their clothes, on their little bodies bruised in the game.

"Look what you've done to yourselves! Pigs! I ought to give you a good licking right now!"

"We didn't hear you, Aunty, cross my heart."

The boys know that Aunt Paulina won't do anything she says. They are used to those ill-humored threats. They don't answer back so as not to hurt her. They run into the house cheerfully, shouting, chasing each other, squeezing the last drops out of their game broken off so inconclusively. Their aunt watches them adamantly, the dim lamp in her hands shedding a pallid light over the rough furniture, the whitewashed, dusty walls, and the tunnel of tiles overhead, lined with cobwebs and grime. The parched earth floor in the dwelling is cracked, cots not pulled out yet pushed against the walls, and the potbellied jug placed high up on a shelf at the back door leading outside to the patio. The boys undress in silence, exuding a quiet happiness, and they are thinking of their grandma's threat: "If you keep on misbehaving I'll send you back home to your mama, I won't put up with naughty kids." They like the country, they don't want to go back to the city so soon. They need their mother and they miss her, especially at night, but by day she is just a recollection without nuances, completely supplanted. In the city they won't have horses, they won't have a river with water in it, nor as much room to romp around in.

"You can't go to sleep like that, you filthy boys. You better get yourselves right down to the spring before it gets darker."

"But it's so cold, Aunty. We'll get all numb."

"I hope you freeze yourselves stiff, you pieces of . . ."

The spring is just a few steps from the house, going down. They go past the henhouse, the rugged orange tree on the slope, the pile of burnt rocks smelling like the seeds of *marañón* fruit. At the edge of the ravine is where the pool is. The boys are trembling with cold. It is freezing in the shade.

"Let's drain it so that clean water will come out. You'll see, it's warm."

Aunt Paulina bends down, kneeling by the side of the hollow, and scoops up the water in a gourd, tossing it into the muddy current. The young woman's hair falls over her shoulders, and each time she bends over the motion reveals the solid build of the muscular body hardened by the labors of the field. The water gushes forth quite clear and reaches the usual level.

"Why don't we play cow-and-calf?"

Her voice is soft, its tone tranquil. She caresses the mischievous heads of the boys and presses them against her breast lovingly.

"Sure, Aunty."

"You won't tell anyone, now, right?"

"Not even Grandma Rufina?"

"No, no, not anyone, that wouldn't be good. It's just a game among us three. I won't scold you anymore if you keep the secret."

"Sure, Aunty."

Aunt Paulina unbuttons her blouse and loosens her brassiere. Her nipples appear like hard, dark suns; they just reach the level of Juan and Carlos's faces.

"See, I'm the mama cow and you are my little calves."

The boys visualize the image of the cow in the corral, that afternoon. They understand the game, the calf between the cow's legs, clinging to the fat udder, suckling and shooing flies away with its tail. They understand. The cow is mooing tenderly, eyes lost on the horizon of the stable, chewing its cud. That is their aunt's game, easy and fun. Pressed so close against the warmth of the cow's body, they ward off the night cold.

Their aunt makes a mooing sound too, like the cow.

The boys are romping around, the air smells like the new sun, like a light dew, like chicken excrement, like roasted tortillas, like coffee freshly brewed. Their grandma is fixing breakfast. The dogs, begging, become entangled in her white skirt. Aunt Paulina is washing up the utensils and watches her nephews out of the corner of her eye as they run around close to the roasting stones where the seeds are blackening.

"Juan, Carlos, quiet down, or else."

The boys stop their romping and look at their aunt without blinking, without fear. They corner her silently, the cow in the corral, and cows don't beat their calves, they munch on grass while the calves play around in the pasture. Disturbed, their aunty smiles in the corral of her memories. Games are games. She gazes once more at her utensils, powerless. Juan and Carlos are racing down the slope of the ravine.

Carnival

Jorge Turner
Translated by Leland H. Chambers

For Joaquín Beleno and Ramón H. Jurado.

I stand there looking at her, the room is tiny, it's hot, in the middle of the table is a vase with withered roses, I want to leave, but she says to me: Sit down awhile, don't be that way, why are you in such a hurry, I tell you, if you go out alone I'm going out on my own hook; it's not a threat . . . But I think it really is a threat. I go to leave. She says, why the roses when the table is so wobbly? She says her heart is broken, like the table leg.

I lean down, I straighten the leg . . . it's all right for now, if nobody shoves the table there's no reason for it to fall down, the scar on the table leg looks like the little scar on my cheek. I'm still bent over and she goes on telling me that I'm a son of a bitch, that I do everything badly, that I should mend it with glue, not to shrug my shoulders because that's insulting, what a miserable carnival Tuesday.

I'm not going to stick around here like an idiot, so I leave, and in the patio the light puts down its last yellow brushstrokes and the neighbors are getting into the festival atmosphere, and the dance is starting, spontaneously, without a director:

With this wind
that blows on me,
with this wind
I'll reach Pocrí.

The women are singing in chorus as they put ornaments into the hair of their petticoated daughters:

Yorilah, yoriley,
a lovely wind
to sail away.

I've managed to leave her at home. I hardly greet anyone. Some boys tie themselves together with paper streamers, some are shouting, a few set off rockets that are echoing, joyful and momentary . . . as I step out into the street.

The sky is growing darker, like her face when I leave her. Lightning? It's not lightning, it doesn't appear like the opening and shutting of your eyes, instead it's a swift fan of light dying among the clouds. As always, the powerful Zone searchlights are exploring the air over Panama.

Along the narrow sidewalk they go along in Indian file. Most of the disguises are wild, savage in fact. Blacks in loincloths and painted with indigo are dancing to the beat of imaginary tom-toms, fencing with brooms instead of knives. What buttocks on the *mulata* in the line moving along in front of me. It's incredible how they fall when she moves. I'd really like to see her in a loincloth, in a topless bikini, in her bare skin, I'd like her to tell me how her heart is broken too. The beating of the tom-toms marks her again with the soft wild rhythms of her protuberant haunches. Harmony of spontaneous flesh with no need for a baton. Her ass is swaying back and forth like a big bell-clapper: "For you, for me, for you, for me."

The mocking face of Momus is swaying back and forth in the faces of the people. The right to have fun without my wife, who lives to get on my nerves: sit down awhile, the house is too hot, and this, that, and the other thing . . . Chinto is fixing me up with a costume. I tell her she's a pain in the ass, but I've left her a thousand times and a thousand times I go back. They've closed the little store where I buy cigarettes, they must have gone to the dance. My ordinary, pale-faced wife with her deepset eyes. It's easy to stop smoking, the next time I promise to do that I'll never take it up again. Her buttocks that split open. Really hot, the kind of woman with a small head and a big ass. You'd better leave off cigarettes when they start hurting you. She's got me tied to her with her cunt, but she hasn't given me any kids in five years. Here's Chinto's place.

I ask Chinto, "How's it going, you got it ready?" and he answers me, "Yes, sir" in English, and I start dressing up, I talk with Chinto without mentioning my wife, I dress up like a clown in the movies. Several kinds of cosmetics. Methodical makeup to get a snow-white face, frozen smile around the mouth, a cross over the eyelids with an eyebrow pencil. The wig of reddish hair is fitted on. Instead of a circus, it's the dances under the tents. My caricature is reflected in the mirror and my new personality makes the image of my wife disappear, and I tell Chinto thanks a lot and "good-bye," in English.

The carnival atmosphere is beginning, the people passing by are laughing, I frolic around, free of my wife. Always sticking around everywhere close as a leech, or complaining because she has no money: head of sawdust, bottomless piggy bank, as if she were so good. Tired all the time: when I get up to go to my fucking job every morning, I fix my own breakfast because she's still sleeping, and she's asleep again when I get back in the afternoons. How come she's always tired? Is she going to bed with some other guys?

It's hard to dance in the crowded tents, but the entertainment is nice. Protagonists: panting black women showing their ivory and gold laughter dancing with feverish rhythm close to the orchestra, *cholas* moving their buttocks in counterrhythm like iguanas caught by the tail, old women grinding their rusty butts and shaking their cobwebs, girls pushing their breasts and their asses around . . . the centripetal force of their shining flesh. Everywhere you look, constant throngs, back and forth, grotesque movements combined with graceful ones, a growing, sticky odor of armpits and sex, together with the smoke of fried fish and the smell of *empanadas*.

The conjugal routine is completely demolished. Virginal prejudices do not enter into the carnival wildness. Conquests seem at your fingertips, but the best thing is, calmly, very calmly, the novelty of the catch. Why hurry with the hook when there are enough shoals of these fish for a long time?

Way over yonder I was drinking rum, I drank rum closer by, here I'm drinking rum. And here, in the La Cocaleca tent, I feel dizzy. I should cut down, because it's going to be my turn. I'll have a double, after that I'll stop. From here where the bar is, I look at the women as much as I want. As soon as the double goes down I'll ask for a cold beer, and then, really, I will stop. That woman over there by herself is disguised as a madwoman, but she attracts me.

I am drunk, but if I finish this beer my bashfulness will go away. Strange woman. Face completely white, country-style hat down to her ears, long dress of black taffeta. The orchestra is about to play. I give up the idea of asking her to dance. No, that's no way to get over this bashfulness: I dip my head down slightly, and the white mask responds affirmatively with another inclination of the head: panting!

The alcohol vapors bring about a diminishing of my senses, nonetheless she really makes a good partner, she follows the steps in my repertoire. I am transported, dancing on air, not on the wooden floor of the tent. With every twist and turn she is more mine, while I am less myself because of the alcohol and the carnival spirit.

In the fog I recognize myself sometimes, my head turns in a crazy whirlwind, but my craving for this woman who seems so aroused keeps me going, this woman who dances well, who won't deny me what I ask . . .

I open my eyes under the impression someone is hammering on my head; the worm-eaten wood of the ceiling isn't the wood in my own house; it's hot, there's no wobbly table nor vase with wilted roses, the tiny room, ah . . . the carnival, a bed made of boards, the stained sheets, the smell of semen, but alone and no *mulata* with buttocks like a bell clapper.

In the corner I see the old woman seated on a bench smoking her tobacco with the glowing fire within, she spits on the floor . . . and I leap from the bed . . . completely naked.

She says to me, "Don't go back to bed, don't cover yourself. Why do that? I've seen a lot of men in their birthday suits, I rent whores to them, I'm an old woman now."

I'm embarrassed anyway. I make an effort, get up again.

The old woman tells me, "Decide what you're going to do. The carnival is keeping me awake, hurry now, I have to lie down to rest (she keeps looking at my body), you and all the other drunks sleep like stones."

The partition of the wall doesn't reach the ceiling, I hear the moaning of a couple making love on the other side of it.

The old woman doesn't know anything about my money, my clothing, she doesn't care if they stole everything from me, she doesn't know my companion of the night before, though she seemed kind of ugly to her . . . when she was young there was always a crowd around her because in those days the men had much better taste.

I tell her to think now, please, how am I going to get out of here without clothes. She repeats she can't do anything, her husband died years ago, she doesn't have any friends, she doesn't know any man who would lend me his clothes. And I tell her I'm desperate, that I'll lose my job, my bread-and-butter, if I don't do something quick, that I have one hell of a headache and to settle it would she get me a bottle of aguardiente, that I'll pay for it later. And she answers me, "Un-unh, un-unh, un-unh," as if doubting my words and making fun of me.

She goes out of the room. She stays a long time. On returning she brings a bottle of rum, I take the cork out and raise the bottle, I swallow without breathing. I feel better, but I'm drunk again. I ask the old woman to take her clothes off. She stands there without moving. I undress her by force. She doesn't resist and warns me that she is too old for these things, not like before. Her body looks as wrinkled as her face, with her breasts empty and all stretched like prunes.

I'm tall and slender, she's short and dumpy. Her greasy dress is too short on me, but I have to put up with it. In the street I get my bearings. I'm not very far from my own house, and it's early in the morning, still dirty with confetti and paper streamers from the last day of carnival, the city is returning to the normalcy shattered by the clownish euphoria.

I'm not so drunk that I'm not conscious of my outlandish appearance. I weave about. The people passing by make remarks. I keep my head up to hide my embarrassment. The distance to my house gets longer.

A group of boys approaches: "Clown lady, clown lady!"

I pay no attention. One of them shouts out, "Clown lady, clown lady, carnival is over, carnival is over!"

They all chorus, "Clown lady, clown lady, clown lady."

I ignore them. But why is it *clown* lady? Yesterday I was disguised like a clown, today like a woman, though it's not my fault. But why *clown*? My fingers touch the greasy surface of my face; the makeup from the day before is still there. The reddish wig is still set on my head.

"Clown lady, clown lady, don't take off your wig!"

The mocking keeps up. The boys abandon their pursuit when I enter the courtyard. I slip a little, nearly falling, the neighbors are laughing . . .

Finally I get into the little room, breathe heavily with relief, notice the table. It has fallen again. I squat down to fix it. At that point I look toward the bed. Oh, no . . .

Sleeping as always, my wife is there, paler than usual, eyes set deep, lasciviousness sketched on her mouth. Despite the heat she is wearing a long dress of black taffeta, and on her swaying breast, moved by her difficult breathing, appears a white mask.

Notes on the Authors

Guatemala

Arturo Arias: Born in Guatemala City, Guatemala, in 1950, Arias teaches at San Francisco State University. He won the Casa de las Américas award for best essay (1979) and best novel (for *Itzam Na*, 1981) and was coauthor of the screeenplay for the celebrated motion picture *El Norte* (1987). Arias is author of short stories: *En la ciudad y en la montaña*, 1975; novels: *Después de las bombas*, 1979; *Itzam Na*, 1981; *Jaguar en llamas*, 1989; and nonfiction: *Ideologías, literatura, y sociedad durante la revolución guatemalteca.*

José Barnoya García: A physician and surgeon specializing in urology, Barnoya was born in Guatemala in 1931. He was educated at the Universidad de San Carlos in Guatemala City, with specialized study in Boston and New York. His books include *La última Navidad y algo más*, 1967; *Primeros pasos de una niña cualquiera*, 1968; *Entre la risa y el llanto*, 1969; *Cosas de niños*, 1970; *Amigo mártir*, 1974; *La huelga de Dolores*, 1970; *Siempre vivas a la muerte*, 1981; *Al cruzar la calle*, 1981; *Unos cuantos cuentos*, 1982; *Letras*, 1983; and *Panzos y unas historias*, 1986.

Franz Galich: Born in Guatemala in 1951, Galich studied at the Universidad de San Carlos in Guatemala City. He is now a professor at the Universidad Centroamericana, Nicaragua. Galich is author of the short story collection *Ficcionario inédito*, 1978.

Dante Liano: Born in Guatemala in 1948, Liano was educated at the Universidad de San Carlos in Guatemala City and the University of Florence in Italy. He formerly taught at the Universidad de San Carlos, the University of Bologna, and the University of Milan. Liano is presently research professor in Spanish language and literature at the University of Feltre in Italy. His books include nonfiction: *La palabra y el sueño: literatura y sociedad en Guatemala*, 1984; and short stories: *Jornadas y otras cuentos*, 1980; and *La vida insensata*, 1987.

Augusto Monterroso: Born in Guatemala City, Guatemala, in 1921, Monterroso left school at fifteen and worked in a butcher shop. He was encouraged to read widely, which led to his own writing. Monterroso has lived in Mexico for many years. His books include the short story collections *Obras completas y otros cuentos*, 1959; *La oveja negra y demás fábulas*, 1969; *Movimiento perpetuo*, 1972; *Antología personal*, 1975; *Lo demás es silencio*, 1978; *La palabra mágica*, 1983; and *Las ilusiones perdidas*, 1985.

Honduras

Eduardo Bähr: Born in Tela, Atlántida, Honduras, in 1940, Bähr was formerly editor of several magazines of belles lettres in Honduras. He currently teaches literature and Spanish both at the Escuela Superior del Profesorado (Tegucigalpa) and at the Universidad Nacional Autónoma de Honduras. He has won two literary prizes in Honduras, and some of his stories have been translated into several languages. His books include short stories: *Fotografía del peñasco*, 1969; and *El cuento de la guerra*, 1976; and a work of children's fiction: *Mazapan*, 1982.

Edilberto Borjas: Born in Honduras in 1950, Borjas studied at the Escuela Superior del Profesorado and at the Universidad Pedagógica in Bogotá, Colombia. He is author of *Tiradores de pájaros y otros cuentos*, 1981.

Roberto Castillo: Born in Honduras in 1950, Castillo has published in several magazines in Central America. Winner of the *Plural* Prize (Mexico, 1984) for short fiction, he is currently a professor of philosophy at the Universidad Nacional Autónoma de Honduras. His books include a novel: *El corneta*, 1981; and short stories: *Subida al cielo y otros cuentos*, 1980; and *Figuras de agradable demencia*, 1985.

Julio Escoto: Born in San Pedro Sula, Honduras, in 1944, Escoto is author of novels, short stories, children's books, and literary essays. He won the Premio Nacional de Literatura (Honduras, 1967) and the Gabriel Miró

Literary Prize (Spain, 1983) for his short story "Reality before Noon." Formerly director of EDUCA (Editorial Universitaria Centroamericana), he is founding director of Centro Editorial in Tegucigalpa. Escoto's books include novels: *Los guerreros de Hibueras*, 1968; *El árbol de los pañuelos*, 1972; *Días de ventisca, noches de huracán*, 1980; *Bajo el almendro . . . junto al volcán*, 1988; short stories: *La balada del herido pájaro*, 1969, 1985; and *Historias del tiempo perdido*; nonfiction: *Casa de agua*, 1974; and the edited anthology: *Antología de la poesía amorosa en Honduras*, 1975.

Jorge Luis Oviedo: Born in Honduras in 1957, Oviedo is author of short stories: *La muerte más aplaudida*, 1984; and *Cinco cuentos*, 1986; novels: *Xibalba*, n.d.; *La gloria del muerto*, 1987; and *La turca*, 1988; and editor of *Antología del cuento hondureño*, 1988.

Roberto Quesada: Born in Olanchito, Yoro, Honduras, in 1962, Quesada is editor of *Sobrevuelo*, a literary magazine in Tegucigalpa. His books include short stories: *El desertor*, 1985; and a novel: *Los barcos*, 1988.

Pompeyo del Valle: A poet, fiction writer, and journalist, Del Valle was born in Honduras in 1929. He has won several literary prizes, among them the Premio Nacional de Literatura (Honduras). Some of his works have been translated into other languages, including Russian and English. His books include poetry: *La ruta fulgurante*, 1956; *Antología mínima*, 1958; *El fugitivo*, 1963; *Cifra y rumbo de abril*, 1964; *Nostalgía y bellezas del amor*, 1970; *Monólogo de un condenado a muerte*, 1978; and *Ciudad con dragones*, 1980; nonfiction: *Retrato de un niño ausente*, 1969; and *El hondureño, hombre mítico*, 1976; and short stories: *Los hombres verdes del hula*, 1982.

El Salvador

José Roberto Cea: Cea was born in Izalco, El Salvador, in 1939. His university studies focused on journalism and letters. He has held several cultural and teaching posts in El Salvador. Widely anthologized and winner of several prizes in poetry, Cea is author of poetry: *Poemas para seguir cantando*, 1960; *Especie de retratos*, 1960; *Los días enemigos*, 1965; *Casi el encuentro*, 1966; *Códice de amor*, 1968; *Todo el códice*, 1968; *Naufragio genuino*, 1968; *Códice liberado*, 1968; *El potrero*, 1968; *Poesía revolucionaria y de la otra*, 1972; *Poeta del Tercer Mundo*, 1977; *Mester de picardía*, 1977; *Misa mitín*, 1977; *Los herederos de Farabundo*, 1981; *Los pies sobre la tierra de Perseas*, 1984; and *Pocas i buenas*, 1986; drama: *Eternidad del sueño*, 1965; *Las escenas cumbres*, 1968; and *De* *el teatro en El Salvador,* 1988; short stories: *De perros y hombres,* 1968; *El solitario de la habitación 5 guión 3,* 1970; *Entre la realidad y la telenovela,* 1983; and *De la ganaxia irredente,* 1988; children's literature: *Chumbulum, el pecesito de Darwin,* 1983; art history: *De la pintura en El Salvador: panorama histórico-crítico desde la epoca prehispánica a 1986,* 1986; and editor of anthologies of Salvadoran/Central American poetry published in 1960, 1971, 1985.

David Escobar Galindo: Born in Santa Ana, El Salvador, in 1943, Escobar has published many volumes of poetry: *Las manos en el fuego,* 1969; *Extraño mundo del amanecer,* 1970, 1972; *Duelo ceremonial en la violencia,* 1971; *Una pared pintada de hombre,* 1971; *Vigilia memorable,* 1971, 1972; *Memoria de españa,* 1971, 1972; *Destino manifesto,* 1972; *El despertar del viento,* 1972; *El toro de Parro,* 1972; *Coronación furtiva,* 1972, 1975; *Discurso secreto,* 1974 (reprinted as *El país de las alas oscuras,* 1977); *Cornamusa,* 1975; *Primera antología—1968–1975,* 1975; *Libro de Lilián,* 1975, 1976; *Arcanus,* 1976; *¿Hasta cuándo?,* 1976; *El corazón de cuatro espejos,* 1977; *Sonetos penitenciales,* 1979–1982; *Canciones para el Album de Perséfone,* 1982; *Cantos a la noche,* 1983; and *Las máscaras yacentes,* 1984; novels: *Una grieta en el agua,* 1972; *La estrella cautiva,* 1985; short stories: *La rebelión de las imagenes,* 1976; *Los sobrevivientes,* 1979; *Matusalén el abandónico,* 1980; *La trequa de los dioses,* 1981; *Gente que pasa: historias sin cuento,* 1988; fables: *Fábulas/Fables,* trans. Elizabeth Gamble Miller and Helen D. Clements, 1985; drama: *Después de medianoche (After Midnight),* trans. Roy C. Boland (bilingual edition).

Jorge Kattán Zablah: Born in Quezaltepeque, El Salvador, in 1939, Kattán is a lawyer and diplomat. A Ph.D. of the University of California at Santa Barbara, he is currently chair of the Spanish Department at the Defense Language Institute in Monterey, California. His books include nonfiction: *Don Juan: de Tirso de Molina a José Zorrilla,* 1972; and short stories: *Estampas pueblerinas,* 1982; and *Acuarelas socarronas,* 1983.

Hugo Lindo: Born in La Unión, El Salvador, in 1917, Lindo received a doctorate in law from the Universidad Autónoma de El Salvador. He was formerly professor of law and also of literature there as well as at the Universidad Nacional de Colombia. Lindo held several cultural and legal posts, among them minister of education (1961) and ambassador to Chile, Colombia, Spain, and Egypt. He was an honorary member of the Instituto de Cultura Hispánica (Madrid) and a corresponding member of the Real Academia Española de la Lengua as well as of similar academies in Chile, Colombia, and Honduras. He won numerous national prizes as a poet. Lindo died in 1985. His books include poetry: *Poema Eucarístico y otros*, 1943; *Libro de horas*, 1948; *Sinfonía del límite*, 1953; *Trece instantes*, 1959; *Varia poesía*, 1961; *Navegante río*, 1963; *Solo la voz*, 1967; *Maneras de llover*, 1968 (translated by Elizabeth Gamble Miller, *The Ways of Rain and Other Poems by Hugo Lindo*, 1986); *Este pequeño siempre*, 1971; *Sangre de hispania fecunda*, 1972; *Resonancia de Vivaldi*, 1976; *Aquí, mi tierra*, 1979; *Fácil palabra*, 1985; novels: *El anzuelo de Dios*, 1956; *Justicia, Sr. Gobernador!*, 1960; *Cada día tiene su afán*, 1965; and *Yo soy la memoria*, 1984; short stories: *Guaro y champaña*, 1947; *Aquí se cuentan cuentos*, 1960; and *Espejos paralelos*, 1974; and law: *El divorcio en El Salvador*, 1948; and *Integración centroamericana ante el Derecho Internacional*, 1971.

Ricardo Lindo: Born in San Salvador in 1947, Lindo studied public relations in Madrid and psychology in Paris. Formerly El Salvador's cultural attaché in Paris, he is currently involved in educational TV in San Salvador. He is author of short stories: *XXX Cuentos*, 1970; poetic prose (under the pseudonym of Ricardo Jesurum): *Rara avis in terra*, 1973; children's literature: *Cuentos del mar*, 1987; art history: *La pintura en El Salvador*, 1986; and poetry: *Jardines*, 1981; and *El Señor de la casa del tiempo*, 1989.

José María Méndez: Born in Santa Ana, El Salvador, in 1916. Méndez is one of the most prestigious lawyers and jurists in El Salvador and has served on the Supreme Court. He was formerly professor of law at the Universidad Nacional de El Salvador for fifteen years, where he was also rector. Méndez has won literary prizes both in El Salvador and abroad for short fiction. His books include the short story collections *Disparatario*, 1957; *Tres mujeres al cuadrado*, 1962; *Espejo del tiempo*, 1974; and *Tiempo irredimible*, 1977.

Alfonso Quijada Urías: Born in Quezaltepeque, El Salvador, in 1940, Quijada currently resides in Canada. His stories and poems have appeared in various anthologies of short fiction and poetry. He is the author of poetry: *Poemas*, 1964; *Sagradas escrituras*, 1969; and *El otro infierno*, 1970; and short stories: *Cuentos*, 1970; *Otras historias famosas*, 1974; *La fama infame del famoso apátrida*, 1980; and *Para mirarte mejor*, 1987.

Napoleón Rodríguez Ruiz: Rodríguez was born in Santa Ana, El Salvador, in 1910. An attorney, he was formerly dean of the Faculties of Economy and Humanities as well as rector of the Universidad de El Salvador. He is the author of the novel *Jaragua*, 1950; a law book: *Historia de las* *instituciones jurídicas salvadoreñas*, 1951; nonfiction: *Discursos universitarios*, 1962; and short stories: *El janiche y otros cuentos*, 1968; and *La abertura del triángulo*, 1969.

Nicaragua

Mario Cajina-Vega: Born in Nicaragua in 1929, Cajina-Vega has published the short story collections *Familia de cuentos*, 1969; and *Lugares*, 1974.

Lizandro Chávez Alfaro: Born in Bluefields, Nicaragua, in 1929, Chávez has written novels, short stories, essays, and poetry, and has won literary prizes for his fiction writings. He served as Nicaraguan ambassador to Hungary. Chávez's books include short stories: *Los monos de San Telmo*, 1963; and *Trece veces nunca*, 1977, 1985; and novels: *Trágame tierra*, 1969; and *Balsa de serpientes*, 1976.

Pablo Antonio Cuadra: Born in Managua, Nicaragua, in 1912, Cuadra is one of the most important living Latin American poets. He studied law for a time and worked as a farmer-cattleman on family ranches near Lake Nicaragua. Inspired early by Sandino, he later supported the elder Somoza and worked against the younger Somoza, first accepting and then breaking away from the Sandinista government. Longtime editor of the opposition newspaper *La Prensa*, he was a member of the Vanguardia group in the 1920s and 1930s, as well as the founder of several literary magazines. Cuadra is author of several books of poetry: *Poemas nicaragüenses*, 1934; *Canto temporal*, 1943; *Tierra prometida*, 1952; *El jaguar y la luna*, 1959, 1971; *Cantos de Cifar*, 1971; and *Obra poética completa*, 1986.

Horacio Peña: Born in Managua, Nicaragua, in 1936, Peña presently resides in Austin, Texas. His published books include short stories: *Diario de un jóven que se volvió loco*, 1962; *Enemigo de los poetas y otros cuentos*, 1976; and *Las memorias de Beowulf*, 1978; and poetry: *Ars moriendi y otros poemas*, 1967; *La soledad y el desierto*, 1970; and *Poema a un hombre llamado Roberto Clemente*, 1973.

Sergio Ramírez: Born in Masatepe, Nicaragua, in 1942, Ramírez lived in Costa Rica and Europe for many years, returning to Nicaragua in 1979. He served as vice-president of Nicaragua throughout the Sandinista regime. Several of his stories and novels have been translated into English. His books include novels: *Tiempo del fulgor*, 1969; and *Castigo divino*, 1988; short stories: *Cuentos*, 1963; *Nuevos cuentos*, 1969; *De* *tropeles y tropelías,* 1972; and *¿Te dio miedo la sangre?,* 1977; nonfiction: *Las armas del futuro,* 1987; biography: *Mariano Fiallas: biografía,* 1971; and edited anthologies: *La narrativa centroamericana,* 1970; and *Antología del cuento centroamericano.* 2nd ed., 1977.

Mario Santos: Born in Managua, Nicaragua, in 1948, Santos is author of *Los madrugadores,* 1975.

Fernando Silva: Born in Nicaragua in 1927, Silva is author of the novels: *El comandante,* 1969; and *El vecindario,* 1976; and the short story collections: *Cuentos de tierra y agua,* 1969; and *Cuentos,* 1985.

Costa Rica

Luis Bolaños Ugalde: Born in Grecia, Alajuela, Costa Rica, in1944, Bolaños is a poet, fiction writer, and literary critic. A Ph.D. in Latin American literature from the University of Arizona, he is now professor at the Universidad Nacional Autónoma (Heredia, Costa Rica). Bolaños published the first study demonstrating the existence of an oral indigenous literature in Costa Rica (1980), a tradition previously unrecognized. He is a founding member of the Instituto de Literatura Infantil of Costa Rica and winner of several literary prizes for poetry and short stories. He is author of a book for children: *Globitos,* 1979.

Alfonso Chase: Born in Cartago, Costa Rica, in 1945, Chase is a poet, essayist, and professor of literature at the Universidad Nacional de Costa Rica. His books include the novels: *Los juegos furtivos,* 1967; and *Las puertas de la noche,* 1974; short stories: *Que vivimos,* 1973; *Mirar con inocencia,* 1977; *Ella usaba bikini,* 1991; and *El hombre que se quedó adentro del sueño,* 1993; and children's stories: *Fábula de fábulas,* 1979; and *Historias del tigre de agua y el colibrí de fuego,* 1992.

José Ricardo Chaves: Born in San José, Costa Rica, in 1958, Chaves is presently studying French literature at the Universidad Nacional Autónoma de México. Formerly a member of the editorial board of the magazine *Revenar,* the organ of the Asociación de Autores de Costa Rica, he was winner of the 1983 Jóven Creación short story contest. Chaves is a frequent contributor to literary supplements of several newspapers in Mexico and Costa Rica. His books include the short story collection *La mujer oculta,* 1984; and the novel *Los susurros de Perseo,* n.d.

Carlos Cortés: Born in San José, Costa Rica, in 1962, Cortés has studied journalism and communications and has been editor of magazines and literary supplements in Costa Rica. He is presently the cultural coordinator of the magazine *Rumbo*. Cortés has won several literary prizes for poetry, as well as the Carlos Luis Fallas Prize for a novel in 1985 and the Juegos Florales Centroamericanos prize in Guatemala in 1988. His books include short stories: *El ojo de un nihilista*, 1989; poetry: *Diálogos entre Mafalda y Charlie Brown*, 1982; *Erratas advertidas*, 1986; *Los pasos cantados*, 1987; *Salomé descalza*, 1989; a novel: *Encendiendo un cigarrillo con la punta del otro*, 1986; and three anthologies: *Antología de Miguel Hernández*, 1980; *Canto abierto: asamblea de poetas*, 1983; and *Para no cansarlos con el cuento: narrativa costarricense*, 1989.

Fabián Dobles: Born in Atenas, Costa Rica, in 1918, Dobles is one of Central America's outstanding writers. Many of his stories have been translated into other languages, including Russian. His books include novels: *Ese que llaman pueblo*, 1942; *Aguas turbias*, 1943; *Una burbuja en el limbo*, 1946; *El sitio de las abras*, 1950; *Los leños vivientes*, 1962; and *En el San Juan hay tiburón*, 1967; poetry: *Tú, voz de sombra*, 1944; *Verdad del agua y el viento*, 1949; and *Yerbamar*, 1966; and short stories: *La rescoldera*, 1947; *El jaspe*, 1955; *Historias de Tata Mundo*, 1956; *El Maijú y otras historias de Tata Mundo*, 1957; *El Targua*, 1960; *El violin en la chatarra*, 1966; *Cuentos de Fabián Dobles*, 1972; *Cuentos escogidos de Fabián Dobles*, 1982; and *La pesadilla y otros cuentos*, 1984.

Carmen Naranjo: Born in Cartago, Costa Rica, in 1931, Naranjo studied philosophy and letters at the Universidad de Costa Rica, where she currently is a professor. She has held numerous posts of national importance, such as ambassador to Israel (1972–1974), minister of culture, youth, and sports (1974–1976), director of the Museum of Art (1982–1984), and presently, director of Editorial Universitaria Centroamericana. She has published numerous articles and has won important literary prizes. Naranjo's books include poetry: *La canción de la ternura*, 1964; *Misa a oscuras*, 1965; *Idioma del invierno*, 1971; *Homenaje a Don Nadie*, 1981; and *Mi guerrillera*, 1984; novels: *Diario de una multitud*, 1965; *Los perros no ladraron*, 1966; *Camino al mediodia*, 1968; *Responso por el niño Juan Manuel* 1971; *Memorias de un hombre palabra*, 1978; and *Sobrepunto*, 1985; short stories: *Hoy es un largo día*, 1972; *Nunca hubo alguna vez*, 1984; *Ondina*, 1984; and *Otro rumbo para la rumba*, 1989; and nonfiction: *Por Israel y por las páginas de la Biblia*, 1976.

Julieta Pinto: Born in San José, Costa Rica, in 1922, Pinto is a graduate of the Universidad de Costa Rica and founder and former chair of the

Departamento de Literatura at the Universidad Nacional Autónoma (Heredia, Costa Rica). Her books include a novel: *La estación que sigue al verano*, 1969; and short stories: *Cuentos de la tierra*, 1963; *Si se oyera el silencio*, 1967; *Los marginados*, 1974; *A la vuelta de la esquina*, 1975; *El sermón de lo cotidiano*, 1977; *Abrir los ojos*, 1982; *El eco de los pasos*, n.d.; and *Historia de Navidad*, 1988.

Uriel Quesada: Born in San José, Costa Rica, in 1962, Quesada is professor of statistics at the Universidad de Costa Rica. He has published stories and essays in newspapers and magazines and has won several literary prizes in Costa Rica. Quesada is author of the short story collection *Ese día de los temblores*, 1985.

Marco Retana: Born in Costa Rica in 1938, Retana has been the winner of several literary prizes in Costa Rica. His books include short stories: *El manicomio de los niños*, 1973; *La noche de los amadores*, 1975; and *De orates y semejantes*, 1982; and poems for children: *La Chocola*, 1980.

Samuel Rovinski: Born in San José, Costa Rica, in 1932, Rovinski is a writer of poetry, short stories, novels, drama, screenplays, and essays. He studied cinematography at L'Ecole Louis Lumière (Paris, 1972–1973) and has held important public posts connected with the cultural life of Costa Rica. Rovinski has won literary prizes in drama and the novel, as well as for one of his screenplays. His books include drama: *La Atlántida*, 1960; *Los agitadores*, 1965; *Gobierno de alcoba*, 1970; *El laberinto*, 1974; *Un modelo para Rosaura*, 1974; *Los fisgonas de paso ancho*, 1975; *Los pregoneros*, 1978; *Los intereses compuestos*, 1981; *El martirio de pastor*, 1983; *Gulliver dormido*, 1985; *Tres obras de teatro*, 1985; and *La víspera del sabado*, 1986; short stories: *La hora de los vencidos*, 1963; *La pagoda*, 1964; *Cuentos judíos de mi tierra*, 1982; and *El embudo de Pandora*, 1988; and novels: *Megapolis beta*, 1973; and *Ceremonias de Casta*, 1975.

Victoria Urbano: Born in San José, Costa Rica, in 1926, Urbano received her Ph.D. in philosophy and letters from the University of Madrid. For many years she was professor of Spanish language and literature at Lamar University (Beaumont, Tex.). Urbano was author of more than two hundred articles on various subjects in Europe, the United States, and Latin America. Two of her early plays were produced in Madrid. Founder and lifetime president of the Asociación de Literatura Feminina Hispánica, based in the United States, she was also editor of the literary magazine *Letras Femeninas* and winner of numerous international prizes and distinctions before her death in 1984. Among her books are

262 Contemporary Short Stories from Central America

poetry: *Marfil* (stories and poetry), 1951; *La niña de los caracoles*, 1961; *Platero y tú* (poetic prose), 1962; *Los nueve círculos*, 1970; and *El genesis de amor* and *Soledad primera*, 1979; nonfiction: *Juan Vásquez de Coronado y su ética en la conquista de Costa Rica*, 1968; *Una escritora costarricense: Yolanda Oreamuno*, 1968; *El teatro español y sus directrices contemporáneas*, 1972; and *El teatro en Centroamerica, desde sus orígenes hasta 1975*, 1978; short stories: *Y era otra vez hoy*, 1972; and an edited anthology: *Five Women Writers of Costa Rica*, 1978.

Panama

Lucas Bárcena: Born in Arraiján, Panama, in 1906, Bárcena is self-educated. His books include poetry: *Cristal*, 1930; *Iris*, 1933; *Prisma*, 1939; *Caracól*, 1944; and *Antología poética*, 1959; short stories: *Tierra íntima*, 1949; and *Cuentos y prosas minúsculas*, 1970; and nonfiction: *Reseña histórica del distrito de Arraiján*, 1987.

Ricardo J. Bermúdez: Born in Panama City in 1914, Bermúdez is an architect and studied at the University of Southern California. Formerly professor at the Universidad de Panamá and dean of the School of Architecture, he has served as minister of education. A member of the Academia Panameña de la Lengua, he has also won the Ricardo Miró National Literary Prize for poetry and short fiction. Bermúdez is the author of poetry: *Poemas de ausencia*, 1937; *Elegía a Adolfo Hitler*, 1941; *Adán liberado*, 1944; *Laurel de ceniza*, 1952; *Cuando la isla era doncella*, 1961; *Con la llave en el suelo*, 1970; and *Poesía selecta de Ricardo J. Bermúdez*, 1982; and short stories: *Para rendir al animal que ronda*, 1975.

Rosa María Britton: Born in Panama in 1936, Britton studied medicine in Cuba, Spain, and New York, specializing in gynecology and oncology. Director of the Instituto Oncológico Nacional de Panamá for ten years, she lectures frequently and has published numerous articles on her specialty in medical reviews. Britton has won the Ricardo Miró National Literature Prize five times. Her books include novels: *El ataúd de uso*, 1983; and *El señor de las lluvias y el viento*, 1985; medicine: *La costilla de Adán*, 1985; short stories: *¿Quién inventó el mambo?*, 1986; and *La muerte tiene dos caras*, 1987; and drama: *Esa esquina del paraíso*, 1987; *Banquete de despedida*, in press; and *Mi$$*, in press.

Enrique Chuez: Born in Santiago de Veraguas, Panama, in 1934, Chuez is professor of history at the Universidad de Panamá. He is author of short stories: *Tiburón y otros cuentos*, 1964; *La gallota*, 1969; and *La mecedora*, 1976; and novels: *Las averías*, 1972; *La casa de las sirenas pálidas*, 1983; and *Operación causa justa*, 1991.

Claudio de Castro: Born in Colón, Panama, in 1957, De Castro has published numerous short stories in newspapers and magazines in Panama and has won several literary prizes. He has published several collections of short stories: *La isla de mamá Teresa, el abuelo Toño, y otros cuentos*, 1985; *La niña fea de Alajuela*, 1985; *El señor Foucalt*, 1987; *El juego*, 1987; and *Fotos de Henry Cartier*, 1987.

Ernesto Endara: Born in Panama in 1932, Endara has won the Ricardo Miró National Literary Prize several times for drama and short stories. He is the author of *Cerrado por duelo*, 1977; *Una bandera*, 1977; *Teatro, 1960–1970*, 1983; *Demasiadas flores para Rodolfo*, 1986; and *Donde es más brillante el sol*, 1991.

Jaime García Saucedo: A literary, theater, and film critic, García was born in Panama City in 1938. He has taught courses in journalism at the Universidad de Panamá and is currently professor at the Pontífica Universidad Javeriana, Bogotá, Colombia. García is the author of poetry: *Poemario*, 1982; short stories: *De lo que no se dijo en las crónicas y otros relatos*, 1982; and nonfiction: *Textos aplicados al lenguaje de la comunicación social*, 1982.

Enrique Jaramillo Levi: Born in Colón, Panama, in 1944, Jaramillo was educated in Panama, at the University of Iowa, and at the Universidad Nacional Autónoma de México. A poet and fiction writer, he has taught Latin American literature and creative writing at universities in Panama, Mexico, and the United States. He established Editorial Signos, a publishing house, while in Mexico (1982), and later moved it to Panama, where he also founded and edited the literary and cultural magazine *Maga* (1984–1987, 1989–present). His stories and poems have been translated into English as well as several European languages. After serving as head of the Departamento de Letras at the Instituto Nacional de Cultura (Panama) and as director of the University Press at the Universidad de Panamá, he is now teaching at the Instituto Tecnológico y de Estudios Superiores de Monterrey, Querétaro Campus. His many books include short stories: *Catalepsia*, 1965; *Duplicaciones*, 1973 (rev. and enlarged, 1982; 3rd ed., 1992); *El buho que dejó de latir*, 1974; *Renuncia al tiempo*, 1975; *Caja de resonancias: 21 cuentos fantásticos*, 1983; *Ahora que soy él*, 1985; and *La voz despalabrada*, 1986; drama: *La* *cápsula de cianuro*, 1966; and ¡*Si la humanidad no pintara colores!*, 1967; poetry: *Los atardeceres de la memoria*, 1978; *Fugas y engranajes*, 1982; *Cuerpos amándose en el espejo*, 1982; *Extravios*, 1989; and *Siluetas y clamores*, 1993. In addition, he has edited several anthologies of Panamanian and Mexican poetry as well as three volumes of articles dealing with the Panama Canal question.

Raúl Leis: A sociologist, journalist, and educator, Leis was born in Panama in 1947. Winner of several national prizes in journalism as well as the Ricardo Miró National Literary Prize for drama on several occasions, he has also won prizes for children's literature. Leis has been editor of the magazine *Diálogo Social* for ten years and is presently professor in the School of Sociology at the Universidad de Panamá, as well as director of the Centro de Estudios y Acción Social Panameño. He is author of, among others, *Viaje a la salvación y otros países*, 1974; *Viene el sol con su sombrero de combat puesto*, 1976; *Colón: en el ojo de la tormenta*, 1979; *El nido de Macua*, 1982; *Voces de lucha* (interviews with labor leaders), 1984; *Comando Sur: poder hóstil*, 1985; *Viaje alrededor del patio: cuentos de vecindario*, 1987.

Bertalicia Peralta: Born in Panama City in 1939, Peralta was formerly coeditor of the literary magazine *El pez original* and is now director of public relations of the Universidad de Panamá. Winner of literary prizes for poetry and short stories, she is widely anthologized in both genres. Peralta's books include poetry: *Canto de esperanza filial*, 1962; *Sendas fugitivas*, 1963; *Atrincherado amor*, 1964; *Los retornos*, 1965; *Un lugar en la esfera terrestre*, 1971; *Himno a la alegría*, 1973; *Ragul*, 1976; *Libro de las fábulas*, 1976; *Casa flotante*, 1979; *Piel de gallina*, 1982; *Frisos*, 1982; and *En tu cuerpo cubierto de flores*, 1985; and short stories: *Largo in crescendo*, 1967; *Barcarola y otras fantasías incorregibles*, 1973; and *Puros cuentos*, 1988.

Dimas Lidio Pitty: Born in Potrerillos, a province of Chiriquí, Panama, in 1941, Lidio has lived in Mexico for several years as a political exile. His fiction has been included in a number of anthologies both in Panama and abroad, and some of his stories have been translated into other languages. Winner of the Ricardo Miró National Prize for Literature on several occasions for poetry, a novel, and short stories, Lidio is author of *Camino de las cosas*, 1965; *Sonetos desnudos*, 1978; *Crónica prohibida*, 1980; children's literature: *El país azul: cuentos y poemas para niños*, 1969; short stories: *El centro de la noche*, 1977; *Los caballos estornudan en la noche*, 1979; and *Recuentos* (with Pedro Rivera), 1988; a novel: *Estación* *de navegantes,* 1975; and interviews: *Realidades y fantasmas en América Latina,* 1978; and *Letra viva,* 1986.

Pedro Rivera: Born in Panama City in 1939, Rivera is a poet, short story writer, and documentary filmmaker. Director of the Grupo Experimental de Cine Universitario at the Universidad de Panamá, he has been the winner of the Ricardo Miró National Literary Prize several times for poetry and once for short stories. Rivera is the author of short stories: *Peccata minuta,* 1970; and *Recuentos* (with Dimas Lidio Pitty), 1988; and poetry: *Mayo en el tiempo,* 1961; *Los pájaros regresan de la niebla,* 1970; *El libro de las parábolas,* n.d.

Jorge Turner: A lawyer, journalist, university professor, and diplomat, Turner was born in Panama in 1922. A founding member of the Sindicato de Periodistas de Panamá, he is currently professor at the Universidad Nacional Autónoma de México and was formerly Panama's ambassador to Mexico. Turner is the author of a short story collection, *Viento de agua,* 1977; and a nonfiction work, *Raíz, historia, y perspectiva del movimiento obrero panameño,* 1982.

Notes on the Translators

Lynne Beyer: A poet, former journalist, and translator, she has contributed original poems as well as translations to several magazines and anthologies. A chapbook, *The Future Comes*, was published by Pinched Nerves Press in 1993.

Pamela Carmell: With an MFA in translation from the University of Arkansas, she is a free-lance editor and translator and now teaches Spanish in St. Louis, Missouri. She is coeditor of a forthcoming anthology of Spain's poets of the Generation of the 1950s and is currently translating a novel, *Este era un gato* by Luis Arturo Ramos (Mexico). Carmell's books include *Woman on the Front Line* (poetry) by Belkis Cuza Male, trans. Pamela Carmell, 1987; and *The Last Portrait of the Duchess of Alba* (a novel) by Antonio Larreta, trans. Pamela Carmell, 1988.

Leland H. Chambers: Professor emeritus of English and comparative literature at the University of Denver, he has published translations of fiction and poetry by Spanish and Latin American writers in numerous literary magazines. He was awarded an NEA Translator Award for 1991. His book translations include a collection of short stories, *Holy Saturday and Other Stories* by Ezequiel Martínez Estrada, 1988, and two novels by Julieta Campos, *The Fear of Losing Eurydice*, 1993, and *She Has Reddish Hair and Her Name Is Sabina*, 1993.

Sabina Lask-Spinac: She formerly taught English at Rockland Community College in New York and was the author of articles on the teaching of English and on modern Hebrew poets. Her translations included poetry by Uri Ziv Greenberg and Yehuda Amichai. Lask-Spinac was killed in a car accident in June 1990, shortly after completing the translations in this volume.

Elizabeth Gamble Miller: Associate professor of Spanish at Southern Methodist University, she is a specialist in Salvadoran literature as well as contemporary poetry. She holds the title of Académica Correspondiente of the Academia Salvadoreña de la Lengua and also belongs to the Asociación Prometeo (Madrid) and the Academia Iberoamericana de Poesía. Miller is on the editorial board of *Translation Review* and is editor of the *ALTA Newsletter* (American Literary Translators Association). Her translations of Salvadoran, Spanish, Mexican, Cuban, Chilean, and Argentine authors have appeared in anthologies and magazines. Books she has translated include *Hugo Lindo: Solo La Voz/Only the Voice* (poems), 1984; *Fábulas/Fables* by David Escobar-Galindo, trans. Elizabeth Gamble Miller with Helen D. Clement, 1985; *The Ways of Rain and Other Poems* by Hugo Lindo, bilingual edition, 1986; *The Enchanted Raisin: Chilean Short Stories* by Jacqueline Balcells, 1988.

Sylvia K. Schulter: A translator/interpreter, Schulter has done her first published literary translations for this volume.

Charles Philip Thomas: Professor of Spanish at the University of Wisconsin at Oshkosh, Thomas is the author of several articles on Chilean theater. His translations of contemporary Chilean and Puerto Rican plays have appeared in literary magazines. Performances have taken place in Chicago, Cleveland, San Antonio, Milwaukee, Portland (Maine), Santiago (Chile), and Denver, and at Vassar College, Kalamazoo College, Marquette University, the University of Rhode Island, Kenyon College, and the University of North Carolina at Greensboro. His translated books include *The Praying Mantis and Other Plays* by Alejandro Sieveking, n.d.; and *The Secret Holy War of Santiago de Chile* (a novel) by Marco Antonio de la Parra, n.d. A forthcoming book is his study, *The Theatre of Marco Antonio de la Parra: Translations and Commentary*.

Don D. Wilson: Professor of humanities at Hartford State Technical College in Connecticut, he is a publisher (Singular Speech Press, Canton, Conn.) and a translator of poetry from many languages. Wilson was the winner of the Richard Wilbur Poetry Translation Prize in 1989 and received a Fulbright award that took him to Bulgaria in fall 1991. His translated books include *Lucretilis: Pleasant Hill of Horace* (Latin poems) by William Johnson Cory, 1982; *Milk Like Wine* (poems from various languages), 1987; and *47 Poems by Flavia Cosma* (Rumania), 1992.

Clark M. Zlotchew: Professor of Spanish at SUNY College at Fredonia, he is also a faculty exchange scholar of the State University of New York. Zlotchew is the author of numerous articles on Borges and contemporary Latin American literary figures, the nineteenth-century Spanish novelist Benito Pérez Galdós, and Hispanic linguistics, as well as author of short stories both in English and in Spanish. His translations of poetry and fiction have appeared in many literary magazines. Zlotchew's books include: *Libido into Literature: The "Primera Epoca" of Benito Pérez Galdós*, 1993; *Estilo literario: análisis y creación*, 1993; and *Voices of the River Plate: Interviews with Writers of Argentina and Uruguay*, forthcoming 1994. As a translator he has published *Seven Conversations with Jorge Luis Borges*, by Fernando Sorrentino, ed. and trans. Clark M. Zlotchew, 1982; *Light and Shadow: Selected Poems and Prose of Juan Ramón Jiménez*, trans. Clark M. Zlotchew and others, 1987; *The House at Isla Negra: Prose Poems by Pablo Neruda*, trans. Clark M. Zlotchew and Dennis Maloney, 1988, and its bilingual 2nd ed., *The House in the Sand: Prose Poems by Pablo Neruda*, 1990; and *Falling through the Cracks: Stories by Julio Ricci*, 1989.

Permissions
Acknowledgments

Grateful acknowledgment is made for permission to include the follow-ing stories, previously published in Spanish:

Guatemala

José Barnoya García, "Tránsito," Leland H. Chambers, trans. "El tránsito," from José Barnoya García, *Letras* (Guatemala City, Guatemala: Universidad de San Carlos, 1983).

Franz Galich, "The Rat Catcher," Pamela Carmell, trans. "El ratero," from Revista *Alero*, no. 4, Cuarta Epoca (Guatemala City, Guatemala: Universidad de San Carlos, 1977 [?]).

Dante Liano, "An Indolence of Feelings," Sylvia Schulter, trans. "La pereza de sentimientos," from Dante Liano, *La vida insensata* (Guatemala City, Guatemala, 1987).

Augusto Monterroso, "The Circumstantial or the Ephemeral," Leland H. Chambers, trans. "De lo circunstancial o lo efímero," from Augusto Monterroso, *La palabra mágica* (Mexico City: ERA, 1983).

Honduras

Eduardo Bähr, "Tarzan of the Apes," Clark Zlotchew, trans. "Tarzan de los gorilas," from Eduardo Bähr, *El cuento de la guerra* (Tegucigalpa, Honduras, 1976).

Edilberto Borjas, "The Last Act," Clark Zlotchew, trans. "Ultimo acto," from Jorge Luis Oviedo, *Antología del cuento hondureño* (Tegucigalpa, Honduras: Editores Unidos, 1988).

Roberto Castillo, "The Attack of the Man-Eating Paper," Clark Zlotchew, trans. "El hombre que se comieron los papeles," from Roberto Castillo, *Subida al cielo y otros cuentos* (Tegucigalpa, Honduras: Editorial Guaymuras, 1987; 1st ed., 1980).

Julio Escoto, "Reality before Noon," Clark Zlotchew, trans. "Abril antes del mediodía," from Julio Escoto, *La balada del herido pájaro y otros relatos*. 2nd ed. (San José, Costa Rica: Servicios Editoriales Centroamericanos, 1985).

Jorge Luis Oviedo, "The Final Flight of the Mischievous Bird," Sabina Lask-Spinac, trans. "El último vuelo del pajaro travieso," from Jorge Luis Oviedo, *Antología del cuento hondureño* (Tegucigalpa, Honduras: Editores Unidos, 1988).

Roberto Quesada, "The Author," Sabina Lask-Spinac, trans. "El autor," from Roberto Quesada, *El desertor* (Tegucigalpa, Honduras, 1985).

Pompeyo del Valle, "The Forbidden Street," Sabina Lask-Spinac, trans. "La calle prohibida," from Jorge Luis Oviedo, *Antología del cuento hondureño* (Tegucigalpa, Honduras: Editores Unidos, 1988).

El Salvador

José Roberto Cea, "The Absent One Inside," Elizabeth Gamble Miller, trans. "El ausente no sale," from José Roberto Cea, *De la ganaxia irredenta* (San Salvador, El Salvador, 1988).

David Escobar Galindo, "Restless," Elizabeth Gamble Miller, trans. "El impaciente," from David Escobar Galindo, *Matusalén, el abandónico* (San Salvador, El Salvador: Editorial Ahora, 1980).

Jorge Kattán Zablah, "The Raccoons," Elizabeth Gamble Miller, trans. "Los mapaches," from Jorge Kattán Zablah, *Acuarelas socarronas* (Barcelona, Spain: Ediciones Rondas, 1983).

Hugo Lindo, "That Confounded Year . . . !," Elizabeth Gamble Miller, trans. "Maldito el año," from Hugo Lindo, *Espejos paralelos* (San Salvador, El Salvador: Ministerio de Educación, 1974).

Ricardo Lindo, "Cards," Elizabeth Gamble Miller, trans. "Naipes," from Ricardo Lindo, *Rara avis en terra* (San Salvador, El Salvador: Ministerio de Educación, 1973).

José María Méndez, "The Circle," Elizabeth Gamble Miller, trans. "La tertulia," from José María Méndez, *Tiempo irredimible* (San Salvador, El Salvador: Ministerio de Educación, 1977).

Alfonso Quijada Urías, "To Tell the Story," Elizabeth Gamble Miller, trans. "Para contar el cuento," from Alfonso Quijada Urías, *Para mirarte mejor* (Tegucigalpa, Honduras: Editorial Guaymuras, 1987).

Napoleón Rodríguez Ruiz, "The Suicide of Chamiabak," Elizabeth Gamble Miller, trans. "El suicidio de Chamiabak," from Napoleón

Rodríguez Ruiz, *La abertura del triángulo* (San Salvador, El Salvador: Ministerio de Educación, 1969).

Nicaragua

Mario Cajina-Vega, "Gloria Lara," Don D. Wilson, trans. "Gloria Lara," from Mario Cajina-Vega, *Familia de cuentos* (Buenos Aires, Argentina: Editorial Sudamericana, 1969).

Lizandro Chávez Alfaro, "Pregnant City," Don D. Wilson, trans. "Ciudad encinta," from Lizandro Chávez Alfaro, *Trece veces nunca* (Managua, Nicaragua: Editorial Nueva, 1985).

Pablo Antonio Cuadra, "August," Lynne Beyer, trans. "Agosto," from Pablo Antonio Cuadra, *Obra poética completa*, vol. 8 (San José, Costa Rica: Libro Libre, 1986).

Horacio Peña, "The House," Leland H. Chambers, trans. "La casa," from Horacio Peña, *Las memorias de Beowulf* (Managua, Nicaragua, 1978).

Sergio Ramírez, "On the Stench of Corpses," Don D. Wilson, trans. "Del hedor de los cadáveres," from Sergio Ramírez, *De tropeles y tropelias* (San Salvador: Editorial Universitaria de El Salvador, 1972).

Mario Santos, "In the Midst of the Downpour They Took Away My Cousin," Don D. Wilson, trans. "En medio del aguacero se llevaron a my primo," from Mario Santos, *Los madrugadores* (Managua, Nicaragua: Impresiones Técnicas, 1975).

Fernando Silva, "Francisco," Lynne Beyer, trans. "Francisco," from Fernando Silva, *Cuentos* (Managua: Editorial Nueva Nicaragua, 1985).

Costa Rica

Luis Bolaños Ugalde, "Rite," Charles Philip Thomas, trans. "Rito," in *Maga: Revista Panameña de Cultura*, #11 (October–December 1986).

Alfonso Chase, "The Path of the Wind," Charles Philip Thomas, trans. "El hilo del viento," from Alfonso Chase, *Mirar con inocencia* (San José: Editorial Costa Rica, 1977).

José Ricardo Chaves, "Burned Soldiers," Leland H. Chambers, trans. "Los quemados," in *Uno Más Uno: Sabado—Suplemento Cultural*, no. 561 (July 2, 1988), Mexico City.

Carlos Cortés, "Funeral Rites in Summer," Pamela Carmell, trans. "Los funerales del verano," from Carlos Cortés, *El ojo de un nihilista* (San José, Costa Rica, 1989).

Fabián Dobles, "The Trunk," Leland H. Chambers, trans. "El baúl," from Fabián Dobles, *El violín en la chatarra* (San José, Costa Rica: Editorial Pablo Presbere 1964).

Carmen Naranjo, "Floral Caper," Charles Philip Thomas, trans. "El truco florido," from Carmen Naranjo, *Hoy es un largo día* (Buenos Aires, Argentina: Ediciones de la Flor, 1986; 1st ed., 1972).

Julieta Pinto, "Disobedience," Charles Philip Thomas, trans. "Desobediencia," from Julieta Pinto, *Los marginados* (San José: Editorial Costa Rica, 1974).

Uriel Quesada, "Behind the Door," Leland H. Chambers, trans. "Detras de la puerta," in *La Nación* (Oct. 2, 1988), San José, Costa Rica.

Marco Retana, "The Back Rooms," Charles Philip Thomas, trans. "Los cuartos de atrás," from Marco Retana, *De orates y semejantes* (San José: Editorial Costa Rica, 1982).

Victoria Urbano, "The Face," Sylvia Schulter, trans. "El rostro," from Victoria Urbano, *Y era otra vez hoy* (San José: Editorial Costa Rica, 1978).

Panama

Lucas Bárcena, "The Sweetheart of the Spirits," Leland H. Chambers, trans. "La novia de los duendes," from Lucas Bárcena, *Cuentos y prosas minúsculas* (Panama City, 1970).

Ricardo J. Bermúdez, "The Horse in the Glassware Shop," Leland H. Chambers, trans. "El caballo en la cristalería," from Ricardo J. Bermúdez, *Para rendir al animal que ronda* (Panama City: INAC, 1975).

Rosa María Britton, "Love Is Spelled with a 'G'," Leland H. Chambers, trans. "Amor se escribe con G," from Rosa María Britton, *La muerte tiene dos caras* (San José: Editorial Costa Rica, 1987).

Enrique Chuez, "The Woman," Leland H. Chambers, trans. "La mujer," from Enrique Chuez, *La mecedora* (Panama City: INAC, 1976).

Ernesto Endara, "Family Photograph," Leland H. Chambers, trans. "La fotografía," from Ernesto Endara, *Cerrado por duelo* (Panama City: INAC, 1977).

Jaime García Saucedo, "Gloria Wouldn't Wait," Leland H. Chambers, trans. "Gloria no espera," from Jaime García Saucedo, *De loque ne se dijo en las crónicas y otros relatos* (Mexico City: Editorial Signos, 1982).

Enrique Jaramillo Levi, "Duplications," Leland H. Chambers, trans. "Duplicaciones," from Enrique Jaramillo Levi, *Duplicaciones* (Mexico City: Editorial Katún, 1982).

Raúl Leis, "Señor Noboa," Leland H. Chambers, trans. "El Señor Noboa," from Raul Leis, *Viajes alrededor del patio: cuentos del vecindario* (Mexico City: Editorial Signos, 1987).

Bertalicia Peralta, "The Village Virgin," Leland H. Chambers, trans. "La virgen de la aldea," from Bertalicia Peralta, *Largo in crescendo* (Panama City: Ediciones Quijote, 1967).

Dimas Lidio Pitty, "Our Boss," Leland H. Chambers, trans. "El jefe," from Dimas Lidio Pitty, *Los caballos estornudan en la lluvia* (Panama City, INAC, 1979).

Pedro Rivera, "Games," Leland H. Chambers, trans. "El juego," in *Antología crítica de jóven narrativa panameña*, ed. Enrique Jaramillo Levi (Mexico City: Federación Editorial Mexicana, 1971).

Jorge Turner, "Carnival," Leland H. Chambers, trans. "Carnaval," in *Cuatro escritores panameños en México*, ed. Enrique Jaramillo Levi (Mexico City: Editorial Signos, 1982).

The following stories have been previously published in English, with the copyright retained by the translator:

Eduardo Bähr, "Tarzan of the Apes," *Tamaqua* (Fall 1992). Trans. Clark M. Zlotchew.

Lucas Bárcena, "The Sweetheart of the Spirits," *ARETE: A Forum for Thought* 1/6 (May/June 1989): 54–55. Trans. Leland H. Chambers.

Ricardo J. Bermúdez, "The Horse in the Glassware Shop," *Aileron* #12 (1991): 36–42. Trans. Leland H. Chambers.

Claudio de Castro, "The Chameleon," *New Laurel Review* (Fall 1992). Trans. by Leland H. Chambers.

Pompeyo del Valle, "The Forbidden Street," *The S.A.A.C.T.E. Journal* 9/1 (Fall 1991): 31–33. Trans. Sabina Lask-Spinac.

Ernesto Endara, "Family Photograph," *Sonora Review* #20 (Winter 1991): 64–66. Trans. Leland H. Chambers.

Julio Escoto, "Reality," *War, Literature, and the Arts* (Spring 1993). Trans. Clark M. Zlotchew.

Enrique Jaramillo Levi, "Duplications," *Translation* #21 (Spring 1989): 123–125. Trans. Leland H. Chambers.

Jorge Luis Oviedo, "The Final Flight of the Mischievous Bird," *The S.A.A.C.T.E. Journal* 9/1 (Fall 1991): 25–30. Trans. Sabina Lask-Spinac.

Alfonso Quijada Urías, "To Tell the Story," *New Orleans Review* (1991). Trans. Elizabeth Gamble Miller.